Jane Gardam has won two Whitbread awards (for *The Queen of the Tambourine* and *The Hollow Land*). She was also short-listed for the Booker Prize with *God on the Rocks*, which was made into a much-praised TV film. She is a winner of the David Higham Award and the Royal Society of Literature's Winifred Holtby Prize for her short stories about Jamaica, *Black Faces, White Faces*, and *The Pangs of Love*, another collection of short stories, won the Katherine Mansfield Award. *Going into a Dark House* won the Macmillan Silver Pen Award. In 1999 she was awarded the Heywood Hill Literary Prize for a lifetime's commitment to literature.

Jane Gardam was born in Coatham, North Yorkshire. She lives in a cottage on the Pennines and in East Kent, near the sea.

Crusoe's Daughter

Jane Gardam

An *Abacus* Book

First published in Great Britain in 1985 by Hamish Hamilton Ltd
Published by Abacus 1986
This edition published by Abacus 1997
Reprinted 2001

A CIP catalogue record for this book
is available from the British Library.

ISBN 0 349 11410 2

Printed and bound in Great Britain by
Clays Ltd, St Ives plc

Abacus
A Division of
Time Warner Books UK
Brettenham House
Lancaster Place
London WC2E 7EN

www.TimeWarnerBooks.co.uk

For my mother, Kathleen Helm.

'The pressure of life when one is fending for oneself alone on a desert island is really no laughing matter. It is no crying one either.'

Virginia Woolf, *The Common Reader*

I am Polly Flint. I came to live at the yellow house when I was six years old. I stood on the steps in the wind, and the swirls of sand, and my father pulled the brass bell-knob beside the huge front door. Together we listened to the distant jangle and to footsteps padding nearer. My father did a little dance on his short legs, and whistled.

Then there followed sharp scenes of confusion and dismay. 'Shut the door. Shut the door. The sand, the sand!' and figures stood about the hall on coloured tiles.

We were not expected. My father was bringing me to live with my aunts – bleak Miss Mary, gentle Miss Frances. They were my young mother's elderly sisters. My mother was dead.

A fat maid led me away to drink tea in the kitchen and then I was led away again by the gentle aunt to a huge and vaulted chamber which must have been the little morning room. With the gentle aunt I did a jig-saw the size of a continent. I did not look up as high as the aunt's face but watched our four hands hover over the oceans of mahogany.

Now and then a door across the hall would open on incisive conversation and once a woman with a green face who carried black knitting and was dressed in black knitting came and glared round the morning room door at me. She said, 'She looks tubercular,' and put her handkerchief to her mouth and went away.

Perhaps my father stayed at the yellow house for a number of days. I remember an afternoon walking with him by the sea, dodging waves, and his figure dozing (disgracefully in the morning) in a button-back chair beside the catafalque of the drawing-room chimney-piece.

And one evening he sang. I knew that he sang very dread-fully but at the same time he danced, and I knew that he danced well – a heavy little man on dainty feet. Sailor's feet. He pirouetted and twirled about the room and Aunt Frances in a rabbity tippet played the piano. It was a sea song.

Aunt Mary sat apart. The little knitted woman retired to the other end of the room and bent to her needles in an arbour of potted ferns, and the maid coming in with coals for the fire put them down and hid her head in her apron at the singing. This I found out soon was very unlike her, for Charlotte was bland and nearly invisible. But she had once been in a choir.

I sat on a stool and knew that my father was having all these funny people on.

It was 1904 and my father died two months later on the bridge of his ship in the Irish Sea, on the coal-run to Belfast. They told me that he had rejected a place in the last life-boat and had stood in the traditional way – to attention in his merchant sea-captain's uniform – but holding and swigging a great stone bottle of gin. He had always been known as a droll man, said Aunt Frances.

The doorstep, the cold waves, the button-back chair were my only memories of my father – these and the journey that we had made together towards the yellow house. My mother had died just before I was one, and the following five years I had spent with various foster-mothers in sea-faring places where the Captain might possibly dock but more often did not. These people were hazy and the last of them the haziest of all, though she should not have been since she was a dipsomaniac who spent much of her life beneath the kitchen table. I spent much of my life on the kitchen floor, too, alongside the three or four – I think – other children in her care. I learned how not to fall in the fire and how to negotiate the locks on the larder door in order to eat. She hugged me sometimes.

Captain Flint, arriving unexpectedly one day, removed me to a first-class railway carriage (he was improvident) and in a series of these we made our way from Wales to the North East.

I remember light and shadow over pale fields – black towns, cold moors – stone walls swooping through rain and a night in what must have been a railway hotel, for there was a blackened glass roof below a window. Steam leaked up through this in spires. There were booms and echoing clanks. Fear and joy.

On the rich fur of the penultimate carriage seat, with its embroidered tray-cloth on which to rest the head – though far above my head – we sat, the Captain and I, side by side. On the rack above me was a very small suitcase. On the seat beside me was a Chinese work-box full of Chinese sewing things – my father's coming-home present: his last voyage had been long – and a scruffy doll or so, and a china mandarin.

The train lolloped between plum-coloured brick, the railway sheds of the North. Very noble. Then came high tin chimneys, centipedes of clattery trucks, serpents' nests of pipes, then mud-flats with whitish pools. There were furnaces, rolling and flapping out fire, and glimpses of diamond bars held fast in enormous fire-tongs in the heart of flames.

Out of the carriage window on the other side of the train, fields stretched out to colourless hills with a line of trees along the tops. The light showing through them made them look like loops of knitting pulled off the needles. The train rocked and my father whistled through his teeth.

The last train stopped at stations which were only wooden platforms. Gritty-faced men got on and off at these but nobody came near the first-class carriage. Whenever the train stopped it was quiet enough to hear the voices of the men talking through the carriage-walls and when they passed our window I saw sharp faces and bright eyes and heard the squeak of the battered tin tea-cans they all carried. All the men were black, but not black like the black seamen in Wales who sometimes came to the foster-mother's house and when they washed were black still. These men were only very dirty and trickly with sweat which left white marks. Those men in Wales used to throw me up in the air when I was little and catch me. Big white teeth.

The train ran out of the grit and the chimneys when the last of the men got out, and between high sand-hills. In between the sand-hills, far away, there were cold gleams of sea.

Then the Captain shared between us a huge meat pie. He took it out of an oily cardboard box and pulled it into two parts with his hands and laid the pieces carefully on the Chinese sewing box. I felt interesting contradictions in my

11

father. 'This', he said, 'is a *great* pie. There are *good* meat pies. This is a *great* meat pie.'

It was Aunt Mary, the older sister, who told me he was dead, waiting very tall just inside my bedroom door until Aunt Frances had finished brushing and plaiting my hair. I don't remember the words, only the white starched bow beneath Aunt Mary's chin. Under her indoor hat her hair was silvery fair, and on her chin the bristles were silvery too. Behind her on a shelf was the Chinese work-box with the mandarin sitting on top. Its head slotted into a hole in its china shoulders and it nodded in time to the up-and-down ribbon bow. A cold wind was blowing through the open bedroom window. A glassy, flashing, pitiless morning, the sea roaring.

I said (I think) 'Can I go out now and see the hens?' and ran past Aunt Mary into the yard. Through the diamonds of the chicken-wire the bow and the mandarin still bobbed and wagged. 'It is so,' they said. 'It has occurred. It must be borne.'

The chickens hopped on and off their perches and talked to each other in long rusty sentences and I wound my fingers about in the wire. Then Aunt Frances came and took me indoors and gave me lemon jelly on the kitchen table – in the middle of the morning. The little green-faced woman watched from the landing window as we crossed the yard.

*

It was the light at first that was troublesome – the light and the space of the yellow house. Light flowed in from all sides and down from the enormous sky. In Cardiff and Fishguard there had been little sky and the only light was reflected from the rainy slates of the terrace across the street.

Here the wind knocked the clouds about over the hills and the marsh and the dunes and the sea, until the house seemed to toss like a ship. I remember that I clutched on to things a good deal.

For to a head not much higher than the door-knobs, the ceilings and cornices of the yellow house might have been up in another atmosphere. The distance between the loose-tiled hall and the foot of the staircase was a landscape, and the newel-post and the banisters had to be held tight. The drawing-room was a jungle of tables and rugs and foot-stools and glass-topped cabinets, and the dining-room a terror. People sat there, silent, at great distances from one another, their mouths chewing slowly round and round. My eyes were on a level with heavy rows of forks and spoons. The knives were for giants. Doom was in the dining-room.

Solemn grace was said before and after the food, so solemn that the sun took notice and never shone in, as it did in the rest of the house, even when it could be seen outside flashing cheerfully to Jutland.

I knew I felt all this when I was six because of the height of the privet hedge outside the window, a poor thing, withered by salt. It never grew higher than three feet in all its years, but then it blocked the view.

All these early mysteries are very clear – forks and privet; and looking through the side of the glass fruit-bowl and the tapping acorns high above the blinds.

Yet I cannot at all remember the day my father went away. Perhaps I never knew it, or perhaps he went away at night after I had gone to bed. Yet I remember very clearly indeed what happened the moment he had gone.

Bowls of water were placed on the kitchen table which had first been covered with newspapers and a lump of opaque soap like rancid butter was put out, and some black liquid in a bottle and a tremendous washing of hair began. I shrieked and Charlotte rubbed and poured and swirled about and said, 'Well, she can shriek, anyway,' and Mrs Woods – the knitted green woman – stood watching at the kitchen door. She said 'Work it well into the roots.'

Then, after torrents of rinsing, I had to sit with my back to the table, the hair spread all over the newspapers – Charlotte began to tug and drag a comb through it, a comb with tiny teeth, like the backbone of a fish. A dover sole. I shrieked again and said some words from Cardiff. Charlotte made a gulping noise and Mrs Woods cried out like a parrot.

'Are there any?' asked Mrs Woods.

'There baint,' said Charlotte.

'Are you sure? The Welsh are very dirty.'

'Never a one.'

'Would you know one, Charlotte?'

'Aye, I would. They're running with them down the cottages.'

Mrs Woods then went quickly away and I sat on the fender while Charlotte rubbed the hair all dry.

'It's not bad hair,' she said. 'There's that to be said. It'll be the clothes next.'

I remember the clothes. They came out of dark shops far away in a black town which may have been Middlesborough. Two thin ladies made more of them, in a house built for princesses – it had a spire and was at the end of a white terrace somewhere along by the sea after a slow ride in a horse and trap.

Long, long afternoons, Aunt Frances sitting near me eating Sally Lunns, as I turned and turned about on a table and got pricked with hemming-pins. One of the sewing ladies had had complete circles of rosy paint on her cheeks and each wore a wig. Once one lady stroked me all over and purred at me like a cat when Aunt Frances was out of the room and I cried and kicked out and said the words from Wales again, and the lady went red outside the circles of paint, and that had to be the last visit.

Then, the bundles on the bed, the open clothes-presses with clean paper linings, the heavy woollen vests, the body-belts and bodices and long drawers and frilly bloomers and petticoats with harnesses over the back and flat linen buttons; and the stockings and the garters and the gaiters and the button-hooks; and the coats and the bonnets and mittens and tam-o-shanters and the Sunday brimmed hat; and the shoes for the house and the shoes for the open air, and the thick wool over-stockings and the goloshes and a pair of boots that seemed weighted with lead.

Charlotte said, 'Best not fall in the marsh in them. You'll sink like an anchor.' The boots were iron black. All the other clothes were dun.

When the drawers and the press and the wardrobe were full and I was completed in all my layers like a prime onion, 'That', said Charlotte, 'is something like!'

'I think she looks very pretty,' said Aunt Frances when I was produced in the drawing-room.

'It's the best we can do,' said Mrs Woods.

Aunt Mary said nothing for she seemed to notice nothing.

14

'It's odd,' she said. 'I can never get very excited about clothes.'

I felt that I understood. I felt uncomfortable and stout, and that there was a very great deal of me. I seemed to be looking down at a globe with two weighted sticks hanging below it. I sat on the button-back chair and swung these weights.

'Humpty Dumpty sat on a wall,' I sang.

'Don't dangle yourself about, Polly,' said Mrs Woods. 'Not in those beautiful boots.'

'I've not much of a neck, have I?' I asked Charlotte, looking in the glass at bedtime – another great mound of clothes waiting on the bed to set me up for the night.

Charlotte said, 'Well, maybe it'll come.'

*

Not once, not once ever, after the short cries of surprise on the first morning did it ever occur to my aunts – the Miss Younghusbands was their name – that I should not be there for ever.

There was no question. I was theirs. I had arrived and should stay. Never in all the years did they suggest that they had been good to me or that there was the least need for my gratitude, or that I had in any way disturbed their lives.

Very quickly in fact I became muddled about whether I had ever lived anywhere else, and the time before the arrival on the sandy step was very cloudy. I seemed to have been born at the yellow house, delivered there neat and complete without the embarrassments and messiness of conception or birth.

The total sureness of Aunts Mary and Frances about this was so great and so calm that it spread about the yellow house, and not even Mrs Woods made any demur, not even when I was with her on her own, which I managed to avoid as much as was possible. Charlotte appeared to accept all that came her way. Life simply proceeded.

There was no mention of loving me of course, nor of any particular affection, but that was nothing, for I wouldn't have known what to do with love had it been offered. 'She is a very *good* child,' they said. 'What a very *good* little girl she is,' – and they said it in front of me, which I found very nice.

15

After the dark, ramshackle years, to be charged with goodness was agreeable. It was like being tucked into bed, which Aunt Frances sometimes did, and sat on the end of it, too, and smiled at me and told holy stories about things called the apostles and the saints as I drank my milk. 'Not a very *demonstrative* child,' they said sometimes, and in front of me. 'Not at all like her mother. But that may be just as well. We could not cope with another Emma. A stolid little thing. But she is *good*. And considering – '

I listened and watched and began to allow myself to be taken charge of and was rather put out to find very quickly that the goodness, though a gift from God, was something I had to see after. For it appeared that I might lose it. I must hold tight to it. I must clutch at it like the newel-post of the stairs, like the string of a kite. I must examine it like my new clothes. As soon as I saw signs of wear and tear it would be well to report.

Saturdays were the time for this, after the three ladies had all been to church for their own confessions. I was asked to sit by Aunt Mary in her study window and we talked of sin. I knew from the very beginning that these occasions were the only ones when she was disappointed in me, and in herself, for she saw in them her own failure. I dreaded them.

*

'Now Polly, is that all?'

'Yes, Aunt Mary.'

'You have really tried to remember?'

'Yes, Aunt Mary.'

'Don't kick the window-seat, Polly. Shall we sit in silence for a moment?'

When we sat in silence all sorts of things welled up from long ago, but I didn't know if they were exactly about sin.

'What are you thinking, Polly?'

'Nothing, Aunt Mary.'

But I had been seeing the dipsomaniac at the old and filthy stone sink suddenly up with her skirts and peeing into a basin.

'Shall we say a prayer, Polly?'

'Yes, Aunt Mary.'

And there was the man who used to come in the afternoons

16

and do things to her in the kitchen. Lie on the saggy couch and roll on her and spread out her legs and make noises and be cruel to her but she didn't mind.

'I want to talk about angels,' said Aunt Mary. 'You do know, don't you, that there are angels? You believe in angels?'

'Yes, Aunt Mary.'

'If you are very good you may see one. They are invisible most of the time, but when you are *very* good – in a state of what we call "grace" – then you might catch sight of one. They can be known by their bright raiment. What is raiment, Polly?'

'Clothes.'

'You have raiment, Polly.'

I thought of my raiment. The mountains of vests.

'And if you keep it bright – ?'

I thought of the body-belts. I thought of the man's trousers dropped on the kitchen floor.

'If you keep your raiment bright – the raiment of your soul – then you may even see your very own guardian angel. You may catch the gleam of a shining feather.'

'Where, Aunt Mary?'

'Anywhere, wherever you are.'

I had a vision of myself in several inappropriate settings – clinging for example to the enormous wooden curves of the seat of the water-closet, tightly in case of disappearing and being washed away to sea. One couldn't imagine an angel in the water-closet. But I should have liked to see one even there. It might be more possible perhaps out upon the marsh.

While my aunt spoke of hagiography and sin I let my gaze go wandering. The study shelves were filled with books. High up went the books. High up went the books into the shadows. The wooden window-blinds were kept down almost always to protect the books from the sea-light and the sun, and they were dusted twice a week, though seldom read, for they were valuable. The shelves were old dark-red paint and set at different levels to make the books comfortable, yet the shelves were the servants of the books, not the other way round. Every title could be seen. Nothing was squashed, or leaning or lying collapsed, or upside down, and the bindings were old and dark. When you pulled one out, the boards were brighter than the spine, with a bloom on them – rose and blue and

17

chestnut and roof-lead green. They had the look of books that had once been greatly used and loved, and if my sins had not been too bad that week and if I had been able to think up a few more to get rid of, Aunt Mary would read to me from one of them for a little while.

Aunt Mary taught me my lessons every morning in the study and Aunt Frances taught me the piano every afternoon. Mrs Woods gave me half an hour of frightening French and later on some German, too, in the morning-room which was always out of the sun by tea-time. After tea I went usually to sit in the kitchen with Charlotte. Charlotte taught me nothing and went about the potato-peeling and pudding-beating as if she were alone. But I watched her.

I watched everyone. When Aunt Mary saw me watching she met the look with an austere one back. Aunt Frances would return the look with an immediate smile and a nod. Mrs Woods would turn away.

Charlotte just gazed. That is to say that her face did not change at all for she always kept what looked like a smile upon it – anyway a smile until you looked again, and then you saw that it was only a drawing back of pink lips that must once have been rosy, the result was an expression of aimless docility.

The face from a distance looked quite pretty and Charlotte had a reputation for good nature, yet I knew quite early I think that what Charlotte carried about between nose and chin was something rather surprising. It was not a snarl exactly – but something like that. A disguise of some sort. A mask. As smiles went it was a dud.

I discovered soon, too, that there was some other mystery about Charlotte. One day, in perhaps the second year at the yellow house, I climbed the attic stairs to Charlotte's bedroom when she was out visiting her sister in the cottages in Fisherman's Square, and under her iron bedstead I found a sack full of old crusts. Crustless bread was Aunt Mary's only extravagance and thousands upon thousands of crusts were stuffed into the paper sack, the top ones turning green and curling into twists. I said nothing to anyone of this and made sure not to think of it again.

Charlotte herself was always washing and scrubbing and scouring – tearing down curtains, whipping off tablecloths, hanging heavy rugs on ropes across the yard and belabouring them with carpet-beaters. Clothes enough for an institution blew board-dry in the wind three times a week, terrible as an army with banners when you considered the ironing. 'Oh, we'll never get another Charlotte,' my aunts would say. 'We know how very lucky we are,' and Charlotte drew back her rosy lips in the non-smile.

Yet Charlotte never seemed clean. She wore her clothes in a bundled way. Her hair was always greasy, her cap held on with oily pins. There was something rather squashy-looking about her feet, and although she did not exactly smell, there was something.

I never felt she liked me – as I never felt that Mrs Woods liked me, although they both sang in a minor key the song about my general goodness – and Mrs Woods sometimes became a little animated when I felt out of sorts, for illness played some mystical part in her religion. Our Lord had suffered. We are told to do as He did. *Ipso facto*, to Mrs Woods; illness was blessed. For perhaps five or six years – perhaps many more – I thought that 'suffer the little children' meant that Jesus had been all for measles and mumps, and this made me thoughtful. In spite of all the care and generosity and approbation and the lovely security that breathed everywhere in the compelling yellow house, I became wary of God there. Oh very wary, indeed.

*

And time went by at the yellow house. One after another the years must have come and gone, summers flashing over the marsh and winters powdering it with snow. The house – it was called Oversands – was very tall and large and foreign-looking with deep roofs and two gable-ends which needed cypresses. It reflected my grandfather Younghusband's honeymoon in Siena for he had begun to build it on his return, supervising various Medici-like grilles on pantry windows and the panelling of the great front door which he had always longed to make a replica, in majolica, of the Baptistery doors of Florence. 'A joyful man,' Aunt Frances called him. Each morning, she said, he would burst from the yellow house and rush into the sea dressed in semi-deshabille – parson's stock and black old-fashioned dinner-plate hat – which he cast off as he ran. His were the books and his the huge photograph with beard of Jove that hung over the study mantelpiece. He had been a great singer of hymns and a student of old stones.

Oversands stared at the German Ocean and its back was turned towards the land. 'Grandfather was a sea-gull man,' said Aunt Mary, mystifyingly, until I realised that she meant he needed to watch the sea a great deal for the black-headed gull which was his speciality. Between its back-door and the Cleveland Hills was only the marsh.

On the marsh there were a few but surprising buildings set far apart: a church, a nunnery, an unfinished folly and away over towards the hills in a drift of trees, a long, noble place – The Hall. This had a little domed building beside it gleaming gold when the sun shone.

Across the wide bay was the clutch of fisherman's cottages sunk down almost into the sand, and inland from them some sudden terrace houses – where the dressmakers lived – a terrace cut off in the prime of its life and looking as if it wanted to be spirited off to Bath.

On the northern horizon there was a kind of bruise in the sky which was the Iron-Works, the demon kitchens my father and I had clattered through in the train, and when the wind was from the north these made alarming roaring noises now and then, and great surging sounds like tidal waves; but usually the marsh and everyone who lived on it was very quiet.

Only the North-East wind was disturbing and this blew almost every day of the year. It piled up sand in front of Fisherman's Square in a barrier reef which had to be dug away as part of life, normal as washing day. It flung sand into the transparent curls of the bread and butter in the white terraces and in among the naked marble crevices of the incumbents of the golden dome who were fortunately dead, for it was a mausoleum. It howled and bansheed on stormy nights around the nunnery which was run partly as a convalescent home for the poor from the Iron-Works villages over the dunes, giving the patients headaches as they lay out on its healthy balconies; and it blew hardest of all into and onto and through and round the yellow house which was closest to the sea of all of them, shaking its window sashes, hurling pan-lids off Charlotte's shelves, whisking and pulling at

Aunt Mary's unusual clothes. Aunt Mary wore Florence Nightingale veiling – the old nursing uniform from the Workers' Hospital – and looked like a black bride. These garments were her statement and her pride, proclaiming that she was not only the daughter of a dead archdeacon, but had once been In Charge of Burns. The wind made Mrs Woods shake her head and reach for her embrocation. It whined and snarled in the rafters of the huge unfinished folly, the house the millionaire-ironmaster had been building for years as one of his seaside retreats.

But when it dropped, the marsh was utterly still except for birds and bells. The birds swung about and cried, watching the sea and land and the few figures moving over them. The bells kept the time – the church bell with a sombre boom that turned each hour into a funeral (it was very High), the bells from the nunnery canonical and complex, and a bell from the Hall stables far-off and uncertain – clear and thin and old and lovely.

Sometimes the marsh dazzled. Sometimes it was so pale and unnoticeable that it seemed only an extension of the sea. The fishermen said that a hundred yards from land, it vanished completely and the waves heaved up over it and appeared to wash the hills. The church-spire stuck up out of the water and the bells chimed eerily from nowhere.

But living on the marsh it was visible enough and had great beauty. Blue-green salt-marsh grasses, shadowy fields of sea-lavender reflected and were reflected in the sky, and the buildings between the salt and fresh-water flats and the rolling skies gave definition and authority to what otherwise would have seemed in the power of the haphazard. Nuns and fishermen went about their business – the fishermen sailing their boats on little wheels across the sand, the nuns, flickers of black and white along their balcony, moving between the scarlet blankets of the sick, or now and then about the beach where they could sometimes be seen laughing, wickedly holding their sandals in their hands. They pushed each other and squealed like bumpkins, though only in the shallowest pools.

Aunt Frances and I walked on the marsh and on the beach almost every day of my first seven years at the yellow house. Aunt Mary came with us on the marsh now and then, but did not seem aware of it. 'We've seen the sea,' she said one day. 'What shall we do now?' Charlotte walked abroad on it, but as little as possible, and Mrs Woods crossed it only to go to church. The news of the value of ozone had not reached us. 'Marshes kill,' said Mrs Woods. 'I have lived in Africa, I understand stagnant water.'

There were very few outings, very few occasions planned for a child. Even Christmas passed almost invisibly. But one day in spring when I was eight years old one great outing was announced. Aunt Mary and I were to go to tea at The Hall with Lady Vipont, Aunt Mary's old colleague. Not a nursing colleague exactly but someone very closely connected with nursing in a Christian sort of way. After that Lady Vipont had founded the curious nunnery on the marsh, The Rood, and then the convalescent home. At some very remote time she had been a young woman, Aunt Mary living not far from her. They had ridden ponies together. Lady Vipont had been greatly influenced by Grandfather Younghusband and listened often to him discussing stones. They had had holidays together at Danby Wiske at what sounded like the dawning of the world.

'You're for tea at The Hall,' said Charlotte.

'Who lives there?'

'One old lady. And one young child. Her grand-daughter. Not much older than you. Though she's usually at boarding school.'

'Is she an orphan?'

'She's something. Something queer. Her grandmother – Lady Vipont – has the handling of her. You're to go as a holiday friend.'

'What's her name? Is she like me?'

'Her name's something peculiar. She's eleven.'

'Is there to be a girl there?' I asked Aunt Mary in the hired barouche.

'A girl? Oh yes. A little girl. Lady Vipont's grand-daughter Delphi.'

We rattled up a weedy drive with tall trees drooping and came to an archway and through it a courtyard with a round building and a chapel beyond that. At the other end of the courtyard, between two broken urns on piers, were pale shallow steps. A young man in some sort of livery was standing there with his mouth open and poking about at his teeth with a twig.

When we got out – Aunt Mary in her nursing robes as usual – he stopped his work on his teeth but began scratching about at his behind, then ambled forward and stood, uncertain what to do, in his satin breeches. Aunt Mary said, 'Lady Vipont? Miss Younghusband and Miss Polly,' and while he thought what to do next there appeared round the corner of the chapel a great wheelbarrow, and two girls laughing. The wheelbarrow was full of hymn-books. The girls stopped when they saw us and dropped the handles of the barrow and turned to each other. Face to face they both exploded and spat out laughter again and I knew that they were laughing at us.

'Will you come on this way?' said the tooth-picker with a sketchy dip of the head, and Aunt Mary and I were removed into the house where, in the vastest and coldest of marble drawing-rooms, sat some semi-transparent bones with black silk hung on them. Lady Vipont sat looking out at the ashy terrace and the ashy sky.

'Mary dear – and the little one. Polly – Emma's Polly!'

Aunt Mary sat on a gold chair covered in gold satin, shredding here and there. From between the shreds bulged grubby stuffing originally placed there by eighteenth-century fingers. I stood behind this chair.

'May Polly join the children, Lavinia?'

'Children?'

'There were children in the courtyard. With a barrow full of hymn-books.'

'Oh my dear Mary, no! Not hymn-books!'

'They were unmistakable.'

'Not *hymn*-books,' said the upright glassy little lady to the two girls who then came in to the room – a bronzy girl and a silvery girl. Behind them there seemed to be the shadow of a boy. A gawk.

'Delphi – what is this about the wheelbarrow?'

'It's for fires. They're no use. They're all mouldering. They've got mushroom-spores flying out of them. They make you wheeze.'

'Now Delphi, *who* told you to take the hymn-books?'

'Commonsense did. If we don't use them for fires we've got

nothing. Nothing till the trees are felled and who's to do that? We'll wait till they fall. You'll freeze this winter. And they're foul hymn-books. We never use them.'

'This is Polly. Polly Flint. This is Delphi and her two little friends from er. Off you all go and play.'

I went in my draggle of heavy clothes, my regimental gaiters and weighted boots, slowly, one step at a time behind the big girls who ran ahead of me, laughing.

The shadowy boy in the background seemed to give off a sort of friendliness, but outside he called, 'I have to go now,' and disappeared. 'We'll be in the mausoleum,' called one of the girls – the bronzy one with red hair, 'after we've got another load.' She had strong, short arms and she bent to the wheelbarrow in which the silvery girl was sitting holding its sides and they ran shrieking over the cobbles, past all the stable-doors with their rickety hinges. 'Stop,' called the girl in the barrow at the steps of the round building and rose carefully, gracefully to her feet. She was tall and narrow. She stepped deftly out.

'She's Delphi, I'm Rebecca. Rebecca Zeit,' said the bronzy one. 'Hello, child. We're stealing hymn-books from the chapel.'

'The awful chapel,' said Delphi. 'Grandmother's chapel. Full of dead birds and coffin-stools and terrible echoes and broken stoves.'

'We're going to light the stoves. And we're going to look at dead ancestors. Do you want to come and look at dead ancestors? Delphi – could we bring our tea out here? To the mausoleum?'

'If you like.'

'Would they let us?'

'If I say so. I'll go and tell them.' She was gone.

'What's a – what you said?' I asked the red-haired girl Rebecca.

'Mausoleum? It's where dead people are put if they're important enough and all in the same family. Come and see.'

'I don't want to see dead people.'

'It's only statues. The skeletons are all under the floor. Come on – it's very unusual.'

'No, I'd rather just look about outside.'

'Look about inside. Don't you want to have a new experience?'

'No.'

'Delphi – she daren't come in. Make her come in.'

Delphi, coming back, passed me however without a glance. She was a tall girl, very spare, white-blonde, not exactly smiling. Her hair and legs were very long and she had no eyebrows or lashes but a heavy mouth and broad, shiny eyelids. There was a flimsy, brittle look about her as if she never went into the sun. She was like a pressed flower.

As she went by and up the mausoleum steps with her hands full of food she turned funny flat eyes on me – huge. She laughed but did nothing to urge me to follow her.

'Why is there no tea? Tea to drink?' the Rebecca girl was complaining, and I looked in through the doors, then leaned, awkward against the door-post and saw Delphi arranging hefty jam-sandwiches and slabs of seed-cake along the top of a tomb. I thought, 'A guest *ordering* things when she's out to tea!' I remember thinking how dreadful if they ever came to tea at Oversands.

'Too long,' said Delphi. 'Can't wait. We'll have water. You – what's your name? Polly – go and get some water out of that horse-trough.'

'What do I put it in?'

'Use your head.'

'I can't use my head – '

But the pale flat eyes did not smile, so I wandered off and found a bucket and dipped it in the trough and brought it into the mausoleum, totteringly.

'She's brought it – look,' I heard Rebecca say and Delphi turned round and stared. They they both collapsed again with laughter. 'Clear spring-water for tea,' Delphi said. '*What* a clever little girl! But shouldn't she wash the floor with it?'

'No, stop it Delphi,' said Rebecca, and I wanted to cry because I was listening to a foreign language I couldn't understand and knew that they felt their power. 'Go on – wash the floor, wash the floor – see if she can bend in the – oh lor! – the *gaiters*.'

And that is all I remember of the visit. Just that – and a hateful memory of wetness and paddly black water running over marble. On one of the tombs I remember a bottle of horse liniment cocooned in cobwebs with some marble roses and the head of a cherub. I must have looked up above their heads because I heard, 'Oh my! We're very haughty,' and I think I saw a tall, high dome with heraldic emblems in the plaster dropping flakes of blue and gold and scarlet turned to old rose pink, like flakes of coloured snow. And the inside of the dome's plaster was woven with swallows' nests and droppings were splattered. Near a broken pane a clump of harebells flourished and in the dome itself was a great and horrible crack stuffed with dangles of roots from the greenery growing above on the roof. Quite a sizable, cobwebby silver-birch was sprouting behind a marble man dressed only in sheets.

'Did you have a nice time with the children?' Aunt Mary asked.

'Yes, thank you.'

'*What* a pretty girl, little Delphi. She'll be a great beauty. It's difficult for beauties.'

'She's not a beauty now,' I said. 'She's very ugly indeed.'

'What dear? Well, I'm sure you looked very nice, too. And *so* good.'

*

I came in off the salt-marsh one day soon after my twelfth birthday with my hands full of flowers and grasses. I had found some sea milkwort and Aunt Mary was delighted. We were making a *hortus siccus* and I think at that moment she felt I was her own. 'Oh Polly!' she said. 'How lovely! And soon you're to be Confirmed.'

'No.'

The word rang round the study and bounced off Archdeacon Younghusband's face. It left him with a stunned look, reflected in my aunt's and in my own.

'No?'

'No, Aunt Mary.'

'But my dear child, why?'

'I – Just no, thank you.'

'But whyever not?'

I did not know whyever not but I knew that the answer was no.

'Is it Father Pocock? Don't you like Father Pocock?'

I had not thought about it, but considering now I found that this was so. But it was not the reason.

'It's not Father Pocock,' I said. 'I'm awfully sorry. I don't want to be Confirmed.'

'Don't say awfully dear unless it is in the accurate sense which I fear it is not. Do you feel that you are too young? Father Pocock could speak to you about that. What's that?'

I looked at the carpet.

'I just said, "How? He couldn't change it." '

'Change it?'

'My age. Twelve's twelve.'

'Nearly thirteen. He could speak to you of Grace.'

I stared ahead at the books. The matter rested.

*

Every few months however it was dragged alive again, and each time not I but some other girl answered, 'No.'

'I'm sorry to be so rotten,' I said.

'Don't say rotten, Polly. It means decayed. Have you *truly* thought about this? About salvation? You have heard so many wonderful sermons. You have lived for six years in this house.'

'Yes. And it's no. I'm terribly sorry.'

I prickled with fear and triumph every time. I was like a new tennis-player facing a champion and whamming back the ball where she couldn't reach it.

'Confirmed, Polly – '

'No!'

*

'No. Aunt Mary, I'm terribly – '

'Don't say terribly dear. It is not appropriate to penitence unless you are using it in the Greek sense, meaning large, which is obsolete now. Come let us say a prayer together and then we'll read some Tennyson.'

Confirmed I would not be.

'Is it because of the smells?' asked Charlotte in the kitchen. The old ladies were all out visiting the nunnery. The Rood. The kitchen was hot and I was sleepy after being on the marsh all afternoon. Charlotte was boiling up her knickers in a big black pan on the fire and I was looking drowsily at the pan and thinking 'Holy Rude' – and feeling wicked. Guilt lurked all over the yellow house.

'Smells,' said Charlotte. 'Incense. Sundays.'

'Oh no. I love the incense.'

*

Sunday was the day of processions. The first one was at seven-thirty in the morning when my aunts and Mrs Woods gathered silently in the hall and then over the marsh they went to church. At nine o'clock they processed back for the glory of the week – breakfast, for on Sunday we had coffee.

This coffee was the one glamorous event in our lives and it was excellent, for Mrs Woods' dead husband had been in coffee in Africa and she was very much a specialist. The coffee was sent by rail to her in person from London, and she paid for it. Perhaps it was her rent, for my aunts would have never thought of asking for any money from her, since she was, we were told, 'in total penury'.

Mrs Woods made the coffee herself and carried the pot from the kitchen herself and there was a great deal of stirring and pausing and peering and sniffing and sedate smacking of lips before the three other large cups of it were poured and passed.

I adored the coffee. It meant primary colours to me, and glorious sunshine, though how I knew it did I don't know, except that I suppose I had begun to learn something from the archdeacon's globes in the study, and of islands and tropical shores, and coral reefs from any sea-faring book I could find. Africa was beginning to sound desirably wild. 'Coffee is where Woods excelled,' said his widow as we kept a reverent silence.

Colour and heat.

Try as I might, I couldn't associate Mr Woods with colour and heat or with anything that was not decidedly pale and chill. Transparent, I imagined Mr Woods, an amoeba, an emergent tadpole. The darkness which surrounded Mrs Woods, one felt, must have soaked him up. She had taken me to see his grave once – very small and lonely in the superior part of the new church's graveyard. It was a particularly small grave decorated with an upturned glass blancmange-dish. Inside the dish was a wreath of everlasting

28

roses made out of what seemed to be candle-grease. 'Woods,' she had said stoically, pointing at the dish, and I saw him small and helpless before the cutting edge of her will, comforted only by his coffee, longing for the gaudy forest. I hoped he'd found coffee in heaven.

After breakfast came procession number two – and hat, coat, gloves, prayer-book, gaiters, sober face. At half past ten away we went, with me following this time behind, for I was allowed to the eleven o'clock service as it was Sung, and only the very holiest of the priests – Mr Pocock – actually received the Communion. I sat as good as the rest, and to look at me you'd never have guessed that I was un-Confirmed.

Eleven o'clock.

Incense.

Greek and solemn music, an hour-long sermon and a sort of tribal dance in the wind at the church-door with Father Pocock bending about towards us all and all of us bending about towards him. Laughter and little hand-shakes. Big stupid smiles. Guilt at disdain. Then home over the marsh again – no guilt there. No guilt ever on the marsh, just joy. And then Sunday dinner.

And the great blast of it through the blue and red glass of the vestibule door: the beef and the minted potatoes, the riches of gravy, the knock-out blow of the cabbage.

Then the duff. Charlotte called it a duff, the aunts called it a steamed sponge. Mrs Woods called it 'very indigestible'. The duff held the shape of the basin and jam or sometimes chocolate sauce ran down its sides. It always came in the yellow jug with the dazzling parrots on it filled with yellow custard. The jug made me think of my father. I never knew why. I loved it.

After which we all retired to our rooms, though I don't think Aunt Mary slept. I think she knelt at her prie-dieu because I saw her there once through the door when Charlotte went round at four o'clock with the reviving cups of tea. Aunt Mary knelt tall, her skin waxy. She still wore her white cap with the ribbon under the chin. The room was always so cold that the drop on the end of her nose might well have been frozen there.

Then, at five-thirty, procession number three for Evensong, and I went to this, too, after a ceremonial locking of the house;

29

for this service – it was the 'servants' service' – Charlotte also attended, leaving ten minutes ahead of us by the back door and sitting with some other maids in the gallery. She returned by herself, too, rather later than us, for she was allowed time off on Sunday evening, so long as she had put ready the supper properly on the sideboard – cold beef, cold duff, cold custard – and we helped ourselves, sometimes kindly carrying through the dishes for her to wash up.

Then I went to my room to do my preparation for Aunt Mary's and Mrs Woods' lessons tomorrow. And then I went to bed.

At nine I heard Charlotte creak up the attic stairs and cross the boarded floor above me and the bedsprings twang above the crusts. Then the three ladies came to bed – first Mrs Woods and Aunt Frances who often talked together at the turn of the stairs at the end of my little corridor – Mrs Woods sharply, and once or twice I heard Aunt Frances crying.

Then Aunt Mary's slow feet followed, and a clonking noise against the banisters because she always brought up as bedfellows the silver spoons. Burglars are not meant to take spoons out of bedrooms.

And then I watched the mandarin if it were light enough, and listened to the sea and the wind over the marsh until I fell asleep.

*

When I was still twelve, not yet quite thirteen, one particular Sunday in March, we had embarked upon our journey over the marsh for the eleven o'clock service when I saw an angel. It was a huge gold man looking at me from the tower on the unfinished house.

First there was the flash of light off its wings which were curved over its head like a boat and enclosed a halo which was translucent and rose-pink. Then the clouds flew across the sun and it was gone.

I turned from it and looked back towards the sea. 'Just ordinary,' I said; 'an ordinary morning,' and I held my arms out on either side and became a bird for a time. When I said that there wasn't a thing Father Pocock could do about my age I had spoken wisdom, for ages merge. Twelve is not too old to be a bird, and I knew that Mrs Woods who thought otherwise, stomping in front of me, would never turn her head once it was launched towards the Eucharist.

'I'm just playing about,' I told the marsh and walked backwards for a time and put my boot into a pool up to the ankle and felt it being sucked down in the rushes. I pulled it out and watched the hole it had made close over with a slap. 'Now there'll be a to-do,' I said to the boot – again aloud so that the angel upon the folly might take note that everyday things must go on.

Anyway it was probably a trick of the light.

I looked again at the unfinished house and there seemed only to be some sort of machine on its tower, probably a pulley for the new slates.

'Angels, how ridiculous!' I said and continued playing birds up to the lych-gate. I let all three of my earthly guardians vanish into the dark porch before I followed them because of the boot. The final quick bell was beating like a heart, saying hurry hurry, it's almost beginning. Then it stopped, which meant there – you've done it now! You're late.

An excited, wicked, pleasant feeling usually swept over me when this happened, which wasn't often – today there had been some serious matter about a leaky hot-water bottle in Mrs Woods's muff which had damped her. I heard the organ give its first cry and stepped in towards the dark, thinking 'Two hours – two whole hours of life going to waste,' and turned back again to say goodbye to the fresh air.

From the roof-top the angel regarded me again – huge and firm and gold. He shone with comprehension and strength and I knew that he loved me and was on my side.

*

So that at lunch-time later that day I said that I wouldn't be able to go to church in the evening. Or probably again. Ever.

We had reached the duff. It was what Charlotte called a nice marmalade and the custard was extra thick. 'Particularly delicious,' Aunt Mary had said of her three small saintly bites.

Six eyes looked at me over their helpings and Aunt Mary said, 'You are not well, Polly. You haven't eaten your

31

pudding.' It happened that I did have rather a pain but I said, 'I am well. But I am afraid that I can't go to Evensong.'

'Please,' I said in the silence, 'I simply can't.'

'We could of course, Polly, *order* you to come.'

'Please – '

'My dear of course you'll come,' said Aunt Frances.

'She must come, and Father Pocock must speak to her afterwards,' said Mrs Woods. The tight veil of her morning hat had left diamonds all over her cheeks and these always lasted as far as the duff. Today they were looking very deeply ingrained under a flush such as I'd not seen before. 'This of course is because she is not Confirmed.'

'I can't come,' I said to Aunt Frances sadly. If we had been alone I would have told her then about the angel. 'I've a feeling – '

'You are ill,' said Aunt Mary, and Mrs Woods perked up.

'No. I'm not. It's just – '

'Yes?'

'The eleven o'clock all seemed so – '

'This morning was a little – long,' said Aunt Frances.

'No it all seemed so – I felt that I was being told that it was – well a bit of a waste of time.'

'Felt *told?*'

'Yes. That it was all – stupid, somehow.'

'Stupid!'

'Yes. All the dreary people dirging away. And the sad music. On such a lovely day. I've wanted to say for ages – .'

'Polly!'

'That awful giant crucifix with the dead body and the blood-drips all carved in wood. And that ghastly face with the thorns all hung over one eye.'

'Go to your room.'

I went, and Aunt Mary followed. 'You are to stay here until supper-time. After Evensong I will speak to Father Pocock.'

When she was gone there was a pause and then a creak in the passage and then Charlotte came in. I knew she had been listening downstairs – she often listened at the dining-room door. She said, 'Well, you've done it. Whatever's got into you?' and sat down on the end of my bed which sank beneath her. She scratched her thighs through her apron and regarded her fat feet and flexed them. She had not sat on my bed before. She felt that my rebellion had drawn us closer and I felt frightened a little.

'You don't look so well,' she said. 'Peaky. You're blue under the eyes. D'you want a drop of something?'

'No thank you, Charlotte.'

'Drop of gin.'

'Gin?'

'I keep a drop for my bad times. Wait on.'

She brought me an inch and a half of clear-looking water in a tumbler. 'Knock it down,' she said, so I did and gave a yell and began coughing until I thought I'd die. 'It's awful. It's poison. Is it a punishment?'

'Punishment? It is not. Who'd do you favours? My word – punishment.'

Warmth was tearing about inside me. I lay still. Joyful heat sprang down my veins until even my fingers and toes were delighted. 'Oh my! Charlotte!' I said.

'Nothing like it. Go to sleep.' She went off with the empty glass. At the door she said, 'Are you right?'

'Yes. Much better. I had a pain.'

'Thought as much. Why didn't you tell them?'

'It wasn't the pain. It was the angel. I saw an angel on the marsh.'

'Oh yes.'

'It told me – well, that I can't go on with them. With church and so on. It's silly. Now.'

'The angel said this, then?'

'In a way.'

'I'd angel it.'

'What?'

'I'd angel it. The idea! Go on, you must. You're twelve. As I must at near forty. Beggars can't choose. You mind your step. It's fine for angels.'

'But I don't believe in it. All the – oh please never tell them, but – all the church. I've found out you see. It's acting lies to go on. I have acted lies, Charlotte. For years and years.'

'Then you'll have to act lies more. What harm's it do? You'll never change them downstairs. Act along with them,

33

poor souls. It's least return. You can't break with them at twelve. All they've got's God – and you.'

When she'd gone I drifted into a haze of gin, and thought about it. I knew that I did not like Charlotte. I knew that there was something she kept hidden and hostile inside her. At the same time I knew – though how? – that she had known a world outside Oversands, a bad uncertain complex knockabout world and the one I wanted.

I dozed and woke to the face of Aunt Frances looking down miserably at me. 'Come down, dear,' she said. 'We've sent for Father Pocock now instead of after Evensong. He wants to have a little talk with you.'

'I can't.' I shut my eyes.

'Polly, please.' But I lay still and imagined the angel, huge, untroubled as he rose off the far roof-top and stood supreme in the fat clouds, smiling.

Aunt Mary and Mrs Woods came next, together. Mrs Woods as usual with her face a little turned away and keeping over near the door.

'Polly, at once please,' said Aunt Mary in her very rare Commander of Burns voice. 'Whatever do you smell of? Come along.'

'I've a pain.'

'You have *not!*' said Mrs Woods, her face flushing again the alarming red through the African sallow. 'Father Pocock is being kept waiting. A child to keep Father Pocock waiting!'

'This is presumably the mother,' she added, to the wall.

I looked at them both as the angel's ankle-wings and golden soles passed up into the clouds, staining them for a moment with radiance. Then I smiled at Mrs Woods, for I was suddenly unaccountably happy and quite without a sense of sin. And she did look so ridiculously dreadful.

I rolled sideways out of the bed – I was in all my clothes – and said, 'Oh well, all right then Mrs Woods, I'm coming,' and tumbled upright onto the white sheepskin-rug and found that blood was pouring all down my legs.

I don't know which of the three of us was more frightened. Mrs Woods was suddenly not with us any more. Aunt Mary in her nurse's drapes drew herself up to the height of the ceiling and said, 'I shall get Frances,' and vanished, too, and I stood drunk and shaking and thinking of the crucifixion.

'I'm bleeding to death,' I said to Aunt Frances as she tiptoed in. 'No, no dear, you're not,' she said. 'I'll get Charlotte.'

So I wrapped myself in a sheet and huddled on the rug and lay down and heard my teeth chattering. I rocked myself and I caught the mandarin watching me. I knew that it was wrong that he should see. I hid my face in my knees.

But when I looked up again he was still staring with distaste so I crawled to his shelf to put him away out of sight and dropped him on the black hearth stone and he smashed to pieces.

Charlotte arrived with bandage things, looking important, and made the bed with fresh sheets and said, 'Well, it's a fine set-on, this. I wonder whatever they're telling the parson? I've had to take them all in a tray of sherry. Two o'clock in the afternoon! I suppose they'll say you're ill.'

'I am ill, Charlotte. I'm dying. There'll have to be a doctor.' I could hear my teeth knocking about in my jaw.

'Can I go back to bed? I've broken the mandarin.'

'I see that. But you're not dying. Don't you honestly know?'

'Know what?'

'About growing up?'

'Only about being Confirmed. Is it because I won't be Confirmed?'

'No. It happens to everyone. Christians too. But it's happened to you young.'

'Everyone? To everyone? To good people? To Father Pocock?'

'Not to men. To women.'

'All women? To you?'

'All women. Even to them downstairs once over, poor old faggots.'

I forgot that I was bleeding to death.

'Charlotte! Shut up.'

'You shut up yourself,' she said, 'great lady. If you want to know what's up with you get back into bed and I'll tell you,' and she began to go about the room picking up the shattered mandarin, rolling up the terrible shame of the sheepskin rug as she gave me her version of our common female doom. I listened with horror, not only at the obscenity she was telling me but because it was she who had been chosen to tell me; and because she knew the shock it was and

35

that she was enjoying herself enormously and would enjoy the retelling in the Evensong gallery even more. *'Now'*, I thought, 'I shall always hate her and now she will always despise me.' I closed my eyes and pretended to sleep.

She crept to the door at last and uttered the last foulness. 'Keep yourself nice and warm now. At these times. That's my way anyhow. Nice and warm. Don't wash yourself too much and never take a bath. You're a lady now. Keep well wrapped up. I know I do.'

The idea of Charlotte. These bits of cloth. Where did she put hers? Oh unspeakable. Were they in the bag with the crusts? The house achieved its Sunday afternoon silence and I suppose I must have sunk into some sort of unconsciousness, too.

*

When I woke it seemed many days later, though the sun was still at afternoon. I was feeling very well – wide awake and tough and quite unlike myself. Perhaps I was still drunk. 'Angels,' I thought. 'Blood. It's dreams.'

'It didn't happen,' I thought, 'any of it,' and I went to the bathroom and noisily, with the door open, I filled the iron bath to the top from both taps. At that time of day it was almost cold but I undressed and jumped in. Still silence in the house, though I splashed tremendously. Sherry perhaps – and shock. I dried myself and left my clothes all over the floor, tied a towel about me and went back to my room and put on a completely new set – everything of the best, topping it all off with my velvet Christmas dress and indoor pumps rather than the stygian boots. I sang a bit and made plenty of noise going down the stairs and getting into my coat in the hall. I pulled down a wool tam-o-shanter over my head, arranged my pigtails over each shoulder and marched into the study. Canon Younghusband's eyebrows seemed to rise and fall as I pulled a great fat edition off one of his shelves, for no book was meant to leave his shrine, let alone the house – or indeed even the shelf it was on if it was a Sunday and it was a novel.

The book was *Robinson Crusoe*, a book that I knew very well. Today it was going where it and I would feel at home. I pushed it inside the front of my coat and set off, giving both inner and outer door a slam, for the wide sea-shore.

*

The wind was tremendous over the dunes but the beach was in full sunlight and I walked fast and then ran and then walked again until I began to be aware of my fingers and toes again after the bath.

The aches and pains of the past few days had gone and I felt springy. Rather pleased with myself. I considered my body and that it was taking decisions by itself as it must have done, and my mother's must have done when it got born, as presumably it would when I died. I felt excited. There was much less to fuss about in life than I had thought. The big things it seemed were to be taken out of my hands.

I wanted to kiss someone.

Robinson Crusoe hard against my chest, I climbed the sea-wall and jumped down and began to run across the huge white beach. The wind battered me, the sun shone on me and the sea was far away with a silver line along the edge of it. The horizon was broken, so broken and curved that it seemed strange it had taken everyone so long to know that the world was round – smoke then ship came sailing towards me, ship then smoke went sailing away.

But, perhaps we had always known really. Perhaps in some aspect of us, we all know everything. Perhaps in some sort of memory I had even known this business of the blood. Perhaps everything is arranged.

The bay disappeared in the direction of the fishermen's cottages and mist, and in the other direction it stretched to the Works standing along the estuary like a line of ironclads. Steam drifted from them in plumes and turned into cream and purple clouds which took charge of the sky. The Works were 'a disgrace', said Mrs Woods, 'against nature', but Aunt Mary said there would be starvation here without them. Aunt Frances said that they made for our wonderful sunsets. I thought only that they were a marvel.

The chimneys of them now stood out against the dropping sun and I sat down in the middle of the beach on some dry sea-weed and dug my heels into it and opened *Robinson Crusoe*. 'Evil,' I read, as I had read before –

37

EVIL

I am cast upon a horrible desolate island, void of all hope of
recovery. I am singled out and
separated, as it were, from all
the world to be miserable.

but

GOOD

. . I am alive and not drowned
. . . I am singled out . . . to
be spared from death, and He
that miraculously saved me
from death can deliver me
from this condition.

'I am singled out'. 'Separated'. Years of solemn sermons
floating scarcely listened to over my head came floating back,
striking warning chords. Pride. Beware Pride – But I always
had felt separated, singled out. It was why she'd gone for me
so in Wales. Why she'd thrown the chip-pan and hit me. Got
me out of bed and screamed at me. 'Watching me all the
time,' she had said, 'you in your separate place.' Then she
would hug me.

I blinked then at the beautiful page of *Robinson Crusoe*
because I had only just remembered the chip-pan and the
screaming. That page would always now be her great face. I
must be right. Somewhere inside we do know everything
about ourselves. There is no real forgetting. Perhaps we know
somewhere, too, about all that is to come.

I watched the wind send tremendous ribbons of sand
snaking the beach like whips.

EVIL

I am divided from mankind, a
solitaire, one banished

but

GOOD

I am not starved and perishing
on a barren place, affording no
sustenance.

38

The sea's edge ruffled up now and then in a splash. I willed the day to grow even colder and tax me a bit more.

> ### EVIL
> I am without any defence or
> means to resist

but

> ### GOOD
> I am cast on an island where
> I see no wild beasts.

I should have liked him, I thought, Robinson. He liked to set things straight. To put down the hopeful things. So sensible and brave. So strong and handsome. He made a huge effort at self-respect. He was a man of course, so it would be easier. He didn't have blood pouring out of himself every four weeks until he was old. He would never feel disgusting.

> ### EVIL
> I have no soul to speak to or
> relieve me. . .

Nobody much was about on my beach either. I saw a distant sea-coal gatherer with his hand-cart, then a far-away grasshopper sitting up on a high bicycle with small children grasshoppers following on theirs – fashionable people from the terraces, 'people we don't know socially', as the aunts said. Behind them was only the sea – the long, crocodile rocks.

The wind dropped and the beach was full of small blue scallops of light as the sun went lower in the sky, saucer-shaped dents. A million, and each one of them shone. 'Having now brought my mind a little to relish my condition,' I read, 'and given over looking at the sea. . .' and I looked up myself and saw, far away towards the Works, a bouncing dark dot.

I thought it was a bird at first, but then at once knew that it was too big. Up and down it danced on the sand, growing all the time, and soon I could hear something – perhaps just the clatter from the foundries blowing across unevenly in the wind.

But the noise was not a clatter. It was a thudding, and quite soon it was a crying and calling. Head-on the small black triangle bounced and for seconds together seemed to get no nearer, but to be some little insistent machine or spring capering on the same spot.

Then it was quite near and it was a pony and trap, the trap polished very smart, with graceful shafts and a basket-work body slung between high wheels. Two people sat in it, a girl and a boy, the girl holding the reins and the boy with a long arm across the seat behind her. The girl was hatless and her hair was flying. The boy was watching how she did as the pony galloped, its head stiff and sideways and white froth blowing round its black mouth. Under the wheels the sand splattered out from all the blue saucers of light. It was a picture of joy.

When they came near the boy called out, 'Woah, Hey up!' and looked over in my direction, and called again, and the gallop slowed to a canter and then a trot and the pony made a circle and the trap came squeaking and bouncing near to me and stopped. It stopped, then started again. Stopped. Then came up within a few feet of the seaweed, crunching the sand, everyone gasping.

'Good afternoon,' said the boy. 'Are you a mermaid?' The girl said nothing but shook her dark red hair about and fussed over the reins.

'Freezing with a book,' said the boy. He behaved like a man. He was nearly a man. He looked as if everything in the world was well known to him and followed a good set of rules, which he kept and was happy. Yet there was wariness about him too, as if perhaps all he knew had been thought out only on the outside. When he smiled he looked as if he found ridiculous things very nice and when he didn't smile he looked serious and good. The girl who had bigger, less careful eyes and a beak of a nose looked as if she didn't smile very often. She was examining me slowly and I saw the eyes were green. I did not like her. I also remembered her, for it was Rebecca Zeit who had burned the hymn-books.

'What's the book?' asked the boy, looking down, tall and kind. They were far above me. I started reading again. He said, 'Oh I'm sorry. I'm Theo Zeit. My sister, Rebecca. We're from the new house. The one on the marsh that never gets finished. It's to be our holiday home. The one with a tower.'

After a while I found I had said – still looking at the book – that I was Polly Flint. From the yellow house. Oversands.

I read

but

GOOD

God hath wondrously sent. . .

'We must get back,' he said, 'we're fearfully late. We're pick-nicking up in the rafters. Then we've a long way to go home.'

Still silence. I so longed to speak. I wanted so much to smile at him.

He clicked his teeth at the pony and leaned and put his hand over his sister's on the reins and shook them. 'Off we go Bec. Goodbye Miss Flint.'

'Goodbye,' I said to my book.

As they moved off he called, 'Where did you say you lived?'

'The yellow house.'

'How old are you?'

'I'm over twelve.'

'What's the book?' called Rebecca.

'Robinson Crusoe.'

She said nothing and I looked up then and thought, 'She's not changed. She likes to be the one who knows most. He's nicer.' He must be that shadowy boy who had gone off some-where instead of playing with us.

He called as the trap started away, 'We'll leave you a footprint.'

I heard the carriage creak, the pony walk, then trot and then the hoofs drumming again, going away to the south now, and when I let myself look again, the trap had turned once more into a bouncing dot. I read

GOOD

God wonderfully sent the ship
in near enough to the shore.

I read on and on but I still seemed to hear the drumming and the story became only words I was looking at as the sun flicked out behind the Works and the day faded and was over.

*

The following Wednesday it snowed and I had a headache and Charlotte's nephew came to Oversands as he did every Wednesday on his way home from school. A long walk it must have been too, all the way from the West Dyke where most of the fishermen's children went to school, if they went at all.

He was called Stanley and his Wednesday presence was as inevitable and unchanging as the rest of the timetable at the yellow house. The clocks were wound on Sunday evening, the milkman paid and given tea on Monday morning, sitting in the kitchen in the steam of the first washday of the week. Tuesdays were celebrated by the visitation of Mr Box of Boagey's, the provisions-merchants over the marsh, Mr Box taking the order for delivery in a long greenish notebook and wearing a long greenish coat which was never removed in the house. He sat at the kitchen table eating Eccles-cakes and drinking tea while Charlotte stood over him smiling her smile.

Mr Box was a ferrety man and made me uneasy because he had slippery red lips and wet eyes and because he changed – intensified – Charlotte. They always stopped talking when I came into the kitchen. Once they were not in the kitchen but there was a crash from the pantry and a scuffling and when I went running to see, Charlotte was in there with him and looking at me in a way that said: 'There's plenty for you to learn yet. If you ever do.' Mr Box said, 'Just checking on the little extras,' and sniggered.

Wednesday was a weekly festival of house-cleaning and Thursdays were for Father Pocock, the day when Aunt Frances wore a different dress and her cameo brooch and her mother's ruby dress-ring; and sometimes there was a big event, like a nun to tea.

Friday was the day of the garden-lad who was also the milkman's-lad and Mr Box of Boagey's lad. He was a silent glum boy who was meant to tidy up the privet hedge and saw wood for the week though he never sawed quite enough. He lurked in the sheds around the yard and looked at me over the stick pile. Once he saw me unexpectedly and dropped a spade on his foot. Once – it was in spring – he came out of the chicken-house and said, 'Give us a kiss then,' turned dark red and ran away. Once he gave me some milk for a present. I was about nine. It was too deep an event to share

– there were not many presents at the yellow house – and I drank the milk alone in the coal-house and washed out the jar and put flowers in it and set them on my mantelpiece. I thought deliciously of the milkman's-lad for many weeks as I went to sleep, although I've never liked milk.

The milkman's-lad like most of the children round about – though I saw very few of them – looked as if he needed the milk himself, for he couldn't have weighed more than three stone and his toes stuck out through his boots.

Charlotte's nephew was very different, though he was as undersized and probably as undernourished as the rest. He must have been about seven when I first noticed him but there was already an authority and vigilance about him. He was very heavy footed and his feet grew heavier and surer as he drew nearer to our back door on which he never knocked. Stamp, stamp, along he marched; click went the latch and in he came, gathering up the sixpence Charlotte always had ready for him as he passed by the draining-board. He would look across at Charlotte and nod briskly, rather like Father Pocock, professional accepter of donations to a worthy cause. Then he would sit down thump in Charlotte's rocking-chair and let his hands hang down between his large red knees.

Down the side of one of his skimpy, much-darned socks he kept a ruler and in the pocket of his jacket a row of sharp pencils. 'He'll go far,' said Charlotte, 'Stanley's ambitious.' He had a purple nose and his hair fell limp like a whitewash brush all round his head from a bald spot in the middle – colourless hair and scant. His nose ran, always, at all seasons and he grunted a lot. Even if one of my aunts came into the kitchen he never stood up, and, oddly, they never asked him to and Charlotte never suggested it. He slurped up cup after cup of tea, pouring it into himself by way of the saucer, and ate everything put before him – stale cakes, old scones, cold milk-pudding from as far back as the Wednesday before. It was all kept for him. Once I remember an elderly fish-pie – or rather its remains, the old crusty bits round the dish you have to soak off for hours before you wash it up. Stanley had them hammered off with a knife-handle in five minutes. Anything freshly cooked that morning – new bread, a still-warm cake, a lush plum tart – down they all went with the rest and with no comment. If it was food, then Stanley ate it. He was more like a dog than a boy, though with little of the bounce and gratitude of dogs.

As he left, every Wednesday, Charlotte would put an apple in his pocket with his freshly darned socks and he would shoulder his satchel, settle his balloon of a cap over the miserable hair, say, 'Bye then, auntie,' and be gone. The apple would be clear of the pocket by the time he reached the chicken-house and his mouth hugely open over it by the time he reached the yard gate. I said, 'Maybe, he's got worms,' but Charlotte said, 'No. I'd not think so.'

'Is Stanley poor?' I asked Aunt Mary.

'Oh yes. They're very poor. Charlotte's sister married very badly. A very insignificant man. They live in Phyllis Alley.'

Phyllis Alley is an offshoot of Fisherman's Square and had been built and named to give the area a more sylvan tone, though looking at it, there seemed no difference. Fisherman's Square had had the cholera not many years ago, and there was still sometimes typhoid fever and typhus. Fishermen, being used to water controlled from afar, are not good at the arrangement of drains, and the cesspits and the drinking water of the Square and the Alley were mingled together. Mrs Woods often spoke of the wells and the middens of that part of the marsh and they made her eyes shine.

'What does Stanley's father do, Aunt Mary?'

'He doesn't do anything now. He was at the Works, but he was in the explosion. He lives in bed and his wife does washing and the children gather crabs and get the scraps from the butcher. We help as we can of course. There are four other children.'

The Wednesday visits must have been going on for years before Stanley spoke to me, and I had quite stopped seeing him. He was as the kitchen-table, the clock, the steel fender, the tea-caddies, or the row of pewter meat-covers clinging like giant oval limpets to the wall.

'Regular as the swallows,' said Aunt Frances once, 'dear Stanley,' and she slid a penny into his hand. 'You are sure and fair as the primrose in spring.'

I looked at her surprised and Charlotte's lips pursed up, and two of her heavy hairpins fell into her pastry. But Aunt Frances was not making fun. She never did that. She was smiling at Stanley and her face was looking beautiful. She

44

put out her hand and touched his head and Stanley stopped kicking about at the fender and smiled up at her and a look passed between them which said, 'We like each other.' It was a less upsetting look than the ones between Charlotte and Mr Box and not the sort to keep you awake at night like the smile of the milkman's-lad: yet when Stanley's eyes found Aunt Frances's, I felt jealous. It was the moment I learned that our bodies are only furniture. That attractiveness has nothing to do with looks or years.

'How old is Aunt Frances?' I asked Charlotte.

'You don't ask things like that.'

'Yes, but how old?'

'She must be forty,' said Charlotte. She slammed fiercely about with pans, 'Every day of it. Maybe fifty.'

'How old's Stanley?'

'Stanley's ten next month. The tenth.'

The first time Stanley spoke to me was the Wednesday after the angel and the blood, when I was sitting head-achey at the kitchen table doing French for Mrs Woods. Charlotte, as usual, had been baking and the room was the warmest in the house and smelled of the lines of loaves and cakes that stood about on every surface, gold and brown and cream. All the loaves stood on their upside-down baking-tins with their tops puffing out like clouds and it was comfortable because you could stretch out and pick little crazed bits off when Charlotte wasn't looking. Outside the blizzard blew and snow fell and was even settling quite deeply on the marsh, which was rare. There was an exciting light across the yard and the sea roared. I had a cold and was glad to be left to myself. I didn't intend to stir. I didn't even look up at Stanley's crumping step and the attack upon the latch or see him when he stamped his snowy feet on the mat and picked up the sixpence. Through the French I heard the usual voices – Charlotte's, less syrupy, more Yorkshire, when she was talking with her own family, and Stanley's, gruff and low; and the shake and scuffle as his coat was taken off him. I paid no more attention than when the cat had been let in.

After a time though I heard a rhythmic angry bashing which continued. And continued. I looked up and saw that Charlotte had left the room and Stanley by the fire was holding the long poker and hitting the top bar of the grate with it – bang, bang, bang, bang, bang, bang. His face was turned to me – the thin cold nose with the dew-drop, mouth open, hair still sopped. He said, 'What yer at?'

'It's my homework.'

'You go to a school, then?'

'No. They teach me here.'

'It's all homework, then?'

'Yes.'

'We don't get it. What ist?'

'It's French.'

'French?'

'Yes.'

'Can yer do it?'

'A bit.'

'Read us some.'

I read some and after a while looked at him and he was sitting with his head cocked as if he were straining to hear something else. He looked sharp. The skin over his cheek-bones was very bright.

'Gis a bit more ont.'

I read on.

'Tell us it, then.'

So I had to translate it. I liked that. French and German were easy – as easy as Welsh had been once. I went slowly for Stanley, but even so, he kept stopping me to hear it over again.

'So one's tother?' he said.

'Yes. It's called translating. D'you like it?'

'I could like it,' he said, 'I could like translating.'

'Aye, it's grand,' he said in a moment. 'Translating's grand.'

And then he threw down the poker, picked up a cinder, pulled the ruler out of his sock, put cinder to ruler and flexed it at me.

'I like it grand,' he said. 'You want to go easy – you. See?'

'What?'

He gave a huge thick sniff, narrowed his eyes and said, 'Rot you,' focussed the cinder and fired.

It hit me on the cheek and hurt and I shouted out, jumped up and flung the French book at his head. He ducked down and the book flew into the fire which was very hot and bright

46

from the baking. There was a cheerful flap of flame and the book was gone.

It happened so fast, so beautifully, that we both stood still in awe. Curved-back, coffee-coloured pages with borders of sparks were poised in the red coals for a second, then collapsed and were air. Stanley said, 'Sorry, Polly Flint,' and looked at me and I saw that he had dark blue eyes and they were frightened at last.

I ran away out of the kitchen then and down the passage and up the stairs to the drawing-room where Mrs Woods was sitting alone, eating muffins from a silver dish. I said, 'My French book's burned. It's burned in the fire,' and she stared at me with a wodge of muffin in her hand. She said, 'This is a matter for your Aunt Mary. You *dropped* it in the fire?'

'No,' I said. 'Yes. I dropped it in.'

'I see,' she said, and began to eat the muffin. I ran out of the room and to my bedroom and got into bed.

Fortunately it was the beginning of influenza – or something in the nature of the week had informed the influenza it might be worth calling in. What I remember after getting into bed is very muddled. Grey people stood around. Darkness fell, sleet rattled its nails across the window as I shivered with cold and burned with sweat. Across the marsh the nuns and Father Pocock were busy with the bells and the wind howled around my headache and mysterious tears, in an eternal argument to do with French books, flames, wickedness, flames, angels, flames, crucifixions, blood, flames, and footprints in the sand.

Now and then Charlotte's voice came through. 'It's just because of the blood. It's now that the blood's come.' 'Cold baths,' said someone. 'Cold *baths!*'

The mandarin returned and brought his friends. They nodded in conclave on tables and shelves and in mid-air. The seventy times seven Samurai. The angel kept away.

Then slowly everything was replaced by a comforting sense of defeat. A happiness. It was a happiness outside myself and after a time I realised that it was emanating from Aunt Mary. It was her happiness seeping about the room, and she was happy because she was being skilful, nursing someone, doing what she was particularly qualified to do. From the sheepskin rug she had fled. That was a dark mystery, not spoken of,

47

stirring the many things that Father Pocock's ministry was working to discount. But sickness of the body was a matter which training and skill could overcome, and she stood beside me in a long encouraging apron, glossy with starch, a watch pinned to her chest, wiping my hot forehead with a damp cool cloth and commanding red flannel, feeding-cups, a fire in the grate, hot water, action. The fire dappled the ceiling at night and she, herself, crept in through the small hours to make it up with her own hands, her hair in fat white plaits swinging over her white tent of nightdress and shawls.

In the mornings, when I grew better, snow-light shone in at the window and the world was still.

When at last I was sitting up again, though just in the bedroom, Aunt Frances said, 'You musn't worry about the book, Polly. Accidents do happen,' and Mrs Woods arrived, or at any rate one of her arms arrived round the door, and placed something on a table. 'Breathing-lamp,' she said. 'Her breathing-lamp!' said Aunt Frances. 'She's brought you her breathing-lamp from Africa!'

'But I can breathe perfectly – '

'Say thank you – quickly, quickly. She never lends her breathing-lamp.'

'Thank you, Mrs Woods.'

'It's to ease you,' said her voice. 'We had it for Woods. Not that there was much that it could do.'

*

They were very slow to let me go downstairs and for a fort-night or more I sat in the bedroom wrapped in iron-grey hospital blankets brought from a lead-lined trunk in Aunt Mary's room and old enough for Scutari. I drank broth and was read *The Cuckoo Clock*. They said, 'Oh Polly dear, you have been so *ill*,' and I felt happier all the time. I forgot Stanley and his queerness that afternoon and the way he had suddenly been unable to bear me.

'What day's today?' I asked, at last back in the kitchen.

'Wednesday.'

'Stanley isn't here yet.'

'Stanley's ill. He took the influenza too, only he's very bad,' said Charlotte. 'He had it on him that day you went mad with your French. He was queer that day. Gave it you, they say.'

'Poor Stanley. Perhaps I gave it to him. I'd caught cold on the Sunday, I think. I had a cold bath,' I said, not looking at her.

'That I know. I saw the bathroom. I wasn't to mention it. You were for killing yourself likely.'

'Have you seen him?'

'I went to see him yesterday and the day before. And Sunday I spent there.'

'All day? However did we manage?'

She wasn't looking at me but out of the window.

'Here,' she said, 'he's sent something for you. We'll hope it's not tainted with infection,' and she stood on the fender and brought a dirty folded envelope down from behind the tea-caddies. In it was a torn end of paper with 'Sorry Polly Flint' written on it, and three sixpences.

Stanley died that night and Charlotte went on Friday to the funeral. She sat still for a long time when she got back, not removing her bonnet and shawl.

*

And with his death the even pattern of days and weeks of seven years at the yellow house ended. On the Friday evening, Charlotte still sat in the rocking chair by the kitchen fire in the funeral crêpe that Mrs Woods had lent her. There she sat.

And there she sat, and Aunt Frances brought her some brandy and talked to her and said she should have stayed longer with her family, and then left her, thinking that was what she wanted.

And the kitchen fire went out, and there Charlotte sat.

When it got nearer to supper-time, Aunt Mary came to the kitchen to say that we could look after ourselves tonight and perhaps just warm a little soup, but Charlotte did not speak.

'You've let the fire go, Charlotte. Dear, oh dear – and *such* a cold day. Now sit still. We shall see to it. I learned all about lighting fires when I was a young nurse. Polly and I will re-light it easily.'

But she could find no sticks. We muffled up in coats and scarves and wraps and went through the snow to the sheds

49

but sticks were still inside huge trunks of wood, for the milk-man's-lad had been cut off by the snow. Aunt Frances found some old newspapers under the copper and I found some safety matches in a cup, and there was plenty of coal. Aunt Mary picked up the heavy axe that stood near the tree-trunks, then quickly put it down again. We needed a hot drink. The kettle hung on its chain over the fire-place, but the water in it was cold.

'Oh dear me, Charlotte,' said Aunt Frances. 'We're very helpless, I'm afraid. We can't light a fire. Could you help us, Charlotte? Isn't there some method of making the paper into twists?'

But there she sat.

'Come along now,' Aunt Mary swung round from the kettle and the grate with a sooty mark on her face but impressive – remembering herself Sister of Burns. 'Charlotte, we need you, I'm afraid. We need a fire so that we can make you a cup of tea.'

A pin fell from Charlotte's head into her lap, but there she sat.

Aunt Frances was in the pantry, peeping about under bowls and gauze covers, looking for soup. 'You need hot soup, dear Charlotte,' she said. 'I expect you've some nice soup here somewhere. . . 'There's always *soup,*' she said to us, bewildered, coming back in, 'always.'

If I had been alone with Charlotte then, I suppose that things might not have gone as they did. I might have touched her. I hated touching her but I just might have done. I might even have hugged her, although she was, even in her best clothes, so very greasy.

And yet I might. I went and hung over the back of her rocking-chair instead and began to tip it gently forward and back. '*No,* Polly,' Aunt Mary said, and Mrs Woods came in.

Except for the Sunday coffee, Mrs Woods never entered the kitchen and she stood blinking now. Snow was falling again outside but today it hardly lightened the room. The stone floor looked leaden and unswept, the rag-rugs grubby and unshaken. The range was cold. No singing of the kettle or clank of the tin clock on the shelf, no kitchen noises.

'Tea is late,' announced Mrs Woods. 'What is Charlotte about?'

'Shush,' said Aunt Frances. 'Shush.'

'Certainly not. The funeral is over. Charlotte has been sitting about in her coat for two hours. Charlotte is a Christian woman. It is her duty to rejoice and continue in her path. Light the fire, Charlotte, and bring us our tea.'

'*Charlotte!*' she said, and banged her stick on the flags and Charlotte blinked behind her glasses and turned her head and got up.

'That's better. Quickly now. Polly, go with Charlotte and chop some sticks. She'll show you. Get the fire going and set a pan of water on it. Then set about the supper with her. There's yesterday's mutton-bone. It is Friday but I think we may have a dispensation from fish tonight. In the midst of death we are in life. Stanley has reached a better world.'

Then Charlotte got up and walked over to the kitchen door and got hold of the latch that Stanley had for so long man-handled. She looked at the draining-board, and then she took off Mrs Wood's crêpe and folded it and put it down where she had been used to put the sixpences. She looked at it.

Then she said to Mrs Woods, 'And who'd bed thee? Who'd ever give thee a bairn? Who'd ever want to bed thee? And what bairn'd ever want thee? What man'd look at thee – a desolate, withered, frosted crow.'

Then she went out of the back door and we never saw her again.

*

In the swirling and gasping and fainting about that followed I had the picture of my two aunts looking at each other quickly and hard and then looking away, printed on my retina like the black sun after you have stared the real sun in the face. There was a sort of muffled moaning and I was alone in the kitchen. The baize door silenced all beyond it and the snow silenced all outside. I sat down on the cold fender and then in time left the kitchen and walked tiptoe, tiptoe, along the clacking tiles to the hall. The house might have been empty. I sat down at Grandfather Younghusband's desk in the near dark.

Huge leather top, double glass-and-brass inkstand, papier-mâché pen-tray picked out in mother-of-pearl, blotter which had supported the great manuscripts of the *Collected Sermons*,

The Folklore of the North Yorkshire Moors and *Thirty Years for Christ in Danby Wiske;* the signed photograph of the last but six, Archbishop of York, another of a steel and jet woman filled with wadding – my grandmother; and the brown-pink smudge that was the cheap photograph of my mother.

I looked at this. Such a tiny woman. There am I lying on her lap, ten months old. The lap is small. I am large and fat and floppy. Look at the fragile bird-bones in my mother's head, the deep eye sockets, lovely tight-drawn-back and piled-up hair. What a romantic dress she's wearing with the lace around the shoulders, and the rose. She sits with a foreign landscape all about her – peaks and clouds and misty lakes.

But there is a crease down the middle of them. It is not a foreign place, it is a photographer's back-cloth in Liverpool. The lace, Aunt Frances has said, would have been draped around her from his property box and the rose is cloth. Outside the studio is the Liverpool lodging-house, the smelly landing and the awful plumbing: money running short and still no letter from the Captain. No work – she was a teacher, but unable to teach because of me.

Vigorous Polly. My mother is exhausted. She is the little sister who has always been made much of. Mary and Fanny's plaything. A school-teacher before she married. A wonderful teacher, they all said. But the baby is too much for her, in black Liverpool, all by herself. She can hardly hold it, laid out on her knee. She isn't even looking at it.

Her eyes appeal instead to the photographer – 'Why have I got this great ungainly thing?' she says. 'I never wanted it. I am a child myself. Why does the blood have to start running down the legs?'

I heard voices at last outside the study door. Dead Emma's sisters coming downstairs after putting Mrs Woods to bed. Whispering.

Aunt Frances: 'Don't. She can't help it. It's because Polly heard.'

Aunt Mary: 'It's not that. Agnes would have found it terrible whoever had heard. Even I. Even you.'

Aunt Frances: 'Polly – would she understand?'

Aunt Mary: 'Of course not.'

Aunt Frances: 'Did Polly understand about Stanley?'

A pause. A rattling about in the umbrella-stand. Aunt

Frances said, 'We should have taken him. It was wrong to take in the mother and not the son. They should have stayed together. We divided them.'

'The sister was a good woman. She made no differences. Stanley liked Charlotte. He never doubted she was his aunt. And it meant he could live in a family.'

'What a family.'

'Of his class. With a man about. Boys need a man about.'

'Drunk all day in bed.'

'Stanley and Charlotte saw each other every week of their lives. And she had *sinned*, Frances.'

'Oh – sinned.'

'Sinned.'

'I must go and find Charlotte.'

'You must not. She'll be back with her sister. There's still sickness in that house. You'll carry it back with you again. Haven't we had enough?'

Aunt Frances: 'Where will she get anything? Any work?'

Aunt Mary: 'I'll speak to someone. The nuns. I shan't of course be able to give a very good account of her. I shall have to pray about whether I am to conceal the outburst.'

Aunt Frances: 'The boy was her own. We took him from her. Where is Polly?'

Aunt Mary: 'In her bedroom. No. We put things right, if there was ever any wrong when we took in Polly. We saved a child in Polly. I'm going to Father Pocock. Look – Father's door is open. Shut it.'

The study-door was pulled half-shut, but I could still hear them.

'Father can't hear us, Mary.'

'Thank God. Thank God.'

'For glory's – D'you think nothing of this sort happened on the Yorkshire moors? Haven't you read his folk-lore book? I've often wondered about Mother if you want to know. Emma was nothing like either of us and she came when father was almost a fossil. And Polly's like none of us either. But Father and Mother would *never* have separated a mother and child. Never, whatever else went on.'

'Father was a saint.'

'However can we know?'

'Frances, *shut* Father's door. He is out of reach. We can expect no message from him. He was a man of God.'

The study-door was then properly shut, the vestibule-door, the front-door shut, and through the study-window I saw Aunt Mary go gliding by round the side of the house, the white bow at a frenzied angle. It was almost completely dark in the study now and Grandfather's portrait a blank. I looked to where *Robinson Crusoe* stood upon the shelf and thought of that straightforward, strong and sexless man sitting alone in the sunshine. How easy and beautiful life had been for him.

*

It is usually just fancy when you say that someone 'changed from that moment'. When a change starts is a matter for the angels, and even they may disagree. Historians can never be certain of anything. Dates as we know are meaningless. The Great War 'began' in 1914 and the world 'changed'. But when did the change really begin? With a student who by chance was sitting in a café when the Archduke's carriage turned down a sidestreet by mistake?

Long, long before.

And so with people. Often the intention is definable – the moment when we say, 'From now on I shall do this, do that.' But the change itself proceeds waveringly – and of course often does not proceed at all.

But changes – huge changes – do take place, and in spite of the libraries of Freudian evidence to the contrary, the deep stamp of past years and even of dreams can be eradicated, washed away, and new people can emerge: and it will be a bad day for novels when this is not so.

After the departure of Charlotte, Aunt Frances changed, and the moment was as precise as a birth and as astonishing and as complete. A plumpish woman, conciliatory, with a face that always nodded and smiled agreement or kept whispers of discord to another room, became, all at once, brisk, energetic, unflinching. Her physical appearance changed. She grew thin. Her body became more defined under its clothes. The clothes changed, seemed to be cut tighter and made from stiffer stuff. Frogging like a soldier's appeared across her day-dresses and her soft foulards for tea-parties looked almost tailored. Her dress-maker suits which had always looked rather too big and hemmy disappeared and she wore tailor-made coats of tweed. Roses vanished from her summer straws and the spectacles which she had kept semi-secretly in the floppy bag that went about with her (that went too) she kept all day upon her nose.

She began to go out a great deal, to take up church work of her own. She even 'took on a District' which meant that she and I carried large quantities of soup about a number of streets at the Works – and the streets were indeed at the Works – deep in among their furnaces: back-to-back rows of gritty, filthy houses, with women standing on their doorsteps watching us walk along, scratching the backs of their folded arms or their heavy dull hair; tired landladies of eight or ten men who slept in shifts in their tiny back bedrooms, and often drank every penny of the rent.

The new Aunt Frances strode into these houses dispensing medicine and advice as well as soup, even over the medicine she did not consult Aunt Mary. She took sweets for the children, old clothes, her own old picture-books, our left-overs of cake and biscuits and stews in jars. She never spoke of these visits at the yellow house, even to me after we were home. Often as we came back we passed Lady Vipont from The Hall in her semi-holy uniform sliding past us in her motor car, a maid beside the chauffeur with other soup-cans on her knee, but neither did Aunt Frances speak of this, nor of any other new acquaintances, and brought a face to the dining-table full of private thoughts. Fortunately for us, for Aunt Frances would probably have been the only one of us able to take on the management of the yellow house after Charlotte, we now had the Vicar's Alice to look after us.

*

For the day of the departure of Charlotte did not end with the revelations through the study door. When at last that night I had crept out of the study, cold and sick, I had found Aunt Frances still seated out in the hall, under the great crucifix Grandfather Younghusband had brought home from his Italian honeymoon, upon an upright chair.

'Oh Polly!'

'I heard.'

'Oh Polly. Oh my dear!'

We looked at each other and she covered her face.

'Your aunt and I are wicked women. We are Dives to Charlotte's Lazarus.'

'You couldn't be Dives, Aunt Frances – not you. You'd never leave somebody starving at gates. And you gave him a penny, often.'

'So *cruel*,' said the chrysalis Aunt Frances.

'But Aunt Mary and Mrs Woods must have thought about it and worked it all out for a long long time – prayed to do right?'

'No. They make decisions so fast. I wasn't consulted, oh, I should so have liked some children in this house.'

'Aunt Frances, do you *like* Mrs Woods?'

The chrysalis looked frightened.

'Why does she have to live here?'

'She has always been very fond of us, Polly. Could you light the lamps? She has no money, you know. She was left in penury. Now we'll see if we can boil a little pan of water on the drawing-room fire. We might make some tea or warm some milk. Aunt Mary will soon be back.'

'Could I tell you something?'

'Well anything, dear.'

'It's – Aunt, could I go away? I want to. All the time. I didn't know until now. I think it's father having being a sailor.'

'But wherever could you go at thirteen?'

'Anywhere. To sea if I could. I know I'm lucky. To be living here. I do love you, Aunt Frances, but – '

'But we are your family. You are our sister's child.'

'What was she like?'

'Your mother was very – young.'

'You can't call people ages.'

For a flicker she looked sharp. The chrysalis was beginning to thin.

'Emma's age never changed. She was always young. As a child she was genuinely young of course: very full of life.'

'But I'm young and I'm empty of life. I just am. I sit thinking about myself all the time. I can't – sort of ever forget myself and how I have to be. All the hymn-words spring up and the Collects, Creeds and Epistles. There doesn't seem anything else.'

'Oh there is, dear.'

I was surprised to see out of the window that a drunken fight was taking place, out in a narrow street – sailors, screeching women, policemen. Dirty people crowding to look down out of opposite windows. It all faded.

'I'd like to know about it. I did once I think.'

She looked puzzled and then said, 'Yes, I know. I never did.'

The milk swelled up to the top of the pan and poured insolently over the drawing room coals.

'What a fearful smell,' came Aunt Mary's voice from the hall.

'Oh please be good,' said the chrysalis, thickening up again.

'There must be more than being good.'

'How like Emma.'

'It is *dull*.'

'It is very wicked,' said Aunt Frances, sounding uncertain, 'to find life dull. It is we who are dull by bringing to life insufficient light. Father Pocock – Polly, if you would only consider being Con – '

'No.'

'Just for the Instruction. The Theology. To learn of the eternal ecstasy waiting for the redeemed – ' her voice was hollow, it echoed like the bell at church; I felt that she was listening to it without confidence – 'and he could give you an hour or so of Latin – '

'*No!*'

'I have here', said Aunt Mary sweeping in, 'Father Pocock's Alice. She is lent to us. What a good, good man! Oh dear – there is milk on the fire-irons – even the coals in the scuttle. Alice just take away the soiled pieces of coal to the kitchen, please, with the pan and then bring a cloth to the hearth. The milk on the coal is unsightly. What is this, Polly?'

'I tell Polly that she should not find life dull.'

'Indeed no. Most certainly not. After today. But at least the day is nearly over now and we have Alice. At least temporarily. Soon there will be a nice fire in the kitchen again.'

'I will go with her,' said Aunt Frances. 'She shall start properly with proper help and she shall sleep in the spare room at first – yes – until Charlotte's room is ready for her!'

*

57

As Aunt Frances stepped into the light in her new vigour, Mrs Woods receded further into shadow. Aunt Mary stayed in her twilight and I was kept so busy with my new duties that I had no time to see myself in any light at all. The music-lessons dwindled as Aunt Frances spent more and more time with the nuns at the Chaplaincy of The Rood, but the French and German were piled on hard – especially the German. For two days of the week only German conversation was allowed – German which Aunt Frances could not speak. This I soon understood was so that Mrs Woods might make a bond with me – or rather so that she could feel that she had me in a bond. But Aunt Frances did not notice and my German days she simply spent away from home. And so passed two years.

Then one day a second metamorphosis took place at break-fast-time – though like the Great War we later saw the long and clanking chain that had made its way right up to the table-leg. Mrs Woods came into the room one evening quite lavender with cold from her walk home from the Celebration of the Holy Innocents and said, 'So Father Pocock is leaving us!' and Aunt Frances fainted clean away.

'Oh, I didn't know. I thought everyone must know. I had no intention of causing shocks,' said Mrs Woods. Her chest was going up and down. The lavender had turned to two flushed marks on her ivory cheek-bones and a smudge of purple round the mouth.

For it seemed that Aunt Frances – and nobody had ever dreamed of it, though (a clank from the table-leg) I did seem to remember some things Charlotte had half-said when I was a child – that Aunt Frances and Mr Pocock had been deeply concerned with one another for many years.

Looking back, I remembered the familiar silhouette of the two of them together, sometimes on the marsh, Mr Pocock accompanying her half-way home from the weekday service; and the dress and brooch for the Thursday tea; but as the Thursday tea had been the only social engagement of the week the brooch had never seemed to us unbridled. Only perhaps in one or two silences in the drawing-room when I had come in unexpectedly – I had always of course knocked; I thought that they had probably been saying some prayers – and in the way that Father Pocock always ignored Aunt Frances at the church-porch at his public greasy handshaking, had there been anything out of the common. Aunt Frances until Stanley's death had often been ignored, and if she did anything un-ignorable, Mrs Woods had at once set her straight about it. The sound of these intense, feverish settings-right upon the stairs as the two women went up their separate ways to bed had been an agony to me for years. When the voices were raised sufficiently to hear words, I had often gone down beneath the bed-clothes, not at all knowing why, and once when things became too much even for the eiderdown and three blankets to muffle I had run along the landing pretending a visit to the bathroom and passed Aunt Frances, flushed, standing up four-square to Mrs Woods, who was looking at her with what seemed hatred and banging her stick on the rug until the sea-asters and arrow-grasses trembled in their oil-green bowl.

'You know how I *love* you,' Mrs Woods was hissing.

I flew. Nobody mentioned the scene. Ever.

*

When the faint was done and Aunt Frances had come to herself again and been patted on the hands and put in a chair, I asked to go to bed and did so. I did not see, therefore, what happened next, but found out later that Aunt Frances had come upstairs soon afterwards, changed into her outdoor clothes and taken herself off across the marsh to The Holy Rood and had stayed there for four hours. Much later in the evening – it must have been in the middle of the night – I heard Aunt Mary and the spoons coming up to bed. She paused and came into my room.

'Polly?'

I didn't answer and she stood by the bed and said, 'Dear Polly. Oh, poor dear Emma. Oh, how difficult.'

'We must think of St Paul,' she said, turning and staring out at the wet night. ' "Better than to burn." Though I don't believe that Father Pocock could ever really burn. And Frances so quiet.

'I shall of course be totally on Frances's side. Totally. Even if it means she is to go to India. I believe you would agree with that wouldn't you?'

I knew that she was talking to Grandfather Younghusband not to me, and when she had gone away, to get rid of the feeling that he was still standing about, eyes blazing above the springing beard, I lit the lamp and looked about the bedroom.

Nothing. Nothing. An empty room. The wind and rain. And Aunt Frances going to India.

Out of habit I said some prayers then, wishing there had been someone real to consult who would send me an immediate and precise answer, or some comforting gift – as when Robinson Crusoe had spoken to me and the wonderful brother and sister had appeared, so affectionate and glorious upon the beach. Some telegram from somewhere.

But none came.

*

In the morning my aunts sat straight and calm at the break-fast-table and although it was Saturday were drinking coffee.

'Coffee!'

'Yes dear,' said Aunt Frances, 'I thought coffee today,' she smiled.

I hadn't realised that anybody but Mrs Woods could make coffee. I had believed it was a rite only to be learned abroad. Yet this was as good as Sunday's.

'I think, Mary, we should have coffee more often, don't you?'

'Coffee? Oh it would soon run out. Agnes buys only so much – '

'There is coffee at Boagey's and at Dicky Dick's, the lino-shop. He is extending. There's no need to send for it by the railway.'

'I'm sure there's no *local* coffee Frances. And what a price! It would be far from usual.'

'Nonsense. It should be usual. Coffee. Edwin has it every day. I'll make enquiries. I'd like to think of you all having plenty of good things when I'm gone.' (She had said nothing to me.)

We looked at her carefully and Mrs Woods came into the room, looking bleak. We waited for the outburst, for the smell of coffee was wonderfully strong, but all she did was to run a finger over the sideboard as she passed it and say, 'Filthy.'

And at table she examined a spoon and said, 'Naples.'

'It is perfectly clean,' said Aunt Frances.

'Since we had vicarage servants we have lived like Naples.'

'Have you ever been to Naples, Agnes?'

'I have known the filth of many foreign countries.'

'Have you been happy anywhere, Agnes? We have had the Vicar's Alice here for over two years. You haven't complained before.'

'I think she should go back where she came from. It was when she came that the rot began.'

'You'd be very silly to send her away. She's quite settled. Edwin doesn't need her. We spoke of domestic arrangements last night. Yours and ours.'

'Yours and ours?'

'Mr Pocock is leaving us, Agnes.' Aunt Mary examined her marmalade. 'You were perfectly right. He is going to India. The new priest will be making a clean start. He may even bring a wife. And Frances is also to leave us.'

'A wife? Oh, not at The Rood. Not a wife among the nuns.'

'I don't see how a wife would affect the nuns. It's usually the parsons that distract them,' said Aunt Frances.

'The Rood is too High for a wife. A married priest!' said Mrs Woods. 'And great goodness, is this my coffee? It is only Saturday!'

'We thought a little treat today. To celebrate. . .'

'To celebrate what? To celebrate *what*, Frances? What is this nonsense of Frances leaving us?'

As I left not one of them moved, nobody whispered. Nobody stirred. But when I passed the window, behind the diseased privet, I heard Aunt Frances laughing – a young laugh, light as a girl's.

*

Oh, I missed her so. The wedding was frightful. It seemed that Father Pocock had been vaguely preparing for the Mission Field for some years but that Aunt Frances had only known about it as his vaguest of general intentions.

As was the proposed marriage. Neither had been more than gently touched upon between them and when the results of his years of vague correspondence with old ecclesiastical cronies had at last began to solidify and necessitate publicity and the signatures of bishops, Mr Pocock had all at once

61

become quite remote from the yellow house. Most strangely so.

'How pinched about the lips he has looked lately,' Mrs Woods had said only the week before the revelation. 'Of course he fasts a great deal.'

'Surely not at Christmas and Epiphany,' said Aunt Mary. 'It's still weeks before Lent.'

Aunt Frances said nothing.

Since Christmas, Father Pocock had scarcely been to see us. Presumably all three ladies had seen him at their weekly Saturday confession, but Aunt Frances's walks to the chaplaincy and the nuns had become brisker than ever. She had stayed for shorter and shorter times. It was some months now, I suddenly realised, since Father Pocock had even been to tea with us. There had always been reasons – but still. Aunt Frances despite her briskness had lately been looking rather white. She was not as she had been after Charlotte – in open misery, walking about with a shadow all around her, weeping for Stanley and her sin, but all, we saw now, had not been well. In the new freedom which Aunt Frances's confidence had given us, Aunt Mary at her prayers, Mrs Woods at her secret broodings and I at my books – all of us had stopped seeing her. She was just steadily, briskly, usefully there.

Now she was rosy, talkative, merry. I thought, 'Of course. That's how she used to be, long ago. When I first came. We had all forgotten,' and it was terrible to think that Aunt Frances might never have been herself again and that we might never have noticed that she was gone.

But it was terrible, too, to know that being herself again was caused by nothing one could feel happy about, and by nothing in the very least romantic (I was reading Scott and Charlotte Yonge at this time) but only by her marching out on a very wet night in the most un-feminine way – and bearding Father Pocock. *Bearding* him.

It is terrible for a woman to beard.

If it were not so unthinkable one might almost imagine that she had proposed to Father Pocock herself; brought him – like someone in Wales or Fisherman's Square – up to scratch: pale flabby candlegrease Father Pocock with hands like a seal's flippers and a puffy pink sea-anemone mouth.

And there was the business Charlotte had mentioned and which Scott, Jane Austen, the Brontës and Charlotte Yonge never: 'Who'd bed thee?' Charlotte had said. Did Father Pocock understand this aspect of things? The sleeping arrangements, the lying side by side and whatever it was that happened next? And the blood? Well, presumably Aunt Frances had stopped. She was old, after all. And he must know. He had read the Bible. About the woman who had gone on non-stop for twelve years, poor wretched thing. So it might have been worse. But what would Father Pocock have made of the couch business in Wales?

What would Aunt Frances have made of it?

Did she even know? I didn't know much, but ought I perhaps to pass on to Aunt Frances what I did know?

But the whole thing seemed yet more terrible again when he came to lunch – Aunt Frances organised it for that very Monday, giving him only the Sunday to compose himself – in formal celebration of their betrothal. There he was at our dining-table, so old and pale, smiling tranquilly round and praising the steamed chicken. Mr Casaubon – so much, much worse than Mr Casaubon, for Dorothea's husband had had a massive mind, a searching scourging soul. He had breathed rare air like Moses on the mountain-top. I could understand the whole of *Middlemarch*. The passion for a scholar. It was a bit like Jo marrying Dr Bhaer in *Little Women*: you felt sick about it, but you understood.

But Father Pocock! He looked down at Aunt Frances over the cabbage, so kindly, as if by marrying her he were going to give her a very great treat that had all been his own idea. Where Mr Casaubon had breathed out Olympian sagacity, Mr Pocock gave off a bright, little self-confidence brought on, one felt, by the relief of having had his mind made up for him. 'We shan't be eating as well as this you know, ha-ha,' he said, 'in India,' – meaning 'How you must love me' – and fluffing round the sea-anemone with his napkin. 'We shall think of all this richness in our little hut.' He was as proud as if he had acquired some small stone saint and breathed it into life.

Aunt Frances said, however, in the quick new voice, 'Hardly *hut* in Delhi, Edwin. And I'm really looking forward to proper curries. They say they're quite a different thing.' And there was no doubt at all that although she – she who had read me Tennyson – had engineered this whole dread business herself, Aunt Frances was happy. Her room became full of open sea-trunks, her days of complex, delightful visits. She was endlessly at the dressmakers of the turret room, and twice she took me with her to York, the furthest I had travelled since I was six – where she brought quantities of gigantic male cotton underwear with buttons fastened all down the front in the most outspoken positions ('You can't expect the nuns to buy them and poor Edwin has no sister').

'The main *body* of things of course,' she said, 'we shall get from The Army and Navy Stores in London. All the tropical vestments will come from Mowbray's' – for the honeymoon was to be a working one, spent mostly at the Society for the Propagation of the Gospel in Tufton Street. 'I shall see to the worldly matters while he gets on with the spiritual things,' she said.

She made great lists of most unlikely objects – she must have done considerable previous research, in the vague hopeful years, all neatly ticked off and costed out. 'It must all be very expensive,' I said once, and she said, 'Oh, Edwin's very well-to-do. We don't have to worry about that. There's more than enough and we shall be able to give away a great deal, too, I expect' – and she gave the quick happy nod she used to give Stanley when she slipped the penny into his hand. 'Oh, I shall *enjoy* being rich,' she said in a way I felt unusual in the fiancée of a missionary.

*

She was married in royal blue and her Leghorn straw hat with big pink peonies on it, made of silk. The wedding was quiet, and on a cold wet morning – it had to be early as they had the connections for the London train to catch. Only Aunt Mary and I and a curious-looking Pocock cousin, the maid Alice, the parson (a colleague from Mirfield) and a trickle of nuns, were in church. There was the usual devout woman at the back who always comes to a parson's wedding and cries and leaves before the end: and Lady Vipont who slipped in just before the bride and sat apart in The Hall pew. Mr Pocock became excited at this and tried to make signs to her from the bridegroom's position: but she didn't look at him and left before the reception.

Also, I thought that just before the service began I might possibly have seen Charlotte, somewhere behind a pillar, but then I may have been mistaken.

Mrs Woods was unwell and unable to attend. And since she needed the yellow house to be quiet in, the reception was held at The Rood. Aunt Frances drove to the church in a motor driven by Boagey's First Class Wedding Services and Aunt Mary and I went with her – two cars seeming unnecessary. Aunt Mary, not a whisker in sight, sat beside the bride in a very antique and beautiful dress and a great hat of ivory silk that had been wrapped in black tissue for several people's lifetimes. She looked astoundingly beautiful and I gazed at her all the time from my tip-up bucket-seat. I could not even look at the bride.

Beside me sat an old friend of the family I had not met before, Arthur Thwaite, who had been something special in Aunt Frances's girlhood and was to give her away. He lived, I had heard, on the Yorkshire moors and I had hoped for a Heathcliff character, but he had a monocle and a drooping moustache and kept clearing his throat.

After the ceremony the motor swished through the rain to the Chaplaincy at The Rood to sherry and paste sandwiches and a piece of wedding cake. Aunt Frances bustled about, exhorting the nuns to make the most of it all – though she didn't put it so boldly – and they did, laughing I thought like children younger than me, but not quite easy with her now, and not paying quite the same reverent attention to the groom as when he had, for example, conducted their Litanies.

He, however, had not noticed. He had shone with good humour, not noticing anyone, not even Aunt Frances much, and the arc of his stomach – perhaps it was the new under-wear – moved with more than usual gravity among us and high above us all.

At the reception nobody paid much attention to Aunt Mary or to me either – I think Aunt Mary's sudden beauty had made us all shy – and I stood for most of the time with Mr Thwaite – the Heathcliff – who looked dolefully out at the rain and said at intervals, 'Fearful weather.' The Pocock cousin approached – the best man. He had a very large head which he appeared not to be quite right in. He seemed an amiable man, but when Mr Thwaite cleared his throat for the third time and said, 'Fearful weather,' yet again, he went away.

At last we all climbed back into the bridal car and the guests gathered upon the steps, a few of the less decrepit convalescents hanging over the balcony above. I sat between my aunts now, with Mr Thwaite and Mr Pocock facing us. Mr Pocock, so large above the tip-up seat that he seemed to be poised in air like God on a ceiling. He waved in various directions sombrely, Aunt Frances merrily, the nuns threw a little rice and we set out for the station.

As we hissed across the marsh, the tassels of the window-blinds scarcely swinging in Boagey's Rolls Royce, the bride-groom said, 'We shall see great changes, Frances, great changes when we return. Mark my words there will be an influx soon. An *influx*. Slum clearances are on the way. There will be huge developments. I fear we may not see our marsh again, or not as it has been.'

Nobody could think of anything to say to this and we proceeded in thoughtful silence. Then Mr Thwaite cleared his throat and said, 'Really frightful weather,' and I burst into tears.

*

At the station she said, 'Oh Polly. Don't cry. You shall come out to us. You know you shall. For a long, long stay. For ever if you want. In a year or so. When you're eighteen. You're not to fret. You're to be very brave and think and think about India. I'll write every week. I'll never miss. I love you, darling, darling Polly, I shall miss you so. You are my very own.' But she looked so triumphant as she wound down the railway carriage window to wave, with Father Pocock's great pale face above her, that I sobbed on. I tried not to. I wanted to leave a nice memory of myself. But I couldn't stop.

I couldn't stop because I knew that whatever she said she was not what she had been. She was lying. For she was not in love. Not in the very slightest. She did not love him. She had lost her true uncalculating self. She was brimful only with the importance of being a married wife.

*

At breakfast the next morning Mr Thwaite gave a cough and said, 'Thought of taking the girl home.'

Aunt Mary blinked at him.

'The girl,' he said, 'Polly Flint. Polly. Little break. Back to Thwaite.'

'Take *Polly?*' She sounded as if there was a host of other girls about the house. '*Polly?*'

'Little change. Little break.' He then subsided. 'Mind if I leave you? Library. Pipe.'

We looked at each other. 'Polly dear – this is very unexpected.' And Aunt Mary, her beauty muffled again in her black, looked about for her sister. It was the loss in her face at seeing the chair empty that made me say, 'Of course not. Of course, Aunt Mary, I can't leave you. With Mrs Woods ill! Of *course* not.'

I meant it, too. Mr Thwaite was a mystery and I liked the mystery: the way he commanded his interior life and was so hopeless with his exterior one. And I was beginning to like him. But when it came to it, this was no time for me possibly to leave Aunt Mary and the yellow house.

'Well, he'll stay here for a day or two,' she said. 'Let's just see what transpires,' and she rang for Alice to come and deal with the breakfast things and put coal on the fire. 'Go to the study, Polly. I'll go up and see how Mrs Woods is. Just see what he – poor Arthur – has in mind.'

The vestibule door was open and we both stood in the hall for a moment looking at the piece of tesselation in the porch where a letter might lie. 'She couldn't have written yet,' said I, 'it's only tomorrow.' I wondered if Aunt Mary was too old and good to be thinking. 'What happened? Whatever happened? How did she do? She was with him all through the dark.'

Mr Thwaite was sitting easily at the great desk in the study smoking when I went in. 'A fair collection,' he said as I slid through the doorway and sat down on a convex, cold leather chair just inside the door.

'Of books. Younghusband's books. Whose are they now?'

'Well – ours. Aunt Mary's I suppose. Like everything.'

'Very valuable indeed,' he said. 'Some very delectable editions. Do you read them?'

'Oh yes.'

'Very often?'

'Oh yes. Most days. Part of every day.'

'What – the old philosophers and saints?'

'Yes.'

'Clerics? Divines?'

'I'm not exactly – I haven't started the Divines yet.'

'And how old are you?'

'Nearly sixteen.'

'How much younger you seem.' He made a great rough noise in his throat, 'How would you really enjoy a visit to Thwaite? Plenty of books – more up to date than this – not my sort of thing, but they might amuse. Consider it.'

'Fan and Mol used to like it,' he said. 'So did your mother.'

'Fan and Mol?'

'Your aunts. And Emma.'

(Fan and Mol!) 'Did you know my mother?'

'Very well. I knew her mother, too. An old connection.'

'You must be much younger than my mother's mother,' I said.

'Yes. But much older than the three girls.'

It took a moment to understand that the three girls were Mary, Frances and Emma, one dead, two deeply aged – quite forty.

'What do you do with your life?' asked Arthur Thwaite.

'In the mornings French and German with Mrs Woods. Then piano – I do – used to do – piano – ' and the great tears came and trickled down my face at the thought of the emptiness now.

'Yes, yes. Never mind,' he said. 'Play Schubert with her do – did you? So did I.'

We sat about and the Vicar's Alice clattered round outside and the rain still whispered down. Otherwise silence blanketed all.

'So now – ?'

'I don't know. I'll just live.'

'The lady in charge of the languages sick and in bed. The lady in charge of the music married and gone. What point is there? You are alone? What shall you do?'

I said, fiercely, that I was not alone. I was with Aunt Mary. I was needed. He puffed and scratched about in the pipe.

'Not very good for you,' he said. 'Not very healthy. Sitting with old women. Only sixteen.'

'Gather', he said, 'your aunt wants a break, too. Said so last night. When you had gone off to bed. The other old – lady not well. Not friendly.'

'She hasn't been for some time. Well, never really.'

'It's all been rather a shock for Mary. She has not had a holiday for many years you see.'

'Oh then I'll go with her. I'll come with her to Thwaite. Whenever you like. I didn't know she felt that.'

'Rather think Mary has – some sort of nunnery business in mind for herself. Oh just for a time of course. . .'

'But – Mrs Woods? And the Vicar's Alice?'

'I rather think that if you were to come with me, all might sort itself out very nicely here. Mrs Woods, I gather the doctor thinks, should be looked after for a time. Nursing home. And Alice can do the spring cleaning. Mary will go into a Retreat somewhere. She has one in mind.'

'You mean, they don't know what to do with me?'

He looked angry and I liked him more. 'Certainly not. No. Never leave high and dry. Very fond of you. First concern. There'd be no anxiety about you though if you were to come to me and my sister Celia. For a time. Just some short time.'

'When?'

'Well, at once. Perhaps even tomorrow. Unless you want to wait for a letter from – Mrs Pocock of course.'

I said, 'Oh no thank you, Mr Thwaite. Of course not. I'll come whenever you want. If Aunt Mary wants me to. Should it be today?'

'Perhaps in the morning. Could you gather your possessions?'

'Oh yes. Yes, I could. If Aunt Mary wants – ?'

'Ha.'

'For how long?'

'Shall we say a month? To be extended to three if you are happy?'

'Oh – yes. Yes. Is it very far? Of course, I'll come.'

'Not at all. Not at all far. Though everything does seem rather far from here.'

*

69

And how very comfortable I was with this old fusty man. In the train the next day, trundling across the plain of York, I was able to ask – a first class carriage and us alone in it – 'Why is it, Mr Thwaite, so like after a funeral? I have never been to a funeral. But I feel I've been.'

'Oh, it was a funeral. A sorry funeral.'

The train ran gently into York, wheezed, fizzed, stopped and we changed platforms and set off again in a smaller train to Pilmoor Junction. 'These books you read,' he said. 'Which of them would you say are of greatest – use to you?'

'Which do I like best?'

'That sort of thing. Love. Love best?'

'Oh, Defoe. *Robinson Crusoe*. I read it all the time. I'm a bit peculiar about it. Especially, I think, in troubled times.'

'Have you often had troubled times?'

'It's more that I've a discontented disposition, I think. Crusoe was so sensible. And so unimaginative. He sorts you out. I love him.'

'Read Dickens ever?'

'Yes.'

'Should read Dickens,' he said. 'Get more of a *throng* with Dickens. Great mistake to keep with one feller only. This is where we get out and we hope that the trap is waiting for us. Now Dickens will make you laugh.'

*

A pony-carriage was waiting for us at Helperby station with a nice dog in it. A man sat dozing in the high seat at the front. A whip was stuck in a holder beside him, drooped like a plant. It was a warm sweet day and the sun shone across coloured country.

'Great change in the weather,' said Mr Thwaite.

'No, no. Pretty steady,' said the driver.

I was handed up beside the dog who laid his chin across my knee and Mr Thwaite stepped in alongside as we clopped out of the flowery station-yard between hedges full of birds. 'All well then?' asked Mr Thwaite.

'Wey, aye,' said the driver, as if how could it not be.

The lane wound round and along. The hedges stopped and seas of young green corn rippled for miles. Clumps of late primroses and fountains of cowslips stood on the verges like

70

bridesmaids' bouquets. There were no people about but we passed quiet farms which were well painted, red roofed and large. Horses stood in the farmyards with silky hair groomed into skirts around their ankles, and shook their heads to make the polished bridles clink. Even the chickens seemed well washed. A labourer working a pink whetstone by a gate looked prosperous and rosy. On rises in the landscape we twice passed a great house standing in a park like the paintings I'd seen at The Hall. There was the sound of streams running sweetly in the grass.

We clopped over a wooden bridge with a white-painted railing and the water underneath ran fast and cheerful over polished-looking stones. All the leaves were out – even on the ash-trees – and the sun shone warm into my back. Everywhere there was Sweet Cecily in creamy lace and the new corn growing thick.

Then we came to Mr Thwaite's village – called Thwaite – after perhaps half an hour: and a pond with ducks, a cluster of red cottages and in trees, a Norman church-tower. Then we passed into a lane with a high wall along one side of it made of small dark bricks. Ivy climbed all over it and other things were spilling out from inside. White and yellow lichens exploded over the bricks like stars. We passed some iron gates all netted up with convolvulus and on them two griffins holding shields, their proud faces turned sideways in disdain. The locks to these gates were papery thin.

We turned into a stable-yard where a boy sat on a mounting-block staring at nothing and doves walked with dignity on green cobbles. Other doves paraded over roof-tops and a stable-clock struck four.

'Thwaite,' said Mr Thwaite. 'The same name as mine and the village. Thwaite House. All it means is a clearing in the forest. Exceptionally dull. There may be cinnamon. Come along.'

We left the trap and went through a door into a stone-slabbed passage with a hanging lantern in it and a smell of roses. 'Scones,' he said. 'Cinnamon scones,' and held another door and we walked over more stone slabs, passing statues and huge black furniture and crossed-swords and huge dark paintings and Chinese jars as big as men. Our feet made a very hollow noise and suddenly from far away there came an odd long note of somebody singing.

'For tea, if lucky,' said Mr Thwaite and opened a door into a room where three windows looked out over lawns and cornland to some hills.

On a yellow silk sofa someone was lying. There was a blaze in the grate of a wood fire that never goes out, and there was also the smell of something else, very sweet. Pot-pourri – there was a heap of it in a great dish – but it wasn't that. All I could make out on the sofa was drapery and a movement of white hands and a sense of eyes watching me.

''lo Celia. Back home. Polly. Polly Flint.' Mr Thwaite did the great harumming of the throat and moved to the window. There was a valedictory atmosphere about him: I have done what I have done. I have gone through with it. He looked at the sky. 'Splendid day,' he said. 'Very poor at Oversands. Continuous rain. Very disappointing.'

'Polly *what*?'

'Flint. Emma's. Flint. Polly. Come for a little break.'

'*Flint*,' said the voice. 'Well – Arthur. On your own? Arthur ring the bell. Polly *Flint*. Come over here.'

On the sofa lay a tiny woman dressed in silk. Pampas grasses in a tall jar bowed over her like a regal awning. Her face was thickly painted – bright red mouth and cheeks. Her eyelids and brows were painted and her very black straight hair was pulled tight back across the skull like a Dutch doll, and looked painted, too. Her neck was not much thicker than a wrist and her ears glittering with round topazes were little and pretty like noisettes of lamb.

Her hands were very, very old and had veins standing on them but they were soft and unused, not as small as all that. Rather determined hands. She held one bravely out – it looked ready to drop with the weight of more topazes.

'But do come nearer.'

She examined my clothes one by one – hat to gaiters. She saw my pelisse, cut down from Aunt Frances's and very special. I had worn it at the wedding. It was draped over my childish serge coat. She seemed to count the buttons down my calves and almost ate the big plate hat. She looked lower and I remembered that there was an uncertainty about my left knicker elastic which I had meant to see to before I left.

'Thought of cinnamon scones?' said Mr Thwaite. 'About tea-time? We arrive upon our hour.'

'Polly *Flint*,' said (presumably) his sister. 'How *very* interesting. How pretty. Emma's girl. Not at all *like* Emma. Very different – except perhaps the cheek-bones. How *very* sensible of you Arthur. Has she come for a visit?'

'Seemed not unwise. Not out of the way.'

'Not at *all* unwise. But how clever. You thought of it quite alone? A long, long visit? She does know of course?'

'No time to say very much.' He looked at the polish of his button-boots.

'And did they – poor Frances – get away?'

'Yes. Yes.'

'No mishaps? No delays? No regrets?'

'No,' I said, so decidedly that the shawls stirred.

'Well. How splendid. And the bridegroom very handsome, I've no doubt?'

'Here's the – cinnamon scones. Ha,' said her brother, 'just the three of us, Celia? Nobody else en route?'

'Well, we never know. We *never* know, do we? You'll find Polly, that people come and go here. They pass through this house with total freedom. Sometimes they are with us and sometimes they are not. You will never know for sure whom you will meet upon the stairs.'

It was difficult to reply to this.

It had been difficult to reply to anything in fact – though not many of the things they had said had been really addressed to me. I thought, perhaps it's some sort of hospital. Would Aunt Mary have known if it was a mad house? Would she have let me come? In all the years at Oversands she and Aunt Frances had never mentioned these people. They had never been to see us before. There had not even been a Christmas card. There were no photographs of them in the yellow house.

Perhaps Mr Thwaite was mad. There was certainly something funny about him. All that obsession with the weather. And the silences. And this wonderful house with the gates all locked and covered in weeds. Surely even Aunt Mary would have known if this was a private asylum.

Then I thought, oh my goodness, but she mightn't! She's got it muddled. Oh dear – she's so holy and vague. It was

Mrs Woods who was supposed to come here and they've got it topsy turvy and sent me instead. Whatever shall I do?

But how very comfortable here. It must be a lunatic asylum for the rich. They have them in novels.

'Before long', said the sister, wiping butter carefully from her lips with a lawn handkerchief, 'we shall find you a room, Polly. I'm sure there must be a room somewhere with nobody in it?'

The huge house – I'd seen so little of it but already I felt I would never find my way out of it again – seemed so empty that if I listened I could probably have heard the crumbs dropping on to our plates.

'We are very full at present,' she said. 'Hush.'

A man came in to the room wearing red braces over a thick cotton shirt fastened with a stud, and no collar. His curly head was clipped close like a prisoner but he had not shaved. He stood staring blankly across the room. Then he snapped at the air over his shoulder like a dog after flies and went out again.

I was right.

*

Sister looked at brother. She said, 'A bad day . . .'

'Shall I go and have a word?' asked Mr Thwaite.

'No, no. He has to be alone. He will probably go out. It is a beautiful evening. If you pass him anywhere outside you might just say "duck".'

'Duck?'

'For dinner. He is fond of duck.'

At least one was allowed outside. And the locks on the gates had been thin.

'Excuse me,' I said, 'but could you please tell me . . .'

'Of course. What to call me. I am Celia – Lady Celia – there was a husband once – and so on. I kept the title – it was all there was. As you know, I am a poet.'

'Oh. No – I didn't.'

'Really?'

'I'm afraid I haven't read very much poetry. Modern . . .'

'Ah, that can be rectified here.'

'Novels,' said Arthur Thwaite. 'Great novel reader. Plays piano. Speaks German and so forth.'

'Ah – you are in for a great treat then. A great experience. There is to be a recital here by Grünt tomorrow. You will know Grünt?'

'I'm afraid . . .'

'My child,' she said, hauling up her hand again, 'you are going to be wonderfully awakened here.'

I realised (in the end) that I was meant to take the hand and caught it just as it collapsed. It was ice-cold, colder than the rings on it, and it lay in mine as dead.

'*How* old did you say, Arthur?'

'Har – harumph, sixteen.'

'How *wonderful*,' she said. 'How very wonderful for us all.'

*

Thwaite

Dear Aunt Frances,

I hope that you will read this before you go to India. I am sending it to the address you gave in London. I expect that you will be surprised at the address at the head of this letter and so, in fact, am I.

After the wedding was over Mr Thwaite asked almost immediately if I would like to come here on a visit. He said it was near where you were born and had lived when you were all little and as I was missing you I said that if Aunt Mary could spare me, yes, I'd love to come. And so we came, he and I together, yesterday.

There is no need for me to describe it to you because I suppose that you must know every nook and corner of this house and I do wonder why you never told me about it or about Mr Thwaite. It was so strange to meet him before the wedding, walking in from the marsh in his tweeds and cape and pipe. I felt as if I had always known him. But you never said.

The wedding was very nice. I hope that you and Father Pocock enjoyed it immensely. It was a shame that Mrs Woods wasn't well. I thought that everyone, and especially the nuns, sang very clearly during the service, and the responses were very good. Mr Pocock sang well, too. I did not know that the bridegroom sang at a wedding but you could hear Mr Pocock's voice *ring out*, as at the eleven

75

o'clock service and his shoulder-blades were going up and down like bellows. I heard one of the nuns say that it was a very *encouraging* and reverent wedding.

I did not actually sing, and I don't know about Aunt Mary. Afterwards at the reception, I felt that everything was rather quiet. The idea of your going to India is still very strange to me and sudden and I am sorry that I cried.

Perhaps in the six weeks of your journey to India it might be interesting for you to read about news of home. I thought that I would tell you a little every few days of what is happening to me here. You will be too busy with the vestment-buying and so on to read it now. Also I expect that being married is very interesting and distracting for you. But perhaps you may read this in small instalments on the high seas. I know that you have the Bible with you, like Robinson Crusoe, but I wonder if he sometimes wished for something a little lighter? And so here I am, in my bedroom, at a rosewood desk with a silver inkstand and blotting-paper it would be a sin to blot with. I am longing to tell you every detail.

*

I am sorry, Aunt Frances. I have left this letter for several days.

What I have said is not quite truthful.

You see, I do not want to tell you about this place. When I begin to think how to do it, I see your face. Then I believe that I can see you in the ship, and the sun rising redder and hotter every day as you get nearer Bombay and your thoughts getting further and further from us and your old life. I see you with all your old life forgotten, dim, as was the old life of Robinson Crusoe in Hull. I see you walking about the deck with Mr Pocock, and the dolphins playing and the great seas swinging, mounting, heaving, dropping, and Mr Pocock and Aunt Frances in the midst of them, and above you both the swirling stars. I do greatly envy you this experience Aunt Frances. And so I think – though we do not often talk of it precisely – does Mr Thwaite.

Aunt Frances, will you please forgive me if I speak to you in a way I would find difficult if I were at Oversands with

76

Mrs Woods always just out of sight, and Alice about and Aunt Mary, who is so pure?

Aunt Frances, why did you leave me before telling me anything of any real use to my life? Here I am with Mr Thwaite and Lady Celia and in one sense I do feel very much at home. In another sense I am unsure. I have become even unsure about whether I should have come to live with you at Oversands – where perhaps I have become fragmented and incomplete. I don't believe that I shall ever really fit in anywhere, although you and Aunt Mary have given me what Robinson Crusoe was told by his father was the greatest blessing. A home in 'the middle state or what might be called the upper station of low life which he had found by long experience was the best state in the world, the most suited to human happiness'.

The trouble, Aunt Frances, is perhaps that I am a girl. Had I been a boy – your sister's baby boy, some solid stubborn boy perhaps called Jack or Harry – how would you have done then? You would have sent me away to school and please, oh please forgive me for saying so, Aunt Frances, but the money would have been found. It would have been a Christian sort of school like Rossall or Repton and you would all have prayed and prayed for me that I would become a priest. But because I am a girl, Aunt Frances, I was to be stood in a vacuum. I was to be left in the bell-jar of Oversands. Nothing in the world is ever to happen to me. Since I have met these people here at Thwaite I have begun to see what I have missed.

I love the marsh and Oversands and I know that I live in a very compelling landscape as the Brontës did. But Aunt Frances I am not at all sure about the Brontës. I am not sure that we were ever meant to become knitted into a landscape. After all, I am in no way mystical, I don't even want to be Confirmed. When Robinson Crusoe was married to a land-scape you know, he had a hard time to keep sane. I am being dissolved into a landscape and all hope for me is that someone will come and marry me to make things complete and take me away.

But is marriage the only completing, necessary thing? I keep thinking of you and hoping that you really thought it out – whether marriage is a necessary thing. I expect by now you will be getting used to it. It may seem quite natural by the time you get to India. There is so much I wish we could have talked about before you left. You have such a secret life now. A shutter comes down when people get married.

Here at Lady Celia's, though, there are not many shutters coming down. All is very different and nobody seems at all sure that marriage is a necessary thing. There are many people here, all of them artists – writers and poets and painters and musicians – and they seem to be very confused most of the time. Lady Celia looks after them. They spend a lot of time in their rooms or walking in the grounds, sometimes late into the night, up and down the lawns, forgetting dinner. They must be very serious about their work or very rich to miss such lovely dinners which Lady Celia kindly urges them towards.

There is a lady who plays a harp. She is fat and nice. When she walks she wobbles but her hands are white and small. Then there is a funny little painter who snaps at the air like a dog. The other evening I almost fell over him in the rose-garden. He was watching the sun drop down behind the hills and he said 'Into the heart of darkness or into the heart of light.' I think it was a quotation. It is all very different from Oversands – nobody goes to church at all. 'We are all free here,' said Lady Celia, yet she seems to lie on her yellow sofa holding long threads somehow, and every thread is tied to a guest.

I could not help comparing the snapping painter to Robinson Crusoe. If I had stepped out of the bushes upon Robinson Crusoe in his loneliness, he would, even after years of solitude, have behaved with greater decorum and manners than the painter, who had been talking to people only at tea-time.

Aunt Frances, there seems to be very little simple pleasure here. It does seem very queer that great artists (Lady Celia says that all her guests are famous and some of them great) should be so ugly on the whole and really rather ordinary in their conversation. I wonder if Daniel Defoe was ordinary to meet? I said some of this to Mr Thwaite and he cleared his throat so much that I think he agreed with me. He has a great admiration of his sister and what she does for artists, nevertheless.

We had a piano recital the evening of the day I arrived by a pianist called Grünt. He is very famous and he is, Lady Celia says, 'the greatest living exponent of the works of Chopin'. We all gathered in the drawing-room and after a time he came in and sat down. He hung down his head so far that his nose very nearly touched the keyboard and he sat there, as praying, and we all sat in tremendous silence, except that Mr Thwaite suddenly gave a very great sneeze. First Lady Celia and then everybody else gave Mr Thwaite a look, but Herr Grünt just hung his face down closer to the keys so that the end of his nose actually brushed middle C – and then his long and bony hands reached up and he began to play.

They played quite independently of his body and even his head, which stayed quite close by middle C for a considerable time. Then his head flung itself up in the air and his face became parallel with the ceiling as the hands went on with a life of their own. His eyes were shut. It was rather warm in the room and all the poets began to sigh and groan and shift about a bit. Only Lady Celia stayed utterly still like a statue in robes.

He went on and on. It's a wonderful piano. His head is very big – far too large for his shoulders which slope away. They aren't so powerful as Mr Pocock's and I thought, well, if Herr Grünt were to get married he would not have the wonderful strength to sing at his wedding. *Down* flopped his head again, very close to his finger-tips. Then – plinkety. . . plonkety . . . plink. Very quiet. Very separate. One note. Another note. Little water drops. One, two, three . . . And a long long silence.

Then he opened his eyes and everyone stirred.

They didn't say 'bravo' or clap. They *stirred*, with a very serious, bulgy, bottomy movement and looked at one another with great meaning in their eyes, except for Mr Thwaite, who had taken out his handkerchief and was examining all the hems on it.

Then, a great murmur of awe went round the drawing-room and Herr Grünt rose and went over to Lady Celia and picked up her hand which is terribly heavy with yellow rings and he kissed it and looked at her and her lips moved and everyone began to breathe adjectives; and some people got out their handkerchieves just as Mr Thwaite was putting his away.

And I did so wish that you were there, Aunt Frances. Herr Grünt was actually, and in fact, the *most terrible pianist!*

Aunt Frances I felt so lonely.

I will write to you again. I am longing for your letters when they come from Oversands. I hope that you and Mr Pocock are enjoying your honeymoon and please forgive me if this letter is not a very controlled one, your loving Polly.

*

Thwaite

Dear Aunt Frances,

I am afraid that I am writing you a great many letters and it is so aggravating because I know that by now your letters to me must be collecting up at home. I shan't see them for ages unless Alice posts them on, and somehow I feel that she may not be very quick at that as she's going to be taken up so much with the spring cleaning and then to have her holiday. Mrs Woods was still in bed when I left, though I expect she will be well enough now to have gone to her nursing home.

Aunt Mary, of course as you will know, has gone into Retreat and there have to be no letters. She is so terribly good, not needing them. I must say I do – and I need to write them, too – and I keep wishing that there were more people I could send postcards to. I have sent some to the nuns.

So I am going to have to bore only you with what has happened since the Chopin recital. I don't find it boring, but perhaps it will be to you, so busy at The Society for the Propagation of the Gospel and the Army and Navy Stores. It is very wonderful here, though. Very gracious and beautiful. We live as if we are all extra-special. I'm afraid it isn't very Christian at all.

After the recital the excitement of the day was far from over. Lady Celia suggested that we all should walk on the terrace for a while and she was helped out by Herr Grünt. He was a bit tottery because of the exhaustion of the piece and Mr Thwaite got hold of his arms and they all three stepped out together through the French doors in a row. Mr Thwaite looked very fine and knightly in his evening dress and his moustache – much more noble in every way than any of the artists and writers and I thought again that perhaps ugliness is one of the things that a creative artist has to put up with as a penance for his other advantages. Apart from Shakespeare and Byron and Shelley, most seem to have been rather plain, don't they? And they stare so much.

As I thought these things, Herr Grünt suddenly fell over which made Mr Thwaite fall over too and for a terrible minute it looked as if Lady Celia would be pulled down beneath them. And then she would have been extinguished. But the painter who barks like a dog came and slid himself cleverly underneath her.

Then there was a quartette of fallen people collapsed upon the terrace and some of them great artists. And when Mr Thwaite stood up and stood on Herr Grünt's right hand and Herr Grünt screamed, it really became quite a serious occasion.

People ran about. There was a very substantial man who is a Fellow of All Souls (I think this means a humble person studying to be a priest at a famous church somewhere in Oxford and I expect you will have heard of it) and he cried out, 'They're off! They're off! Finished – his career is finished!'

Everybody ran and helped Herr Grünt to his feet, and he was weeping, and a long lady in purple looked very deeply at a thin lady with a fringe who paints water-colours. '*What* are off?' asked the little white harpist. 'Fingers,' said the FOAS.

Even the butler was laughing – he's awfully nice – called Barker, and he and the housekeeper, Maitland, are not a bit what you'd expect. I have been invited to supper with them one night in the servants' hall.

After the multiple falling over, Barker laughed quite openly. Nobody noticed but me. He laughed in a sober sort of way but for quite a long time.

Then we all went early to bed.

This morning Lady Celia sent for me. She said, 'Child – '

(I think she may just play at being Miss Havisham sometimes) – 'Child, you are very *quaint*.'

I said I was sorry.

'It is not in your control,' she said. 'Quaintness is caused
by circumstance. Nevertheless you ought to wear different
clothes.'

I said, 'Thank you, Lady Celia, but I think Aunt Mary
might not like me to have new clothes at present. I have
had new clothes for the wedding.'

'Those?' she said.

'Yes,' I said.

'Oh,' she said and closed her eyes. 'Green,' she said,
'kingfisher green. Glossy. Shot.'

I said that actually kingfishers were blue. There were
some in The Hall pond at home. I also said that it is
virtually impossible to shoot a kingfisher. As well as being
a frightful idea. Herr Grünt was sitting near, nursing his
right hand which was in a bandage the size of a wasp's
nest and he gave a shocked moan as if I were being remiss.

Then I heard someone laugh and it was the painter; but
Lady Celia looked at him and he snapped the air.

Lady Celia's eyes gave a snap round the room, too, a
fierce one. 'Quaintness may go too far,' she said. 'Help me
up – no, not you – ' (the big purple woman had lunged
forward) – 'Polly Flint.'

So I helped her up and armed her across the room feeling
very clumsy and huge. I'm still growing horribly as you
very well know. At the door she turned and looked at
everyone, one at a time, and they mostly looked frightened
(but not the painter) as if they might possibly soon be
leaving.

Then we began a long journey, Lady C and I, slowly.
Up the main great staircase at last, where she kept stopping
and holding on to the front of her neck. You could see a
vein beating in it and I was scared and said, 'Lady Celia,
are you well?'

'No.'

'Then shouldn't you – stop? Shall I get Maitland?'

'Of course not. I am perfectly well. What is not well is
the company in this house.'

'Oh, I'm sure they're – '

'They are not what they once were.'

'Oh, I'm sure none of them is so *very* old.'

'My family', she said, 'has entertained Tennyson.'

'Yes I see. But I expect he got old in the end.'

'His age was immaterial. Mr Dodgson has been a guest in this house. Many times.'

'Mr Dodgson – oh, did you know him?'

'Of course. He was at Croft. I was a child.'

'Oh – did he talk about *Alice*? And creatures?'

'He hadn't thought of *Alice* then. He kept asking difficult questions. Very queer mathematical things. And he was fond of marmalade.'

'Yes, I see.'

'But it was immaterial. Whatever he said or did was immaterial, for he was going to write *Alice*.'

I said, 'Oh yes. Oh *yes*.' I looked at her – all rings and paint and silly draperies and proud mouth and her old claw hands on her stick. 'Oh Lady Celia, yes.' I said it with terrific agreement rather congratulating her. She didn't like it much.

We were in her bedroom now. 'Sit me there,' she said and I settled her on a lovely watered-silk sofa with a curled end and she spread her shawls about. 'Over there,' she said and pointed at an old piece of furniture. 'Open the press.'

So many materials were stacked inside the press that it looked like a pirate's cave. A female-pirate's cave. Flimsy bits and silky bits and thick velvety bits and long, long lacy bits all crammed in and layered tight, all the colours there are, all textures, all patterns.

One of the very few mistakes in *Robinson Crusoe* is his regret about clothes – one of the jokes is his clumsy furry appearance in the nanny-goat skins. Yet there were clothes brought off the ship. He had them by him. He did not use them. Or scarcely. Perhaps he had never really cared about his appearance. I would guess this was true. One can imagine him as a boy of say fourteen, in Hull, looking not very well turned-out I think. And his parents not being enthusiastic about him at all.

Clothes on the desert island are what I should very much

have missed. Different, beautiful clothes as time went by. Though I never, never seem to be wearing the right ones.

'Oh,' I said. 'Different beautiful clothes.'

'Try the greens,' she said.

'I'd love the yellows,' and I draped one after the other round myself. 'Yes,' she said, 'we could do worse than that. Try a red.' There was a dark red velvet a hundred miles long and I paraded about.

'Frightful,' she said. 'Try the blue. There's a blue there. Kingfisher blue.'

I dropped the red and patrolled in the blue.

'It gives you eyes,' she said. 'A start. It must be the blue. You approve of *Alice?* Many children don't.'

'I love *Alice.* I mean the book, not the girl.'

'Why not the girl?'

'She was a bit stodgy.'

'Why?'

'Oh, the bows and the frills and the big chin and she did answer back so.'

'You are very decisive yourself. Especially for someone who has lived so far from the centre of things.'

'But it's the centre of things for me,' I said, 'and I'm sixteen years old. Alice was a child and everything was very everyday for her. She'd seen nothing odd. She just lived in Oxford.'

'Her dreams say otherwise.'

'She was a child,' I said.

She looked at me for ages and then said, 'Come here. Yes, I suppose you are. Older than. . .' but then she wouldn't say any more. 'You shall have the yellow,' she said, 'and the blue. I believe there is a brown velvet ready-made somewhere too – Maitland can find it – which will do for now. Wear it tomorrow. Ring the bell for Maitland.'

Then in came Maitland all pursed up and there was a great deal of talk about the lovely material and fussing about. It looks as if I am to be dressed as a princess. I sat at her dressing-table. All the silver! Great fat chunky look-ing-glass with fat silver cherubs flying and brushes galore, far too heavy for her and rows of glass bottles with silver stoppers.

There was a box made of pink and cream chips of some-

84

thing shiny – Persian people lying on benches and looking lovingly across at each other. She opened it and scrabbled about. All kinds of glittery things. The maid Maitland fastened up her mouth tighter.

'Maitland,' she said, 'shall we have Polly read us some Tennyson?'

'Yes m'lady.'

'Some Tennyson, Polly.'

An edition was produced. I read them Tennyson. *Maud*. I went on for about half an hour. Then Maitland started clanking the water-jug. Lady Celia had shut her eyes. '*The Lady of Shalott*,' she said, so I started that. I went into a sort of trance over it after a while as I always do with Aunt Mary though it upsets Aunt Mary doesn't it? She never liked it as you do, Aunt Frances. When I came to.

'She left the web, she left the loom

She made three paces – ' Lady Celia said, 'Stop!' and took a little greyish glass bottle and sniffed at it. 'The end,' she said.

So I read the end – the lovely man looking down over the bridge on the poor dead face, all of her so lovely and never even been for a walk. She must have had an awfully pasty complexion when you come to think of it. 'Wonderful!' said Lady Celia. 'Is it not?'

I said that it was wonderful.

'Do you love Tennyson?'

'Oh yes.'

She lifted a necklace out of the Persian box.

'Better than anybody?'

I watched the necklace. It swung. It was seed-pearls, with a little diamond clasp like a diamond daisy. It was small. Made for a girl.

But I had to say, 'No, not better.' And the necklace swung.

'Not best of all?'

'Well, I don't think he's quite as good as Daniel Defoe.'

'Daniel *Defoe?*' she said, as if other Daniels might have got by – the one in the lions den, or the one George Eliot wrote about, or Daniel the Upright and Discerning Judge.

'Daniel *Defoe?* You mean *Robinson Crusoe? Moll Flanders?*'

'Yes.'

'But my child – no trace, no *trace* of poetry. No trace of poetic truth.'

But then, Aunt Frances, I grew terribly angry and said in a fury, '*Robinson Crusoe* is full of poetic truth. And it is an attempt at a universal truth very differently expressed.'

'No form,' she cried, 'no form.'

I said, 'It is wonderfully written. It is true to his chosen form. Because of this verisimilitude it reads like reality. I have read it twenty-three times. In a novel form is not always apparent at a first or second reading. Form is determined by hard secret work – in a notebook and in the subconscious and in the head.'

'You speak of journalism.'

'Yes. Why not? With glory added. And not a lot of gush and romantic love.'

She let the necklace trickle back into the box and there was a long silence and then Maitland said, 'Oughtn't Miss Polly to be going to change?'

So I went out.

I went out rather noisily, I am afraid, because I felt very angry on behalf of Daniel Defoe. And I love you and goodnight and I'll continue probably tomorrow, Your loving Polly.

*

There was a thunder storm on Sunday evening this week and a tremendous sheet of rain across the plain of York. The drawing-room windows were closed and we all watched the lightning and listened to the swish and hiss of the tropical-sounding rain. Whenever the rain eased a little we opened the windows to let in the steamy summer night. When at last it had nearly stopped, the butler came and flung them wide and the sweet smell of flowers and wet grass – and lilacs – swam into the room.

The house was lamp-lit. Lady Celia and the guests sat talking in undertones very earnestly. The purple woman and the fringed water-colourist sat together in a window-seat and the Fellow of All Souls enunciated carefully to Herr Grünt who seemed to be nodding asleep. Mr Thwaite was not there, nor the painter. I wished somebody – not Herr Grünt – would play the lovely piano. I wondered if I should go up to bed, when there was a little noise beside me and I looked up and saw the butler.

It was not so much a noise he made as an easing of the feet. One, two, they went on the oriental rug. Like a cat padding. He held a tray with nothing on it for he had finished distributing Madeira round the room (the purple lady had taken two) and he was looking firmly at me.

'Message from Maitland, Miss Polly.'

'Oh, thank you, Mr Barker.'

'To speak in the sitting-room.'

'Yes I see. When?'

'Now, Miss Polly. If you have a moment. When you have said goodnight.' He looked from me to Lady Celia and back again and at once I went over to her and said goodnight, and goodnight all round, though nobody noticed much.

'Listen to the owls,' cried the purple lady. 'I distinctly hear owls.'

'Owls, owls,' mumbled Herr Grünt and went to the piano and shrill unhappy yearning noises came out of it as I followed Barker out. They cut into the stillness of the drawing-room and all its lamps and whispers as we closed the door, but the music did not catch the true awfulness of the cries of owls whose essential quality is bad temper (Robinson Crusoe was spared owls) and Herr Grünt has not the vitality for bad temper.

After a long walk, Mr Barker bowed me not into the servants' hall but into a smallish room where a fire burned bright but didn't make it stuffy in spite of the storm. Three lamps were turned up as high as they would go, one on a round table covered with thick, cream-coloured oilcloth and tacked in underneath. On the oilcloth a pack of cards was laid out. In a rocking-chair Maitland was darning and on an upright chair opposite sat Mr Thwaite, slapping down one playing-card upon another at top speed. He had removed his dinner jacket and black tie and sat in his studs and silver braces. He looked rosy and at his wrist stood a great glass of beer. 'And so and so and *so*,' he said, to the last cards, and looked round in triumph. 'And so! Out. Finish. Chess? Mr Barker. Ha – Polly. Very unsettled evening. The barometer is almost at risk.'

'Here she is,' said Mr Barker to Maitland who looked at

me over her gold glasses, while her needle flew about over the wooden mushroom she held to the sock-hole.

'A game of chess, Polly?' said Mr Thwaite.

'Mr Barker said that Maitland wanted me.'

'Yes – never mind her for chess, Mr Thwaite. We thought she might like a cup of tea in here with us. You two get down to the chess.'

She stooped forward and crunched the kettle down in the coals. 'We always have a cup of tea about now. And a short-bread. Sit down and make yourself comfortable. I'll have to start measuring you before long for this kingfisher festivity.'

It was funny to see the way she was in charge – not only of me the newest guest but of her husband. On the other side of the baize door Mr Barker looked and behaved like King Rameses of Egypt in Grandfather Younghusband's book of Kings. But she was also in charge of her employer – for Mr Thwaite sat there engrossed, using his head, drinking his beer, filled with the acceptance that life is very good.

'Move your arm now, Mr Thwaite,' she said. 'Let's set down these cups and saucers. Barker, take your shoes off. Put them by the fender.'

Mr Thwaite opened up the chess box as Mr Barker brought the board and they set out the men between them.

'Your move, sir,' said Mr Barker. He set down a glass for himself and a jug of beer among the tea-things. 'Yours last night.' Mr Thwaite looked piercingly at the pieces – and at length moved queen's pawn. 'They're off,' said Maitland, 'that's better. Here's your tea, Miss Polly, and we'll have a nice talk.'

'Lady Celia thinks I've gone to bed.'

'Well then, she'll be content. She's happy when everyone's safe in bed.'

'Is she? Why?'

'She likes to lie thinking of the good she's done – helping everyone, knowing that all these wonderful people are resting.'

'Why does she?'

'She believes that she was born to help geniuses and I dare say that she is right. They go away fatter than they came.'

'It's very kind of her.'

'It's *very* kind of her. Very kind. That's what tends to get forgotten in any discussion of Lady Celia. She may order them cruel but she never stops giving. Behaving filthily, a lot of them.'

'I suppose if they're geniuses – '

'There's no excuse for filthy under-drawers where there's soap and servants. Some never takes them off in a week. Mr Dodgson, of course, was very clean. Here – let's see. Turn to the door – no, there isn't enough for a long sleeve. I said there wouldn't be. You've a good round arm. You'll look well in this blue.'

'I could darn for you if you like.'

'You're here for a holiday.'

'I'd like something to do.'

'I hope you are not going to be bored with us,' Mr Barker called over his shoulder in a much more host-like way than Mr Thwaite or Lady Celia would ever have done. It would never occur to Lady Celia to enquire how anybody was enjoying himself. I was still very embarrassed about not knowing quite what I was meant to do all day and I'd been spending quite a lot of time just wandering about between meals, picking up books in the library and putting them down again. They weren't so engrossing somehow as the ones at the yellow house, being so often books people had written about other books and so many of the pages being un-cut was rather strange. You had to peer in sideways.

Wherever I walked I tended to meet the other guests walking idly, too. Not the water-colourist – she was safe because she had her easel – and not Herr Grünt. He was safe with the piano: but the rest of us, it occurred to me, might perhaps all be playing the same game. The snapping painter never painted. He stood for long periods quite still on the lawn. The purple woman poet I had met that morning, transfixed before a fat blue hyacinth which burned intensely at her feet. I said, 'Oh sorry,' coming round a bush, and then wondered why, for she had not moved a muscle. Later on I found her staring at another hyacinth right down near the great glasshouses. It was a thinner, pink hyacinth, looking rather poorly, beginning to bend a bit and go tea-coloured at the tips. I had had to say, 'Oh sorry,' again and this time she turned and seemed to come out of her trance. 'I *was* the hyacinth,' she said.

'Yes, I see.'

'I *was* it, and it was I.'

'Yes I see.'

'You see? See? If only you could. If only any of us could truly see.' We both looked down at the pink hyacinth which chose that moment to keel over. It is a rare sight to see a hyacinth collapse, being so sappy and stout, but this one tipped slowly and inevitably over like a soldier fainting and its bulb stuck out in the air with all its root threads writhing about like wire-worms. I couldn't help laughing, but she glared furiously – first at the hyacinth and then at me, and when I said, 'Oh poor thing. It's all been a bit much,' the purple woman walked off very grimly twirling her ebony cane.

Thinking about it now, darning, I started laughing again and Maitland said, 'And so what's this?' and I began to tell her, putting down the darning and taking swigs of tea. Deep breathing came from the chess players and the odd little chink from the fire but otherwise the room was quite still and utterly beautiful. I do not mean that there was anything of definite beauty – it was a cluttery dingy room – unpainted for years. There were ugly framed family photographs, an ugly sewing machine, an ugly rag-rug. It was the atmosphere which was beautiful – Mr Barker, Mr Thwaite, Maitland and I and the blue material were beautiful. Four people happy together. Light-hearted and happy in a way that was not very usual at Oversands.

'That'll do,' said Maitland when I got to the bit about the hyacinth falling over. She was trying to make her tight mouth deny itself.

*

'And what of the hair-cutting?' called Mr Thwaite from behind his hovering knight. Maitland said, 'And that'll do from you, Mr Thwaite.'

I said, 'Oh no – please, what about the hair-cutting?'

So he told us the story about when a very famous writer indeed was staying at the house and there was a poet staying, too, who had been here so long that his hair was getting in his soup and he wanted it cut. Lady Celia liked it, however, and said there was no barber nearer than York and so secretly the poet asked the very famous writer just to trim his hair a little on the quiet. While Lady Celia was resting, they spread a bed-sheet on the poet's bedroom floor and the writer came to borrow Maitland's scissors but they were not adequate. He needed very long sharp scissors he said, and Maitland had been rather worried, but had sent for horse-clippers and shears.

'Needlessly,' said Mr Barker, 'needlessly worried. That was not one we ever had trouble with. Melancholy at times, yes. Suicidal and dangerous, no.'

I wondered whether to tell them that when I arrived I'd thought it was a lunatic asylum but then thought they might be hurt. 'I shouldn't think geniuses would be very good barbers,' I said. 'It is quite difficult for an ordinary man to cut hair. Even a practical, very very sensible man like Robinson Crusoe couldn't cut hair. It was a great drawback to him. I always wondered about that though. I'm sure a woman would have found a way. Like gnawing.'

'He made a very fair try,' said Barker, 'A very even finish, the novelist,' and both he and Maitland looked across at Mr Thwaite, and I saw that servants do not laugh before their employer at the guests of that employer. Mr Thwaite said, 'No bad hand at it at all. Trouble was he had a bit of a go at his own afterwards and a lot of hair got scattered off the bed-sheet around the room and they tried to get it up with the hearth-brush and left some soot-marks on the carpet. Then they burned it.'

'What, the carpet?'

'No, the hair. They lit some paper in the fireplace and burned the hair on it and then they gathered up the bed-sheet hair into the grate too and the bed-sheet caught fire.'

'Yes, I see.'

'Then they crammed the whole bed-sheet into the fireplace to try to choke out the fire but there was quite a – well, a very fair blaze. Not many actual flames but rather a great deal of smoke which went billowing out and they flapped it about the room with pillows and things to try and do some-thing about the smell of burned hair and then the pillows caught fire. Somebody sitting on the lawn – we were all waiting for tea – heard them and saw the smoke and cried: "Fire", and Mr Barker and the stablemen had to go running with buckets and a boy was sent to Pilmoor for the fire brigade, but they didn't get here for two hours.'

'Whatever did Lady Celia do?'

'Oh, she was quite wonderful. She never said one word except at dinner. She asked the great writer why one side of his hair was six inches shorter than the other. He hadn't been able to finish you see.'

'What about the poet?'

'He disappeared.'

'Check,' said Mr Barker.

'Serves me right,' said Mr Thwaite. 'Not concentrating.'

'You do have fun here,' I said.

'We have our little moments,' said Maitland. 'Not much for anyone your age though, Miss Polly. No young life. You're the first child I ever remember.'

'I'm not a child. I'm sixteen.'

'You are and you're not. You're younger than many a twelve and you talk older than many a one we've had here of forty.'

'She makes these utterances,' said Mr Barker. 'My wife is a very wise woman.'

'I didn't know you were married to each other.'

'Does it seem so strange?'

'No. It seems perfect.'

Mr Thwaite cleared his throat and said, 'Excellent. A very excellent arrangement.'

'I think everything here is absolutely excellent and perfect,' I said. 'I've never been so happy.'

'You should go to bed now though,' said Maitland, 'child or no child. There's something for you to look forward to tomorrow. Did you know? A new one.'

'No. What – a new guest?'

'Yes. Something special. A poet. The most hopeful thing since Shakespeare, we understand, and he must be. He's to have the green room.'

'I hope he doesn't snap the air.'

'He's scarcely more than a boy,' said Mr Thwaite. 'Celia is very fond of boys.'

'I think she's asked him for Miss Polly.'

'Oh, I shouldn't count on that.'

'For *Miss Polly*,' said Maitland very firmly. 'And there's a new blue linen and a good hat for you you'll find in your wardrobe as well as the new brown velvet. I had a roust about. And I took the liberty of discarding the pelisse.'

*

The motor went off for the poet the next morning – not the trap. This guest was important.

I heard it leave and I can't say that I waited about for its return but as I sat reading on the lawn until luncheon I found that every now and then I stopped to listen and often looked up.

But at luncheon nothing was new. The dining-room was dark – the pale blinds drawn against the sun and Lady Celia playing with curls of toast and examining her sole. There were not many of us. The poets all seemed to be resting and the water-colourist had not returned from her morning session by the wheat-field. The snapping painter had completely disappeared and only Herr Grünt sat dismally at the far end of the table, his long blue under-lip extended as a ledge for his spoon.

Afterwards, I wandered about, wishing for Mr Thwaite. He was said to have gone for a walk somewhere after breakfast and I wished he had asked me to go with him. He had gone across the fields, Maitland said, towards Brafferton and if I took the hedgerow paths and then the river path I might just meet him coming back. He had probably gone by Thoralby and Roundstone.

'Thoralby?'

'The Jewish people are near Thoralby.'

'Jewish people?'

'Yes. They live near Thoralby.'

'You mean a sort of – tribe?'

I couldn't understand her or why she laughed. I had never met any Jews as I had never met anybody black or a Roman Catholic. Jews were in the Old Testament. 'A great family,' she said, 'rich as princes. They are industrialists.'

'But it's all farms,' I said.

'They have bought a manor house here. They have houses all over the place. They've branched out from Tyneside some-where – they're foreigners. Originally from Germany or some place like that. Thwaite doesn't mix with them. Not socially.'

93

'But you said Mr Thwaite might have gone there?'

'Oh, Mr Thwaite mixes everywhere. Mr Thwaite, we don't question.'

'Doesn't Lady Celia know the Jews?'

'No. She wanted to. She thought they might be musical. When she found out they were just industrial she was very disappointed.'

'Yes I see. I'd love to meet some Jews,' I said. 'Do they worship idols?'

'They worship the same good God as you and me and Jesus Christ,' she said. 'Hist?'

There was a crackly noise of the motor arriving and after a moment Mr Barker came in – we were in the kitchen – to say 'Three trains have been met and no guest alighting.' He and Maitland exchanged a long look.

So I set off across the gardens to a gate in the wall and along the hedgerow paths and down to the river and along the meadows hoping to meet Mr Thwaite on his way back, perhaps accompanied by some of the industrial Jews. I imagined them walking together in a little group like on the road to Emmaus, but it was difficult. I felt like poor Robinson Crusoe when he first saw the cannibal boats, staring and staring as hard as he could but making out nothing because he'd come out without his expanding-glass.

It was lovely after the storm – the grasses by the river in shiny clumps and feathery with seeds, all the dandelions and meadowsweet polished and clean and the water running fast in the streams. The meadow smells were not like the marsh smells – the rushes and blites and spurreys and scurvy grasses.

I was wearing Maitland's 'blue' which turned out to be a lovely floppy skirt and top and a sailor-blouse with white on it with a big bow and a straw hat with ribbons. I had undone my hair, all loose and long. Maitland said this was acceptable, since I was in the country – until I was seventeen. At seventeen, up it must go. I kept imagining Mr Thwaite appearing round the next corner with a cluster of disciples – strong fishermen-type people with hook noses? Very brown, and sandals? Country people – except of course, St Luke, who was a doctor. I wondered how doctors dressed in Galilee about 30 AD and if they carried a bag of any sort and I sat down and took a reed and pulled the brown tufty sprout off it and began to suck the worm of white sorbet inside. I licked it and tapped it with my tongue.

It was a very hot afternoon. I took off my hat. I lay down and looked up at the sky. Then I sat up. There was not a sound anywhere. There could be no people for miles. The path I'd been following was hardly a path at all. I took off the top of my sailor suit. It felt stuffy and hard. Then I took off my liberty-bodice and then I took off my vest and I lay down with no clothes on the top half of myself in the long grass and listened to the river running by. I thought of the disciples walking talkatively along with Mr Thwaite. And then I fell asleep.

When I woke up there seemed to be a disciple looking at me – very serious and reflective. He had a twitchy sort of nose and bright black eyes and I felt he was some old friend. But when I sat up he was not there and I knew that he had been part of a dream.

The sun had gone. It looked like rain again. I knew it was much later. I looked astonished at my bare arms and then more astonished at the bare huge rest of me. I must have been mad. Lying half naked in broad daylight in the middle of the plain of York! I scrabbled back into the blouse, pushed the vest and bodice into the skirt pockets, tried to get myself straightened out round the waist. Then I thought I heard voices calling somewhere along the path and I was filled with wonderfully exciting shame. I found the hat, crammed it on my head and ran frantically back along the way I had come.

I ran for nearly a mile until I came to the door in Thwaite wall and slid through it and leaned against it, then walked quickly along inside the wall, past the bonfire place, the glasshouses, the pink hyacinth still displaying its unseeable underparts to all who passed by like the man who fell among thieves. I sidled into the house and up to my room and saw in the glass a ruby-red face on a rough girl like a well fed gypsy with torn stockings, wild hair and her vest hanging out of her pocket.

Outside on the lawn the guests were beginning to gather for tea from their creative activities for the next part of the comforting time-table Lady Celia had provided for them against the assaults of their calling.

Seeing them pacing so soberly, acquiescently forward, I

found that I was crying and the reason for this seemed to be that I had now to go down and join them. I, so nondescript and friendless, and wearing all my clothes. And somewhere, Charlotte peeped from a corner of the room with some triumph and there were some queer shadows behind her from Wales.

Below me, Mr Barker was walking like Rameses over the lawn following two parlour-maids in black and white. He carried a cake-stand and they the heavy trays of silver and the tea-cups. Mr Thwaite had arrived – no sign of the disciples – and his sweet smile brightened at the sight of the cakes and made me calmer. 'I shall have to join in,' I thought. 'I shall have to go down.'

'Beggars can't choose,' said Charlotte from inside the wardrobe as I changed my dress. 'It's not as if there's anything else for you. You've no excuse to be different. You can't write poetry or paint or play very well and you'll never write a book. You've never been to school or felt you were a hyacinth. All you can do is speak German and talk about *Robinson Crusoe*. There's no genius in you.'

So I walked sadly on to the landing and there was somebody there. He said, 'Oh thank goodness – I know absolutely no one. May I go down with you?'

*

Thwaite

Aunt Frances, most dear and best beloved, I have fallen in love. Paul, he is called, Paul Treece, a friend of Lady Celia and the most beautiful of human beings. Oh let me tell you what has happened.

He was standing on the stairs yesterday as I came out of my room to go down in the garden for tea, and he is twenty years old, which is old, I know, but from the first moment it did not matter. He has quite a godlike air but he has not at all a godlike certainty because he said, 'Could I go down with you? I don't know a single soul.'

It seemed amazing. It was exactly what I would have said to him, the very words. I felt that we had changed souls. I said, 'Oh yes,' in a very stiff way and we walked downstairs side by side but very far apart. He walks all bobby up and down and bouncy – and all the time he talks – very fast and excited. He is a poet and in his second year at Cambridge. He is very eager all the time. Out of the sides of my eyes I kept getting a look at him and his profile is – oh Aunt Frances – most utterly perfect. His nose could be a nose in a textbook of fine noses.

On the lawn there were two other new people just arrived – very important new ones making their way to Wooller in Scotland: writers of some very significant sort – a melancholy brooding man and a very thin woman in old expensive clothes with the hem coming down, who was beautiful. Even her raggedness looked queenly. She was rather wild about the eyes which were in very deep caves in her face, and the corners of her mouth turned down in a desperately forlorn and anxious, yet sweet way. Her hands were long and bony and she clutched her tea-cup tight. When Lady Celia introduced us all, this woman looked for a long time and then turned her head away, but I think she was thinking of other things. The man smiled gently and nicely at us.

I perhaps noticed them so particularly because since meeting Paul Treece I have noticed everything with very precise and crystalline pertinence, Aunt Frances, as if a skin had been peeled from everything, a gauze or a glass. Even when Paul Treece turned brick-red with awe at the two writers and sat by the bony woman on a stool at her feet and turned on her a very passionate gaze as he put scone after scone in his mouth (which is a bit red. It's a pity) without looking where it was going, and I went over to sit by Mr Thwaite – even then I thought, 'Nothing, *nothing* will ever spoil this day. We arrived on the lawn together. They will think we belong to each other.'

Mr Thwaite said that it was hot for the time of the year and I asked if he had enjoyed his walk. I told him how Mr Barker had been worried by the chauffeur meeting so many trains, because he loves talking about train-times, and we discussed trains generally for a while. He then said, 'Know who they are, these new cough-drops?'

Mr Thwaite never asks questions – well, so very seldom. You know. He spoke quite loud and it fell very clearly and flatly into the tea-party because nobody was talking much.

That is an interesting thing that I have noticed: great artists do not actually say very much in the ordinary way, but go in for great silences. The more famous they are the less they utter at tea-parties, which makes me think that Paul Treece cannot be a genius as he is the most tremendous talker and was only silent at that moment with awe and scones.

Several heads turned to Mr Thwaite and everyone looked at him with long intellectual stares and I felt so sorry for him until I noticed that he did not seem to care at all. He simply opened his mouth over a beautiful piece of black fruit-cake and munched. Lady Celia said melodiously then, 'When the evenings grow longer, later in the year, we come out here after dinner and listen to the doves.'

Again nobody said anything and the sentence – she has a light slow fluty voice a little like Aunt Mary – hung about among the tea-things for a time and then floated away. In ones and twos then people began to say things blankly – unconnected things, unhurried, and it turned into a discussion soon between a number of people, quite fast like a chorus. Then between only one or two people, and more dropped out until it was just two – the dark new man and the snapping painter who talks Cockney with a bit of a foreign accent (the lady looked up into the trees. She is called Mrs Wolf which is inappropriate for she is more horse or unicorn-like) and it got very difficult for me to follow.

At last the dark man – Mr Wolf, though he is more dog-like – said something that sounded like the ultimate word of truth, and everybody murmured and stirred about like at the end of a concert. Paul Treece was left stranded by the unicorn lady, who had now closed her eyes, so he came over to Mr Thwaite and me – talking – and said, 'Mr Thwaite – what a perfectly beautiful garden. What a house! May I ask if you were born in it?' Mr Thwaite looked quite surprised. Lady Celia's friends don't talk to him much. He said, 'Harrumph grunt grunt ha – yes. Ha. Good old place. Romantic old place. As it happens, yes.'

'I expect that you must be lord of the manor?'

Lady Celia was listening, though she did not turn her head. Mr Thwaite looked across for guidance from her.

'Well – my sister, Celia, has taken on all that – ' he said, leaving things trailing. 'Though I am, in fact.'

'Might I – might we – walk about a little? I'd love to see.'

'All means. Delighted. At once,' said Mr Thwaite, pleased as a cat and got up and went striding off with us after him.

We walked everywhere, Aunt Frances – miles of gardens and shrubberies I hadn't seen, down to the spinneys and along the near bank of the river, Paul Treece talking all the time and bouncing and springing on his feet (which are very big and may become flattish in later life, but never mind. He is very tall) and making little runs here and there. Once he said, 'Oh quickly – don't let us miss this glade, Miss Flint,' (Miss Flint!) and ran to a gate and rested his elbow on it, his chin in his hand. He sighed and said some Latin. 'Horace,' he said.

'Odes One,' said Mr Thwaite. 'Rabbits everywhere. The very deuce. Gun?'

'I beg your pardon?'

'If you've a gun – care for a gun?'

'Oh not at – No thank you.'

'See about one, tomorrow?'

Paul Treece and I found that we were looking at each other at that moment, very steadily, and reading each other's thoughts. I knew then everything about him and I felt sure again he knew all about me. 'Never', he said, 'a gun. I could never handle a gun.'

'May have to,' said Mr Thwaite, 'before long.'

'I am a poet, sir.'

'Ah well. Some of them did. Horace.'

'Horace fled the battlefield leaving his shield.'

'But thought it a disgrace. There'll be other Horaces. Before long. War coming.'

He went off then by himself, saying he must see the farm people and leaving me and Paul Treece together.

With love from Polly – I won't write again for a while, as I think I'd like to see the letters that will be waiting from you at home.

*

99

The next morning I woke up and went to my window and saw Paul Treece standing with his back to me on the terrace, looking out over the meadows and watching the sun rise. It was a rose-pink sky on the horizon with navy-blue above it and the dew on the nearer grass where the mist had not yet touched it was like rime. Paul Treece's bony figure looked gawky in the dawn and his clothes which seemed to be the same as yesterday's – he had not even changed for dinner – looked crumpled as if perhaps he had slept in them or just dropped them on the floor. They were noticeably now too big for him. Also, as I saw him for the first time not in profile, I noticed that he had oval ears, standing out like shells at right-angles to his head and the rays of the sun as I watched shone through them and made them glow.

It may have been the ears that gave me the confidence to dress in two minutes and go down through the early morning house and out to the terrace to join him; though when he turned and saw me all my awe of yesterday came back. I stopped still and said (very silly), 'It's early.'

'It's not six. Look, here's the sun.'

We stood side by side and as the sun burst up, listened to the tremendous palaver of the birds. The red farms on the plain were standing now up to their knees in mist and the river-bed was a gentle snake of cotton-wool crawling away to join the Ouse at Ouseburn to the south. He said, 'It's like *The Mill on the Floss*, isn't it? All the prosperous farms,' and my shyness went away. I said, 'Oh no. It's much prettier. They were great dark ominous places. Solitary. Great barns and things, all heavy and obvious – more like where I live.'

'Oh – is that near Northamptonshire?'

'No. I don't think so.'

'But you know Northamptonshire?'

'I don't know anywhere. This is the only place I've ever been to stay in except for home. And Wales when I was a baby, but I don't remember much of that.'

'But the Midlands?'

I hadn't realised *The Mill on the Floss* was in the Midlands – or anywhere except in a book. I hadn't realised you could use a landscape in a book. I'd thought you had to make new ones. I knew the landscape of books – the weird sea-coast of *Sallee*, the primaeval wastes of *Wuthering Heights*, the rich isles

100

of the Caribs, all the fancy places of French romance; the expanding-glass places of Gulliver. I knew every inch of Looking Glass Land and the underground places that open out from rabbit holes. It was the landscape of maps I found unreal – that's to say useless to fiction. I hardly ever looked at Grandfather Younghusband's globes now, in the study. I feared them rather. I said, 'I'm not even very sure where The Midlands are.'

He said, 'Where is "home"?'

'To the North.'

'I'm from the North-West. But I met Lady Celia in Cambridge.'

'Have you known her for a long time?'

'About three weeks. I met her at a concert. I sat next to her – she was visiting somebody grand. I'm in my second year there. She asked me to stay here.'

'Yes I see.'

'I'm a writer.'

'I expect she had heard of you.'

'Nobody's heard of me. I haven't published anything yet. She is good to poor writers. I was lucky to sit next to her. She invites anybody she thinks is promising. She is quite noted for it.'

'Are all the others here promising?'

'Oh goodness, yes. Some of them are Olympians. Are you considered promising in some way? I expect you're still at school.'

'I'm a sort of relation. I've never been to school. I don't think I'm at all promising.'

'Well, you've read *The Mill on the Floss*. It's a start. Do you read many novels?'

'I've read two hundred and eighty-three.'

'Good heavens. I didn't know there were – Were they mostly romantic?'

'No, I don't think so. I just read them in sets – they're all in the study. Scott, Dickens, Hardy, Richardson, Fielding, Sterne, Disraeli and so on. Most of them I think were my grandmother's though the study was my grandfather's really. He was very stuffy. He read mostly holy things and about stones and so on. The Swift is his though. Swift is very good. I've read all the French ones too, but I don't think he read

101

those. He must have kept them out of sentiment when his wife died.'

'Did you meet Lady Celia in a cultural way?'

'No. I said – I'm a sort of relation. There was something between one of my aunts and Mr Thwaite. She's just got married, so it's rather a tense time.'

'I am coming to *adore* Mr Thwaite.'

I thought, what a very strange thing to say.

*

We walked across the lawn and out of the door in the wall and headed for the water-meadows. Our feet were soaking. Paul Treece's trousers were black with dew half way to the knee and clinging round his legs, not very engagingly. I said, 'You'll catch cold. You'll have to change when you get in.'

'Oh, I shall be all right.'

I felt troubled as we walked on and wondered why. We passed a man out hoeing turnips early and a string of cows, red as the farm-building they were leaving. The cows looked hesitantly, one by one, out of the byre and then stepped from it with a dainty step. They swung very slowly across the yard and into the lane watching us, edging by us with anxious eyes. They smelled milky and warm and blew damp mist from their noses. Cocks were crowing about the land and the sun blazed up, round and brilliant above the stack-yards. How could I be troubled?

We came to a footbridge – a wooden plank on old stone pillars with a hand-rail polished smooth. The water ran quietly, wrinkling round the stones, and Paul Treece stopped on the bridge and stood smiling at the water, his hands on the rail. He was jumpy with pleasure. I had thought that poets were ruminative and sage – like Wordsworth and Tennyson – but Paul Treece was all arms and legs and jitter.

His trousers were drying and I looked down at my own wet shoes and stockings and realised why I wasn't totally happy. When I'd been concerned for his wetness he hadn't given a thought to mine. Also – another thing – one bit of grit can set another scratching – 'I adore Mr Thwaite.'

How could he *adore* Mr Thwaite? He'd hardly met him. It was not manly. Could one imagine Robinson Crusoe saying that he adored Mr Thwaite? Imagine Swift or Thomas Hardy! No, they would not. It did not do.

And how self-sufficient he was, springing about by the bridge. Now he was on the other bank picking things up and throwing them in the air. He was a bit dotty – as dotty as those Olympian Wolves at tea yesterday though at least he wasn't so miserable. Dotty as the snapping painter.

He wasn't the least bit interested in me either. Whatever was I doing walking along the fields with him, hungry and wet before breakfast? He just liked being watched. That was it. He liked a girl looking at him and feeling, 'I am walking in the meadows with a poet.'

He was nothing.

Just then though as I crossed the bridge he took my hand.

He didn't stop talking – he talked all the time and about everything he saw – 'Look – the wheat. Look at the lines of it. Look at the hedges. D'you see how the May is dark red? D'you see how red the hedges are – a different red? Bright. There's so much *red* in a hedge – right from the start. The new shoots in January – well it's January in Cambridge – later here no doubt – what about your part of the world? Are there hedges? The sap is never green you know, rising. It's red. Like blood. That's a fact. And a poetic concept – ' That's how he went on and in the middle of it, had taken my hand.

The talk was sure enough but the hand-holding wasn't very expert and I knew he hadn't done a lot of it before. His fingers were very nice and his hands thin but somehow it was all very disappointing. I had expected that holding a man's hand would be rather better.

'I'd like to go back now, please. We could go back along the path and get home this way, I think.'

We had come to a field end.

'Yes, all right.'

He turned obediently. He was endlessly amiable.

'You seem a very happy person,' I said.

'Happy? Well, yes. Very happy. I don't, as a matter of fact, think – I don't think I've ever been so happy – Cambridge and Lady Celia and – I'm very lucky. Oh dear – '

'What?'

'Is this the right way? The right way home?'

103

'Yes, I think so.'

'You can't see Thwaite from here can you? We seem to be in a valley bottom. Do you read Meredith?'

'No. I haven't heard of Meredith. Look I think – '

'Or Yeats. Do you read Yeats?'

He did a sort of dance. 'To think of it!' he said. 'To think of it. You are so innocent and yet aware. You have everything to come. Yeats and Meredith!'

I thought, he's so beautiful and joyful and I am alone with him in the early morning. I'm talking to him about all the things I most care about, like poets and wonderful books. Why can I only think of breakfast and that Lady Celia must be right – I am not in any way promising?

'Shall we try this way?'

After a time to my great relief we saw a man coming along through the fields in working clothes – black trousers tied at the knee with whitish, hairy string and a shirt without a collar, just a brass stud. Paul Treece was going on very loud, quoting from the writer Yeats but I said, 'Could we just ask do you think?'

'Ask?'

'Where we are. That man. How to get back.'

'Get *back*? Do you want to get back? Do you want this to be over?' All the time he had still held my hand and his big brilliant eyes looked at me very excitedly. I had a sudden comprehension of Fanny Brawne. I wanted to kick him.

'*Please* will you ask this man?'

'Good morning,' said Paul Treece. 'We're slightly lost. Early morning walk. We're trying to find Thwaite again.'

The man put down on the grass a bucket of milk he was carrying. It slopped about, pink at the edges. 'Thwaite?'

'The Hall.'

'What Hall?'

'Thwaite. Thwaite Hall. Lady Celia – '

'You're nearer Roundstone Hall. It's next village. Past Thoralby.'

'But we are staying at Thwaite.'

'Then you're away off your course. You're five miles off. Now Roundstone Hall – '

'That would be no good, I'm afraid. We have to be at Thwaite for breakfast.'

104

'Then it's a fair step. It's way beyond the river. The bridge is two mile back or two mile forward. Good day to you.'

'Five miles,' I said. 'Five miles! It can't be. We can't have walked five miles. We're absolutely lost.'

Something in me wanted him to say that how could we be lost and together, that I needn't worry, that we were so happy.

'Roundstone,' he said, 'Roundstone Hall. Well good heavens, did he say Roundstone Hall?'

'Yes, I think so.'

'Well I know it! I know Roundstone Hall. I know the people.'

'Oh yes?'

'I'm at Cambridge with a chap from Roundstone Hall. He said it was in Yorkshire somewhere. Theo Zeit. Come on, young child. We'll find a breakfast.'

*

The boy and girl of the pony and trap stood on the stairs, the girl not much taller than she had been then – rather short-legged, but the same glorious hair. Theo stood on the step above and so seemed very tall indeed. He looked quietly at us as his sister covered her mouth with a shriek at the sight of Paul Treece.

'Oh good heavens!' Out shot her arms. 'The *Poultice*, The Poultice! It is – how can it be – The Poultice?'

There was the most tremendous smell of polish and newness everywhere. Every surface was soaked in it. Fine mahogany chests and cabinets and chairs like thrones swam with it. A rosewood pedestal glowed with it and the sabre-leafed plant that stood on it seemed polished, too. In the dining-room sideboards like streets, a vast table and twenty chairs were rich with the hours people had spent rubbing at them with wax and soft cloths. The table-legs had flown from some Indian temple and there was a good deal of brass and copper about. At the end of the table a woman sat very upright and amused by us. She had papers beside her and a pen in her hand.

'Well, good morning.'

'Mother. This is extraordinary! Paul Treece from Queen's.

And – Miss Polly Flint. Walking before breakfast and lost. They're staying at Thwaite.'

'Lost – oh dear. How do you do? And before breakfast.'

'They set off very early. About dawn. They've walked in circles.'

'The Poultice is a poet, Mamma.'

'Poultice? Ah, yes. A poet – they have a good many of them at Thwaite I hear. Good morning Miss Flint. You must be a poet, too?'

'No, I'm just – '

'You are just. Well done. Come at once and sit down. No – go with Rebecca and wash. You must be longing to wash. Then come back again – at once – for food.'

'Thank you. I'm just slightly – '

'Worried? There is no need. We shall telephone.'

'They aren't on the telephone. It's not what Lady Celia – '

'Then I shall send a message. Wash. Return and eat. Theo will see to Mr Poultice.'

She was quite little but with a large head, black hair in ropes in a nest on top and a face most dreadfully plain with a floppy undefined sort of mouth that strayed over it. But she had a smiling look about her and gave the general impression that everything in her world was remarkably pleasant. Her hands were very certain of themselves as she tidied the papers and letters beside her. When we came back from a wonderful bathroom white tiled to the ceiling with taps like something in the Works – she was gone.

Paul Treece sat at the table instead in front of a plate mountains high with kidneys, bacon, sausages, eggs. He was talking hard, waving his fork, and his eyes quite wild with excitement. The delicious but not robust food at Thwaite was meant to pass unnoticed, incidental to the spirit, and it came in very small quantities.

Rebecca sat near him watching the mountain diminish and Theo stood by the window, his red head against a velvet curtain which had bobbles all the way down it like thistle heads. He had the same look of general happiness being the order of things as his mother and smiled and said, 'Come and have kippers.'

'Oh – no thank you.'

My heart thumped too desperately for eating.

'Coffee? Tea?'

'Oh, coffee please.'

'It's a bit of a wash, the coffee today. Difficult to get round here.'

'We get ours from London.'

'*Do* you indeed! On that marsh? Do you still live on that marsh of yester-year? Does the coffee come in on the tide?'

'No it comes from Mrs Woods. She has connections with Africa.' Rebecca spluttered. She said, 'Oh God – I'm sorry. Africa!' Theo gave an elderly smile (but not unkind). 'That marsh and Africa,' she said.

So I knew I must defend it.

I looked round at the money – the plush, the carpet, all turkish red and blue, gold-framed pictures on brass chains on brass railings supported by fat gold brackets in the shape of fat gold flowers. A gold-tubed clock set between marble supports under a glass bell, on the chimney piece struck nine. 'Oh the marsh is a *really* rich place,' I said.

They were quiet.

'We're going to have our house ready soon,' said Theo. 'It's on the way to being finished now. It's for us all to get lots of healthy sea-breezes in the summer.'

'Yes, I know. It doesn't seem to be getting on very fast.'

'It's been Mamma's plaything for years. She keeps changing all the plans. She thinks Father ought to have some-where healthy to go to not so far from the Works as Germany – which is where he is now, and very often. At the Spa. The Works are only across the estuary.'

'The Works are getting nearer all the time,' I said, 'and the smoke's nearer too.'

'We shall be neighbours,' he said. 'Next year the plan is that we shall be there for ages – all the summer.'

'It's all astonishing,' said Paul Treece, stretching for fresh toast. He took a great many small bites at it, examining the shape of each and then took a great many quick little sips of coffee. 'I know nothing about any of all this. Nothing.'

The brother and sister collapsed again.

'The dear old Poultice,' said Theo. 'You know he's a genius, Polly Flint? Writes the most amazing stuff. So I'm told. Publishes it in the greenery-yallery magazines. He's supposed to be like whatsisname, the famous one.'

'*What* famous one?' Rebecca was wiping her eyes. She seemed very close to her brother, catching his thoughts. 'Oh, we're being beastly, Theo. Sorry Poult. I'm terribly sorry Polly Flint. You see The Poult knows and puts up with us. You don't. We're utterly hopeless you see, Theo and I. All the Zeits are. At arty things. Even though we're Jewish and German – we can't sing a note or play a thing and we never read a book. And behold the pictures! Dying stags. Mamma bought them from a baronial mansion in Scotland because of the frames. We're *terrible* philistines. Aren't we, Paul?'

'They're *fairly* hopeless,' he said, dolloping on the butter.

'I thought – philistines are a particular Jewish sect?'

'We are philistines and we are atheists.'

'I've never agreed about that,' said Paul Treece. 'You love mankind. You're not atheists. Your family gives away goodness knows what. Millions.'

'Well, we are atheists, aren't we, Theo?'

'You are,' said Theo, 'and Mamma, and so, I *suppose,* is father, but he will never discuss it. He thinks things out by himself. In Baden-Baden. In the mud. And he'd give you his last pair of trousers.'

'Whyever should Polly Flint want father's last pair of trousers?'

'I mean he is the *best,* not just the good Samaritan. And he is probably very sad that he can't believe in God. How about you, Miss Flint? I shouldn't think God comes into things down on the marsh very much.'

I felt cold and the furniture glowed in vain.

'More coffee? Is something wrong?' Theo came and sat beside me and looked at me. Rebecca had been looking at me too, noticing that I was looking awful – elderly, quaint and not pretty. And not a pretty shape. Theo looked as if he was concerned for me, though.

'She's probably not met many atheists,' said Rebecca.

'I never – I don't really ask – '

'I don't suppose there are many people *to* ask on that marsh.'

'Ask in the Iron-Works slums and you'll find atheists,' said Rebecca.

'Some aren't,' I said. 'Well they say "God bless you" some

of them when we go round with soup. Some don't speak for hate of us, but I don't think they're all atheists. Actually at Oversands we – my aunts – are very religious. My Aunt Frances has just married a priest. They've gone to be missionaries in India. They sail – tomorrow.'

Rebecca groaned and put her hands through her great fizz of wild hair. 'I can't bear it.'

'What?'

'I'm sorry. I can't do with all that.'

'All what?'

'Tosh and missionaries. I'm sorry. I have to speak out. I'm not like Theo. He's nice. I'm very bold and crude. Nobody likes me much at Cambridge. I can't keep my mouth shut.'

'You mean', I said, 'you honestly don't believe in God?'

'No. Not a bit. I can't. It just all sounds like fairy stories. There seems absolutely no sense in it. Old men in the sky looking down and watching over us. I haven't the beginnings of an idea how an intelligent human being can believe that. It's why I didn't read Philosophy. History is mystifying enough.'

I saw the queer procession of my aunts, Mrs Woods and me, pacing towards the bell every Sunday, rain or shine to worship an old man in the sky.

'Shut up, Bec. Live and let live,' said Theo. 'I go to church at Cambridge every Sunday, don't I, Poult? My God, He lives in King's College Chapel.'

'He lives in toast,' said Paul Treece, 'peach jam, in Polly Flint and Zeits.'

Theo said, 'Polly – we have upset you.'

'It's all right,' I said, 'I'm not Confirmed.'

'Oh *I* am. I was done *en bloc* at Eton.'

I felt sick and shy again and said, 'Paul, I think we ought to go now. It's so late. We never said we were going out.'

'All is perfectly dealt with,' said Mrs Zeit sailing back among us. 'I'm just sending someone over to Thwaite with a note. I've said you'll be staying here for the day. It's a perfect day for the garden and we've tennis and croquet and some more interesting people from Sunderland coming to luncheon.

'More interesting than what – or who?'

' –m' said Rebecca.

'I'm afraid', I got up, 'I really should like to go. Don't you think so, Paul?'

'Oh well – '

'If you want to stay, do stay. I want to go.'

'But you *can't*,' said Rebecca. 'It's nice here. Come on. They're all old *things* at Thwaite. Creepy crawlies. Pianists.'

'They'll mind,' I said, 'I'm sorry, Mrs Zeit,' and surprised myself by folding my napkin, getting up and walking over to her. 'It's been so kind of you.'

She was wearing yellow silk with ruching and diamond brooches. In the morning. Her eyes were very displeased. Then, instead of taking my hand she held out both hers and took both mine and her eyes smiled again. She held tight. 'My *dear* little girl,' she said, 'have some *fun* here with us.'

But I said, 'No. I must go home.'

*

When I reached the drive, Paul Treece followed me and walked beside me and near the gate a great quiet car crept up behind us with a chauffeur in it. It passed and stopped and the chauffeur got out and held the door for us.

'To Thwaite, sir?'

'Oh – well, yes.'

'I'd like to walk,' I said, but felt that this was overdoing things and got in, Paul Treece beside me. He was silent and only said once, 'Look Polly, Look at the corn.'

I looked but did not really see the miles of silvery stalks and the blobs of poppies and the sky above them. 'See them wriggle,' he said, 'in the breeze. What a lovely summer. There can't have been a more lovely summer since the beginning of the world.'

At length the crumbly walls of Thwaite appeared and we got out.

I knew perfectly well that nobody had noticed that we had been away.

*

The chauffeur, as he opened the motor-car door for us, handed me a letter addressed to Lady Celia and said that he had been told to wait for an answer. I said, 'Oh no – that's all been changed. That letter was to tell Lady Celia we were not coming home – '

He said, 'No miss, that was the *first* note. This one's been written since. It's why you had to set off without me and I had to catch you up. Mrs Z is a right fast writer. There's new plans afoot now.'

The Poultice was standing waiting at Thwaite's door so I took the envelope. 'It might be a while to wait for the answer,' I said. 'Shall I tell Maitland you're here? You can go round to the kitchen and have tea.'

He said, '*No* thank you, miss,' and gave me a look.

In the hall Mr Barker was putting out the post, keeping aside on a salver a pile of very personal-looking letters, some faintly coloured with ripply edges to the flaps. 'Put that one on the top of these,' he said. 'They're all for Lady Celia. They're just going up to her.'

'Oh!' I pounced and knocked his Pharoic arm. I had seen Aunt Frances's writing on a letter laid out on the chest.

'Hold hard,' said Mr Barker. 'That there's not for you, it's for Mr Thwaite. Here's yours.'

I grabbed – but it was not from Aunt Frances. How could it be when I came to think about it. She didn't even know I was here. Her letters to me would be waiting at the yellow house. And this letter was in a cheap envelope, very thin, the hand-writing round and wobbly like a child's and it spelled my name wrong.

'Dear Miss Polly,' it said. 'Sorry to trouble you on your holidays but would appreciate advice about matters here which are not good she is worse even in my opinion not right at all and Miss Mary gone. Have called the doctor and think you should come back yours truly Alice Bates.'

'Lady Celia wants you to go up,' said Mr Barker. He had come down again from the bedroom and stood with his head bowed a little towards me as a butler should, but he said, 'Something wrong, Miss Polly? You're gone to a statue. Mr Treece is away for some coffee. Shall I – ?'

'No thanks. Oh – '

'You're to go up there, she says. If you don't want coffee, go now and get it over.'

'I must see Maitland. Lady Celia will be answering the letter the chauffeur brought. He's waiting. I've time.'

'No – get sorted up yonder, miss. Roundstone waits. We don't faff with Roundstone.'

'Yes, I see.'

Lady Celia's exhausted head was propped on a hummock of pastel-coloured pillows and above them drooped a spray of peacock-feathers and gauzy curtains like in Tennyson. Her breakfast-tray, a still life, was untouched upon the bed and she was looking out of the window and her hand holding Mrs Zeit's letter seemed hardly attached to her. It was a dark bedroom. I stood at the foot of the bed.

She said at last, 'You have called then? At Roundstone?'

'No. Yes.'

'No-yes? What is this no-yes?'

'We got lost.'

'Lost?'

'We went walking. Paul Treece and I. We went much farther than we meant to and then we were told we were near Roundstone and Paul Treece was absolutely thrilled because he knows the people there.'

'Ah.'

'I said it was rude just to go in.'

'You were right.'

'But they are his very *close* friends.'

'Paul Treece has very many "very *close* friends".'

'They're all at Cambridge together. It's all very under – '

'Paul Treece', she said, 'is a go-getter. An enchanting boy, but a go-getter. You should be warned – though I don't see him in great pursuit of you. The Zeit girl and her millions perhaps. He can write poetry – to a certain extent. This is why I invited him. He is very poor.'

'Yes I see.'

'And also he is in love with me. As much as that sort of man ever can be.'

I said nothing. She must have been fifty.

'It is not unusual in this house. It is something I have to put up with very often. It killed my husband – my intense attractiveness to men of all ages.'

'Yes I see.'

'Will you please stop saying, "yes I see". And please understand that we at Thwaite do *not* know those at Roundstone.' There was a sort of electricity in the pillows as she turned

112

her head and glared at me; a patchiness about the face which was not rouge. 'They are people we are not able to know socially,' she said. 'Do you understand?'

How could you know people unsocially?

'Yes. But – ' I was about to say 'But Mr Thwaite goes to Roundstone often,' when I remembered his nice lanky old figure in its breeches going off like a shadow towards the meadows.

She didn't know.

'They all seemed so very – interesting there.'

'They are not. They are not interesting in the very least. Not at all.'

'You mean because they are Jews and foreigners?'

'Certainly not. Thwaite is full of Jews and foreigners. It is because they have no conception of anything we stand for. They laugh at aestheticism. And they deny their God. They find us *amusing!*'

'I hated it about God,' I said. 'It seems so much worse somehow when they are Jews. But some writers don't exactly believe in God. Isn't that what they were all talking about on the lawn yesterday? All that about a primal force? And the Zeits do give millions of pounds to the poor.'

'And told you so?'

'Oh, not – Well, in a round-about way. Somebody said – '

'Exactly. For us such people are without reality.'

'But they all seemed so very real,' I said. 'They all seemed a bit too real. Very – solid.'

'Ha! Solid – solid is exactly it. Up to now we have avoided Roundstone. I have never called. Yet this shameless letter has invited you and Treece to spend the day with them tomorrow. Picnics – no doubt with silver canapé-dishes and everyone dressed up in diamonds and high-heeled shoes. Motor cars. Businessmen from Tyneside in gloves. Please go down and ask Barker to send the chauffeur away.'

'What shall he say?'

'That a reply will be posted. They are *philistines!*'

'Is he to say that they are philistines?'

A flash from the pillow. 'Of course not, you fool of a child.'

I said, 'Actually they know that they are philistines. They

113

told me so. They say they can't help it. I don't think they're at all – subversive.'

'You seem – and come back: throw this letter in the waste-paper-basket by my dressing table – you seem to have got a very long way at Roundstone in a very short time.'

I dropped the letter, and in the looking-glass saw the peacock-feathers and the gauzes and the drapes of birds and flowers, an easel with a portrait on it of someone very rich but of spiritual expression, in a cravat – the husband killed through his wife's magnetism for men. I wondered whether I liked aestheticism very much.

'Oh we did get a long way,' I said. 'You see, I'd met them before, long ago when I was young, the two Zeit children. We got a long way then, too. It was on the beach. I loved them at once, and very much. And I couldn't have gone with them tomorrow anyway, Lady Celia, because I have to go home.'

*

I did not see Paul Treece again before I left, for Lady Celia took him aside with her that afternoon and they were in close conversation all the evening. He smiled in my direction over dinner and after dinner I made off to the servants' quarters where I felt they were sorry that I was leaving, and this was balm.

But I didn't say much. Just sat, held Maitland's knitting wool, listened to the cinders drop, the kettle sing. Nobody asked any questions about my being called home and I wished they would, for it might have strengthened me to say in words why I must go – for I had not explored the reasons why I was so sure. Yet in another way I liked being left alone. It was adult.

Maitland did say when I said goodbye at bedtime – for I was to leave early in the morning – that she hoped all would be well for me. I said that it couldn't be well, exactly, with both my aunts gone.

'Then who's to greet you?'

'I shan't be *greeted*. There's just Alice the maid, and Mrs Woods. Mrs Woods is ill. That's why I have to go.'

'Who is Mrs Woods?'

'She's someone who lives with us.'

'A servant?'

'No, just someone my aunts have been kind to.'

'Ah – a paid companion?'

'Oh no. Not *paid*. She's very important. I don't really know much about her. But I think she's always been important. For years.'

'Well it seems to me it's not very nice of you. You with your own life beginning. We'll all miss you – won't we Barker? We've taken a great fancy to you. Do you realise that? Mr Thwaite – we'll miss Miss Polly.' Mr Thwaite didn't look as though he were going to miss me much. He was examining a bishop.

'It's good to have some straightforward young life here,' she went on. 'Now you're to write to us. Will you write to us?'

'Yes, of course. I think I'll write very often. I think I might need lots of advice. If I'm to be in charge, with just Alice.'

'In charge of this important old companion who is sick – advice you'll need. What's this Alice?'

'Oh, she's – she keeps apart. She's very quiet and hard-working. She came from the vicar, she's my age about. She's the maid. But we think she may have to go, now that Aunt Frances and the vicar have gone.'

Maitland raised a long arm in the air and held her wool aloft for an extended moment. She said, 'You're to write, if *ever* you're in trouble. No one manages alone.'

*

Mr Thwaite surprised me at the station – he had driven us himself in the trap, I and the snapping painter who was returning to London – by saying the same thing in his own way.

'Letter not come amiss,' he said. 'No joke alone for a girl.'

'I'll write to Lady Celia tonight.'

'Apart from bread and butter. Collinses. Personal to me. No S.O.S. ignored, directed to Arthur Thwaite.'

I wanted to thank him, to love him – standing there looking high above our heads, his Don Quixote shoulders in the old Norfolk jacket, blue eyes peering about at the station traceries, examining the baskets of geraniums, the little swinging sign, checking the station-clock with his gold watch, thin as a biscuit. 'Thank you very much for having me to stay. It's been the most marvellous – '

'Here she comes. Right on time.'

Along the dead-straight track, puffs of smoke preceded the round face of the engine. 'Here we are now.'

The painter and I got in.

'Perhaps, let me know?' said Mr Thwaite. 'What you hear from India?'

'Of course.'

'Deplorable business.' He touched his temple with the whip of the pony-trap and swung away, and I saw how blank his face had become.

The painter's train to London did not leave for some time and so, on Darlington station, we sat together on my platform and waited for my train to the marsh.

He looked as mad as ever. He wasn't snapping so much but he twitched his fingers and pulled at his hair and kept getting up and sitting down again. The day was grey and cold – the wonderful weather of Thwaite seemed already to belong to some sealed-off conservatory somewhere, some hot and distant island. Rain began to patter on the high glass roof of the station and a wind blew down the platform from the direction I was going to take. I shut my eyes.

I didn't bother to speak to the painter and he didn't bother to speak to me and I sat with my eyes shut until I heard my train clank in and then I climbed up and put my bags on the rack and let down the window to lean out and shake hands.

But instead of taking my hand he put a piece of paper into it. It was a picture of me sitting on the platform asleep, and it was the most beautiful drawing I had ever seen.

'A young woman on the threshold of life,' he said, and snapped the air and twisted his face about; and I laughed, because although the drawing was so lovely the face was also the most miserable face in the world.

'The doomed traveller,' said he.

And looking at him I saw what a miserable, smug, self-righteous lump I was. What a heavy weight I must have been. And yet, for all that, he had missed none of the few good things. Seeing all, he had forgiven all, and had shown that, though I was young and stupid, there was some sort of hope.

'Oh,' I said, 'oh it's wonderful. It really is *very* good,' and he looked at me sharp and sideways – a 'thank you kindly, Miss No one'. The whistle went, the flag flapped on the slamming doors. 'You'll be someone I'll think of,' I shouted, 'I think you're going to be very famous. It's just *like* me. Oh I wish I didn't understand things only when they were over. I'm not really a misery. Not by nature. Thank you, so very much. I'm a sort of Robinson Crusoe. I'm all washed up at present.'

Doors slammed.

'Robinson Crusoe wasn't so bad,' he said. 'A bit too bloody sane, but not so bad. Goodbye.' He reached up a hard, warm hand then to the back of my neck and pulled my head down to him and kissed me. He stopped kissing me and then kissed me again harder, opening my mouth, pressing my mouth until it hurt, putting his tongue inside so that I gasped out. The moving train jerked him away and was nearly off the end of the platform before I could breathe.

I could tell from his figure walking in the other direction that I was already forgotten.

*

Hearing people talk now, or reading about it, one imagines the four years of the Great War passing in England in benign and golden sunlight, occasional gunfire on the channel-breeze as we tended roses, rolled bandages and drank cups of tea, or handed white feathers about the pleasant streets. We are also told, endlessly, that the war burst and shattered us like a thunderbolt from a summer sky, like Crusoe's demon pouncing upon him in sleep.

Neither is quite true. Even on the marsh we had heard uneasy things for some time – for about four years. For months before August 4th, 1914, Mr Box of Boagey's, the doctor, the vicar had all spoken of a coming war and I remember Aunt Frances telling me years before her wedding when I was still a child, 'Father always said that there will be war with Germany in the end.' I had heard Mr Box tell Charlotte, 'There'll be war again, you'll see. With Germany. I can't stand Germans, but if I had to choose between them and the French as friends I know which it would be. Never the

117

French.' Charlotte said, 'One foreigner's as bad as another. I can't abide Germans neither' – though wherever could she have met one? Or Mr Box a Frenchman? There was still, on the marsh, a faint shadow of pride going about that we had beaten Napoleon, and a curious Nelson-Worship – something to do with H.M.S. *Victory* – always called 'Nelson's Flagship Victory' on the marsh, presumably because so many people remembered local men being pressed aboard her long years after Trafalgar.

Through the spring and early summer of 1914, when the possibility of war was mentioned, I remember no patriotism, only sombreness. Perhaps, of course, on our queer island on the marsh we were different and dour. Certainly we were on August 4th, 1914, which was by all accounts throughout the rest of the country a most glorious golden morning.

With us it was raining. Round the yellow house there hung a cold, early-morning sea-fret and Alice and I looked out at whiteness as we dealt with Mrs Woods's slops and dirty sheets and made ready for the day. Out of her window we could hardly see the little privet hedge. The sea might not have been there, but for its insistent whisper – the long wave from the Gare to the breakwater turning and collapsing, turning and collapsing just out of sight. Not a bird uttered and we could hardly hear the bells.

What Mrs Woods could hear, of course, or see or understand about war or anything else, goodness knows, for she had had a stroke and for more than a year now had lain looking at the ceiling, not speaking, but groaning a great deal when Alice and I lifted her twice a day.

For I must now say what happened when I came walking home in 1913 over the marsh from Thwaite towards the yellow house – a changing marsh, for I had been a month away.

I noticed how it was shrinking. It wasn't just that I was two feet taller than when I first knew it, so that the flowers and grasses were so much further off. The marsh itself had diminished. The chimneys had crept up on us, and so had the workmen's houses on the mud-flats with all their plumes of smoke bending together away from the sea. And the streets up around the church were closer too and there were more

118

of them. There was a large and prosperous blossoming of lodging houses.

And I noticed what must have been there for a while, a broad tarmacadammed road running along and out towards us before the sea, stopping well short of the yellow house certainly, and cracking here and there with sprouts of persistent grass – brave ugly grass, which might win yet. But it was a road.

The yellow house stood high with its big windows flashing and the sea behind it tossing and the big ships sliding along the horizon waiting for the tide into the estuary. Oh, beautiful house.

I climbed the steps and the door was flung wide to an empty hall and the vicar's Alice turning her head away from me with embarrassed relief.

'Tooken bad five days,' she said. 'I got the doctor.'

'Is Miss Younghusband here yet?'

'She's not come. I wrote. Like to you. The nuns up at The Rood say a Retreat's when you're closed off from things.'

'Yes, but not in a *crisis*. Mrs Woods might have died.'

'Well, Miss Mary's not here. There's been me alone.'

She was very frightened. Wisps of hair and a dirty apron.

'I'll go up. Is the doctor coming every day? You've done wonders, Alice. I came as soon as I could,' which was true. But how in the last few hours I had yearned to be back. I dumped down my bag and went up and held Mrs Woods's bedroom door-knob.

In all the years of my childhood I had never been inside her bedroom but I knew that when I opened the door there would be a smell – the sour, dreadful smell of her. I knew that she would be looking towards the door as it opened, looking at me with the resentful bitter face I'd scarcely ever seen soften or smile. I prayed, 'Help me' and thought – 'Praying – how ridiculous. The people at Thwaite would not need to pray – the Olympian writers who had come to tea, mercurial Paul Treece, the snapping painter. Or the Zeits at Roundstone. Strong effective brilliant people who knew how to enjoy their lives in long summer visits, and endless pleasures – never with morbid thoughts of God. None of them believed in God. They had the wonderful freedom of not believing in God, the freedom denied even to Robinson

Crusoe, otherwise the steadiest man in the world though very likely not Confirmed.

Look where praying had got my aunts. To India with Mr Pocock, to a cell where they wouldn't let you out to look after your friends. Look where it had got Mrs Woods – a husk on a bed with no one to love.

I wondered then about Mr Thwaite, if he prayed, and at once I knew that he did; and it was seeing his mediaeval face in my mind rather than a message from anything higher that gave me the courage to turn the door-knob and go in.

I saw a clean room, very bare, a thin carpet with a broad surround of blank floor-board, a white cotton bed-cover, no curtains, and over the fireplace a cross. The window was wide open and the swish of the sea came in, comforting and steady. The room smelled salty. She was not looking at me but straight upwards, the side of her face drawn slightly down and dribble was coming out of her mouth. She was wearing a thick white very clean night-dress, her arms out of sight under the quilt. She seemed exceedingly small. By not a blink or a flicker did she show that she was glad to see me, or could see me at all. The expression of ferocity in her eyes had gone. They held none. Her hair on the pillow I noticed for the first time was thin and there was a pink blob on the top of her head where it had worn out.

The horrible thinness of the hair had to be looked away from. I said, 'Mrs Woods. Hello. I'm so sorry. Whatever have you been doing – frightening us all? Well, I don't know! You can't be left alone for a minute.'

What was all this? Kindness? I was awkward with kindness. I had never learned it. You have to learn kindness very young indeed. Kindness had been sketchy in Wales.

'We must brush your poor hair,' I said (We!). 'Dear me, we must set things to right.' I hated her still.

And a tear formed then in Mrs Woods's good eye, welled up over its red under-lid and spilled crookedly down her awful cheek.

*

Aunt Mary did come back to the yellow house but not then. Not for some time and her return was almost a worse surprise than Mrs Woods, for like the marsh she seemed to be shrunk and poor, unrecognisable as the tall beauty in the oyster-silk at the wedding scarcely more than a month ago.

Stepping out of the taxi she seemed pinched up, strange, and old, in the familiar crazy black veiling. She scarcely noticed me as she came into the house, glanced at the pile of letters in the hall and passed them by, looked at Alice as if she were uncertain who she was and examined the barometer for a long time. Then very slowly she took off her gloves.

At last she said, 'Polly?'

I tried to hug her but she pushed me vaguely away. 'No, dear, let me just think.' She went across the hall and looked round the study door and stood there for ages. Then she crossed over and looked in at the dining-room. 'Oh how nice!' she said. 'I hope the spoons are safe?'

I said, 'Mrs Woods – '

'Yes. Never mind. Another time,' and we went up to the drawing-room and Alice brought tea.

'Are you all right, Aunt Mary? Was the Retreat – nice?'

'Very nice, thank you.' She sat upright holding the flowery tea-cup.

'I had a – marvellous time. I met all sorts of famous people. It's a wonderful place, Aunt. Thwaite. You never told me. It's a vast house. There are suits of armour and things. Lady Celia – '

'Lady Celia,' said Aunt Mary. 'Hah!'

'Oh – don't you like her?'

'Celia Thwaite, we do not talk about. She is a destroyer. She has ruined lives.'

'Goodness – Yes, she might.'

'She did. She has. Arthur Thwaite was born to marry a good woman. At the wedding – '

'Oh – oh yes. I see.'

'Celia is a wicked woman given over to sin.' The ring of the old Aunt Mary made me feel better. 'If you don't mind, Polly, we shall not speak of her again.'

'No, of course not. But', I said, 'I can't see why he – Mr Thwaite – listened to her? About getting married?'

'He is weak. All men are weak. Pocock – your father. Not of course your Grandfather Younghusband, but he was one apart. Women are the strong ones, Polly, but we are not

121

allowed to show it. We have to await men's pleasure. We can never ask *them*. If we do there is a fiasco. Like Frances – '

'Oh, have you heard from her? There are letters from her in the hall – all to you. None to me.'

'I heard before I left the Retreat. Something or other to do with the armed forces. Shopping in London.'

'Oh please, can I bring the rest of the letters in?'

'Not just yet.' She sat looking queerly at the brown and gold pansies on her tea-cup. 'I've been so happy while I've been away,' she said.

After that she took to wandering about. For the next few days she drifted round the house looking out of all the windows. Then she spent hours sitting still. She ate almost nothing. Once she went to see Mrs Woods, but soon wandered out again and when the doctor called, though she seemed to be listening to him intently, her eyes were on other things. 'Mrs Woods may well live for many years,' he said. 'She is improving all the time. We're getting her up – Polly and young Alice – now. She will soon be getting downstairs again. I don't think, since she's not – er – , that there should be much extra washing. So that we need not think of moving her. I shan't recommend hospital at present, or nursing home.'

'There is no money for either,' said Aunt Mary. 'It would have to be the nuns. Or the workhouse. She is penniless.'

The doctor tipped his sherry-glass about. 'The nuns only take the convalescents of the working poor.'

'We are the idle poor,' said Aunt Mary. 'I am nearly penniless too. Frances and I had very little and Frances has taken her share to India. I have only the house and no one would buy that. We are as poor as Our Lord.'

One night I woke up and found Aunt Mary standing in my bedroom looking out of the window again. It was moonlight and she stood still, watching the sea. After a minute she went out. She looked even thinner, madder, with her great white nightdress floating all about her, one hand holding a candle and the other the case of spoons.

I lay awake then until the sun began to rise, thinking about her and about everything that had happened to me since I was born, and how perhaps a dog, a couple of cats, a handful of goats and a parrot might be quite jolly companions.

*

A week or so later she came into the study and said, 'Polly, if I went back to the Retreat, could you manage? It is very cheap and I don't mean it to be for very long. I do so miss it there. Just until I feel better? I don't seem able to underst— to organise anything here any more.'

I said, 'Yes, I see. Of course. I'm sure with Alice – She's very good.'

'I don't want to do *wrong*,' she said. 'You're not seventeen. Could you ring for Alice?' Her eyes glared and stared.

'I'd miss you very much,' I said.

'Alice, come in. Could you and Miss Polly manage alone for a little longer? If I were to go back to the Retreat?'

Alice looked at me as if she were about to have her throat cut. 'Yes Miss Younghusband. Yes, I'd think – '

'I cannot be as near to God here as I should like. Miss Polly understands, although she is – sadly – un-Confirmed. Now I shall go and write the letter.'

When she had gone out Alice said, 'Oh Miss Polly!' and I said, 'Is she ill, Alice? What shall we do? She's not *here* any more.'

'We must bide with her,' said Alice.

'Alice, I'm frightened.'

'I'm frightened, too, miss, but I'd think it might be her age.'

'What does that mean?'

'Well, her age. Her time of life. We go funny, women.'

'*Funny?*'

'My Mam did. But she'll come through it. Bear up.'

'Yes, I suppose so.' (Would I ever know anything? What was this 'funny'? There was nothing about women going funny in novels. Perhaps if Robinson Crusoe had been a woman – Did men go funny, too, and who was there to tell me?)

'We'll fettle grand,' said Alice uncertainly, but she was watching me. I saw kindness in her face and something better – something that meant she could be strong if need be. She had only to get used to an idea. 'Oh, we'll fettle grand,' she said. 'We got me Mam through right as ninepence. She took a great fancy to bloaters and we humoured her. She takes in washing again now – strong as a lion, and so'll Miss Younghusband be.'

But she was wrong for Aunt Mary died a month later from a tumour on the brain and was buried in the churchyard near poor little Mr Woods, which would not have pleased her.

*

To tell Aunt Frances was the first concern. I wrote at once, of course, but knew that it would be weeks before the letter arrived in Delhi – long before she did, for the Pocock's were travelling very slowly. Rome and Naples had been visited and at present they must be steaming across the Indian Ocean. I thought that at the funeral I might be able to ask Mr Thwaite about the telegraph to cable to ships, but Mr Thwaite had bronchitis and could not attend the funeral. After worrying about it – and being advised about it by the Church and The Hall and Mr Boagey and Mr Box and several of Aunt Mary's nuns – even going to the post-office to enquire of Dicky Dick who had expanded the lino-shop to become the first postmaster to the new esplanade terrace (he had no first-hand information about cabling facilities but gave me tea) I decided that there was no need for haste after all.

Aunt Frances could not come back. Even if she could have done, what sense in it would there be? I was only wanting sympathy.

So I wrote a note to the Society of the Propagation of the Gospel in case they had someone else going to Delhi who might be a comfort to her in her sad loss, and tried to keep my head.

I took to going to church regularly after Aunt Mary's death, sitting in her pew, using her white prayer-book, thinking about her a good deal. The church-people were kind. They turned round from the pews in front with wide smiles and sympathetic nods and at the church-porch the new young priest thrust out at me his Cardinal Newman jaw and his hand gripped mine like a vice.

He came to the yellow house to see me, too, often stayed after bringing Mrs Woods her Holy Communion and threw back several glasses of sherry, sprawled out in the button-back chair.

After Evensong once – I even started going to Evensong, though I suppose I did let my mind wander rather – watching the new priest tearing about the chancel, scrabbling in his vestments for his handkerchief, singing cheerfully like a Methodist – after Evensong once, a large important woman asked if I would like to do a vase, but as I didn't know what she meant I said no, and there was rather a cooling off after that.

Then one day I went to the church and met a great blanket of gloom as I stepped through the door. I was handed a prayer-book by Mr Boagey bent in to a hoop, and the ladies here and there had handkerchieves about them as openly as the vicar and nothing to do with hay-fever from the marsh. The vase-lady turned from the pew in front and covered my hand with hers and when Lady Vipont slid into The Hall pew, it was like the arrival of the cloud that worried Noah. 'Thank God', said the lady of the vase, 'that it was painless and swift.'

It appeared that Mr Pocock had died at sea. The vicarage had heard only that morning.

'My child – you didn't *know*! We were sure – ! We heard just before the service – a telephone message to The Hall and The Hall to the Vicar. We would have come to you at once – '
After the service clusters of ladies stood talking in whispers in the church-yard and only the nuns, being professionals, looked composed. And only the nuns said 'Your poor dear aunt. Oh Polly, your poor dear aunt. And still a bride.'

Alice said – we had a brandy together in the kitchen – 'Look at it this way, Miss Polly. She'll not want. He was a rich man. That's not nothing. Miss Frances was liked by all when she was poor and now she'll be the belle of the ball. And she's so young-looking, too!'

'But she'll be coming home, Alice,' I said, just realising it. 'She'll be home again. Oh Alice!'

And then the most astonishing thing happened.

Superstition, habit, respect, what you will, I could not write a letter on a Sunday with the sepia eye of Grandfather Younghusband on me from the wall and the holy eye of Aunt Mary from the clouds and so it was Monday morning before I had the letter of condolence to Aunt Frances ready for the post.

Alice and I did Mrs Woods that morning as usual. I wrote the letter and decided not to wait for the postman to call, but walked across the marsh to Dicky Dick's myself. It had not been an easy letter to write and I brooded all the way on whether or not I had hit the right note – Aunt Frances had always known very well that Mr Pocock and I had not been the best of friends. He had no idea what I looked like for a start as he had always been intent on something far above my head; and he had hardly addressed a word to me since the business of the refusal of Evensong. I said what I could – the terrible shock, the short time together, and so forth, and described the dreadfully sad atmosphere in church yesterday and the long prayers we'd had for both of them, alive and dead. The last bit was the real bit. Oh when, when, when will you get home? Darling Aunt Frances, when?

At Dicky Dick's I got another cup of tea and a long discussion on burials at sea and foreign germs. Then we moved to the new vicar and how the nuns were threatening a strike on laundering his albs. 'As to his cottas,' said Mrs Dick, 'they say they're shameless. They don't know what he does with them – and his surplices ripped and filthy round the hem like a Roman. It's the way he rives about in the pulpit. And that sneezing. Mr Pocock, God rest him, always behaved so stately.'

'Here's post for you, Miss Polly,' said Mr Dick, 'from foreign. Just arrived.'

I seized and ran – and on the marsh peeled the large envelope from the front of my coat where I had slapped it against me – and gazed. It was. A letter from Aunt Frances. To me. Addressed to me. At last. I ripped it open.

It was heavy and stiff, not like the letters on the hall-table to Aunt Mary, which, still unread by me, had accompanied her to the Retreat. In fact it was not a letter at all, but a photograph taken on board ship and it showed Aunt Frances dressed as a pierrot in a stiff white ruff and a pointed hat with black pom-poms, a satin skirt and bodice cut tight. Surrounding her were other pierrots, male and female, some of them smoking cigarettes in long holders and holding wine-glasses at angles. Everyone had a very shiny face. A large man in the middle who was wearing a monocle which accorded strangely with the pom-poms had the shiniest face of all. He was holding a bottle and had his arm round Aunt Frances's waist and on the back of the photograph in Aunt Frances's hand-writing were the words, 'High Jinks on Deck.'

It was after tea before I told Alice. She said as she came to take my tray, 'She's managed three scones and honey and she's walked to the window. My feelings are she could do them stairs now even by herself, if she had a mind. You're quiet?'

'Yes. I've had some news. I forgot to say.'

'*Forgot*? Now what's this then? Letters?' (I thought, Alice is changing.)

'Well, it wasn't a letter. From Miss Frances. It was a photograph. Taken on board the ship.'

'Oh Miss Polly,' she said, reverting to status. 'Oh, how lovely. Oh, she'll be glad she had that taken in time. Just the two of them together. Especially after no photos at the wedding. Even our Min had wedding photos. You'll have to take it round to all of them at Church.'

'I don't know that I will, actually. Mr Pocock's not in it.'

'Oh dear, I expect he was sickening. Oh!'

She looked at the photograph closely. For a long time, then turned it over and then back.

'Which one is Jinks do you think, Miss Polly?'

'I don't know. It's rather puzzling isn't it?'

'Miss Frances looks rather – over-done. I don't think I should show it to Mrs Woods.'

'No. Maybe I could show it to the new vicar?'

'Well, we could,' she said. 'They say he's a man of the world.'

' "We",' I thought. 'Yes, Alice is changing. They'd all have had a fit about "we".' And then I thought, 'Whatever should I do without her?'

'I had this from Aunt Frances,' I told the vicar the day of the post-Communion sherry and he choked violently in the button-back chair and went wheezing and hacking round the room beating his chest and ended up with his head against the marble chimney-piece. 'God in Heaven!' he cried and remembered himself before looking at the photograph again with a grave mouth, his eyes streaming.

'D'you think it's some sort of mistake, Father? I hardly recognise her.'

'She does seem rather – over-excited,' he said, getting out the handkerchief.

'Alice has a brother who was stoker on a liner. He told her

127

that people do get rather excited on board ship. It's the vibrations of the engines, though I don't see quite why.'

'Harra – yes,' he said. 'Did you see the postmark?'

'It was posted ages ago,' I said, and left it at that. He kept looking at me however, and at last I had to say, 'Aden.'

'Aden?'

'Yes.'

We looked away from each other then, because we both knew that last Sunday we had prayed for the repose of Father Pocock committed to the deep, and that the deep referred to had been the Mediterranean. An ocean which the Aunt Frances in the photograph had left far behind her.

*

To the best of my knowledge, that vicar who stayed such a short time with us and whom I missed very much (there was a hay-fever and incense revolt) never told anyone about the photograph. I put it deep in a drawer where it stayed for many years, taking it out only once, a month later, when we heard that Aunt Frances had died of amoebic dysentery on the way to Chandrapore. I looked at it for a long time then and felt mystification as before, but a sort of elation, too, at the dizzy joy in her face.

*

The war began for us, then, with a rainy morning and mist wrapped about a stunned house of death and disease and metamorphosis; and also with the front doorbell giving a loud and tremendous jangling cry.

'Law, I can't answer it, look at me,' said Alice at the dirty fireplace and held out black hands. I said, 'I'll go, it's all right.'

'That you'll not. Whatever would they have said?' She tried to push bits of hair back under her cap and left a black mark on her forehead.

'I'm going,' said I. 'You go off and wash before you go up to the bedroom. I'll come and help soon. You're a show, Alice,' and I opened the door to Paul Treece.

He looked eager, rose-pink and dripping.

It was more than a year. The sight of him meant Thwaite and Roundstone, and there was a great surge of excitement in me. Simultaneously there was the surge of disappointment at the girlish slope of his shoulders, the ears, the over-brightness.

'Polly – Miss Flint! I came over at once. I had no idea you were so near. I'm at The New House. With the Zeits. I was staying for a visit. None of that now, of course. I'm joining my regiment this afternoon.'

'You're frightfully wet. Come in. I didn't know you were in the army. It drenches you, the mist. You're flooding the tiles.'

'I didn't stop for a coat. I thought I'd get right over to you at once.'

(Goodness! Goodness, goodness, Paul Treece!)

I said, 'I heard the Zeits were coming at last. But it's been so long. I don't go out much.'

'No. I heard. You're alone looking after a crowd of sick aunts. They're very sorry – the Zeits. I was to say so. Look, I've a letter here. You're to go over. I'll be gone though.'

· 'I can't go over, Paul. Come through to the kitchen and I'll get you a towel to dry your hair.'

He rubbed at his hair like a small child, going round and round his head in circles.

'I didn't know you were a soldier.'

'I jumped the gun. Made enquiries. I got my papers this very morning.'

'You said you couldn't bear guns.'

'That was long ago.'

'I saw this coming. Well, it has to be done.'

'Saw what coming?'

He took his face out of the towel – his ears vermilion, the hands in the towel bony and big – 'But you know? You've heard?'

'No.'

'We're at war. It was all up yesterday – well, it was all up in June. The declaration was this morning.'

'I heard nothing. Did the bells ring?'

'No. There was nothing. It's just seeping around. They have a telephone at the Zeits.'

'We're – rather cut off out here.'

'Well, it's the war. There's no doubt about it. No choice if we're to keep with France. May as well get it over – it won't last long.'

'A *war*.' Trying the word over, it sounded mad. Such a random thing. A boy with a gun in Bohemia, one afternoon. The lunatic world.

'It comes from so far away. Such a foreign, hysterical sort of thing. It happens all the time in historical novels, the shooting of dukes, but the world doesn't join in.'

'It's not nothing to Austria. It's as if our Prince of Wales had been assassinated in Ireland.'

'Well, yes I see. That would be frightful. But it makes me think we should be on their side.'

'What a desert isle you live on.'

'Come through,' I said. 'We'll take the tea to the study. D'you think – d'you suppose we'll actually notice it? Up here?'

'All the men will disappear,' he said. 'They say a hundred thousand are going to France. Theo Zeit says there is a plan to make a new army – overnight. Everybody – the butcher, the baker. It will be mediaeval. Magnificent. Otherwise I dare say it won't change your life here very much – unless there's a bombardment from the sea. But that couldn't happen in the North-East I'd think. You'd be a huge target here of course – in this house – you're almost in the water.'

'Yes, almost.'

'You must mind these books,' he said. He was moving fussily around the room, touching the shelves. 'Take care of them. Maybe you should let the Zeits look after them at Roundstone.'

'What's happening to the Zeits?'

'Nothing yet. Theo isn't in any hurry for the army. He's very quiet. You know how he is. Rebecca's all agog. Talking of nursing already. But there's a snag or two. For all of them. Not very pleasant.'

'Oh?'

'Well – foreign blood and so on you know. They're Germans, after all. German Jews. Schleswig-Holstein or somewhere extraordinary – there are a good many in the North-East. They've been here for a generation. Everyone calls them German though. And since Theo's father died – '

'Oh did he? I didn't know. I never saw him. Mr Thwaite liked him so much. I'm sorry.'

'Grand old country gentleman. Typical English country gentleman, if you didn't know. He collected butterflies. She was the power house always. The genius Ironmaster was Theo's grandfather and Mrs Zeit took up the reins. Theo'll take over in time of course and be magnificent. He's a marvellous chap – you can feel it, can't you? He keeps his own counsel. You can never get very near him. But everyone likes him. He'll have a hard time. The Iron-Works are in poor shape aren't they?'

'There have always been people thrown out of work there, I think. It stays like that. We don't really know much about the Works on the marsh.' (And all the time I was saying: Paul Treece, Paul Treece is here and Theo not two miles away.)

'Theo will change things. He may stay here now. There may just be some trouble about him getting into the army you know. He may be more useful here at home.'

(Theo upon my doorstep. Theo near me all the time!)

'Could I?' He took down a book and looked at it with love. He stroked it and smelled it. 'When I come back from the war,' he said, 'I shall sit still all my life in a room full of books.'

I liked him again. He was standing in profile too.

'I see you here,' he said, 'a hundred years behind your times, reading Jane Austen – what an edition! – through endless afternoons. Sitting up straight, as you do!'

'I don't like her much.' (He's noticed how I sit.)

'Good heavens, don't you? Of course, I'd forgotten. Defoe's the one isn't he? Is he still? People usually move off from *Robinson Crusoe* after childhood.'

'I shall never move off.'

'Perhaps you will always be a – ' But he caught my look, I dare say. I'd noticed this before in people. I hoped it wasn't something I'd learned from Mrs Woods.

'Now why on earth is that, I wonder?' he said instead. ' "The granite rock of English fiction" and so forth, but not *high* in the imaginative stakes. Not *exactly* given to flights of poetry.'

'Neither's Jane Austen. And imagination – you're mad. Have you ever tried to imagine it? Twenty-eight years of life, minute by minute, solitary, out of touch, nothing but the Bible and some animals? Not a soul to open your mouth to with hope of a proper reply for nearly thirty years? And all those years in holy dread? And the creation of a whole landscape? Out of nothing? He wasn't much of a traveller, Defoe, you know. D'you think he'd really seen bears and the Indies and cannibals and the sea-coast of Sallee?'

'Goodness me. There are *qualities* of imagination you know. Jane Austen's was water-colour. Subtle. She had the poetry of the intricate mind.'

'Oh get on,' I said – and looked round to see if it was someone else speaking. For a moment I thought I'd said one of the words from Wales. 'Water-colour. *Etching,* more like. And I'm a bit lost with intricate minds to tell you the truth. I like large obvious minds. I suppose it's because I'm large and rather obvious but – I love people who are very rational. Who *do* things. I admire it. Not that *I* am rational – I have to work very hard at it. I'd much rather go soaring off somewhere in the imagination, but you can't face things that way. It's not brave. Robinson Crusoe was very brave. And strong and oh, so clever.'

'How long since you read it, Mistress Flint?'

'I read it most years. I read Defoe all the time, but *Crusoe's* separate from the rest. He's a separate, real person Defoe struck upon by accident. A sort of divine accident. I think that this is how most characters who are going to survive get born.'

'But he wasn't brave,' said Paul Treece. 'You said there was terror on the island. There was terror all the time. He was afraid of everything. Sleeping up trees, building fortresses with secret back-doors – and after years – years – when he'd not been troubled by any living creature, he gets the shakes over a dying goat. After he spotted the foot-print he had the shakes for two whole years. And he only started praying out of fright. He prays non-stop for twenty-eight years – *out of fright*. He never sits still. He's a bundle of nerves. He lives in fear, refined and pure. He's magnificent when the shooting starts, I agree. Smell of cordite, whites of eyes and so forth. But for a quarter of a century, waiting for the fun to start, he's a dithering, boring coward.'

'Perhaps he did have some imagination then.'

'Oh well – I don't know. Instinctive cowardice I'd call it. How would you have liked to spend the years with him?'

'Very much.'

'You could hardly have loved him? You'd have been his good woman. He'd have been worse than the dreadful father of *La Famille Suisse*, which is saying something. Nobody really loved anybody – have you read Part II?'

'Yes.'

'Crusoe and women? He never needed a – gave a thought to a woman all those years. As for Friday – what about the way he treated Friday? Called himself a Christian and didn't even ask his name. Gave him a new one he'd thought up himself.'

'That's not un-Christian. Christians are always changing their name.'

' "Friday" – how ridiculous. "Good Friday" I suppose. Someone will be calling it all religious allegory soon I expect. Maybe it was – though I'd doubt it, in a journalist. The Crusoe-fixion. Ha!'

'Of course it's not. And Defoe wasn't just a journalist. I don't think Crusoe was very religious as a matter of fact. He was possessed by guilt and discontent and this tremendous inborn lust for travel. He was the last man on earth to endure imprisonment on an island, but he came to terms with it. He didn't go mad. He was *brave*. He was wonderful. He was like women have to be almost always, on an island. Stuck. Imprisoned. The only way to survive it is to say it's God's will.'

(I had had no idea that I thought all this!)

'I agree with you about the praying,' I hurtled on. 'It wasn't love of God, like we're meant to have. It was awe and fear and at last just habit. That's why I won't get Confirmed – it would be just habit. That's why I think marriage is so dull – after you're married it becomes just habit. But they're both a sort of crutch to help you along. You get in a mess without them. Habits.'

'Habit and journalistic device,' said Paul Treece. 'The Godly element in Crusoe was only put in to hang a few sermons on. People would read anything then if it had a sermon in it. Times change. I tell you – Defoe was a journalist. You've glorified this book into a gospel.'

I wasn't really listening. I was hot in the face and felt that I had to talk on and on or burst.

133

'Actually, with my aunts the habit didn't work.' I said, 'It wasn't strong enough. They missed out on marriage or they muddled it and the praying got – oh, too important. They both went mad a bit I think. It's more difficult you see. Women's bodies are so difficult and disgusting, though they're supposed to be so fragrant and beautiful and delicate. We have to try so much harder than men.'

'I've lost you, I'm afraid,' he said, looking dreadfully embarrassed suddenly. Before I'd mentioned women's bodies he'd been looking handsome and excited and happy – and as delighted to be talking about Defoe as I was. Now by talking about my body I'd stopped the only real conversation I'd ever had in my life.

'The painter at Thwaite understood,' I said.

He recovered and his ears dimmed.

'D'you know what Dickens said?' He put the *Sense and Sensibility* back on its shelf. 'Dickens said that *Robinson Crusoe* has never made anybody laugh or cry.'

'Why does everybody read it then? I go on reading it. I have done since I was eight. Everybody loves it. Crusoe's everybody's hero. I laugh and I cry. I expect Dickens was jealous. Most people don't remember when they first heard of Crusoe – that's the test. He just always was. He's very human and at the same time almost a god. He's my *utter* hero.'

'Oh, you get these books,' he said, 'books to possess you. You ought to rid yourself of him or he'll stick fast. He'll retard you. It's like love. Often the book that gets you is the first you've really read for yourself – or maybe you pick it up at an important moment in your life – at the time of some passionate event. Like ducks. Little ducks, you know – the first thing they see when they step out of the egg, they think is their mother. Even if it's a cow, they'll follow it about. I live on a farm, I've seen it. It is an imprint. "Love" is only an imprint, most of the time.'

'I'd love to live on a farm,' I said.

'That's part of the Crusoe complex. The good earth. Distrust it.'

'How do you know so much about books?'

'I was born that sort.'

'Yes. So was I. I was lucky to come here.'

134

'I've had to suck up to people to get any books,' he said. 'I'm fairly shameless. A parasite and a go-getter. Otherwise no books. We're pretty poor at home.'

I thought, 'He is an honest man.' I was beginning to love him again.

'But I'm not a duck.' I said. 'I don't think *Robinson Crusoe* is my mother.'

'That's something.' He came up near to me and touched my hair and ran a finger round the edge of my face. He patted it in a motherly sort of way.

'But it's true about love,' he said. 'It's the girl who happens to be there at some important moment who becomes the obsession.'

'That's a bit unflattering.' I moved a step back.

'Like that morning,' he said, giving a little jerky jump forward. 'That extraordinary dawn. And the cows. And the rolls of mist on the river and the pink milk. They cast a spell.'

'Yes. There was something then.' But I thought of years before, when the pony and trap came up out of nowhere on the sands as I had sat freezing on the seaweed.

He said, 'I'd better be off, I suppose,' and stepped back again. In the new talkativeness and sureness, I said, 'You're very cautious for such an emotional man. And a poet.'

The quiet book-room had grown quieter, the big windows blanker and whiter. The mist was beginning to shine and the sun would be through now soon. 'I always seem to be with you in mists,' I said.

'Yes. Well. I had better be off. I wondered if perhaps I might write?'

'Write? But don't you?'

'Write to you. You might write back if you have time. I dare say we'll need some letters wherever we're going. Of course, I don't want to compromise you in any way – '

'No. I suppose not.'

'I have asked a number of girls to write. I wouldn't want to – embarrass you. You're very young. I mean – it's early days.'

'Yes, I see.'

'Here's Mrs Zeit's letter.' He handed it over, looking above my head. 'I say, that's a lovely drawing of you.'

'It was done at Lady Celia's. Well – on the way home.'

'A surprise. I didn't know you were so pretty. What's the matter? Have I said something wrong?'

'About six things,' I said, 'but never mind. You'd better go.'

'I'm sorry. I'm not good at it. Talking with a girl alone. I do talk too much I know. They say I'm rather naïve. I write better.'

'Yes I see.'

'It's odd – you shut away out here. You're not at all naïve.'

'I thought I must be, quite.'

'No. I'm very direct,' he said. 'You like the direct. Defoe.'

He stood about. I thought, 'Oh Lord, go away. You're hopeless. Go. You're hopeless after all.'

He turned at the foot of the steps as if he'd never move again and stood still, examining his wet boots. Water was being almost visibly sucked up from the marsh to join the soaking air. I said, 'Wait,' and ran back to the passage where there was a cape hanging from when Grandfather Younghusband strode the landscape in it, and I gave it to The Poultice. His body became invisible inside it, a soft, poor tortoise in a noble shell. 'Oh *jolly* swish!' he said. 'I'll tell them to let you have it back. Don't like getting wet particularly. I'm not sure that I'm going to be all that keen on the outdoor aspect of this next business. Still – I expect I'll be all right when the shooting starts. Like himself.'

'Goodbye Paul. I will write.'

I watched the triangle of the immense cape vanish into the lifting mist, bobbing here, bobbing there through the long pools and the salt-hills. It moved in cheerful jumps and splashes I could hear him after he had disappeared.

*

His letters were slow in coming, but when they eventually began to appear, continued thick and fast, first from his O.T.C. camp, then from the local battalion he had joined as a private in order to get more quickly into action, and finally from France where he found himself a second lieutenant within the space of three months. The letters were very perfect – the handwriting neat and confident, sentences beautifully constructed, adjectives consciously correct. There were no endearments, only carefully-judged phrases of appreciation

136

which had been looked over for a long time and sometimes, I felt, changed to give better cadences. Whole letters may have been re-drafted to achieve this – there was never a crossing out. They were exercises. But little did I care, for I read them quickly, only interested because they were letters I had received from a man. I liked the look of them waiting on the hall-table. I often didn't open them for hours.

For during the next months, as the soldiers fell in thousands, off Belgium, I was at The New House every day, being welcomed with flamboyance by the Zeits. I turned pink and merry overnight and got Alice to put up my hair, which had become shiny and curly and taken on a life of its own. Rebecca approved me and Theo was there.

Theo was there all day. Every day. At every meal. He was quiet while the sister and mother talked and talked – so cleverly, so fast – but he seemed always to be looking at me and when I caught him looking at me he never looked away, but smiled. We walked in the gardens together and we sat together indoors and he saw me home across the marsh at night. In October he and Rebecca went up to Cambridge but I still went to the house to help Mrs Zeit with her war-work – she held something called 'The Depot' in her morning-room, and rather-awed, respectable local ladies from the terraces rolled bandages there. Flowers came from Theo once to the yellow house, thanking me for helping his mother. He returned home before his term had ended and was closeted with her for hours.

Walking back to the yellow house with him one evening, looking at the belching Works he said, 'I don't want them. I don't see them as mine. Well, the war will decide things I suppose.'

'Shall you – do you think you'll enlist?'

'It's all confused at present. I'm not sure I shall be allowed to. We have a German name. We didn't change it like most people. They are embarrassed for us – and suspicious of us. It would look like fighting our own side we're told – though I don't feel it. We're waiting.'

'Yes. I see you can't feel very passionately patriotic.'

'No. Have you heard from the redoubtable Poultice?'

'Oh yes,' I said. 'Often.'

'Are you – d'you mind my asking – engaged to him?'

'Oh heavens, no!'

'I thought you might be. I'm sorry. You looked so very much together the day you came walking in to breakfast in the country.'

'Oh that was just accident. It's like that at Lady Celia's. The others there were all famous and old so we were rather thrown together.'

'Arty-crafty place isn't it? It'd suit the poor old Poultice.'

'I think he loved it.'

'Did it suit you?'

'Well some of it.'

'Bit of a delicate flower, isn't he, actually? If we're really honest. Something of a joke.'

I said nothing. He said, 'I've put my foot in it. Dear God, I'm sorry. And you must be so worried about him. He'll be back soon you know. He'll get some leave.'

'He wanted me to go up to London for his embarkation leave but of course I couldn't.'

'Really? I'd think it would have been fun for you. Well, "it'll be over by Christmas", so we are told. Endlessly.'

We walked on the beach and went out in the trap and visited The Hall – but nobody was there. The shutters were up. There was a chain across the mausoleum door. The sun shone every day as if it were a festival year – a deep, beautiful autumn. Rebecca left Cambridge and briefly visited us, then departed with set jaw to London on political matters, she said. 'She's anti-suffragette,' said Theo, 'like so many bossy women.'

He taught me to play tennis on the new court and laughed at me for being so stately, not making it seem foolish. I spoke German with him and with Mrs Zeit – they said they would forget it all soon and could only speak it when the servants were not about. 'How beautifully you speak,' she said; 'a perfect accent,' and I said, 'That's Mrs Woods.'

But I had forgotten Mrs Woods. I had forgotten home altogether – the household, the housekeeping, Alice. I went home only to sleep and pray for the next day to come fast.

I woke up very early one day and wondered why. It was sunny and still. I felt that something had just stopped and went to my window and saw outside the yellow house Theo sitting in the pony-trap in the early light. He was not attempting to get out but simply sitting, staring ahead. He had a queer, patient, staid look about him and seemed to be staring at, but not seeing, the old convalescent home where soldiers were now marching on a newly-made parade-ground, up and down, up and down. The tinny bark and echo of the sergeant-major bounced towards the house occasionally. Surrounding Mr Pocock's old Chaplaincy by the nunnery, a city of tents had gone up, spreading out onto the marsh itself. The broken-ended esplanade had been extended.

Theo was sitting so remarkably still, even for him, that I dressed and rushed out to him without doing up my hair and he turned and looked down at me.

'Are you warm enough?'

'Yes. It's a lovely day.'

'Could you – jump in?'

'Yes, of course.'

The front door stood open behind me for the sand to fly freely in, and I had not looked even to see if Mrs Woods was all right, and I had not seen Alice, and I was not wearing a hat. He leaned down and helped me up beside him and we moved off inland, turning away from the lane-end that led to the Zeits, away from the sea. We meandered inland towards the church, but veered away from it again, and on past a farm and haystacks, then northward towards the Works. We sat watching them across the stubble – fields which were growing new flowers among the straw, for the summer would not cease. It was quiet except that I thought that I had never heard so many birds. He said, 'Polly, we've just heard from Rebecca that Paul Treece is dead. He was killed a week ago.'

The birds went on and on and the smoke from the chimneys stood in the blue sky. The horse shook its head vigorously and clattered a shoe. It moved to the hedge and began to pull up and crunch the grass beside it. After a time Theo put an arm round me and I put my head on his shoulder. He smelled of soap and man. I had not smelled man before. I began to cry, not because The Poultice was dead but because of my wickedness in being so excited by the smell of Theo Zeit.

He turned the trap with one hand and we drove back very slowly to The New House with my hair against his face. I believe that people passed us and saw, but I didn't move and nor did he. When we reached The New House drive I still did not move, but there was a flash of light from somewhere above us and I jumped and sat up; but he still held on to me.

'It's all right. It's the telescope. It's being dismantled. Government orders. They think we're German spies.'

'I once thought I saw an angel up there.'

'I saw you once from there. You were trying to fly like a bird.'

'I was twelve. It was years ago.'

'I thought you were lovely.'

I disentangled myself and sat up straight and tried to sort out my hair.

'Could you take me home?'

'Not yet. You're to come to us. Mother ordered it,' and she was standing on the steps in her funny over-decorated dress, all brooches and necklaces, her face lifted up like Hecuba with tears on it, her short, plump arms held out. I thought, 'She looks as if she's going to sing,' and nearly laughed.

'My dear, dear child!' Such hugs and kisses as I had never known, and had no notion what to do with. But I felt them less than I felt Theo standing near and watching me; and I cried again at my wickedness at having been made happy by a death.

I hadn't even thought about the death yet. I would get to that when I went home.

'Would you very much mind if I went home?'

'My child, very much, very much.'

I sat down to coffee and then breakfast with cheese and small sweet cakes, but I didn't like to eat them. Maids padded about outside the door, people spoke in whispers. Down the creamy cheeks of Mrs Zeit the tears flowed and she was unashamed. I thought, how foreign she is.

But Theo sat beside me.

'I must go and get tidy,' I said and Mrs Zeit took me to her bedroom and I sat at her dressing-table before a forest of photographs: powerful short men with short beards, women with chins and frilled crinolines and mountains of crinkly hair and firm, gigantic bosoms. Rebecca, a sparkling child, and Theo – no one but Theo – a baby with watchful loving black

eyes. He wore a satin suit and sat firmly on a satin chaise-
longue.

'You are to stay here with us for a little while, Polly, my
dear. A day or two.'

'No, I must go back. There's Mrs Woods.'

'Polly, soon we are to talk about Mrs Woods, you and I
together. It is time that something was decided about Mrs
Woods.'

'She's got no one.'

'Which is no reason that you should sacrifice your young
life.'

'Please, I don't want to talk now.'

'Of course not. Of course not. But we shall be talking soon.
I have decided. We are to talk about your future. About the
university. Yes. I have decided. It is to be Oxford I think.
Please do not look at me so. It is to be Oxford for you.'

I said that I wanted to walk home and Theo came with
me as far as the terrace. I felt his gentle eyes watching my
back all the way down to the faraway gate. I tried not to
think of this – to think only of Paul Treece – dead Paul
Treece, the ears, the sloping shoulders, the hands that had
touched the books, had touched my hair, all rotten, limp,
bundled into a hole in France. I managed for a minute or so.

At the gate I turned back to wave to Theo but found that
I had been wrong, for he was not there.

I helped Alice when I got home. We changed Mrs Woods,
talked about meals, domestic things. 'D'you want a rest?' said
Alice. 'You look right lowered.'

'There's somebody killed,' I said. 'It was the young man
who called the day of the Declaration of War.'

'I remember him,' she said. 'He was artless-looking. Well.
He'll not be alone out there. Mr Box of Boagey's has gone
and many another more. There'll be many and many a
hundred yet. It said in the papers "The Greatest European
War in History". It's hard to believe, isn't it – being a part
of History?'

*

I went each day to the Zeits for four weeks then and for four
days after that, and the late autumn was still golden and hot
and berries shone on the trees and hedges. The house was

141

busy with comings and goings. We were allocated the billeting of Belgian refugees, though I never saw any. Great consultations went on usually behind closed doors and I sat at Mrs Zeit's desk, writing the letters, checking endless rather obscure lists while she went about the rooms, talkative and busy – often talking apparently to herself. She set up another desk for herself near a giant telephone and Theo, amused, delighted with her, often caught my eye including me in his affection. She was in total command. Sometimes, however, the discussions behind the locked doors left uneasiness in the air when the doors were opened.

'We still don't know what they're going to do with us,' he said.

'What could they do with you?'

'Stick us in prison. Intern us.'

'Oh Theo, how ridiculous. You're English. You're as English as I am.'

'Yes. I'm sure it won't come to it. It's all very haphazard. Shall we go down and look at the sea – as near as we can get? We're rich, you see. There's jealousy. In Newcastle they're interning all Germans who aren't naturalised, whoever they are. Newcastle's where we started from in England – the family. When we left Europe. It's hard to believe we don't belong.'

We walked by the sea and we walked in the fields and as late as early November we sat out after dinner on the terrace. When it grew colder they found me an old fur coat. It was silky. 'They're sables,' he said; 'you are a princess.' He kissed me sometimes. I found that I was very good at kissing after a time, as good – rather better – than he.

A letter came from Paul Treece with a poem in it called *At the Gate of the Past*. It arrived a week after he was dead, posted the day before he died. The poem floated along on the top of my mind and I did not allow it to go deeper. I carried it everywhere with me, and although I was never so indecent as to let it be seen, I knew that my motive for having it always in my pocket was not a pure one, and in the end, I did casually mention it to Theo. 'You were in love with him,' he said, so solemnly that my heart lifted.

'No,' I said, 'no I wasn't, not in love.' But I said it with an inflection on the 'I'.

142

'You and he were very close though. Books and so on. Weren't you? I felt it. I suppose you'd known him a very long time.'

'Oh – a year or so.' (Not, 'I had met him twice.')

'You've known me longer. You've known me for five years and I've known about you for longer than that – since the day you were being a bird, behind all the old birds.'

'Not *known*,' I said.

'I'm afraid I don't read much. Only the Sciences. Well – just the books everyone has to.'

'You'd read *Robinson Crusoe*. You said so on the beach.'

'Well everyone knows about the footprint. That's not a novel though, is it, *Robinson Crusoe* – isn't it biography? He was real, wasn't he?'

I was sleeping at the Zeits now, only going home occasionally. There was to be a Christmas party at The New House – just a few close friends of the children, Mrs Zeit said – and I had written to Maitland – we wrote every month or so. She wrote funny formal dry little letters back and always said that I was to say if ever I needed anything. For the party she had sent me a dress – with Lady Celia's blessing, so that I was supposedly forgiven for the defection at breakfast last year. The dress was of pure silk muslin, golden-brown, with needle-work bands and a high neck stitched with blue silk thread. I was thinner than when she had measured me at Thwaite and Alice had been altering it. I went home for this dress only and Alice was as pleased as I was with it. So we arranged for Boagey's to bring a car for me on the night of the party and at The New House we worked at preparing the party all the day before until we were tired. In the evening Theo said, 'Come out. Put on the sables, Mistress Flint, and we'll look at the stars.'

It was a frosty night at last, but I was warm, and we walked about the marsh and on the sand-hills. We lay down in the sand-hills and under the sables he undid my dress. I said, 'We'll be seen. There are soldiers. I don't think we should be here anyway. Even if we are just walking.' But we did not go. We stayed there for hours.

'We'll go home,' he said. 'You're staying tonight. We have the whole night ahead of us.'

And so I went to bed at the Zeits and waited for him. I

143

wore my silk nightdress, Maitland's last Christmas present, and I brushed my hair two hundred times as Aunt Frances had taught me. The big clocks downstairs struck eleven and then twelve and at last, oh at last, some time after that, the handle of my bedroom-door began to turn.

Mrs Zeit came in to the room and sat on the end of my bed.

'How we shall miss you, Polly. Oh we shall miss you so. As a daughter and as a sister. The whole family will miss you. We'll be gone in three days you know – only three days left before London. Now, we want you to know. We *all* want to help you. We're not going to let you waste your life here.' She picked up the sables which were lying across a chair and put them comfortably over her arm.

I said, thank you.

'Somehow or other we are going to get you to Oxford. Now what do you think about that? Go to sleep. Go home in the morning and don't think of coming in again. You've worked so hard for the children's little party. Just have a good rest at home until it's over. And if we just *don't* see you again before we leave, you must not think we have forgotten you. We shall never lose touch, dear Polly. Good night my child.'

She left the room, stroking the furs, and I lay awake until the pale, cold morning came and, still dark, the maids began to stir about the house.

Theo was very affectionate when we said goodbye, and kissed my cheek and Mrs Zeit kissed me, too, as the chauffeur held open the Daimler door. Mother and son stood side by side upon the steps, she with the kindest of faces, he to attention, looking over our heads, not exactly smiling but not quite achieving the blankness he was aiming at. But perfectly in control.

'We can't have you walking home,' said Mrs Zeit, 'after all you've done. *Such* hard work. And the car can go on afterwards to the station and pick up the guests.'

At first, in the car, I allowed only the most immediate things room. How to tell Alice about the dress. Whether I should tell her that I'd made a frightful mistake. That it had never been intended that I should be at the party. But I saw the disappointment and hurt for me in her red, rough face, and then the fury rising up and knew I couldn't bear it.

As the car slid past the church and the ghosts of my saints, I prayed, I think for Alice first: 'Dear God, set this to rights. Oh, amidst the chaos of nations and the deaths in France and the great disasters in the turning world, and although I am still un-Confirmed into the Church of England I pray through Jesus Christ our Lord that this miserable hurt in my worthless grain of a life may somehow or other be resolved and used at last.'

*

'Why, the poor old sowl!' said Mrs Treece, 'And after years. Just gone in a minute! Well, it happens. Gone in her sleep. But just as you stepped in from visiting? You'd feel badly, not being with her at the end.'

'Well, yes I did. You see she was the last of the people I've known since I was a child. I felt so guilty. You see, she and I had never been friends. She'd resented me when my aunts took me in. She'd always adored one of my aunts you see, and when I came, that aunt began to adore me instead, and – '

'Nose out of joint,' said old Mrs Treece. 'Well, she's to be prayed for. Strokes is terrible things. I remember my father lying.'

She was so small that her feet scarcely touched the floor and the rocking chair she sat in stayed upright and steady. She wore black of course, for Paul – black ankle-strap shoes like a child's, over woollen stockings, and even the upright, soldierly collar round her child-size neck was trimmed with black lace as was the long apron over her woollen dress. Out of it all her face shone clear and rosy and her hair shone silverish. She was peeling big potatoes over a newspaper and washing them in a bowl beside her before dropping them into the pan on the fire.

Outside the farm kitchen it was snowing fast and the snow had gathered in the same corner of each of the nine little panes of the window over the stone slab sink where we washed the dishes. The fire was bright with precious small-coal for the cooking and I sat on the fender in my friendly brown-velvet dress, my back warm against the copper where the water heated in a deep dark font. A chicken was roasting in the fireside oven, for it was Christmas Day. My invitation to

145

stay at the Treeces' farm had been waiting for me at home the morning of my banishment, when I had walked in upon Mrs. Woods's death.

'And her funeral a sad tale, likely?'

'Oh yes, it was. There were so few there. Some nuns – she was very keen on nuns, though she never really got to know any of them separately. She hadn't the touch for friends at all, poor Mrs Woods. She was awfully clever. She spoke three languages and she'd been all over the world. But she'd got into the habit of being grim.'

All my life I have felt that I would find it very easy to talk to people if I could just once get started and here, at last, on a farm in the North-West fells, with Paul Treece's mother I was achieving it – though only, perhaps, I thought, because she keeps to her own unselfconscious track. And maybe it was her grief that had made her so totally uncritical, so accepting. It might well not last.

At present however I felt that I had lived with her for years.

'The poor old *sowl!*' she said again. 'No friend to mourn her? Paul has his mourners, and in high places.'

'Yes he has.'

'Paul knew some of the greatest in the land, even before he went to college. His room's full of letters from people very well born. Writing, clever people.'

'Yes, I'm sure.'

'Which is how I found you out, Polly, among all the letters from universities and lords and ladies. I went and sat up there and I read everything that there was in that room, on and on. On that first day his father and Laurie left me. They fettled for themselves. Maybe three days, all by themselves. There was bread and ham and a bit of cheese and some potatoes. What I did, when the telegram came, I took cloths to cover the pictures and the mirrors and I opened the windows all over the house. Bitter weather, bitter. I went up and sat in his room. It's always been the coldest in this old place, Paul's room, but he never ailed a thing, never. Mind, he wasn't here these last years, scarcely, and I did think he was looking terrible thin just before he went to France.

'I liked it being cold up there in that room as I read. The room was full of him. Electric. You know how he was? Electric. Oh – so tidy! I never seen a pencil not set straight. His books all graded along the bed-shelf and on the ledge and on his floor on newspapers and little slips of paper for dividers and on his table all his exercise books right back from school and through college. Oh he was a wonderful scholar, his writing that neat and clever-looking. Well, we never could think where he could have come from, Paul. No more could his teachers. Latin was nothing to him. French he could write as fast as English, all the little marks this way and that way, neat as print. I'se seen him up there writing Latin as young as twelve, freezing with his ears turned rainbow. I knitted him a cap once, but I don't recollect him wearing it. I would take him up his supper when his father wasn't by. His father'd say, If he can't come to table he does without. He wouldn't let him have a lamp, neither, with the price of lamp-oil. I've known him have a lamp under the clothes up there when he was still at school – for his homework. It's a wonder he wasn't cinders. Yet he was always lucky, Paul, till now. He seemed charmed. Lately his father was proud of him and he could do what he liked. Didn't even expect him to help with the farm work – well he weren't much advantage when he did, dreaming about. Paul was a mystery to his father, and to many another, but he's properly mourned – not like your poor person.'

*

I had walked from the Zeit's Daimler, praying and thinking of dresses, and up to Mrs Woods's bedroom, to find Alice turning from the bed.

'When, when?'

'Now. It must have been just now. I was up with her at breakfast. She had some breakfast. She's dead.'

'She *can't* be – ' I wouldn't look. I had never seen anyone dead. 'How do you know?'

'Look.'

'I can't.'

'You can and should. Stay here. I'll go for the doctor. Take her prayer-book. Read some prayers will you?'

'I can't.'

'Very well then, go downstairs. Get yourself a hot drink. I'll be back when I can.' She was out of the room.

147

I paced about the house then and Mrs Woods was everywhere. She stood on the stairs, she sat in the chair by the ferns, she peered round the study door with her knitting, her walking-stick tapped across the coloured tiles; she gave commands at the kitchen door. When I looked out of the windows there she was, huddled over her hot-water-bottle, scurrying over the marsh to church. In the dining-room she sat glaring at a child with her nose level with the forks. Outside my bedroom she whispered on the landing and out in the yard she was looking down from between the net curtains of the staircase window, holding one of them back on a finger. In the end my feet took me to the one place she was not, her bedroom, where a nothing lay under the cotton counterpane – a nothing with a young face, quite gentle and pretty, and the room calm.

*

'Now just go through to the dairy,' said Paul Treece's mother, 'and on the stone you'll see pork sausages. We'll fry them for the chicken on the fire. The bread sauce is at the bottom of the oven and there'll be room. The plum pudding's well away. There's room for another pan. It's a fine pow-sowdy. I'se not my usual self this year. Most-times I'se brisker. Maybe it's soon to be bothering with Christmas, but Paul wouldn't have wanted us overcome.'

'Why did you choose to write to me out of all the other people? Didn't you tell the other people?'

'No. Some seems to have known. There've been some messages. None of his letters – they sent them back to me from France with his things – even his fountain and his photographs and his brushes – none of his letters from other folks was so homely as yours. Being from famous people I suppose they couldn't be. Very dignified they mostly was, as if to someone lower, but time would have changed that. When I comes to your letters, thinks I, here's a quaint-spoken, old-fashioned girl and fond of Paul.'

'Yes, I was.'

'And like to have married him.'

'Well, – '

'I thought, "I dare say out of all the grand ones she'd have been the lucky one. All she had to do, this one, thinks I, was

148

play her cards right and she could have had him." He'd tell't me of you.'

'Oh – did he?'

'He'd tell't me of others – ladies and sirs and Bells and Wolves, this and that. Says I, "Paul, they're all foreigners to me. However you keep up with them I'll never know. Money-wise alone it can't be easy, with only the scholarship." I didn't ever like the way he was stopping with first one and then another, not giving back a penny. That's another thing I couldn't think where it came from. It's not like our family. I kept it from his father. I went by myself to his college for the graduation, long since. His father might have drawn attention to hisself – not liking south-country folk, them not ever doing any work.'

'Did you meet his friends at Cambridge, Mrs Treece?'

'Not so many. They were stand-offish I dare say. I looked for thee, Polly Flint, or one like thee. One that loved Paul.'

'Oh, I didn't – '

'Say no more. I can tell. When I read the letters I said, "She's the one I want about me now." '

She had forgotten the potatoes and let her hand holding the little worn triangle of knife drop to her lap among the peelings. She looked at the fire. I said, 'Let me finish,' and took the things from her. 'Sit still. I'll see to it' – I, who was hopeless and hadn't cooked a potato in my life.

Then the door opened and Paul's father and brother came in from feeding calves, carrying buckets, and stamped snow off themselves, clattered and called about, paying us no attention. They kicked the dogs into a corner and Paul's father stuck his wet cap up between a sagging black beam and the ceiling to dry. Paul's brother slapped the dirty bucket under the sink ready for us to wash up after our dinner. Their boots left pools about the patches of linoleum which were so sparse on the cold slabs that the floor seemed to be occasionally painted with dim flowers and leaves and squirls and bare in patches, like the traces of an antique pavement.

We sat to dinner quietly. There was a rough black settle covered in a pattern of red birds. There was not much of a cloth on the table, shreddy linen, but very clean. We drank from mugs not glasses. The knives and forks were poor and crooked but shining. The pudding was served with a queer

149

plain sauce like starch. 'It's a good pudding,' said Paul's brother, shovelling it in. 'It's a grand pudding.' 'It's carrot and potato,' said his mother. 'There's plenty currants in it,' said the brother, looking defensive, watching me for disgust.

After dinner the farmer took off his boots and heaved himself on to a high wooden meal-chest at the back of the kitchen and fell asleep. His feet, pointing at the ceiling were in socks as thick as chain-mail. Mrs Treece and I washed the dishes and then the animal-buckets at the sink and the brother Laurie sat at the fire, grinding branches into it from the stick-corner until the sparks flew. At length he leaned back and slept too.

What had Paul done on Christmas afternoons? I thought of him reading Yeats in the cold bedroom, writing careful letters to the famous, poetry of his own.

'Do you go to church ever at Christmas, Mrs Treece?'

'No. We never bother. Only harvest festivals.'

'We're very religious where I live.'

'Well, some it suits. The parson's been over about Paul. Not that he knew what to say for all the practice he's had. Eleven in Paul's carriage from this parish sets off for France, and nine of them dead in a week. What could he say, if ever? What it's for's beyond me. I make no pretence of under-standing. I'll go up now to change my dress.'

I sat opposite the sleeping brother. He was short and thick-set with huge hands, hanging loose between his open thighs, his head flung back and sideways, his hair soft and young. His coarse trousers were rolled up and his stockings like his father's had big darns in them which were beautiful. He lay heavy and still, uncaring and unaware of me or any stranger. A year younger than Paul, this boy and he must have been babies together playing on this rag-rug, learning to speak with the same country accent, before Paul unlearned it again, going together to the same village school. Paul had never mentioned Laurie.

Laurie's eyelashes were like Paul's. His ears were usual. He had a nicer mouth – a sleepy, hungry mouth with the lower lip fuller than the top one. Looking at the mouth I began to think about Laurie.

'What ist?' he said, waking up. 'It's goin' on dark. It's bare three o'clock. Canst thou mek tea?'

'Yes. I'll make tea. Shouldn't we wait for your mother?'

'She'll bide. She'll be sleeping maybe. She's slept little. It's in yon caddy.'

He pointed up to a red tin with the King and Queen looking out from it in patchy gold on the chimney-piece. It was so high that I had to stretch even standing on the fender, and he watched me and did not help. I found the teapot and warmed it and threw the slops out of the kitchen door as I'd seen his mother do and some of them blew in at me again. Then I poured the water from the huge kettle on the chain over the fire – it needed two hands – and then set the teapot on top of the copper-lid to stand. Laurie said, 'That's a good lass. Thas't not a bad lass.'

'Thank you.'

'You and Paul was sweet-hearting, then?'

'Well – '

'He'd never had one. Tell truth, I never thowt he would. He was missing in that direction.'

'Did you – were you quite close?'

'Aye, under the year.'

'I meant close. Close friends?'

'I could never make him out. Aye, we was friends. Did you have a ring from him?'

'Oh no. Nothing like that.'

'You knew he was from farming people?'

'Oh yes. I told him I'd love to live on a farm.'

'You did, did you? What made you think that?'

'I don't know. I'm telling the truth though.'

'Have you changed your tune now?'

'No.'

'D'you know we works twelve hours a day all week and never a holiday? My mam walks eight miles to a shop to save a penny on the bus – and she's scrubbed this floor for twenty years, not being money for a hired girl – and her a boarding-school girl herself when she was young. Well born. She's an old woman now at forty-nine. We never get an egg – they go to be sold. Most of last year it was potatoes, potatoes. You're rich, aren't you?'

'No. I haven't any money except a little bit I was left and a house.'

'A house is rich – and that dress is rich. This house in't

our own. We's tenants. We could be thrown out tomorrow. Paul would have come rich, mind, you could see.'

'Why did he go to the army so soon, Laurie? He didn't have to.'

'Christ knows.'

'You won't?'

'Not required and won't be. I'll be reserved occupation. Catch me, anyway.'

'I suppose Paul went for his country.'

'My country needs me in it.'

He leaned forward soon and took my hand and watched me, and his hand began to tighten. Then the old man stirred on the kist-top and Mrs Treece came in without her apron, pleased to see the pot of tea.

'Could you not stay longer?' she said at the New Year. 'We's got used to you. You've brought comfort.'

'Aye, you've done that,' said the farmer, surprising everyone, 'you've brought some comfort.' The simple words seemed to surprise the speaker too. For the first time in the brave house I felt near tears.

'Why not stop on?' Laurie was watching me carry down my bag and the big parcels of Paul's papers and books which his parents had quite fiercely said were mine. He watched me wrap myself up in gloves and scarves and lift up my things into the cart behind him. 'I can't. There's too much to do at home. Alice is all alone.'

'You'll come again mind?'

'Thank you very much.' (I knew I never could.)

'I'll drive you then.'

We squatted side by side in the front of the cart drawn by the brown cart-horse. I kept Paul's box of papers between us, and watched over the bundles of books tied together with hairy twine. The floor of the cart was caked with old dried mud and between the cracks in it I watched the rough road go by between the long hedges up the hill. The high wheels went wobbling round – they had once been painted red and yellow and must have looked like a carnival, when Paul was a baby. A daily fairground. I saw the baby watching the coloured wheels turn and the red shoots of the hedges all about them.

Laurie let me get down from the car alone and then passed

me all the things and some butter and eggs wrapped in oily paper. He watched me go with the old station-master helping me up the station yard and I waved goodbye and stood in the waiting room stamping my feet and looking out at the miles of snowy fell.

The sun shone. The station stove made a clinking and dropping of coals and there was a louder clinking and xylophonic dropping of water outside, for all along the pretty carved edges of the station buildings the icicles were melting. Then I could hear the train coming.

As I gathered my things together again, Laurie suddenly appeared and took my bag from me with a funny sideways, sly-look, not speaking and I thought, Good gracious, after all he's shy.

I opened the carriage window and he looked up at me and said 'If you was to sell that house you could come here and live. Think on. Think on now. I'll say nothing further.'

'Thank you very much.'

'I'd not have thowt to fetch up with a woman of Paul's, mind. Seems we wasn't so different after all.'

'Thank you very much.'

'What say then? Think on?'

I said nothing and he began to hop and run by the train. He had anxious, over-bright eyes. I saw Paul in him now so clearly for a moment that my own eyes filled properly with tears and this time the tears fell. For I knew that Laurie and the Treeces were not for me.

'It's grand here in spring and summer,' he called. 'You'd like that. The lambs and that. And harvest time. It's a grand country. I'd not leave it.'

He'd think later I was a strange girl, crying, never answering him, though he'd not think of me for very long.

*

The most famous heart-stopping incident in *Robinson Crusoe* is, of course, the foot-print, yet it was never to me the most terrifying. A glorious idea, with no known parallel in fiction, as simple and splendid as the idea of the book itself, at once an astounding and completely credible sight.

Yet I was always slightly disappointed by it – that it was just a print, not Friday's print as everybody has come to

153

think. Just the print of some quite anonymous foot, probably crunched up on a later occasion around the cannibal fires.

Secondly it had always seemed disappointing that years had to pass by before any living foot followed the promise of the print of one – even though the casual lapse of time is consistent with Defoe's unhurried pace, his grandly confident unrolling of the years.

But much more frightening seems to me to be another occasion: when Crusoe, after his first foray in his home-made canoe, gets shipwrecked again on an unknown part of his island and hears his own voice calling out his name.

'Robin, Robin, Robin Crusoe, poor Robin Crusoe! Where are you, Robin Crusoe? Where are you? Where have you been?'

(His parrot.)

'However, even though I knew it was my parrot, and that indeed it could be nobody else, it was a good while before I could compose myself. First I imagined how the creature had got thither, and then how he should just keep about the place, and nowhere else. But . . . I got over it and . . . he . . . continued talking to me, "Poor Robin Crusoe! And how did I come here? and where had I been?" just as if he had been overjoyed to see me again: and so I carried him along with me.'*

*

Would Alice have kept about the place I wondered, coming home from my own foray to the farm, away from my island? There was really no reason for it. Whyever should she stay now in the great yellow house out on the marsh, all alone with me? There was other work to be got with the war. Soon she would be able to make twice – four times – the money. And she was only about my own age. There was no purpose in her staying to wait on me there, as there was no purpose in my own life there, either, come to that. Or anywhere.

What I was to do with my life now I hadn't the least idea.

And if my life at the yellow house was odd – and dull and lonely except for my books – how much worse it must be for Alice. She had never given much sign of liking any of us particularly and I knew that I had never been a real friend to her, not seeming to know quite how to begin. Yet she had toiled and slaved and nursed and cooked for us and seen to my clothes and cared about my new mysterious life at the

154

Zeits. My last weeks there had made her eyes sparkle when I told her of all the glamours. I had still of course not told her that these glamours were done and I shamefully rejected, treated as a dismissed servant, as we would never, never, have treated her.

I had begun to be a little afraid of Alice, I realised, as I walked home over the marsh with as many of my belongings as I could carry from Paul Treece's farm. I wasn't sure exactly how I should feel if I found a dead house and a letter of farewell from her lying on the hall-table.

Perhaps a freedom?

But the chimneys of the yellow house smoked, and as I walked in with my butter and eggs and bundles of poems, there she stood, saying, 'Well, you're back. Praise be. I wondered if you'd stop. I'd half a fancy they'd seduce you away – and then where'd we be?

'There's been a great bombardment here,' she said. 'Hartlepool – and dozens dead.'

She was wearing a most unlikely hat, like a long felt bluebell stuck with a painted fish-bone pin, and she had a hand on her hip and was smoking a cigarette. 'Butter and eggs,' I said, looking away. 'Such nice people, Alice. Did you have a happy Christmas? It's good to be back,' and I knew as I spoke just why I was frightened of her.

'Yes I see. *That's* a good thing then,' she said, examining the parcel.

It was my own voice using my own words.

She was in charge – and had probably been in charge, though I had not known it, for ages. Gone long ago were the wisps, the grubby sharp face and the big skivvy aprons. How long since I'd seen them? Alice was her own woman and had been so at least since the day of Mrs Woods's death when she had turned from the bed and ordered me what to do.

But when I got used to the change I liked it.

*

And I clung now quite desperately to my island. I went nicely about, day after day, industrious in the yellow house, behaving like the soul of serenity. The house needed a lot of looking after. Even in the midst of war, at that time it was not so strange for a woman to give her life to a house.

155

Also, I invented work. I had kept the schoolroom habit of sitting at a desk surrounded by books each day for years and now, with Paul Treece's things about me too and his manuscripts, I began to write myself, starting, of course, with *Robinson Crusoe* which I decided to translate into German.

It was a totally pointless exercise but demanding in its way and I took pleasure in the pile of glossy exercise books I bought and in my clear handwriting covering the pages. I wrote page-numbers in red ink and underlined in green. Then as time passed I discovered the satisfaction of footnotes. These I also wrote in red with an inked black line between text and note. There was a vast amount of double underlining.

I translated for four hours each morning, the translation was fast, but its transference to the page I tried to make so beautiful that it was very slow, and soon I was as abstracted as a monk at a Book of Hours or a child with his first crayons.

After lunch I often worked at The Poultice MSS which I copied out and arranged in order. Nearly all was poetry – pastoral, direct. There was some love-poetry – alarmingly passionate. Strawberries and nipples. It made me thoughtful. Rather shocked. There was a series of poems about some simple but very confident girl who lived inside her head and drove men mad. It seems that she was very desirable but as far as I could make out, half asleep. He had said that he knew a lot of girls.

Some of the poems were strong and witty and there was a lovely fortitude in them which reminded me of *Robinson Crusoe* and I began to see that under the mud of France there was dust that might have become of great account.

Then, in the evenings, I read. There had been some critical works in Paul Treece's library and they interested me, being the first modern ones I had seen. While it seemed to be an extremely arrogant way of getting into print I think that they may have been the start in me of a greater organisation of my ideas. This was a sort of physic.

I made notes about everything. Whenever my mind and heart began to stir I made notes more feverishly, meticulously still and uselessly for the demon at my back was not Paul. It was of course still Theo.

But no letter had come from him. No message had come from any Zeit. No card, no word, no whisper, no local gossip.

His face, at first I blotted out with hurt and shock, helped by seeing another kind of suffering – the raw suffering – at the farm. Now however it kept returning, surprising me at aimless moments – on closing a book, or looking up quickly at the tap of the acorn on a blind-cord in the wind. Often I heard the Zeit pony and trap at the door and looked out at an empty road.

Since the winter night, lying there with him, I had not been able to walk on the sand-hills and would take a huge half circle round them to the town, and the soldiers guarding the camp, and the sick in the old convalescent home watched me. I heard one soldier say once, 'Is she a bit peculiar that woman in that house?' and in Boagey's Son and Nephew a loud lady said to old Mr Box, 'Whatever happened to that young Miss Flint? She was wanting a bit, wasn't she? Slow?'

But I was still there. No recluse. Not seeking solitude to weep in. It was only the sand-hills I couldn't face.

Sometimes I tried to talk to the people I met on the marsh. The convalescents were no longer the Warrenby poor our soup had failed to cure, but the wounded shipped from France and the North-East ports and distributed about. They lay out in the convalescent home, such as could, under grit-brown blankets in crowded rows. Some sat in the sandy blowy grounds staring. Others wandered the marsh, wooden and apart. It was they who turned from me when I came near.

The New House stood empty. Because I had never been quite alone there with Theo it was possible still for me to bear to walk in its gardens. Through the long windows of the drawing-room spindly gold chairs were stacked in heaps, abandoned presumably after the Christmas party. I could see the magnificent piano (which no Zeit had ever played) covered with a thick dust-sheet tied in at the feet and the chandeliers of 'the best rooms' as Mrs Zeit had called them, hanging in huge bags heavy as swarms of bees.

There was a lackadaisical care-taker. He had been the church's sexton, ancient and sly, and I had never liked him. He used to dig the graves with an awful relish and slowly deck their walls with leaves of privet and sea-lavender held in with big black hair-pins. He would watch you at ankle-level as you passed. Alice once said with rare venom, 'I'd like to kick the face in of yon.' 'Bitter,' he used to say even on pleasant days. 'Bitter weather again, Miss Flint. I hear Mrs Woods is failing?'

At this time I seemed unable ever to get quite free of images of mortality and met the sexton everywhere, at last coming face to face with him in The New House drive where the imported orange gravel was now all hazed with green weeds.

He said, watching me, 'They're putting them sand-hills out of bounds. There's young girls out there shameless with the soldiers. Going at it like tortoises. I've thrown water over cats for less.'

I didn't go back to The New House after that, but often wondered about tortoises and exactly how they went at it. When my own memory of the sand-hills came to me there was no longer the lurch of pure joy as he unfastened my dress. Only tortoises.

'Are tortoises funny?' I asked Alice. 'You know – unnatural?'

'I don't know as I've seen many outside Boagey's Pet and Corn shop.'

'You know – sexually peculiar?'

She gave me a queer look.

In the spring of 1916 when the slaughter of the Somme was such that each army sometimes ran out to retrieve the other's dead, Alice and I were busy with the sexuality of tortoises. We cleaned the library, getting down the books from every shelf for the first time in memory – possibly ever – and behind a row of works of the Reverend Thomas Fuller, up against the ceiling, we found a small copy of a novel by Cleland and I took it to the window and examined it. I stayed there for a very long time.

'Aren't you coming to your tea, Miss Polly?'

'Just a minute.'

'Your supper's ready. Whatever've you found?'

'Read it,' I said, 'take it to your bed.'

The next morning we did not look at one another in the eye. Washing away at the shelves from the top of the steps, she said, 'That *Fanny Hill*! Life's full of surprises. I'll say that.'

'Did you – know all that, Alice?'

'Aye – some of it.' She was still servant enough not to ask whether I did.

'I didn't,' I said. 'I didn't know any of it. Well I knew some things. It sounds a lot better than I'd thought. D'you think people really go on like that?'

'I'd think so. Mind, it was in History. They seemed to have enjoyed themselves more then. All the long skirts and that. Romantic. Well, exciting-like!'

'They didn't seem exactly to get in the way.'

We began to giggle and laugh. 'Where's the book now?' I said. 'I want to read it again.'

'I'm ashamed of you, Miss Polly.' Alice had turned a brickish colour. 'You can't have it till I've read it again.' So we sat together in the kitchen that evening, reading bits silently then staring at each other, then dissolving with joy.

'However did it get up there? D'you think it was the Archdeacon?'

'Archdeacon nothing,' said Alice. 'Didn't you see? It says Gertrude Younghusband, large as life on the fly-leaf. Shameless!'

'Maybe she wrote her name in it before she'd read it?'

'Well, she didn't burn it up or throw it away.'

'*Alice!* Gertrude Younghusband was my *grandmother* – the Archdeacon's wife!' We both went and looked long and hard at the matron in whalebone with the imperial nose on the Archdeacon's writing-desk.

Alice began to have a great many more evenings off after this. I, less extreme, only started to teach myself to cook. *Fanny Hill* had cheered us and though it should have made us restless in some way in fact it made us rather calmer, and more assured, so that for the next two years until almost the end of the war we seemed to swim in rather more hopeful waters.

For the next two years.

'For the next two years', like Crusoe, 'I cannot say that any extraordinary things happened to me; but I lived on in the same course, in the same posture and places, just as before.'

*

Then one day in 1918, Alice ran into the kitchen where I was beating something in a bowl and bread was rising rubbery white in ten tins.

'There's someone here.'

159

'Who?'

'I don't know who.' But she looked very wild. 'It could be Mr Zeit.'

'*Could* be?'

'I don't say is. Here – give us that skillet.'

I walked through to the front of the house with my sleeves still rolled up and my apron on and my hands floury. In the hall was nobody, nor in the dining room, nor in the library, nor upstairs in the drawing room. I stood in the hall before the glass again and rolled my sleeves down, wiped my hands upon the apron and took it off. Outside on the scrag end of marsh that was all that remained stood an army-green motor with driver. A man sat in the back, very old and empty-looking about the eyes, but they were still Theo's.

'Can you drive with me somewhere?'

It was cold. I went in for a coat. Then I sat by him in the car and saw how his hands shook like the hands of the men at the convalescent home and that he clasped them together and still they shook. When he spoke it was with long pauses between words and sometimes the words got stuck and he spluttered and gulped. I asked, 'How long were you in France?'

'Since you saw me.'

'Is your leave long?'

'It's been long. I'm about ready to go back.'

'Are you?'

'Well there's a Board next week.'

'Aren't we going to The New House? We've gone by.'

'No. It's full of soldiers now. It was commandeered.'

'Yes. I heard. Where are you all? Where are we going then, Theo?'

'Mother's up in Newcastle. She was interned you know. For nearly two years. But she's running the North again now.'

'Yes, I see. I hadn't heard.'

'Rebecca's in France, nursing. So is Delphi Vipont from The Hall – and fairly hopeless at it I gather. I thought we'd go to The Hall now. Bec wants me to collect some things for Delphi.'

The Hall was so much of a ruin that even the army had not wanted it. Parts of its roof had gone in, its shutters hung crooked or were gone, its drive was so choked that Theo ordered the driver to go and leave us at the gates which were overgrown, immovable, and we climbed through between one of the stone posts and the great broken hinges. We walked through the courtyard and in through the front door, stuck open under its swaying fanlight. The long stretch of rooms, one opening out of another, stood empty. Rats had eaten holes in their floors, a volcano of soot sat in each beautiful grate, the milky marble above dulled and daubed with bird-droppings. 'It's all to be pulled down soon,' said Theo. 'There'll be nothing here. She's too late for her keepsakes.'

We walked about. Old newspapers were stuck to the black and white of the eighteenth-century saloon, the staircase was splintered. He tried to help me up the stairs but I had to help him too, he seemed so uncertain.

His hands were so cold. In the bedroom we opened a shutter and found a four-poster bed all by itself on the bare floor still with a dark old counterpane and hung with crimson silk, each fold of the silk with a velvet edge of dust. A prie-dieu stood beside it and it all had a daunting ecclesiastical look.

'It must have been Lady Vipont's. She was very holy.'

Theo said, 'Delphi must have started in that bed.'

His hands were shaking again and he sat on the window-seat. Across the window wistaria hung so thick and gnarled that the window had to be pushed hard against it to open at all. Rain fell on the green leaves, pattering, though the sun still shone through them. Large glassy drops hung on the long grey flowers. 'I've thought of you every day,' said Theo, 'but it was thinking of someone else's woman in another century.'

'You sent no message. It's been nearly four years.'

'No.'

'Have you written no letters? Not to anyone?'

'Only to the parents of my men. When they die. Saying that they died bravely. I only write lies.'

'I've heard nothing. Nothing. Not from any of you. You all vanished. You might all have been dead. You threw me away.'

He said, 'I am dead. We are all dead, Polly. This country died.'

We lay down on Lady Vipont's bed in each other's arms

161

until it grew dark and we said almost nothing. In the great cold house I became warm and I felt my warmth warm Theo and he held me fast. We did not make love, yet we lay as one person for hours. We lay till dark.

Before we left he said at the top of the stairs, 'I'll just look for something, in case – ' and went off, feeling and looking about in a room or two. 'There's a bit of old junk in the back of a cupboard. She wanted something from the mausoleum really.' We passed the mausoleum all boarded up and tied round with barbed wire. 'D'you remember in there?' he said, 'All pearl and pink. D'you remember that day? The hymn-books? Beccy running? You like a round flower?'

At home he said, 'Go in quickly. Go. I'll write this time. I promise, when I can write letters again the first will be to you. I'll see you next leave. The war can't be long now.'

Then he said, 'I do love you, you know.' But the words seemed to be very difficult to understand. We both stood considering them as if we were hearing an old primitive language.

When the car had gone I stood outside the yellow house until Alice came out and said 'Miss? *Was* that Mr Zeit? I can't think it was Mr Zeit,' and I didn't know what to reply.

*

He did write and at first quite often. The letters began to arrive three weeks later and continued for about a year. I answered every one and sent two or three extra in between.

In my letters I told him everything in the whole world so far as I understood it: about Wales, about the marsh and about the sad years when everybody prayed or died or vanished. I told him about my wish that I might be a good Christian but my certainty that I was not ready to be Confirmed, about my sinful disgust at Mrs Woods and God's answer to my prayer with her death; about my fear and awe of Alice – how I knew that she had hated looking at and touching Mrs Woods and feeding her with a cup and putting little bits of food in her awful mouth as much as I did. The lifting her. The washing of her. Yet never once had she flinched or mentioned it.

I told how I still missed Aunt Frances and of the mystery of her silence to me after she had gone away; and how I had felt at home so seldom – only in the old sexy memories of Wales, the housekeeper's kitchen at Thwaite and walking on that one morning with Paul Treece. I told him how sick I felt and worried because I had not liked Paul Treece's looks, had not wanted to touch him. I told him about Virginia Woolf and the poets and famous people at Thwaite, and the memory of my father; dancing and singing the sea song; of Mr Pocock, and the table-top swimming with polish in the dining-room, so that I had looked out over a shadowed lake, with the brooding presences around its edges, like in Wordsworth's *Prelude*.

I told him how my life was now divided before my lying with him on Lady Vipont's bed, and afterwards; and I wrote how much I loved him in such a tremendous and passionate way that I often stood looking at the post-box after the letter went flop inside it, thinking, 'Could I have written that? Could any woman ever have written so much to any man before?' I saw his face which never told a thing, reading it and I thought, if he is killed, will all the letters go back to Mrs Zeit? Yet, I continued to tell everything, everything, as I am doing in this book, and as women are not supposed to do.

Then, thinking of what women are not supposed to do, I would go quickly away and write another letter saying yet more. About wanting him and needing to sleep with him, though I did not say sleep. Wanting, wanting, I said – and in just what ways, day and night, indoors and out, wherever he sent for me. I drew deeply on my knowledge of the novel which my grandmother had prized. I wrote unlike a granddaughter of a Victorian Archdeacon, unlike even the women in D. H. Lawrence whom Alice had taken to lately (Well, Lawrence's women hardly say anything.)

Had Moll Flanders, Cleopatra, Emily Brontë loved Theo Zeit they could not have told him so with more passion and with less restraint. And they were I dare say the wiser women.

Theo's dry, short letters grew more and more difficult to read – the writing smaller and smaller, almost tormentedly careful. Then they stopped.

They stopped not after any especially naked one of mine. I thought, 'He is killed.' Then after two months, 'Had he been killed I would have heard by now.' I re-read his last letter slowly, slowly. There was no clue. I re-read all the letters then and I found that they had been nothing. I was left with nothing and I had then a great terror that I had been mad. The bed in The Hall had been fantasy. '*Was* that Mr Zeit?' Alice had said, 'Surely it can't have been?' I had dreamed it. I did not fully remember what happened. I did not remember how he got home. I had dreamed.

A hole in the air.

I read and re-read the letters, on and on. At the end of each one he had always said 'love'. I clung to this wonderful fact: that he had always said love.

And I began to feel sorry for him – that he had been burdened with letters like mine. All the things I had said were the things that he so prudently would have felt were best unsaid. I had based my great trust that we felt and thought and saw alike on the fact that when I was twelve years old he had said that he would leave me a footprint, and that when he went away the last time he had said that he loved me.

Such a correct and truthful man. Such a nice man. Everyone said so. Would he tell lies? Oh, of course he would not.

So I thought on my island.

*

There was one night – I had been translating Crusoe for hours, colouring in the chapter-headings, underlining with very exquisite care, letting the fire die, the lamp go down, my feet grow cold. All sound in the house and outside it had ceased. Only the clocks.

I said, 'It is time. It is time, Polly Flint. It's time this stopped. He is nothing. You are sick. No woman need suffer like this. It is wicked and mad. Forget him.' And telling myself this with great authority, some of the burden did fall away, as did Robinson Crusoe's on awaking from his fever to a spell of God's peace.

*

The next morning, since I had gone to bed at almost dawn, Alice brought me up my post and there was a letter from

164

Rebecca Zeit to say that she was coming to The New House to arrange for the sale of it, or of what the soldiers had left of it, and might she come and see me.

Her writing was huge and black and spluttery and she arrived a day or two later, exactly as she wrote. I heard her voice right up in the drawing-room calling out to the taxi outside to come back in an hour. 'In *one hour*,' the voice called like a bell, 'now *exactly*, Mr Boagey, not more, not less. Yes.' The door-bell jangled loudly and I heard her laughter as the wind took all the mats in the hall and wafted them about. Alice showed her up and she swooped forward in a great flurry, still talking, though whether to Alice or me or to herself wasn't clear.

She had turned into a still rather alarming but rather merry woman in tight-fitting clothes, with fur at the neck and cuffs, very fashionable: an ugly, long-draped jacket, short skirt, and her hair short as a man's but still curly crammed under a beautiful helmet hat. She talked and she talked, seeming unable to keep still. Bright green eyes searching about.

'You're *exactly* the same! Exactly. Oh, Polly, I don't believe it! You've been here all this time. *Nothing* has changed!'

'I couldn't leave.'

'The old woman – the aunt-person. Did she die?'

'In the end.'

'But couldn't someone – ? Wasn't there anybody? She wasn't even a *relation*.'

'No. But – '

'Yes, of course. I remember – you were terribly Christian at the yellow house. But you're not all alone here, Polly?'

'Well, we've had some officers billetted – '

'You must have *noticed* the war?'

'They bombarded Hartlepool. At the very beginning. But I was staying away on a farm.'

*

We had tea.

*

'And no romances? With the officers?'

'I hardly saw them. Alice looked after them. I'm not very romantic.'

165

'Yes, I remember. Factual downright Pol. *Robinson Crusoe*. You were always the plain woman.' She realised what she'd said and tried to set it right, 'I mean the straight woman – salt of the earth. Dependable. You'd have been wonderful in France you know. But perhaps you're lucky.'

'It is over without me. It is over and we've won.'

'It's over,' said Beccy, 'that's all.'

'What will you do, Beccy?'

'I'm stuck nursing in a private nursing home – but I'll stop now. Get back to Cambridge and finish.'

'Yes, I see. Is Mrs Zeit – ?'

'Oh, Mamma has survived. But it won't be long now – '

'She's ill?'

'No, no – Mamma's never *ill*. No, the war. We've made a decision. We're going back to Germany – all of us. It's mother's idea. We all agree though. It won't be easy here – everything of ours in England's sold up – it was mismanaged, neglected. Mamma was interned you know. Theo in the Army. She's suddenly feeling very continental – very German-Jewish. She wants to work for post-war Germany.'

'But can you? Live there after it all? After all you've seen of Germans?'

'Yes. What makes you think they're so different? Somebody must start somewhere showing that all countries are the same. Just people. If we bleed Germany dry now there'll be another war in a generation. You'll see.'

'Do you tell people this?'

'No, no. I must say we don't. It would not be the moment.'

'Why d'you tell me, Beccy?'

'Well, you're not just anybody are you? It's funny, I've always felt you were a sort of part of our family. Yet when it comes down to dates and times I suppose it's almost nothing. That day on the sands – you know – I felt we'd known you always.'

'Yes I know. It was the same for me.'

'And I think you were even closer to Theo. You and Theo – I think you knew him better than I did.'

'Knew?' I was standing and held on to the back of the chair. 'How is Theo?'

'Oh Theo's perfectly all right. He was wounded pretty early on you know. Bit of shellshock, but he never quite broke up.

Had a good long sick-leave. Very brave, our old Theo – could have got right out of it if he'd tried. Of course, you never quite know what Theo wants. He's survived – playing it fairly carefully. D'you remember that queer Treece person? He lasted no time at all. It wasn't just that Theo was careful, though. He's lucky. He's the sort who'll never get cancer or TB or be run-over or have accidents. D'you know, Mamma and I never really worried for him. Isn't that weird? He's amazingly his old sweet silent self as a matter of fact – oh, look here, ducky. Here's the taxi, I must go. It's been lovely to see you, Polly. Mamma often talks of you. I think she feels the least bit guilty you know. She had such schemes for you – to push you into a university. D'you remember? She still makes these wild decisions.'

She was firmly pulling on gloves.

'There wouldn't have been the money for it, Beccy.'

'Oh, she'd have seen to that. And she'd have seen that you had the right qualifications – she'd have got you coached. She had a pull with Somerville. Modern Languages – that's what it was to be, wasn't it?'

'I've no idea. And I couldn't have gone. As things were.'

'Mamma would have seen to the old woman. It was the war. It swamped her. All of us. She had a worse time than me in the internment camp you see – ostracism and so on. Two years. And it was so *ridiculous*. She can't bear to be ridiculous. But I do know she feels guilty about you – just a teeny bit mis'.'

'There's no need. I would not have been helped.'

'Oh, Theo's getting married. Maybe you knew? Delphi Vipont of course. Never been quite my sort – or Mamma's and we've told him for years she's not his. Besotted with her. As ever. Well – its been a life-long thing. D'you know she never wrote to him *once* when he was in France. She was pretty wild. The Viponts lost everything in the war, you know – so he's a haven for her now.'

We were at the taxi. She looked me quickly up and down and gave me the sharp, assessing, bird-look I remembered. She said, 'It's been lovely. Look – we'll see each other again, Polly, won't we?'

*

167

It is considered usual that anyone in great solitude of mind for many years will run mad. Alexander Selkirk, after only four years upon his island ran mad as a hare, as did most of the other historical characters who may or may not have been Daniel Defoe's inspiration for *Robinson Crusoe*. Indeed, it is a sign of a human being's sanity, perhaps, that he should run mad in such circumstances, and perhaps Crusoe himself was insane when he arrived on the island, for his twenty-eight years in residence show only the growth of a most extraordinary and unnatural steadiness.

This growing, rather frightening sanity proceeded from a very affectionate analysis of himself, his ability to stand apart, to watch and to muse upon his shaggy and unlovely figure walking the great beaches, perched upon the ferocious cliff-tops, treading the forest and saying: 'Well, I don't know. Look at me. I have God and myself to talk to. How much better to have God and oneself to hand than almost any other of one's acquaintance. "That man can never want conversation who is company for himself, and he that cannot converse profitably with himself is not fit for any conversation at all." '

Oh, the stability of this great Yorkshireman! After the two years – *two years* – of digging the trench for the sea to introduce itself to his great beached boat he finds that the sea will never reach it. He stands sagely and calmly by and says: 'How great is the human condition. A man may learn from his mistakes.'

Occasionally the passions flower. Occasionally they even threaten to take charge. Yet they never do take charge – not wholly. For as they manifest themselves they are monitored, dissected, pondered – and dispersed.

There are some secret, moving springs in the affections which, when they are set going by some object in view, or even not in view . . . that motion carries out the soul in such violent, eager embracings of the object that the absence of it is insupportable.

When that happens, the hands of Robinson Crusoe clench, and Robinson Crusoe watched them clench, so hard into the palm that anything in them (he reflects) would be crushed.

Crusoe feels Crusoe's teeth involuntarily clamp together so that he can hardly part them again. 'Doubtless,' says Crusoe, 'these are the effects of ardent wishes and of strong ideas formed in the mind.'

'How very interesting,' says Robin Crusoe, and tick-tock, in time, Crusoe's body, Crusoe observes, begins to behave itself again.

Monumental, godlike Crusoe. Monumentally and deist-ically taking control of his emotions. And I, Polly Flint, after the knowledge of my loss, set out to be the same. Theo's face and being and presence at her shoulder, Polly Flint blots out, and lets the noble and unfailing face and being and presence of Crusoe become her devotion and her joy.

Crusoe is her idol and her king.

Crusoe's mastery of circumstances.

Crusoe, Polly Flint's father and her mother.

Crusoe, the unchanging, the faithful.

Crusoe, first met at the cracking of Polly Flint's egg.

Crusoe, the imprint.

Crusoe, her King Charles's head.

Will Polly Flint ever attain Crusoe's magnificent simplicity?

Will Polly Flint ever attain his wonderful exploration of emotion as a means to morality and truth?

Will Polly Flint ever attain his wonderful endeavour to bring things to a divine balance? 'Bringing the years to an end as a tale that is told?'

All these became, after the vanishing of Theo, Polly Flint's whole cry.

Sitting in the yellow house with nothing in the world to do. Polly Flint. Twenty years old. Might there be time?

*

I became very odd. Oh, really quite odd then.

*

The officers who had begun to be billetted at the yellow house in 1917, I had, as I told Rebecca, left entirely to Alice, who had had charge of the money we were paid for their keep. Only when they were gone did I realise that without them we should be on the way to starvation.

'There's nothing for it now but lodgers,' said Alice.

'Would we ever get them? Right out here?'

'Yes. If we advertise the ozone. We'd get fifteen shillings a week full board. Each.'

'Perhaps we should try just one.'

'We should try more. We should try three.'

'Could you manage, Alice? You know I couldn't spare time from my book?'

'I could manage if we go shares.'

'Shares? Of course. Oh Alice, don't I pay you enough?'

'Twelve shilling a week is all you can afford to give me. But we've possibility here of a decent living, Miss Polly.'

'Lodgers. It does seem extreme.'

'It's the only hope for us. We'll start getting Miss Frances's room up, then the spare room and then I'll make a clearance of Mrs Woods's.'

'Haven't we done that yet?'

'I never quite cared.'

'Yes, I see. Could I – ?'

'No. I'll see to it. We'll sell everything since nobody's emerged to take interest in it and there's no will.'

*

'*Precious* little,' she said a week or so later. 'Rags, tatters, bibles. Her cross could go to the nuns and her clothes I've taken as charity down to Fishermen's Square though they didn't look overjoyed at the sight. You can't seem to get rid of bibles. It seems a sin to burn them – '

'Oh, burn them. It's only superstition.'

'The knick-knackery I did sell – a picture or two and a sewing-box. I got two pounds so I bought some whisky. It's wise to have a bit of whisky in a house. For emergencies.'

She put bottles down on my desk. 'These,' she said, 'were fastened into her prayer-book with a band,' and she propped against the bottles twelve fat letters unopened and addressed to me. They were Aunt Frances's adventures after her wedding which Mrs Woods, in her dark queerness, had kept between herself and God – long loving letters which had been seen by no one and each one saying how she was looking forward to my going to India.

'I always thought she'd flitted down into the hall and round about sometimes at the beginning and nobody knew it. Right down to the hall-stand. It's why she had the second stroke I wouldn't wonder,' said Alice. 'And never to open them as well as never to say! That's horrible cruel and unforgiving. That's very bad.'

Perhaps it was unfortunate that the happiness the letters gave me would always be associated with the simultaneous arrival of the medicinal whisky. Or perhaps this was just part of the pattern, too.

'Her room's real bonny now,' said Alice, 'and there's a Miss Gowe come to see it, or rather her sister did. Miss Gowe's arriving tonight.' (It was a month later.) 'She works in the post office. To *live* here,' she added. 'You understand?'

'We'll have a drink to celebrate,' I said.

'Another three are arriving next week,' said Alice, pouring. 'My dad says a bottle holds seven drinks. That looks rather a lot. We'll say nine about. My, it's strong!'

'It's splendid. Who are the three?'

'Two commercial gents and a schoolmaster from The New House School. Insignificant little feller so I've put him above you.'

'But that's your room – Charlotte's old room.'

'I've moved down into Miss Younghusband's.'

'Yes I see. Well, thank you for doing so much, Alice.'

'We'll be rich by next year. Rich enough to see to the window-sashes on the sea side anyway. And in time to the roof.'

'Is the roof bad?'

'You should see the ceiling in Charlotte's bedroom. I'm only taking six shillings from the schoolmaster.'

And Alice from this moment turned into the White Queen flying here, flying there about the house from dawn until long after dark with bundles of washing (laundry extra) and bedclothes and trays of food. They were easy lodgers – or Alice saw to it that they were – the commercial travellers turning out to be pale washes of men, something to do with office equipment in the Stockton and Darlington railway where they spent long days. Miss Gowe was a fat, grinning creature, all cardigans and said to be in charge of postal telegrams at Middlesborough, though it seemed rather unlikely, her powers of communication being scarcely developed.

The schoolmaster was called Selwyn Benson, a near

171

transparent silver-fish of a man, but Alice said that all the masters at the new school – bought from the Ziets – were either flotsam from the trenches or too frail to have gone into them in the first place. Mr Benson was in the first category presumably, for he shook and flipped past us in terror, up the stairs and down, and froze if we spoke. At night I sometimes heard him crying in Charlotte's old bed and Alice said that when she took up his breakfast tray he often hid behind his wardrobe door, poor little lad.

There were odd folk everywhere after 1918, for many years.

'You'd not think we'd won this bloody war,' said Alice, 'My dad says after Mafeking you knew who was the heroes.'

'*What* did you say?'

'Bloody,' said Alice. 'Sorry, Miss. It's all over the buildings. 'I can't help it. The marsh is all buildings now. It's to be amusement park and that next – and a public rose-garden. It's to make employment. There's to be a hurdy-gurdy and penny-on-the-mat. We'll hear it all right even out here. Between us and the town. Well – it's the only good thing mebbe the Germans has done to give employment.'

'Daniel Defoe,' I said, 'that's to say Robinson Crusoe, spoke well of the Spanish even though the War with Spain was scarcely over.'

'I don't want to hear, Miss. You know my views in that direction. It's time you finished with that romance. You can't get another squeeze out of it, I'd think. Can I go now? There's shopping and the orders. And we need another bottle.'

*

Often I watched from the study window as Alice set off to the town on these housekeeping expeditions in the following months, prancing on her high heels with her imitation fox-fur around her neck and a fondant pink toque upon her head and wondered where Alice, the tired young mouse, had gone – but blessed both of them.

As time went on I saw that a young man from over the marsh often stepped out from the esplanade shelter to meet her. He held a respectful trilby and after placing it carefully back upon his head, took her arm. There was something familiar about him, but it was a long way off, and I was now most furiously busy with no time at all to brood about love.

For the difficult and miserable outer world had by now receded, and almost disappeared. 'Thus in two years time I had a thick grove; and in five or six years time I had a wood before my dwelling, growing so monstrous thick and strong, that it was indeed perfectly impassable.'

Only my monthly letter from Maitland at Thwaite pierced a ray or two of ordinary daylight through my trees, and a spotlight broke through with the occasional letter from Mr Thwaite and a short radiance on his annual visit to us.

Lady Celia was gone. She had died in the war, and was buried in the family vault in the church at the end of Thwaite's old gardens. Maitland minded. Her letters were sad, and sadder because Barker and Mr Thwaite himself did not seem to mourn her as they should. 'And as for them artists and warblers, for years taking her salt, not a sign from them, though Mrs Woolf and poor little Mr Gertler wrote at the time, Mr Gertler enclosing a very nice drawing of her, showing her good points. "My lady had her place", I wrote back to Mr Gertler, "in a tawdry world." '

I answered all Maitland's letters always at once, even on my bad days, wondering whether I had been right in thinking Lady Celia frightful – vain, cold and full of machinations. She had stopped her brother's marriage to my beloved Aunt Frances who otherwise would not have gone so conspicuously mad on board the ship to India. No – Lady Celia had certainly, I thought, been filled with sin.

But perhaps it was in analysing Maitland's letters and Lady Celia's character that I began at last to come to terms with the idea of sin, though I was, of course, taking a very good general instruction in the subject still, in the great book, *Robinson Crusoe*.

For *Robinson Crusoe* is a study of the reality of sin. All his misfortunes spring from it. It is sin which occasioned his first disaster in the Yarmouth Roads to his last shipwreck on the imprisoning island. He sinned from childhood against his father, leaving the good, quiet middle station of life in which it had pleased God to place him. He had sinned in his yearning for the sea which was always his enemy.

Indeed, all his unhappiness was caused one way and

another by the sea, it seemed to me, his persistent need for it. Considering this, at the end of each day I took to pacing our own beach and watching the movement of the waters around my boots as they wandered in the red-rusted barbed wire.

'Young man,' had said the captain of Crusoe's first ship, 'you ought never to go to sea any more. You ought to take this as a plain and visible token that you are not to be a seafaring man.'

And because Crusoe acted against God's decree, venturing on a mission contrary to his duty, like Balaam, like Jonah, like Job, like Ishmael of *Moby Dick*, like St Augustine, he foundered. Until his repentance at last.

But why was it a sin for Robinson Crusoe to yearn for freedom, adventure and traveller's joy? Why was it wrong for him to reject his boring Yorkshire home, the middle-class sensible day-to-day life of Hull? Obey his instinctive longing for the sea?

Because God had said so.

Like Job, when he accepted this, things became better for him. In fact, marvellous. At the end of Book I even more so. And at the end of Book II, Crusoe has achieved nobility.

Oh, I envied him. Oh, I envied Robinson Crusoe not his suffering and his repentance, but his having the powers to put up a fight, and his powers of analysis, his seamanship, for knowing exactly where he was. And his being tempted, proved that he was, at least in God's eye, God thought he was worth testing.

Yet here was I, totally unregarded by God, sitting out my life at the yellow house.

Oh, I envied.

I envied Crusoe his sin, his courage, his ruthlessness in leaving all he had been brought up to respect; his resilience, his wonderful survival after disaster.

I envied him his conversion, his penitence, his beautiful self-assurance won through solitude and despair.

I envied him his unselfconsciousness, his powers of decision, his self-reliance – he never dreamed after any specific creature – I envied him his sensible sexlessness which he seemed so easily to have achieved. But most of all I envied his being in God's eye.

I envied.

Seated at my desk, day after day, with only the click of the lodgers' feet on the tiles, the occasional opening and shutting of a door as Alice went hurrying by; the bottle and the glass in front of me and the shadows of people I had known just over my shoulder out of sight, in the corners of the room, watching me, not greatly concerned for me, I envied him.

*

'Miss Gowe's sister's here and wants a word with you.'

'Tell her I'm busy.'

'I have. She says she's staying till you come.'

'What's she want?'

'She's up in arms for her sister.'

'What's that to do with me? Alice – can't you – ?'

'No. I can't. Miss Polly, come.'

The sister sat with Miss Gowe in Mrs Woods's old room. Miss Gowe nodding nicely, smiling and waving nervously at a chair.

The sister glared. She had a glossy mouth and fine arched eye-brows painted with a pointed brush and her crossed legs showed a yard of cream silk-stocking. Miss Gowe, in her dowdy woollies had become a part of my home, but the powdery silky sister made sure that I was aware that I was in Aunt Frances's old shawl and somebody else's bedroom slippers and my fingers all ink and that was getting fat.

'This house is.not suitable for my sister,' said the sister. 'It is isolated, eccentric and the food inadequate.'

'Yes, I see. Does she want to go?'

'She will have to go.' said the sister.

'Yes, all right.'

'Unless,' she said quickly, 'there is a reduction of terms.'

'Yes, all right.'

Alice had come in behind me and gave me a prod in the back. 'How much?' she asked.

'My sister is paying you fourteen shillings a week,' said the sister. 'Are you not, Winnie?'

Miss Gowe gave a shy little snigger.

'Fourteen shillings a week. I suggest ten shillings and sixpence.'

'Yes, all right.'

'Twelve shillings,' said Alice loudly.

They settled for twelve shillings. The sister swept away down the stairs and turned to us at the front door. 'I have to say this!' Alice held the door wide for her. 'There is a certain stigma attached to my sister, living in your house.'

'Stigma?'

'Stigma. I hear what I hear. Perhaps I should tell you that the Gowes are Scarborough people. I, myself, now live at Harrogate. In Valley Drive.'

'Yes, I see.'

'Alice,' I asked, 'bring yourself a glass. Why are we inferior to Valley Drive? And why must we keep Miss Gowe?'

'We need the twelve shillings if the roof's to hold up. And as to Valley Drive – Miss Polly, look at you. Look in the glass.'

I looked at my whisky.

'No, Miss Polly, in the glass.'

*

But of course I did not. Metaphorically I covered every glass like Paul Treece's mother when the telegram came so that the spirit should not confront itself.

I returned to the manuscript – I was busy now, since finishing the French and German translations of *Robinson Crusoe* a year before, in 1930, on an analysis of the book as a Spiritual Biography, seeing it in relation to other spiritual biographies of the seventeenth and eighteenth centuries, busy with the red ink, busy with the green, and Mr Thwaite brought me beautiful notebooks to write in every year.

*

Mr Thwaite's placing of the brown-paper-parcel of notebooks on the hall table was the first act of his annual visit to us every August 1st. It is quite difficult to describe the pleasure of these visits of Mr Thwaite because of any man in the world he must have been the quietest and some might say the most colourless. Yet he had authority of a subtle kind – never once asking if he might come, simply arriving each year at four o'clock on whichever day of the week August 1st might be, and remaining for three weeks. He never rang the bell but was all at once in our midst in knickerbockers and Norfolk

176

jacket looking mildly at us from his light blue eyes, Box-Boagey's taxis (Mr Box himself and an assistant) waiting patiently behind him on the step with two portmanteaux and a cabin-trunk with brass bands around it. Mr Thwaite loved clothes so long as they were very old. He always changed for dinner and brought a smoking-jacket and a great supply of garments for his walks by the sea and his excursions mackerel-fishing or casting for whiting from the pier. He had, after great deliberation, of late years bought outfits suitable for the new boating-lake, though he had not yet embarked on the costume for the penny-on-the-mat at the amusement park. For a motorbus outing to Hinderwell-for-Runswick Bay or Filey he wore deer-stalker or sou-wester depending on the weather. When Alice said, 'It's not the old landau, Mr Thwaite. The motorbus has a roof to it,' he said that he never felt roofed in a motor.

He was the most peaceful of presences. You never heard him move about the house, yet when you opened a door you could always tell if he were in the room by the pleasantness that breathed out of it. At meal-times he ate with small bites and great enjoyment, looking long at Aunt Mary's lovely spoons, sometimes holding them up to the light, looking out of the window and after clearing his throat a few times, remarking on the weather and the direction of the wind. He needed no conversation and made little. And never once did he criticise a thing about us – the decaying house, the funny lodgers, the plain, plain food, my whisky bottle which now accompanied me to table. Seldom did he praise us, yet we knew that his visits were a precious part of his life.

'And how is the book coming along, Polly?'

'Oh coming along. There's a great deal of work.'

'Oh, I expect there is.'

Never asked for details, never suggested it might surely soon be finished, never queried its vital importance. I suspected that he might know that in the end no book might materialise at all, that I was clothing myself in armour, hiding in a lair, hiding from pain. He never hinted it though.

'Tremendous work in a book,' he would say. 'We had a great deal of that sort of thing at Thwaite.'

I went out every single day when he was with us, arm in arm with him along the beach, the sea casting down lace

177

shawls before us, then dragging them away. The wind was always cold – even in August it was usually from the North-East – and I would be wrapped up in anything that came my way from the back-kitchen hooks – waddly boots on my feet, my hair dragged up in a bun with the filling falling out, sometimes a hat from ages long ago stuck on my head.

Yet I always felt carefree and pretty, walking with Mr Thwaite. On fine days I removed the boots and paddled and he watched me. Once he said, clearing his throat, 'Polly you are but a child.'

'I'm over thirty. Nearly forty. I'm just behaving myself unseemly as the nuns used to do.'

'Nuns,' he said. 'Ah. I remember those nuns. Poor Frances. They were after her once I believe.'

'Oh I'm sure they weren't. It was Aunt Mary. They just about got her.'

'No, no. It was her own decision, that holy nursing.'

'Well, they've gone now. All of them. The nuns have moved right up into the slums in the Iron-Works now.'

'Mysterious women,' he said. 'But all women are mysterious.'

'I'm not mysterious.'

'No, no. You're not mysterious, Polly. You're a very straightforward sort of girl.'

'Yes. I can't think why they all go on at me.'

'Do they?'

'Alice says I'm wasting my life.'

'Oh, I'd not say that. You have to get your book done. You have to keep the yellow house – the family home. That must be a great strain. Very glad you know – assist – At any time.'

'Oh we can manage. Thank you *very* much though. When the book's done, of course, I shall have to think – '

He said nothing. Sniffed the breeze, watched the ships along the horizon waiting for the tide, the chimneys belching flames across the sand-hills. 'Very beautiful place this,' he said. 'Part of my youth. You are of course – you know – always welcome to live at Thwaite.'

'Thank you.' (Old age, emptiness, even Mr Barker now dead.)

'Thought maybe of travelling? Cruising?'

'Travelling!'

'Just an idea. India, I've often thought. West Indies. Should be glad to take you. Good for Maitland, too. Since she's been widowed and Celia gone she's finding things a little slow.'

'I can't think. I'm so busy. Shall we go home?'

That night the manuscript of the spiritual biography blossomed more wonderfully than ever with coloured inks and various scripts. When Mr Thwaite and I met before bedtime for hot milk we did not speak of cruises but as usual sat hardly speaking at all, listening to the clock tick under its glass dome on the drawing-room chimney-piece between the glass prisms and the photograph of my droll dead father. 'D'you hear of the Zeits? he asked suddenly. 'I miss old Zeit. I still miss him.'

'No. I hear nothing.'

'They went off to Germany. Curious idea. Very – positive – lot, except for the boy. The boy married – not much of a success, I gather. Delphi Vipont. She stayed once – or maybe it was her mother. Couldn't get on with her, one way and another. Beautiful, of course. Life's hard on very beautiful people.'

'Yes. Maybe.'

'Heard she'd left him. Went off with some German. Something in the German government – or the German army. Not clear. It's a pity the Zeits chose that sorry country.'

'Beccy said they felt it was their own country after all.'

'Poor Zeits. Very mistaken.'

'Why?'

'Jews. Not good at present. For Jews in Dusseldorf.'

'Yes, I see.'

'I liked the boy. Quiet feller like his father. The sister was a bright spark. The mother was a bit of a – challenge. There were grandchildren, I gather. Theo's children and the wife, Delphi. Had some children.'

'Oh?'

'Two girls. Born after a long time. Delphi hadn't been very keen. They're with the father. Well – we're not likely to see any of them again.'

'No.'

This was the longest conversation Mr Thwaite ever had with me which he himself had initiated.

How dull he sounds.

*

'No letters between you and that family then?' he said as we switched off the lights (Miss Gowe and the rest had resulted in electricity for the yellow house) and made our way up the stairs. I was clutching the banisters, gripping them every third or fourth step, walking like an ancient. I only needed spoons.

'Something there I always thought,' he said, astonishingly keeping on, gazing intently at the belly of the green flower-pot on the landing.

'Where?' I examined the pot.

'Between you and the boy.'

When I said nothing he made his way to his bedroom, turning at his door to say, 'Talked about you to me once or twice. "Good-looking girl. A stunner," he said. 'Appears he once saw you by some river.' Shutting his door quietly behind him he said, 'One always somehow hoped it might not be over.'

The next day, the next week, until the end of Mr Thwaite's visit that year I did no more work upon the book; and I joined him on the motorbus outing to Filey, dressed clean and neat, Aunt Frances' niece again.

*

It was the lightening of my heart caused by this particular visit that probably marked the beginning of the great change.

For a long time Alice had been asking me if I would see the silver-fish schoolmaster, Mr Benson, to have a little talk. I knew that she must sometimes discuss me with him. He had been with us for four years now and once when they were helping me upstairs I remember them acting towards each other with more than the intimacy that occurs between sober people dealing with a drunk. Mr Benson had had quite a brisk way with him on that occasion, not at all as in his sliding, apologetic days. Often nowadays I would sit upon the bottom stair, sometimes with my whisky-glass, sometimes when I had decided to drink no more, but having had to

180

pause for a while to take stock of things on my way to bed. 'Good evening,' Mr Benson would always say, flipping past me. Miss Gowe and the businessmen – they were not always the same businessmen and had lately changed into more schoolmasters from The New House School, though I never could tell one from another – Miss Gowe and the other lodgers never spoke to me on these occasions, passing tactfully by.

At last, however, there were no other lodgers but Mr Benson. The businessmen or schoolmasters were gone. Not even Miss Gowe, for she had been taken away on a tempestuous wind of disgust one Saturday afternoon, to a terrace house called Boagey's Guest House for Business Women, Separate Tables. It had hot and cold in the bedrooms and, according to Alice, doilies and bits of parsley. And no doubt a landlady acceptable to Valley Drive.

Miss Gowe didn't want to leave us. She had seemed to like the crashing sea outside her bedroom window and the three-handed Bridge with the businessmen and dominies with whom a glass of sherry had not been unknown. I don't think she even disapproved totally of her landlady, for once or twice I saw a gleam in her eye of what might have been envy as I examined my bare feet on the stairs, my hair loose for the night. Sometimes I sang a bit.

Plod, plod, Miss Gowe's feet had gone upon the turkey stair-carpets – faded now, beginning to wear thin on the treads, and the brass rods without their lustre, for Alice could not do everything. Once I had tried to help her by polishing these rods and unfastened every one of them and, with Brasso and cloths, set about them on the hall floor. But then I had gone away to look for sustenance and shrieks and hollow cries had assailed my ears. Miss Gowe had fallen heavily on the loose stair-runner and lay in a bulgy heap upon the tiles. She accepted gladly the inch and a half I gave her to pull herself together and we sat for a time pleasantly discussing this and that until Alice came in from shopping and helped us both to bed.

When Miss Gowe had been removed from us into respectability – with a broken arm – Alice said 'All right then. I'm speaking.'

'You're speaking, Alice.'

'I'm speaking. I've seen it coming. You've seen it coming. It stops, or I go.'

'What stops.'

'The drinking stops. You don't drink when Mr Thwaite's here. Nor for maybe a week after you get a letter from him or from that Maitland. So you don't have to have it. It's not essential yet. I know. I remember my father.'

'It helps my work.'

'Rubbish it helps your work. You sit there sozzled at your so-called work. You're a show, Miss Polly, and a disgrace. Everyone's talking.'

'Who is everyone? Everyone's no one to me.' This struck me as a fine epigram, brilliant and sad.

'Look at you – hair in a tatter, face blubbered out, stockings in drapes. Ashamed. I'm *ashamed* of you. Ashamed to say I know you.'

'You drink, too.'

'That I do not. Not no more. I did and I don't, having pride and sense – and proper work. Do you ever think of your aunts?'

'No.'

'Or your friends of bygone days?'

'No.'

'That lovely soldier dead and gone, God rest him, who thought so much of you. Wrote those lovely poems about you.'

'They weren't about me. How d'you know that?'

'I can read.'

'Help me up.'

'I've read them. As I've read that colouring game you play at. And I'm ashamed.'

'Be quiet. Call me what you like. I dare say I do drink, and much I care. But don't call my work or – '

'What?'

'Well, you can go. I'll dismiss you. Help me off with my dress. I'm going to bed. If you say anything about my work – '

'Always in bed. When did you wash your hair? When did you take a bath? You never hardly leave the house. No – the time's come. Oh, Miss Polly, you were a *pretty* girl, and clever. Where's your will?'

'It never grew. I'm in a mess, Alice. I missed education.'

'Now you're telling the truth. A mess. But you haven't missed education. And stop crying. There's Mr Benson wants to talk to you. There now – Will you do this one thing for me, Miss Polly, and see Mr Benson?'

'What about? I don't see Mr Benson doing much for me. Let me get some sleep.'

'Will you see him tomorrow?'

'Tomorrow, tomorrow –'

'Right. Tomorrow. I'll keep you to that then.'

'You take a lot upon yourself, Alice.'

'Just as well,' she said, 'or God help you.'

'He doesn't.'

'I'm scarcely surprised.'

*

God only helps the strong, I thought, holding my head the next day. Crusoe, so much stronger than I was, helped with visions bringing certainty and joy – Crusoe, who husbanded his supply of brandy for twenty-five years, so that there was even some left for Friday's father when he was recovering from nearly being eaten by cannibals. Crusoe, the controlled, the respected, the beloved of God.

Selwyn Benson, when he knocked at the book-room door did not seem as eager to see me as Alice had led me to expect. He hung his face only a little way round the green curtain that was there to preserve silence from the house for me at my desk. I had combed my hair that morning, my headache was abating, for there had been a letter from Thwaite and I felt, seeing his hesitance, rather in the ascendant.

'Oh come in, Mr Benson. I hope everything is all right?'

'Oh thank you. Yes, Miss Flint.'

'Do sit down.'

He was a very small man. In among Grandfather Younghusband's furniture he seemed a pigmy.

'Would you like – ?' The decanter seemed to be missing. 'Coffee?' (I could hang on a bit.)

Silence fell. I felt a sort of emanation behind the book-room door, the waves of Alice beating. He was no more wishing to see me than I him, but she wasn't going to let him out yet. I wondered if Alice were trying to make some sort of a match.

'We are rather in trouble at the school,' said Mr Benson eventually.

'Oh dear. I hope it isn't going to close. I heard it was doing rather well.'

'Oh yes. Very well. A great many boys. It's mainly boys unable to be accepted by the better-known schools and it's not expensive. It will survive.'

'Oh, good.'

'We are, however, rather – er – short of staff. I understand you have academic qualifications?'

'None.'

'Mr Thwaite and Alice have spoken of Modern Languages?'

'I'm not a man. It's a boy's school.'

'Since the war men have been hard to find. We wondered if, perhaps – a little French?'

'My German's better.'

'Alice tells me that your mother was a teacher. She has the idea that you would be good with children.'

'I don't see how she knows. I've never met any.'

'Alice knows,' he said. We looked at each other. We warmed to each other.

'Perhaps one English lesson a week as well? For pleasure?'

'Yes, I see. I'd like – But is it legal? I thought you had to have qualifications?'

'No.' I could see that he thought this fact appalling. So whyever was he doing this for me?

'Perhaps you might just come to the school to see us? Have a try? Perhaps just tell them a little about your – er special subject.'

'That is *Robinson Crusoe*.'

'Yes.' (He did look doleful, now.) 'Of course, if you feel – '

Outside the door I felt Alice planning to wring his delicate neck. He sat very still in the carved oak chair, looking as if he were never going to move.

'I shall have to get on with my work now, Mr Benson.'

'Yes, of course.' He picked his way across the clutter of the room and gazed round it. 'I might be able to help you as well as your helping me,' he said, 'I might teach you something of indexing – filing.'

*

'Well now – will you go?'

'I think I'm too busy.'

'You're frightened that if you leave that desk you'll find there's been no cause to sit at it, and then you'll have nothing.'

'You're cruel.'

'Aye, I am. And need to be. It's time.'

'I've not had a drink today.'

'Well, that's a start. But you'll be drunk again by bedtime. Drunk with fear – and cowardice and dissolution.'

'I can't go teaching boys, Alice. Look at me.'

'It could be set right still. Just. Out with Mr Thwaite, you looked a girl again. Come on – let me get at your hair.'

'Certainly not.'

*

'What are those scissors?'

'Cutting contrivances. Now – '

'Alice – stop. Whatever are you doing? You've cut off a yard!'

'Put your chin down. Shut your eyes. Now then.'

'Alice!'

'Hold still.'

'Alice.'

On the floor fell dreadful black lumps, heavy as felt. The scissors crunched and crunched.

'Alice.'

'Now here – mind the kettle. I've a sachet of camomile shampoo. Great Heaven, look at the water!'

'Alice – all this has happened to me before.'

'Pray God it won't have to happen again.'

*

'And here's a good washing cotton.'

'Wherever from?'

'The new emporium. In the High Street. The Bon Marsh.'

'Who on earth is Bon Marsh? The marsh is nearly gone.'

'It's French – you ought to know if you're going teaching.

It means cheap. Not that it was. Nothing's Bon Marsh now we've lost the lodgers. Here get in to it. My – you're thin. Well I never, you do look nice. Now shoes – I've got you ankle-straps with bucket backs.'

'They sound awful.'

'Well you can't wear your galoshes on the bus.'

'The bus. To The New House? It's scarcely a mile. I'll go in my old lace-ups.'

'There's these of Mrs Woods. I kept them as curios – I think they're African.'

'I like those.'

And so with bobbed hair with streaks of grey in it and savage slippers and a cotton frock of the very latest design and Mrs Woods's knowledge stored within me, I set forth to become a school mistress.

*

As I walked the well-known mile, waves of cold fright passed through me followed by surges of excitement of a new kind connected with my coming exposition of the great book, *Robinson Crusoe,* to a room full of children – for Mr Benson suggested that I begin with the subject in which I felt most at home.

The fear rose from the fact that the book, being so much more than a book to me, might lie so deep in the bone that it would be difficult to lay bare. The solitary work I had done upon it as spiritual biography, my later studies in the examination of it, not as fiction but as metaphysical landscape, had been written in the precious quiet of a study – a room I had made as remote from outsiders and as unknown to them as the texture and colour of the brain within the skull.

As one piece of work upon the book had been completed I had begun the next, placing the first carefully on a shelf. All my years had given the lie to the writer's lust for fame. I was too deep down, too separate, too simple, too mad even to trouble myself with the distractions of publication or communication and I did not even think, 'Perhaps when I am dead – '

Now I was to communicate some of my immense knowledge, and to children, when I had known no child since I was one myself and that one Stanley, who had responded by throwing hot coals at my face.

Yet I remembered his large eyes, his 'it's grand, it's right grand', and the feeling that he stirred in me before the cinder and the burning of the book that I had taught. Some small flame had spurted and sparked. And the book's curling pages, the shoots and sparkles and the flap of its flames had not stayed in my mind as a destruction but as a triumph, the completion of an act. I only knew now, and it rose out of an unconscious place, from some deep water-table, as I crossed the stile and on to the tarmac road and through the iron gates and up the familiar drive, weedless, rude cement – I only knew now that as I read and translated the French to Stanley, I had recognised an inherited power. 'Your mother was a wonderful teacher, I'll say that,' all of them had said. 'Oh, it was a loss to the teaching profession when she had you.'

And so today I willed as I walked that the power would return. I should tell the boys, these new Stanleys, receptive, rich, already well educated, things that they would not forget.

I would begin by discussing the concept of the novel: the English Novel, how it had emerged from jumbled and simplistic sources some three hundred years ago into the literary form we now recognise, its purpose to give solace and simultaneously to disturb; though its true genesis lies deep within man himself, in his urge to tell a tale. I would describe how, as blobs of jelly and the flat ribbons in the sea became fish, became birds, became mammals and intricate man, so the grunts and the snuffles of the cave became anecdote, joke, tale, tale set to music, saga, song-cycle and glorious traveller's tale. And then arose Defoe from the smelly streets of London, honest man (and criminal) prolific genius (and hack) to produce the great curiosity, the extraordinary masterpiece, the paradigm, *Robinson Crusoe* itself, the novel elect, fully realised and complete like the child Athene springing from the head of the rough god Zeus.

Having said a little of this I would continue in an analysis of the novel along the following lines (someone sloped by me along The New House School drive – it was the sexton, with his sideways look and I greeted him heartily):

1. Development of narrative during C18. Particular

influence of Defoe on English and European fiction. *RC* and its roots – current journalism. The subtle transcendence of these sources. Brilliant manipulation of the reader. We read with the pleasure gained from the best dramatic journalism, unaware at first that we are reading more.

2. Imitators of, then reactors against Defoe, esp. ref. Fielding, Richardson. Outline gulf-stream imitators, sports, curiosities; C18 pattern of novel, its waves sweeping wider: and riding these waves (sub-section) original, unrelated wks. of genius: es. Swift (note Swift's opinion of Defoe!)

3. Rise of the women as novelists: Fanny Burney, Blue-stocking writers, Lady Mary Wortley Montagu. 'Embassy Letters as Fiction.' The only book Dr Johnson read entirely for pleasure.

3(b). Interesting developments: horror novel, sickly childhood of the thriller. Dexterity, passion, brilliance at Haworth Parsonage etc.; the five miracles at Alton, Hampshire by a lady beset by domesticity and a querulous mother.

Final Point Every serious novel must in some degree and *unnoticeably* carry the form further. Novel must be 'novel'. To survive – like the blob in the ocean, the seed, it must hold in itself some fibrous strength, some seemingly preposterous new quality, catch some unnoticed angle of light – and unselfconsciously. It may fail – but better to be sorry than safe. All the time it must entertain. No polemics. No camouflaged sermons.

The novel in the later nineteenth century, I thought I might leave perhaps until the second lesson.

*

There was no reply at the peeling front door of The New School House so I walked round to the back and saw the tennis-court scarcely more in trim than when the army had taken it to pieces in 1914. A net sagged, big plants grew, there were holes in the rusty wire. The orangery the Zeits had not quite completed was still beautiful in outline, but – I opened the door and walked in – the stone flags were dirty and covered with splintery dining-tables and cheap old chairs. All smelled of mince.

A boy roamed about. He told me that the Headmaster's

room was upstairs. I said, 'Will you run up and tell him I'm here? Miss Flint,' and he went. While I was still thinking about my voice speaking to him as if it knew some of the rules, and wondering why my fluttering stomach wouldn't behave likewise, the boy returned and said, 'You're to take 1c. I'm to show you.'

'What a terrible noise,' I said as we approached Mrs Zeit's old morning-room where she had set up The Depot for the relief of the trenches.

'Mr Benson's not here,' said the boy. 'It's in there.' Without opening the door he went off and I walked in.

There were about twenty little boys. I knew nothing of ages but their hair was still floss or fledgling down. They showed great gaps of gum or the stubs of new frilly-edged teeth coming through gums. They had stick-legs with heart-breaking dents in the backs of the knees. Sagging socks. Most of them were rolling in combat on the floor.

Of those who were not, two were on window-ledges being the Royal Air Force and two more banging their desk-lid with a steady and hypnotic rhythm. Others were gathered at the teacher's tall desk and tall stool, scrabbling and kicking each other to get at what was inside, which didn't seem to be much. The blackboard was covered with faces and words beginning with 'b'.

The noise slowly faded as I stood at the door – the desk lids, mercifully, being the first things to die down, like a thunderstorm receding. Boys on the floor began to recline, then to sit up, those at the teacher's desk laughed less, and fought their way self-consciously back into the body of the room. Two last parachute descents were achieved from the window-ledge a little nonchalantly. A white china ink-well flew, smashed, trickled. I sat on an empty desk by the door.

In the moment of something like silence, the fuzzy photo-graph of the firm young woman with fat me on her lap in Grandfather Younghusband's study said decidedly, 'Now Polly! Before they start again.'

'Before you start again,' said I, 'pick up that ink-well. Thank you. You – with the torn shirt – go and clean off the board those filthy words. Yes – and stay there. The rest of you sit at your desks if they are not piles of firewood. Shut all the lids. Thank you. Now – take a deep breath.'

'Go on. All of you. Go on.'

'That's better.'

'Now then – I am Miss Flint. I am like SHEET STEEL. Write that on the board and I want your names every one of you. STOP THAT,' as a foot snaked from under a desk and hooked itself round the rail of the chair in front and jerked. 'Get up there beside the board, too, and write your name. *S*s don't go that way round. Write me twenty.'

'Now then, I'm your new teacher and you'd better be careful because I'm a terrible woman. I know a great deal about cannibals. On desert islands. I eat boys for lunch. Who can spell cannibal? Quite wrong. Go back. Someone else have a try – oh, *very* good. It's a difficult one. What's your name? Gegg? Well I never.'

'How dare the rest of you laugh! What's wrong with being called Gegg? He can spell cannibal. I won't eat him, ever.'

(How very delightful! How utterly delightful this was being!)

'Now then, I'll tell you something to stop you sniggering at things people can't help like their names, unless they're ladies and they can sometimes improve things by getting married, though not always – '

'There was a little boy once in a London school called Tim Crusoe and it was a very unusual, queer name and I expect he got laughed at for it. But one of the other boys in the class when he grew up, remembered it and wrote a story about it, and who can tell me what it was?'

'What's the dead silence? What? Gegg – Gegg knows – "*Robinson Crusoe!*" That's right! What was the story about? Who was he?'

'He had a wooden leg, miss.'

'He had a wooden leg, Miss Flint. No, he hadn't. Yes?'

'Please Miss – Flint – he had a parrot and a hook for a hand.'

'One point for parrot. No point for hook. You're mixing up sailors. You'll be saying Flint next.'

'He saw a foot-print. On a Friday.'

'One point for foot-print but Friday was a person. Why was he Friday?'

190

'Please Miss – '

'Please Miss Flint.'

'Please Miss Flint, he was another boy at Mr Crusoe's school.'

'Mr Defoe's school. Daniel Defoe wrote *Robinson Crusoe*. Over two hundred years ago and we're still reading it today. Why?'

'Because you make us.'

' "Because you make us, Miss Flint." I do not. If you don't want to read it, you needn't. I'll find you something else, you silly young nut. Stop laughing. If you don't want to read it you'll miss a lovely story. I'm going to tell you it first though – it's too long for you to read by yourselves yet. What's that awful noise?'

'It's the bell, Miss Flint.'

'Bell?'

'It's the end. What have we to do for prep?'

'Prep? – Oh – '

(Prep?) 'Oh. write me a story. Even if it's only two lines long. I promise I'll read every single word. Stand up. Say good morning. Put your tie straight, Biggles. And don't all write about Gegg. It'll make him conceited. Goodbye.'

'Please Miss Flint, when're you coming back?'

'As soon as possible.'

'Yippeee!'

*

And then – again – alas.

*

'Please,' said the dispirited boy still hanging Smike-like in the hall of The New House School – and I wouldn't have been surprised to have seen him trailing a broom – 'Please, you're to go up to see the Headmaster.' 'Very well,' said I, flushed with power. 'Show me up, please. Come *back*. Show me *up* please. Oughtn't you to be in class by the way?' (Wherever were these words coming from?)

'Mr Benson's not in today,' he said again.

'Things are different when he's here?' I asked.

'Oh yes, miss, very.'

And there, in Mrs Zeit's bedroom, the room in which I

191

had been cossetted and pitied for Paul Treece's death, where still some slight ghost of Paul Treece lingered, where I had expected soon to be embraced as a daughter, sat the owner of The New House School, freckly, porridgy, flaccid, wan.

'One pound', he said, 'per term, per boy, per class. One class, twenty boy maximum.' He heaved a sigh. 'Five mornings a week all subjects. Supervision of football. Dinner duty on occasion, secretarial duties here for me. Cleaning of this study and the landing outside. Light shopping. Position to be surrendered when suitable male teacher available.'

Down through the mince-smelling orangery, over the cemented terrace, along the empty drive again and not a boy in sight. Silence like an old people's home with the inmates shovelled away, silent as the old nunnery, but none of the nunnery's confidence, happiness or life.

And home.

Mr Benson and Alice waited, and Alice became a whirl-wind of anger and Mr Benson turned and thumped a mantel-piece so hard that glass prisms jangled and a clock under its dome gave a twang of surprise. 'I can't do it. Oh and I want to do it,' I said. 'But it's too much. I'd fail.'

I went off to my desk. There was a whisky-bottle in the drawer. I poured two inches and then another inch, and after a while an inch again.

Oh the humiliation. But they would be indulgent to me now. It was a relief to be here – in my own setting again, safe behind my own hand-built stockade. Oh, Robinson Crusoe, 'ship-wrecked often, though more by land than by sea'. I drooped above the whisky. Soon they would come with my tea. They would be good to me. Dear Alice, so kind to me.

But tea did not come.

Nor yet did supper, which Alice usually brought on a tray. I poured more whisky and went to the kitchen, but no one was there. The house seemed empty. We were without lodgers until the regular summer visitors arrived to see our house-keeping expenses through the winter. I called about the house. No answer.

I walked out on to the sand-hills and there I saw Alice and Mr Benson in very determined conversation, Mr Benson with clasped hands and hung head, nodding occasionally, rather sharply. They had seen me. They looked at me. They looked away. They went on talking.

After a time they got up and came over to me, still talking, and Alice said, 'We'll go in. Come along,' and though Mr Benson drew back to let me pass in front of him, Alice marched in front of us both straight into the house and up to the drawing room. I followed, feeling carefully from one chair to the next, on account of my exposure to the brisk fresh air. Mr Benson stood by Aunt Frances's piano in the middle of the room, looking to the left and to the right.

'Shall I leave you then?' said Alice.

'No, no.'

'I think I'd better. It's your place, not mine.'

'Oh sit down Mr Benson, for goodness sake,' I said and sat down myself, hard on Mrs Woods's chair. Dust puffed out. I could not remember anyone sitting in that chair for years.

Then slowly Mr Benson sat and looked seriously into the grate and I began to feel rather frightened.

Time went by and I began to feel greatly frightened, for Alice sat down, too. She sat down with me in my drawing-room. Alice, the maid.

'Miss Polly,' she said, 'Mr Benson has something to tell you. He has bought The New House School and is to be the next Headmaster.'

'*Mr Benson!* But I met the Headmaster this afternoon. He said nothing – Well, you know what he said.'

'He's a very sad fellow. I don't think he knows what's happening. I was hoping – '

'But then, you're rich Mr Benson! You must have been rich all the time.' I was totally sober.

'No. The school was on the rocks. I borrowed the money. I am quite happy – '

'But – oh, good. Well done. Well, I do congratul – '

'I have something to ask you.'

'There,' said Alice. 'Now I can go away while you get on with it. As is only right.'

I looked at Mr Benson who smiled showing very square determined teeth I had not before noticed and for a moment his face allowed itself to go full rip. He looked joyous. A lunatic thought came to me. He was about to propose.

'I want to ask you', he said, 'to let me have Alice.'

'Oh, I can't possibly spare Alice.'

'I have asked her to be my wife. I asked her a great time ago. I have asked her often. She has always said no, until this afternoon.'

'Oh. Yes, I see. That is wonderful for Alice.'

'It's wonderful for me. Miss Flint, I think you knew. I think you guessed. You are pleased. I always said you would be pleased.'

Alice. A headmaster's wife.

'Oh of course – '

'We shan't be far away.'

'Far away? Alice won't go? You won't leave Oversands?'

'We shall of course live at the school. Of course,' and the square teeth were revealed again.

'Yes, I see.'

'I take up my position next term. We shall have the summer holidays to set the new regime going. I shall be interviewing staff and engaging building contractors. Getting out the new time-table usually takes a week. I have done this for some years already. There will be new boys and new parents to alert and see. A great deal to do and of course the wedding and honeymoon.'

'Oh, honeymoon.'

'We shall be married from Alice's home in Skinningrove.'

'Alice's home? But Alice's home is – '

'Yes. Her mother is determined to give the reception.'

'I didn't know. Of course she goes home at Christmas, but – '

'Her father is a miner, as of course you know.'

'Oh yes. Is he?'

'You will be guest of honour of course.'

'When – ?' I saw my fingers slowly rubbing and pleating together the skirt of my dress – the first sign it is said of old age in a woman. 'When do you? When have you – ?'

'In one month,' said Mr Benson. 'That gives you time to find Alice's replacement. Now, shall we bring Alice back? I shall find glasses and lemon barley-water for us all to drink to future days.'

*

194

'Oh Alice!'

'Oh Miss Polly!'

'It had better be Polly.'

'Oh never. Oh, who'll you get next to replace – ?'

'I can never replace you.'

'Oh Miss Polly, whatever will you do? It was do or die. I had to do it. After today it was kill or cure. It's your only chance.'

I wanted to say, 'But can you stand this man, Alice? His time-tables and talk?'

'And oh, Miss Polly, the price of whisky!'

'Hem, heremmm,' said Mr Benson, 'You will of course be able to start your classes next term Miss – Polly. I can assure you there'll be no cleaning of the landings.'

'It wasn't that,' I said, 'it was the – well, I think as much as anything the shopping. And the uncertainty – I should have had to leave, he said, when a male teacher became available.'

'The nerve!' cried Alice.

'That will not be so. Please take more potatoes, Miss – er – Polly – Flint.' (We were sitting all together to three chops round the kitchen table.) 'One morning a week to start with, the proper scale of pay, with increments as time passes. French and German, but also a little general work which we shall call English.'

'You can do it, Miss Polly.'

'I wonder why you think so?' I felt so tired. 'I loved it this afternoon but – '

'There, then!'

'But I was probably just showing off. Acting. I've had no training – I've never been to school.'

'Some can, some can't – isn't it so, Selwyn? Miss Polly – '

'Alice tends', said Mr Benson, 'almost invariably to be right – though neither she nor I was right this afternoon. We mismanaged that. You should not have gone to the school alone.'

*

Later, as Alice and I washed up together – I dropping the last good plate – she said, 'You see, Miss Polly, Selwyn's scared. He's a right mix, Selwyn. Don't listen to the bombast.

He's just whistling in the dark. He's still a scared man, though I've done a lot for him. France and that could still come back. I'm scared, too, but that's between ourselves – coming only from Skinningrove and no airs and graces. Headmaster's wife – Alice! Miss Polly, we'll need you bad.'

'He didn't say that.'

'He's proud. But he knows it. The school's going to need you for tone. They'll be right vulgar common folk sending their little lads at first, just so they can say they sent them to a private school.'

'I don't think I'll impress them. I don't see me adding any tone. I've noticed people think me very funny.'

'You've got something, though, Miss Polly. There's something to you. It's being brought up by people not usual. Not caring what's thought of them. And brains. That great book you're writing. I tell everyone.'

'Colouring game is what you called it last.'

'I only said it after years. I got so frightened for you. I saw you disappearing. All washed up and marooned and far away. But you won't be now. I know it. I know, I truly know. This is to be the right thing for us all.'

*

So they were married. I gave them Aunt Mary's spoons and my Chinese work-box. Under Alice's care the school flourished and filled and Mr Benson strutted forth in university gown and mortar-board with fierce glances and a kind heart and people began to love them both. Boys spilled about the grounds, swiped balls across the tennis-courts of neat mown green, began to be allowed about the town in smart black blazers and black-and-white caps – and their fathers gave enormous pots and cups of heavy silver for prizes on Sports Days, when Mr Benson wore his blazer of sunset-stripes and a panama hat so large and silky cream it would have graced even Mr Woods of Africa.

Mr Thwaite often attended the Sports Days, and Maitland came, too, dressed in brown tussore and a picture hat and carrying a reticule. Mr Thwaite looked very frail now, his old legs wrapped in rugs against the sandy wind which tossed the names of events and competitors, cried down hand-held megaphones, about the sky. Once Mr Thwaite gave the prizes and a speech which was all about the weather, but the wind took the speech away, too, so that nobody heard it, though they all clapped enthusiastically at the end and told each other how lucky the school was to have him there as he was some sort of lord.

And I, Polly Flint, was always there – at the Sports Days and at the Speech Days and every ordinary day – the week-days and week-ends, early and late, and 'the yellow house' became 'The Yellow House' – a school boarding-house, and I moved into the front two rooms of it. The dining-room table was covered with red felt and then a white cloth on top and ten boys ate round it noisily and enormously. Upstairs in Mrs Woods's room six boys slept with lockers and photographs of home beside them and as many books and toys as they liked. When I walked home after school at the end of each day, the smallest school-house boys always accompanied me as far as the gates, talking hard and prancing. And when I turned back at the stile to wave to them, they were always there. And so passed some beautiful years.

For Alice's marriage had saved me, had shown me my course. 'I saw my deliverance indeed visibly put into my hands, all things easy, and a large ship ready to carry me any whither I pleased to go.'

*

And so, how happy now I had become at the yellow house; and one Saturday afternoon, two and a half years later, there came the most miraculous day in my life. For years of our lives the days pass waywardly, featureless, without meaning, without particular happiness or unhappiness. Then, like turning over a tapestry when you have only known the back of it, there is spread the pattern.

It was the early summer of 1939. I was walking home from school where I had been teaching in the morning, then sorting Selwyn Benson's letters for he was busy with a cricket match and Alice supervising visitors' teas – the maids all terrified of her – and it had grown thundery and hot. I walked slowly. I was thinking of my strange madness of long ago, my obsession with my paradigm, *Robinson Crusoe,* now quite gone, fled like the end of a love-affair, the bird flown from the shoulder. The fever over.

197

Oh such a great many years.

I decided to go home by the church and look at the graves of Aunt Mary and Mrs Woods for I had taken lately – like an old church lady – to visiting the church on Saturday afternoon. I passed the sexton's grave and thought that there should be a black but comic poem about a sexton's grave. I looked at the lonely, meaningless sick-beds of the other graves, pulled weeds out, thanked God that from my purgatory with the works of old Defoe I had emerged with a sense of God and resurrection; and I went into church and sat myself down in a pew at the back.

Women were working in the church for Sunday. Funny old birds. They sounded like birds, too, calling about from one part of the church to another. One was fluttering about the altar and another buffing about at the inside of the holocaustian windows polishing them even brighter, one was tightening up screws in the leading, some twittered round the brasses. Two ostrich-like ladies moved heavily-weighted sticks about over red tiles. Their talk was scarcely words. They spoke in the up and down conversational notes of birds in the evening in quiet woods.

I had grown, the past year, to love this music. To love the church, to begin to take part in this particular kind of song. 'Oh dear, oh dear,' said the lady at the altar, 'everyone's oh-dearing today.' 'Sand everywhere, sand everywhere!' called another, sweeping a lot of it down a grating. 'Sand, sand,' and Christ looked down from beneath the thorns of Jerusalem.

'Here's Miss Flint to help us. Now then, Miss Flint, it's a beautiful day.'

'It's hot,' I said, 'it's hot.'

'There – I've fastened that window,' said the lady with the screwdriver. 'It's been loose since the bombardment of nineteen-fourteen. Oh this church is a show! Miss Flint – if you'd known it once.'

'I've known it from the start,' I said, 'since I was six. But I wouldn't come to it. I was a rebel.'

'Oh, but I remember your Aunt Mary. What a saint. We always said she should have been a nun. And Miss Frances. We all loved Miss Frances. That wasn't much of a marriage – ' And the birds began to sing like mad and louder with excitement when the parson arrived.

He was a new parson, said to have been a local lad, he was hungry-looking, with a Grangetown accent and frayed cuffs to his suit. He put his arm round some of the women and called out greetings. I thought of Mrs Woods who had said you shouldn't talk in church. All the ladies warmed and turned to him, like chickens running at feeding time. I saw Mrs Woods's dark, outraged face – and found I loved that, too.

'Hello, Miss Flint,' said the priest. 'Sheltering from the thunder?'

'Just calling.'

'We're in for some dramatics. You ought to get home. Can I give you a lift over the marsh?'

'Over the marsh? There isn't a marsh any more. It's two steps. I'm all right thank you.'

'In your wonderful house,' he said. 'Have you thought of that, by the way?'

'Thought of the yellow house?'

'If there's war they'll have you out of it. You're nearly in the sea.'

'That's what they said last time, but it came to nothing. We stayed put.'

'It'll be different this time.'

'Will there be a war, Father?' asked an old lady.

'Yes,' he said, 'there'll be a war. Very soon now.'

*

We stood together in the porch the priest and I. I said, 'Look – on the top of the tower on the school. D'you see the telescope? When I was a small child – well about twelve – I saw that telescope for the first time on the way to church and thought it was an angel.'

'Did they sort you out?'

'I didn't tell. Well, only our poor Charlotte. The maid. But look – it's back. The old telescope. Selwyn Benson found it in the cellar.'

'It'll be back down the cellar again when the war starts.'

We walked together across the marsh field. He said, 'Polly Flint. Do you know, I asked you once for a kiss?'

199

'What!'

'I was the milk boy. The milkman's lad. I wish I knew you well,' he said.

'There's little to know.' A surging ridiculous blush, and a stumbling over my feet. (And past forty!)

'You live alone, don't you, except for the school? No family? You never come to services.'

'I think I shall soon. Why don't you come and see me at the yellow house?'

'You're always somewhere else. Always working they say at the school.'

'Well, it was time I worked. I must go now. I've books to mark.' I put out my hand and laid it upon his arm. Triumphant.

'How very hot it is,' he said, and I blushed again as he watched me.

'Goodbye, beautiful Miss Flint.'

So I walked home, having been called beautiful, and had to unlock the door of the yellow house, for this evening it was – very unusually – quite empty, the boarders being still at the Match and the housekeeper having the day off this particular Saturday.

I liked the house empty, now that it was so seldom.

I walked through the light and shadow of the hall with its rows of pegs and children's clothes and lockers and muddle of shoes and smell of boys and into the kitchen to boil a kettle for tea, thinking of vestal virgins, the dying face of Christ, of Jews, of the beautiful happiness in the world, all seen so sharp now, before the new war.

I thought of the shabby young priest; and the blush came again, surging up from my waist this time and spreading all about me, and I stopped what I was doing and stood still and thought – I'd suspected it before. Blood again. Disturbance in the blood.

Ah well, so it's over. No children now. A thousand years since the Sunday of the sheepskin rug. Yet only a moment. The blush came yet again.

And I watched the kettle boil and said, 'It's over.'

I cut myself three slices of bread and butter. Thin. I thought of the days of whisky, when food didn't matter. I went to the sink to wash the butter off my hands and looked

200

out of the window and saw Stanley standing watching me out in the yard.

*

He was sharp-edged and clear.

He wore the clothes in which I had last seen him, over thirty years ago, the week he died.

His trousers were old-fashioned and long, over the knee, and his tie – which I had quite forgotten – was a string of slippery yellow and green stripes. The row of pencils was there, the ruler in the sock. His eyes were blue and attentive and very clear. He had been watching me for some time.

Then the ghost was gone.

It did not fade away. As I looked up, there it was – established. A sharp and definite boy. Then it flicked out and the yard was empty.

But there had been some command – a direction it would have been impossible to describe and which might have been lost had I stopped to think about it. I dried my hands and put the towel beside the sink. Without a word or a gasp or even a glance out of the window again, I walked from the kitchen to the front door.

On the mat were letters left by the afternoon postman and I picked them up. One was inscribed with a red cross in the top left-hand corner and seemed to be an appeal for sponsoring Jewish children being brought out of Germany. A circular. I would look at it later. It was rather odd that it had been addressed to me in person. Miss Flint.

Then I turned to the other letter but needed my glasses. They were in the study and I found them and sat in the window there among all the fat dead files and the dusty books I seldom looked at now.

The second letter was postmarked Germany. Dusseldorf. And it was from Theo Zeit.

But I couldn't read it. His writing, always so small and odd, was here indecipherable. I couldn't believe it at first – stood up with the letter, pulled the paper tight, peered and peered at it up near my face, paced the room with it, held it to every light.

It was in German. Here and there I could make out a phrase. 'Almost ready', 'lost, no chance – ' 'sudden

201

departure', 'planned so long', 'unable to say'. Near the end I read, written quite clearly, 'Soon I shall follow them', and then, 'With my gratitude, blessings, love always – Theo.'

I found the strongest magnifying glass in the house and put the letter on the window sill in the last of the sun, but the calligraphy, always so minute and tense, was now so small as to seem scarcely formed. I went for a torch and blazed it on the paper, then put the paper under a bright light bulb in the desk-lamp. It made no difference.

I put on a jacket to run to the school, but stopped on the step. For all her importance to me I could not take Theo to Alice for interpretation. I turnèd instead to the other letter.

Hepzibah and Rebecca Zeit, the daughters of Dr Theo Zeit of Dusseldorf, are expected on the refugee train from Dusseldorf on Wednesday, May 8, 1939. Their sponsors – cousins who escaped from Germany a year ago – have waited as long as possible, but have had, at last, to leave for America where there will be work. They have run out of money. Dr Zeit has been contacted with the greatest difficulty and he has given the name of Miss Polly Flint of Oversands as temporary sponsor. He will follow the children with the rest of his family as soon as possible. He is only waiting for his last documents. It is thought wise for the children to leave as planned and very quickly. Their train leaves Dusseldorf on Tuesday, May 7 and will carry several hundred Jewish children. Will Miss Flint please be at Liverpool Street Station in London to meet this train and send word at once on receipt of this letter, also sending a guarantee of sponsorship.

I went out then, not to the school, but along the esplanade. And along and along it until it turned inland. I came to The Hall Estate to find the postmaster. His wife opened the door – she was one of the church ladies of the afternoon and I remembered that she'd asked me if I'd like to come to a get-together that evening. 'Well, I never! She's come,' she cried.

*

'Now, what about this? Miss Flint's here. She's come to have a sing. Now come inside, Miss Flint. The kettle's just this minute boiled.'

'It's the telephone,' I said, 'I need the telephone. Very quickly. Could you put a call through for me?'

She looked so disappointed that I said, 'Of course I'd love to come to the get-together afterwards.'

'Well, of course you can use the telephone. Dickie will see to the number.'

'It's two numbers. One near York and the other one in Germany.'

'Germany? Well, I don't know that we've done a Germany. We could manage a York. Dickie, we've done calls to York?'

'Well of course we have. What's this then? Sit down and we'll have a look. Well, the Thwaite's possible all right – that's a Pilmoor Junction number, reached through Trunks at York. It'll maybe take an hour. The Germany, we'll have to enquire. Is that the number?'

Theo's address and telephone number were printed on his letter-paper. The postmaster departed.

I sat in his tiny front room with the get-together, knee to knee, twelve of us on hugely-stuffed chairs and a sofa. It was extremely hot. In the corner sat the post-master's daughter who wasn't right in the head. Her mouth was open. She nodded and gaped and her hands tried to stroke me. Her hands were very cold. She seemed another mystery of this haunted day.

'We were just singing hymns,' said the postmistress, 'verse by verse, passing the book. Shall we go on until the call comes through?' Someone gave a note and the mad girl became even more excited and two old men began to sing,

'Old folk, young folk, everybody come
Join the donkey Sunday School and make yourselves

at home'

and I thought: 'This is enough,' and got up and made for the door where the postmaster was suddenly standing to say with quiet pride that Thwaite was on the line.

*

'Mr Thwaite? It's Polly. No – everything is very well. I think. Mr Thwaite – there has been a letter. I am to take Theo Zeit's children. He has asked me. To live with me. Yes. They are coming on a train full of Jewish refugees from Dusseldorf. On May 8th.'

'The connections should be quite easy,' said Mr Thwaite. 'I have the International Bradshaw beside me.'

'Mr Thwaite. Of course it's going to be absolutely marvellous to have them, but – '

'I liked old Zeit,' said the faint thread of voice, 'I enjoyed it when old Zeit was still about. I liked the boy too. Indeterminate for a Jew – but a good boy.'

'It's just – Mr Thwaite – I have never been to London.'

'Oh, I shall come with you.' The thread vibrated and crackled in the thundery night. 'I shall join you at York. You can get to York safely?'

'Certainly not. I mean, yes, of course I can get to York safely. But you mustn't think – '

'I shall be there. The Tuesday. We shall catch the eleven forty-three from platform four, which means you take the eight forty-five from the marsh to be safe for your Darlington connection. King's Cross six-fifty as I remember. I shall arrange accommodation.'

'Mr Thwaite you are too – You aren't strong enough.'

'I should like to see London again,' said the thin voice; 'it may soon be greatly changed.'

'Dusseldorf', said the post-master, 'is, alas, a different matter. Calls to Germany are not easy just at present. I have booked it in for you tomorrow morning – tentatively. And I fear that it will cost a great deal.'

'That's all right. I'll pay for York now. May I come and wait here tomorrow?'

'As long as ever you like, Miss Flint.'

The get-together was watching me with interest. 'We could go on with the hymns,' said somebody, 'if Miss Flint would like?'

'I've some Jewish children coming from Germany,' I said. 'They're coming to me. It's sudden. To live at Oversands. They're refugees.'

They had all heard the telephone conversation in the back of the shop but put up a fine show of surprise. 'The more the better, the more the better,' said the post-mistress; and her dotty daughter nodded her head. 'Poor souls, poor little homeless objects. There's none of us knows here one thing about what's going on out there. None of us. You're a lesson to us, Miss Flint. I suppose you don't play the harmonium?'

So I ended the day when you needed me, my love, playing

a harmonium and singing hymns in the street that had grown over Ðelphi's stable yard and the mausoleum of long ago.

*

'I sat three days in the back of the post office,' I said to Mr Thwaite and Maitland as the train rocked out of York station, 'but I never got through to Germany.'

The three of us sat in a first-class carriage on bluebell and grey plush, our heads against little lace-edged cloths with L.N.E.R. intertwined in satin stitch, but rather less starched somehow than the ones from Wales when I was six. Mr Thwaite's ancient Don Quixote figure gave the carriage a patrician look. No one would divide a meat pie in it.

Maitland sat very straight in black, on her head a shiny straw-hat with a feather held on by a golden pin. Mr Thwaite was in button-boots and a silvery herring-bone coat, rather long for a hot day; a tall coke-hat sat on the rack above his head and his yellow gloves and silver-topped stick lay on the smaller rack below it. Holiday people in shorts and knapsacks looked in with interest at us as they passed along the corridor. I was probably looking rather queer, too, for I have never quite understood about clothes. They are always wrong. But my stockings were silk.

Mr Thwaite gazed about him with enormous composure and Maitland's mouth was tweaked up very tight which signified emotion, her fingers clutched up on a pouchy port-manteau which she kept on her knee.

We trooped to the dining-car for coffee and chocolate biscuits; we trooped to it again for luncheon and drank 'a bottle of bone' which turned out to be wine. We ate roast beef and ginger pudding and custard. Maitland said that the railways always made a nice ginger, and how she was not sure, for a ginger took a good hour or two to steam. The custard she thought passable, though boiled up and not baked. But we were thinking of the children on the other train, starting and stopping, clanking towards Holland.

Mr Thwaite, watching the weather above Selby, pointing out the Abbey as an afterthought, said that a boiled railway pudding eaten in Doncaster could have been initiated in Edinburgh where the train started. He added with pleasure that we should still be on board for tea.

We drank our after-luncheon coffee, poured by a magician who didn't spill a drop as we flew through flat Lincolnshire. Quiet fields, quiet villages. 'They should be over the frontier now,' said Mr Thwaite, 'if they left Dusseldorf on time.' We all saw faces of parents left behind. 'Safe now in Holland,' he said.

Giants made of cardboard walked in the fields of Rutland. They were decorators carrying a ladder between them and on the ladder the name of some sort of paint. 'Miss Polly's still a child,' said Maitland, 'looking and looking.' Maza-wattee Tea seemed to be the name of all the stations, or Oxo-Bovril-Oxo, and sometimes a gold-and-pink girl would spring out at us from a huge frame box set up beside the line, great sheaves of corn painted all around her and a steaming cup and saucer at her feet. 'What a lot of beverages we have to choose from these days,' said Mr Thwaite. 'We are really very fortunate.'

The countryside slid quietly by, quicker and quicker. Newark was anonymous, Peterborough invisible. Tea-time was scones and jam, tea in pots with rose-buds round the lid, cups squat and wide like chamberpots. They sat deep in their saucers, unrockable in the pleasant afternoon. Outside basked the bland and peacetime South, with three months remaining. Hertfordshire: cows and large trees.

'What huge trees, Mr Thwaite.'

'Ah yes. You will find the trees huge. It's a pity you can't see a southern spring. I should like you to see a spring in Italy one day, Polly.'

'I hope they will have warm clothes,' said Maitland; 'it's very cold with us in winter.'

'They ought to be getting well through now. Almost to The Hook.' said Mr Thwaite, looking at his silvery-gold pocket watch.

Eight wild tunnels. We screamed through them, then slid and settled into booming, hissing King's Cross. The porter couldn't hear our voices. They were lost in the echoing great arc above us and I couldn't understand him. He sounded like a foreigner. But he found us a fat taxi like a coach or a pram in which we sat in a row once more and from which we were bowed to Brown's Hotel.

Mr Thwaite went quickly to bed and Maitland and I were

206

asleep soon too, and at seven the next morning were again in a taxi to meet the German train. 'If we are first there,' said Maitland, 'we shall be first away. The poor things – oh, they will be so exhausted.'

'It will be a four-hour wait,' said Mr Thwaite, 'from seven until eleven. Before they even arrive.'

'But if we can sign the papers or whatever we do – there'll be some sort of desk set up, I suppose – in, say, half an hour, – we might just get a train home this afternoon.'

'It would be too much in one day for Mr Thwaite,' said Maitland.

'Oh, not at all. Not at all.'

'Shall we take all our luggage with us to the station?' I asked them. 'And leave directly from Liverpool Street to save time?'

'I shall have a word with the Hotel Manager,' said Mr Thwaite and reported that the Manager felt that we ought perhaps to reserve rooms for one more night, just in case – and a further room for our guests.

'Guests?'

It suddenly dawned that the children to be collected would be guests. People.

Children.

Distraught children, perhaps sick children, and certainly wretched.

'We'll get them quick home,' said Maitland, 'quick as we can. Get them in their beds by midnight and journeying done. That's my feeling – home to-day.'

But Liverpool Street Station, at seven in the morning, was very quiet when we arrived and there was a blackboard covered with copperplate writing saying that the train from Dusseldorf would be arriving twenty-four hours late.

'We ought to look at things,' said Maitland, 'Miss Polly's never been to London.' But we were reluctant to look at anything, reluctant to leave the station.

'What if they come and we're not here?'

Vociferous Jews were talking in clumps. 'Certainly not today,' said a man with a long floaty beard and a round black hat, which I thought must be a joke. 'We should all go home.'

'Perhaps at least we should go and look at Westminster Abbey for Polly,' said Maitland, so we all took a taxi to

Parliament Square and there were sandbags piled about in fortress walls all along the buildings, about the cathedral itself. It looked dusty inside, subdued, disappointing. There were a great many people praying. Everyone quiet. We walked a little way down Victoria Street and saw the noble doorways of The Army and Navy Stores. 'Oh, it's where Aunt Frances went,' I said, 'to get her missionary things for India. I wonder if they still sell things like that?'

'I'd think not very many at present. But we might have luncheon there, and see,' said Mr Thwaite.

We made our way after luncheon to the department of missionary equipment and it was very empty indeed. On display was a fortress of cabin trunks with brass ribs, a skyscraper of pigskin camp-stools, tiger-proof tents, chromium and crocodile water-bottles and gleaming elephant-guns.

'Poor Frances,' said Mr Thwaite. 'Elephant-guns. So unlike her.' He took a solar topee and stroked it and set it on his head. 'I have always rather desired one of these things,' he said, standing to willowy attention.

'Twelve shillings and sixpence, sir,' said an assistant.

'Ah – Alas – '

'Mr Thwaite,' I said, 'I want to buy you the solar topee.'

'I don't expect I'd wear it much. It's rather a waste of money. In Yorkshire. In view of the coming war.'

'But still, you shall have it,' said I.

Then, as the assistant went to see to the wrapping of the box, Mr Thwaite said what seemed to be a very frightening thing.

'I am going to leave for Thwaite,' he said.

'What? Oh, of course you're not. You can't leave for Thwaite *now*. You can't possibly travel alone – and Maitland and I can't possibly do without you. We need you to be noticeable. With taxi-drivers and everywhere. We need you – to get the children home.'

'No, no,' he said, and cleared his throat so that the safari fire-irons jingled. 'I am – her – um, going to leave – er – Thwaite.'

'Leave *Thwaite!* You are going to leave *Thwaite?*'

'No,' he said. 'I am – er – trying to say, Polly, that I am – in fact, in my will I have already done so – I am leaving you, Thwaite, Polly. When I die.'

'Will you be wanting anything more?' asked the assistant, approaching with the tall box.

*

The next day we were at Liverpool Street at seven once again, but again there was no train. The blackboard was wiped clean.

No one to ask. No Jewish relatives. Nobody. There had obviously been some vital announcement that we had missed by visiting The Army and Navy Stores the day before. We walked about Moorgate and the City Road and London Wall and went to look at the Bank of England for a time, and up and down. 'How do they stand it?' asked Maitland. 'The noise of it all? Look at all the white faces. And what are they all *running* for? Miss Polly, I'm sorry – I must sit.'

'Oh yes. So must I.'

'I'd thought we might look over a few of the city churches,' said Mr Thwaite, who was growing more and more vigorous as the days went by and we grew weaker. 'And there's the Mansion House and Smithfield Market. Oh yes, and several excellent stations I believe. For instance, none of us may see Fenchurch Street in our lives if we don't see it now.'

'Well, see it you may but it'll be alone,' said imperious Maitland, who had confessed in the hotel the evening before that since the butler's death and Lady Celia's, she and Mr Thwaite had become very close. 'Miss Polly and I need a cup of coffee.'

'Or Bovril, Oxo, Ovaltine or even Mazawattee Tea,' said I.

'Perhaps one sherry,' said Mr Thwaite. 'If we can stop Polly from being an utter abstainer.'

'No thank you. Look – it's awful here. Maitland's quite right. Listen to us shouting in this traffic. Let's go back to see if there's some news and if there's not – well, we could go to a park somewhere or go and look at the river.'

'It's the river through Thwaite meadows I'll be glad to see again,' said Maitland. 'If ever we do. We're stuck with this Liverpool Street, it seems to me, for life.'

But at the station there was now a great change. Crowds were pushing, yelling, shoving and being issued with identity tags; and in a moment we were among them and being

209

whisked up into the gallery of some sort of railway building. Below us streams of children were flowing in, and Red Cross ladies. Wild-looking government and railway officials ran among them, clutching armfuls of notes and the air was salty and sour with the smell of dirty hot children and cries in German and English together, and there was quarrelling and weeping. The children poured steadily, slowly into the hall below us as if the tide of them would never cease.

We sat in a row and Mr Thwaite dozed. Maitland and I were now electrically wide-awake. 'He's old,' said Maitland. 'He is old now. Tiredness hits him sudden. He's over eighty. One forgets.'

'I never think of him as any special age.'

'And he has left you Thwaite,' she said, her eyes on the confusion of the world below.

'Oh Maitland – did we dream it? Has he?'

'Yes. I knew already. He's talked about it. After all, you know Polly, he is your grandfather.'

The family next to us were called by a ferocious Red Cross captain with a fine, permanent wave, and bulged and pushed past us wildly, treading on feet.

'What!'

'Your grandfather, of course.'

'D'you mean – '

'Emma – your mother – was his daughter.'

'But how could – Maitland! D'you mean – ? Aunt Frances?'

'No, no. Mr Thwaite never cared for your Aunt Frances very much except as a sister. It was Miss Younghusband he was in love with, your Aunt Mary. She was a raving beauty when she was young – or so I understand.'

'But you can't mean – ' The world tipped and reeled as the uniting families tipped and reeled about us. 'Aunt Mary!'

'No – your Aunt Mary wasn't your grandmother either, though she was old enough – twenty years older than your mother. Your Aunt Mary wanted to marry him but unfortunately – or fortunately since the result has been you, Polly dear – he then fell in love with her mother.'

'What, the – ? The battle-axe bosom? Grandmother Younghusband? The one who had *Fanny Hill?*'

'I know nothing of any Fanny Hill. I don't think she had

more children still, though from all accounts the Archdeacon might not have noticed – '

'But she couldn't. She couldn't! Mr Thwaite must have been so young. And Grandmother so very old.'

'He was twenty. She was forty. I am told.'

'But it's terrible.'

'A little strange,' said Maitland, 'but Victorian life is full of surprises. And the Archdeacon, you know, was almost obsessed with stones – and God, of course. I think I'll just pop out on to the station and see about some more sandwiches.'

I sat looking at Mr Thwaite. Mr Thwaite at twenty, the lover of the warrior mother of Aunt Mary, the ice-maiden. I thought of Aunt Mary in the taxi on the way to Aunt Frances's wedding, her face growing whiter and whiter under the wonderful ancient hat. And Mr Thwaite clearing his throat all the time and looking at the rain. And the tension mounting, mounting, so that at last it broke in the storm of my crying. And how I had been unable to stop the crying because of the awful confusion in the air.

Poor Mr Thwaite – conceiving my mother in some fit of pubic madness (I looked at his face – a long brown map, the eyes closed in their deep sockets just like – well, yes: the photograph of my mother in the cardboard mountains with the crease down the middle, tired out in Liverpool.) Had he loved her – his daughter? Had he even been to see her? He must have had to stop coming to the yellow house quite suddenly after it happened. And no explanation to Aunt Mary.

I mean – how *could* he have explained? How tell a girl he had wanted to marry that he had conceived a child by her mother? Well – but it was Borgian!

Poor Aunt Mary – her spoons and her prie-dieu.

Well then, and what a frightful, frightful man, this Arthur Thwaite. What a villain. And yet – oh no.

But what a grandmother I had had! What a terrible woman. And yet – the loneliness, the husband, quietly turning pages, singing hymns as he bounded into the sea. Gazing at stones. Poor woman.

*

211

So much never to be known.

*

And all that church!

*

Mr Thwaite stirred and woke and looked at me with blue eyes – oh heavens, mine again – and smiled.

'No progress?'

'No progress. Maitland's gone for sandwiches. It's all going awfully slowly.'

'I'll just nod off again then.'

I could not stop looking at him – dropping again easily into sleep, his hands (Oh Lord! My thumb!) crossed on the head of the silver-headed walking-stick.

Oh Lord God – men!

What men I'd known – cautious, inadequate, shadowy, grasping, dull. Maybe it was just bad luck. At any rate Mr Thwaite on one occasion had been none of these things. My grandmother on one astounding night (though maybe more? Maybe dozens? Maybe not even at night?) on at least one astounding occasion had admitted to some forgotten bed at Thwaite or the yellow house or even Danby Wiske – springs squeaking, feathers heaving – oh Lord! – one gloriously incautious man.

'Egg and cress,' said Maitland. 'He's dropped off again. Did I shock you, Polly? Are you sorry to know?'

'No, no – of course not. Did – what did Lady Celia know?'

'Everything of course. She and Mr Thwaite were very close. Always close.'

'You were saying – ' I looked at the egg and cress, the taut dried-out upward curve of the railway sandwich – 'You were saying that you and Mr Thwaite are very close, too?'

'Oh yes.'

'He's been quite a – successful sort of man with women hasn't he? I mean, I always adored him as a girl. It's interesting to know that there are such men. Usually they're only in novels.'

'Oh, he's very successful,' said Maitland comfortably. 'He's always needed quite a full-blooded life you know. Those arty,

212

bohemian people at Thwaite – he found them very milk-and-water.'

*

We sat in our rows in the gallery. The children's names were called out, oh so slowly; and the children in the morass below us thinned out, oh so slowly – talkative children, tired children, very young children – babies really – numbed grey children, fierce tough children and children who looked older than Abraham. All were beautifully dressed in clothes far too hot for the weather and rather too big. Each had a big luggage label round its neck. Some carried parcels, some carried dolls and bears, some leaned against each other on the benches with fingers in their mouths. As time passed, some slept.

At four o'clock in the afternoon there were still sixty or so children left below us. The benches around us full of relations were emptying. We had been brought tea, and something to eat. I ate and drank nothing. I looked. Two children were mine? Which, which, which?

'Why are we so near the end? Haven't they come? I can't see properly. They all have their backs to us now.'

'It is administered alphabetically,' said Mr Thwaite awaking from the present nap. 'We shall be near the end.'

'A great many Jews are zeds,' said Maitland. 'Let's hope these of Polly's are top of the zeds.'

*

But they were not. By six o'clock the great mass of children had thinned to a scatter, but ours were still not called.

Which, which, which.

Theo's children. Theo's and mine.

Seven o'clock. They had thinned to half a dozen, and the half a dozen didn't look very special ones. Six times at least my heart had thumped when I thought I saw Theo's turn of the head, Theo's smile – or Rebecca's red hair, long legs. Very quiet, wan children these last ones, crumpled on the benches now, and I allowed myself to think, in order to prepare myself for disappointment: mine may be resentful, sullen, ugly-minded children. Think what has been happening to them. Worse – I tried to think very rationally – they might look or be like Delphi Vipont – the Delphi who had looked

213

at me forty years ago and at whom I had looked back and our dislike had bitten into both of us.

If two small Delphis awaited me?

But, 'Zeit? Flint?' nodded the Red Cross captain in my ear and I went down alone to the hall and saw two thin girls standing by the desk. One was curly and one was straight. They had the wooden faces of people blotched with tiredness but refusing to cry. The taller girl was clutching a book, she had kept her finger in the place she had reached when she had been called away to me. The little one held a doll, a bear, a china horse, and a lop-eared rabbit and had Theo's eyes.

We said goodbye to Maitland and Mr Thwaite at York, Maitland most anxious and reluctant to go, Mr Thwaite, with a porter behind him pushing the luggage and the topee box, clearly relieved that all was done.

I was totally confident, rattling along in flowing German and as comfortable as if I had visited London every week of my life.

Hepzibah, Rebecca and I.

We changed trains at Darlington into the little train that ran down through the steel-works and out on to the marsh – or where the marsh had been. The great flames and plumes of fire still rose from where they were smelting the iron bars, the same long crocodiles of trucks, long puddles in the mud, long clanking pipes and rough old machines, and on the hills opposite, the woods still grew sparse so that the light shone through them like knitting-loops when you draw the needle out.

But the marsh was almost invisible now. So small.

It was afternoon – the afternoon of the next day and of course, since we were getting near the yellow house it had begun to rain. 'I did so want you to see it sunny,' I said. 'Look Hepzibah – do look out of the window even if it's dreary. It's where Daddy lived. Leave the book for ten seconds.'

'Oh pretty,' said Hepzibah, looking at The New House as the train clattered by. 'What's that thing on the roof?' and then back to the book – which as far as I could see was rubbish.

'A telescope.'

'They're doing something to it,' said Beccy.

'It was your father's. I'm afraid they're taking it down. They keep doing that. It's because of the – '

'The War,' said Beccy looking at the lop-eared rabbit.

'Daddy'll get here,' said Hepzibah firmly. Beccy leaned her head against my side.

'It's quite near,' I said, when we reached our station, 'we can walk if you like. Mr Boagey will bring the luggage on later for us. Would you like that?'

'I won't leave my things,' said Hepzibah, 'I'm not moving without my things.' She was thirteen. There was trouble coming.

'I'm staying with Tante Polly,' said Beccy. 'You go in the taxi, Hep, with the luggage.'

*

So Beccy and I came striding over the tarmac road and across the last tail-end of marsh to the yellow house.

'Is that ours?' she said.

'Yes. Ours. It's a funny old house.'

'It's wonderful,' she said, 'like a big ship.'

And so we blew in through the great front door, held open for us by Alice, with Hepzibah and the luggage alongside her in the hall. The doors slammed and the sea crashed and the windows shook, and we were all safe home.

THE END

A Victorian study. Shelves floor to ceiling, almost empty of books, but a few objects: a sewing box, a sherry decanter, a framed drawing.

A large sash window shows an expanse of moving sky – big, sea-going, creamy clouds. The furniture is contemporary (1986) sparse but pleasant. A gigantic television set has its back to the audience. One corner of the room is shadowy.

Beside the door an answerphone and an old woman – still tall, her hair still thick and brown and swept up on to the top of her head in a frisky twirl. Ankles rather swollen. Her cheeks, once round and rosy, have dropped a bit, pinching up the mouth. She wears a flamboyant shawl.

She speaks into the answerphone:

POLLY FLINT: Could you speak louder? The traffic –
                Could you speak louder? The door is very
                thick.
                Oh dear me, yes. The memoirs.
                I'd forgotten the memoirs.
                Oh dear, oh dear – I should be locked up.
                Well I suppose I am locked up. I've locked
                myself up. Just a moment. Just a moment.
                Will you wait till I find the key?

She flicks down the switch, walks vaguely here and there, dabbing about on the shelves, on the chimney piece.

In the shadowy corner a shadowy figure begins to become apparent. It sits facing the television set. After a time POLLY FLINT *eases her old self down into a chair also facing the set. Outside the yellow house the traffic zips past continually. At its gates there is a busy roundabout. Beyond them the old Iron-Works stand, dwarfed by the huge chemical city which has grown round them, its chimneys like silver pencils, its cooling towers like vast Christmas puddings decorated with a spaghetti*

216

of pipes. They are beautiful and weird. The yellow house sitting in the middle of them is bizarre.

At the back of the house the great front door is little changed but a journalist is sitting on the steps. She has cock's-comb hair, all-in-one leather hose, is knitting a fluffy sweater and smoking a cigarette.

Round the corner after a time a car comes bumping and a black-eyed, dumpy, talkative woman gets out.

BECCY BOAGEY	The traffic's frightful. I can never park outside. Some day I'll sink in this sand. Good morning. I'm Beccy Boagey. I'm the parson's wife.
JOURNALIST	I'm Charlotte Box. *North-Eastern Gazette.*
BECCY	Well, there's no point waiting, dear, I'm afraid. She won't see you. She won't see reporters. She's very old.
JOURNALIST	It's an appointment. She'll see me. I'm not on about this nuclear thing. I was in her Confirmation Class. She knows me. I'm after her memoirs.
BECCY	You'll be lucky.
JOURNALIST	Yes, I will. I am. She likes me. She has a laugh at me. Being called Charlotte Box. I don't know why.
BECCY	She's had a time lately.

The vicar's wife, Beccy Zeit, rings the bell, screams into an answerphone that she's Beccy and please let me in Tante Polly. The metal grille crackles but there is no reply.

	She does this I'm afraid. Locks herself in. Then when she comes to look for the key she forgets what she's looking for.

She gives another great peal on the bell and then sits by Journalist.

JOURNALIST	I don't blame her, do you? Not moving. I wouldn't move. Not to make way for nuclear waste I wouldn't. Making way for rubbish. It's a lovely house. It ought to be preserved or something.
BECCY	I believe it was once, but then there was a compulsory purchase. She dug herself in. With the nuns. The house is let to some

217

	nuns. They've dug themselves in, too. They live round at the back.
JOURNALIST	Oh, they'll never do it – The Government. The nuclear waste. The dumping of nuclear waste. They'd never dare.
BECCY	There's plenty of room for it, you know. There always has been. Under the Hall Estate there are great salt caves you can run lorries round. They've been used for years as store rooms though nobody seems to have known about it.
JOURNALIST	They catch on slow round here.
BECCY	I never saw the salt caves. For this nuclear waste. But we weren't here for very long, when I was young. The war came and we were evacuated to Thwaite School.
JOURNALIST	That started here, didn't it? Thwaite school? You're Miss Flint's some sort of daughter, aren't you?
BECCY	She adopted me. She adopted me and my sister. We were Jewish refugees. My father sent us from Germany. They'd been lovers of some sort. I never exactly heard. I never saw my family of course again.
JOURNALIST	I heard. Weren't they – ?
BECCY	Yes, Auschwitz. All of them. My sister and I came out of Germany on the second from last train. My father hesitated. He was a great hesitater. Though usually he was lucky.
JOURNALIST	You must have been little. Coming all that way to England. Did you only know Miss Flint?
BECCY	We didn't even know Miss Flint. We thought she was a bit mad at first. But she spoke German. We felt safe with her. Soon we loved her. We'd had no mother for a long time you see. She'd gone off when we were babies. She died at Dresden.
JOURNALIST	And your father at Auschwitz. Oh my God!
BECCY	Oh no. My father didn't die in Auschwitz. The rest of the family, not my father. Don't

218

ask me how he survived. I asked him and he said, 'All that I can say is that I do not know.' He had the number across his wrist. He used to cover it with his other hand gripped tight. It's all I can remember of him really, though I was seventeen by then. That and the look of him on the white seat by the privet hedge.

JOURNALIST   Here? He didn't come back here?

BECCY   Yes. Oh dear me – where is Tante Polly? We'll have to go round to the back. The nuns keep a key for when this happens.

JOURNALIST   I didn't know your father came back. They all say Miss Flint's a – well –

BECCY   An old virgin? So indecent. Yes. She is. It was a terrible shock his coming back. It was one morning in the summer and my sister Hep – you know her? Yes. It is that one. The international lawyer. She runs Europe. Hep had got up early to work. She was taking the Scholarship to Oxford – which she won of course with twenty stars – and while she was dressing she looked out of the window, and then she came upstairs to me. I had the little attic bedroom – the crow's nest where the poor maids used to sleep in the bad old days. I liked it. Tante had made it lovely. So then Hepzibah and I both looked out of the window. And then – it was odd. Hepzibah being so bossy and always trying to be in charge. She simply said, 'Come on,' and we went down into Tante's room and stood there, looking down at her in bed. She's rather large you know – or she was. She was lying there asleep, rather splendid. And she opened her eyes on us in the early light, and looked. Then she got out of bed and went to the window and said, 'Stay here,' and put on her slippers and a queer old coat – but she looked beautiful.

And we saw her walk in to the garden to

219

the awful-looking thing on the seat. And they stood looking at each other, and the wind blew Tante's nightdress about. Then she brought him in to us.

JOURNALIST   And he stayed?

BECCY   Yes. He died soon.

JOURNALIST   They didn't marry?

BECCY   I think it had gone beyond that.

JOURNALIST   They were old?

BECCY   No, no. It was not important. Let's get the key from the nuns.

*

In the book-room inside the yellow house POLLY FLINT is seated looking at a television screen which does not seem to be switched on. The bright window is behind her, the clouds soaring along. In the shadow the other shadowy figure is now rather more defined.

POLLY FLINT   I was looking – what was I looking for? I don't know – losing things, forgetting things. The key. And I knew she was coming, the journalist. Dear Charlotte Box. For my memoirs.

CRUSOE   My creator was a great believer in memoirs.

POLLY FLINT   So impossible, so false. Talking about memories.

CRUSOE   Oh, I don't know. My creator had quite a facility. Stood him in very good stead. Memoirs.

POLLY FLINT   Nonsense – he made it all up. Fiction isn't memory.

CRUSOE   But memory is fiction. I tell you my creator had no compunction – well, here I am, for a start.

POLLY FLINT   Making things up from nothing is another matter. An easier matter.

CRUSOE   He didn't quite do that. I'm not sure that I was easy, exactly. I believe I quite tired him. Even God had to rest on the Seventh Day.

POLLY FLINT   Your creator must have been ready for a rest by the end of Book Three. I'll concede that.

220

CRUSOE	He said something of the sort. He said that I tended to take charge.
POLLY FLINT	You are apt to do that.
CRUSOE	Can't think why. I'm very ordinary.
POLLY FLINT	Yes – Dickens thought so.
CRUSOE	Never met him.
POLLY FLINT	I never thought so, though. You've lasted me out, Crusoe.
CRUSOE	You're not dead yet. You may find another yet, Pol Flint.
POLLY FLINT	Not at eighty-seven.
CRUSOE	You never know. Your mind may begin to wander.
POLLY FLINT	It has never done anything else. But you're the only – You have been my great love.
CRUSOE	That was your misfortune. Your heart was never thoroughly in it, Pol. Loving real men. You were after the moon.
POLLY FLINT	One ought to be after the moon. And what do you know? My heart was in nothing else but love for years and years. Like a dumpling in broth.
CRUSOE	My creator liked a homely phrase. Pol Flint – your men were all duds or shadows.
POLLY FLINT	The men one meets are matters of luck. I was properly kissed once. On Darlington Station. I can remember that.
CRUSOE	I know nothing of it. Pol Flint – you know that I never loved you?
POLLY FLINT	Yes.
CRUSOE	I have made you happy. But I have never loved you.
POLLY FLINT	Yes.
CRUSOE	Characters in fiction cannot make new departures. We are eunuchs. Frozen eunuchs.
POLLY FLINT	Maybe we are all just fiction.
CRUSOE	Don't be ridiculous. You are talking like a satirist. Like that fool, Swift.
POLLY FLINT	He thought nothing of you, either. Maybe your creator, maybe Defoe himself, was only

a character in fiction. Nobody really knows. He had a lot of disguises – very queer. All those warts, and the stoop. And in the pillory and prison. He sired you at sixty. An unlikely man.

CRUSOE   A perfectly ordinary journalist. Bit of genius. In a minute you'll be on about what is fiction.

POLLY FLINT   No I won't. I'm over fiction. As I'm over drink. I keep cream sherry for the nuns and watch them sip, all nods and smiles. As I nod and smile when people talk about the importance of art. I cleared the shelves after all. That gave you a shock Crusoe, didn't it? When I sent all the books to Thwaite School? Marooned all over again.

CRUSOE   Well, you kept me.

POLLY FLINT   Of course. And a few others. A few since your day, too, dear Crusoe. But on the whole, it's all over now.

CRUSOE   What, fiction? Or you having affairs with novels?

POLLY FLINT   Both.

CRUSOE   Fiction'll fade out?

POLLY FLINT   It won't fade out, but it will have to change. It's become quite canonically boring – all about politics or marital discord. The minutiae. You should see the fiction they have thought up about you and Friday.

CRUSOE   Yes, well, he could be very trying.

POLLY FLINT   We don't have heroes now. We shan't see your like again.

CRUSOE   You didn't see my like before. I was an innovation. Though I was but a plain man.

POLLY FLINT   Yes. But you became immortal. There are no immortals now.

CRUSOE   No, no. I was just a man. I can't think why I still hang about. I do hang about, don't I? It's not just you?

POLLY FLINT   Oh yes you're still here. They put you in

	films and song-and-dance acts. They've had you On Ice.
CRUSOE	However did they do the footprint? My setting of course was good. He knew all the best sites. And very exciting. He knew about excitement, my creator.
POLLY FLINT	Novels aren't exciting now. Just writers rambling on.
CRUSOE	How curious. In my creator's day writers hated one another.
POLLY FLINT	Oh they do now. Great haters.
CRUSOE	Ah yes. Knew very few.

(*Pause for thought.*)

	I did think it was all rather moving of course. My battle. My courage. The way I dealt with things, all those years.
POLLY FLINT	Let's not boast.
CRUSOE	Our weaknesses begin to show in old age.
POLLY FLINT	But you're ageless, Crusoe. You were new and yet eternal. You were 'novel'. Dramatic. Poetic. You could tell the tale. You nourish us.
CRUSOE	Like bread.
POLLY FLINT	You were my bread. You are my bread.
CRUSOE	That sounds like blasphemy.
POLLY FLINT	Quite a few people see an affinity between you and Jesus Christ. They are given grants for theses on the subject.
CRUSOE	These are blasphemers.
POLLY FLINT	Oh, quite often people confuse their fictional heroes with God. As they confuse their human lovers. Or themselves. It is a great hindrance to a happy life. Emily Brontë did it. So did Proust.
CRUSOE	I don't know them. Should I care for them?
POLLY FLINT	You'd find conversation difficult with Proust.
CRUSOE	Pol – I think you should find that key. The journalist's been on the step for quite twenty minutes. It is a great profession. You should remember my creator and treat it with respect.

POLLY FLINT   I'll look in a moment.

She sits back in the button-back chair. The sky outside darkens. The CRUSOE-shape grows clearer – shaggy beard, tattery garments, great hairy-mushroom umbrella, suspicion of parrot on shoulder. As this figure grows grander and bolder, POLLY FLINT's figure begins to fade. Now she looks old. Her cheeks sag. Old, knobbed hands drop down, slide off her lap. Her head rests sideways at a gentle angle. Her mouth hangs open a bit. CRUSOE has become a Titan.

CRUSOE (*rambling. Even Crusoe grows old*)

You've been a good and faithful woman, Pol Flint, and children love you. A room of empty shelves, but still half in love with books. Is it enough? A quiet life. But Godly – and some of that because of me. As a life, not bad. Marooned of course. But there's something to be said for islands.

POLLY FLINT   Good night.

CRUSOE   You know, when my wife died, there were children. There was a daughter. We don't hear about the daughter. What became of her?

POLLY FLINT   Goodbye, Crusoe, Robin Crusoe.

CRUSOE   Goodbye, Pol Flint.

THE ART OF
ANTHONY TROLLOPE

THE ART OF
ANTHONY
TROLLOPE

Geoffrey Harvey

WEIDENFELD AND NICOLSON
London

Sections of this book originally appeared in
slightly different form in *ARIEL, Wascana
Review, Texas Studies in Literature and
Language, Studies in English Literature* and
the *Yearbook of English Studies*.

ISBN 0 297 77728 9

Printed in Great Britain by
Willmer Brothers Limited
Rock Ferry, Merseyside

To my Mother and in memory of my Father

CONTENTS

Acknowledgements

I should like to thank the staffs of several libraries for their invaluable assistance: the Brynmor Jones Library of the University of Hull, the Bodleian, the British Library, the Folger Shakespeare Library, Washington, D.C., the John Rylands Library of the University of Manchester, and the Killam Library of Dalhousie University.

I am particularly grateful to Professor Arthur Pollard, who encouraged my study of Trollope in its early stages and offered much timely guidance. Thanks are also due to my former colleagues at Dalhousie University, especially Dr Allan Bevan and Dr Gary Waller, for their lively and critical interest in my work. More recently I have received encouragement from my colleagues at Bulmershe College of Higher Education, notably Dennis Butts, and I am indebted to Christine MacLeod for her meticulous reading of my manuscript. Nevertheless, I am of course solely responsible for what follows.

Parts of this book have appeared in a slightly different form in the following journals: *ARIEL* (1975), *Wascana Review* (1975), *Texas Studies in Literature and Language* (1976), *Studies in English Literature* (1976) and the *Yearbook of English Studies* (1979). I am grateful to the editors and to the Board of Governors of the University of Calgary, the University of Saskatchewan, the University of Texas Press, William Marsh Rice University and the Modern Humanities Research Association for permission to reprint.

Finally I wish to record my gratitude to my wife and family for suffering my work on Trollope with such patience.

A Note on References

Since there is no standard or complete edition of Trollope's works, quotations from the novels and the *Autobiography* are taken from the Oxford World's Classics editions, as being those most readily available to the reader, with the exception of *An Eye for An Eye*, which was published by Anthony Blond (London, 1966). Where these are double volume editions, I have indicated parenthetically in my text both the page and volume numbers.

The following abbreviations are used throughout the notes for works cited frequently:

An Autobiography	Anthony Trollope, *An Autobiography*, (Oxford, World's Classics, 1953, reprinted 1961).
Letters	*The Letters of Anthony Trollope*, ed. Bradford A. Booth (London, 1951).
Marginalia	Folger Shakespeare Library, Washington, D.C., Trollope's marginalia in his editions of the early drama.
Papers	Bodleian Library, Oxford, *Trollope*, Papers Relating to His Work, 3 vols., MS. Don. C.9., C.10., C.10*.
Thackeray	Anthony Trollope, *Thackeray* (London, 1879).

I

INTRODUCTION

IN spite of their varying estimates of Trollope's fiction and their conflicting interpretations of his individual novels, critics are virtually unanimous about the existence of a 'Trollope problem'. Most obviously there is the strange ambiguity of his position in the critical hierarchy of Victorian novelists, especially when some half dozen of his novels are by any standards first-rate fiction. Then there is the fact that, in contrast to his fellow novelists, we still have no complete edition of his works. However, the major problem facing critics striving to come to grips with this most apparently substantial yet in many ways most elusive of Victorian writers, has been succinctly summarized by C. P. Snow in a perceptive essay on Trollope's craft: 'Trollope wrote so much and, of all writers, he is the one least adapted for most kinds of academic approach. How do you dig into him? And with what books?'[1] What critics have tended to do is to construct their own Trollope, dipping into his many novels according to their own particular interests. And the Trollopes so created are many and varied – the entertainer, the psychological writer, the moralist, the political novelist, and the social historian. This present study is no exception and in it I propose to discuss my own Trollope: Trollope the artist.

As C. P. Snow intimates, the central question is whether Trollope is accessible to standard critical procedures, for he is not a symbolic or poetic novelist, nor a novelist of ideas, nor indeed a technical innovator in any obvious sense. However, James R. Kincaid, who is optimistic that we now have a criticism capable of dealing with Trollope, believes that 'the growing strength of formalist and structuralist criticism may spring Trollope from the historicist trap in which even his admirers had placed him'.[2] But is it really necessary or useful to 'spring' Trollope from the 'historicist trap'? I do not believe that it is; for perhaps more than any other English novelist Trollope is truly representative of his age, as regards both his choice of material and the form of his fiction. My intention is to show how his art draws its strength from its roots in the Victorian ethos and particularly from the critical debates on the form of the novel which were current during the peak of his writing career.

A fundamental aspect of the 'Trollope problem' is the fact that his personality and his literary career possessed many curious features. His fiction exerted a fascination over the intellectual and the common reader alike. Not only was he admired by such distinguished writers as George Eliot, Henry James, Tolstoy and Shaw, but, as R. C. Terry reminds us, he was a continuing favourite with readers who subscribed to Charles Mudie's great circulating library, which dominated English middle-class reading habits. Indeed Trollope was read quite widely until well into this century, reaching a peak of popularity around 1900.[3] More interesting perhaps, is the contradiction between the man and his novels. 'Some of Trollope's acquaintances', remarks Frederick Locker-Lampson, 'used to wonder how so commonplace a person could have written such excellent novels'.[4] Indeed, several of his contemporaries commented on the dichotomy between the ebullient, fox-hunting extrovert and the subtle, often coolly ironic novelist. In public Trollope was a magnetic, vital, popular figure, but in private he was extremely reticent, even in his correspondence. And this habitual reserve was not broken even in his *Autobiography* which, if anything, deepens rather than elucidates the mystery. Indeed, he asserts quite bluntly that he has deliberately omitted giving us a record of his inner life.[5] And as far as his art is concerned, his references are exasperatingly casual because, as he claimed jocularly, he did not believe that he would be read into the next century.[6] The truth is, I think, that the *Autobiography* is really a very defensive document. It was commenced in 1867, the year of Trollope's greatest popularity after the enormous success of *The Last Chronicle of Barset*, and was written almost as a way of explaining to himself his amazing good fortune and of justifying his chosen profession. So it serves to perpetuate the paradoxes: the discrepancy between Trollope's treatment of his novels as marketable goods and his desire to vindicate his calling by writing a history of the novel, and between the cavalier way he refers to his own work and the care and discipline he advocates to everyone who asks his advice about writing.

Self-doubt goes a long way towards explaining why Trollope took such pains to conceal his indisputable commitment to his art. His defensiveness, both as a man and as an artist, can be traced to his childhood. There were the three miserable years at Harrow from the age of seven until his tenth year, where he felt awkward and disreputable because of his stupidity, his shyness and the poverty of his dress, and where the feeling was impressed upon him that he would never manage to succeed like his fellow pupils.[7] Then followed a period of utter friendlessness at Winchester College while his family moved to Cincinnati, and a shame-faced return to Harrow, this time as an even shabbier boy, when the family fortunes declined. Self-distrust became engrained in him during this desolate time of his life. Like Dickens, he was a gentleman's son who was not treated as such by his school-fellows. He felt isolated and intensely lonely, and it was during this period, as he reveals in his *Autobiography*, that he escaped into a private world of make-believe which became the foundation of his later writing. And these sad, enervating years were followed by an equally desperate period as an usher in a school in Brussels (where his duties included teaching classics to thirty boys) until, following the deaths of his brother, his father and his sister, he was sent in 1834 at the age of nineteen to work in London as a junior clerk at the General Post Office. We learn very little from the *Autobiography* about this period, which lasted seven long years; however Trollope's treatment of young men living in London in *The Three Clerks, The Small House at Allington, Phineas Finn* and *Ralph the Heir* presents a cumulative picture of intense loneliness, uncertainty and lack of purpose.

Even though Trollope himself is reticent about them, we should not underestimate the effect on him of these early experiences. One obvious consequence was the fact that when success finally overtook him in the 1860s he grasped it firmly and enjoyed it to the full. During this decade he had twenty novels in various stages of publication. He also cooperated with Thackeray on the *Cornhill*, founded the *Fortnightly Review*, wrote plays and essays, was elected Chairman of the Garrick Club Committee, stood for Parliament, and acquired many friends highly placed in the professions and in London literary circles. The assaults made on his self-respect during his boyhood had served to nurture his ambition. When the opportunity presented itself he endeavoured to succeed in a wide field of activities – in the public service, writing, politics, editing and amateur scholarship. But the habit of self-deprecation, which was deeply engrained in him, was intensified rather than assuaged by success. The more triumphant he was, the more fragile his success seemed, and the more vulnerable he felt. This is perhaps best illustrated by Frederic Harrison's anecdote about Trollope describing his method of work to a gathering at George Eliot's home. Trollope and George Eliot were close friends. She respected his writing and indeed revealed that *The Way We Live Now* had given her the courage to persevere with *Middlemarch*. But she was an intellectual and Trollope was not. Because he felt intimidated he told his story about writing for three hours every day at the rate of two hundred and fifty words every quarter of an hour. George Eliot replied that there were days when she could not write even a line. " 'Yes', said Trollope, 'with imaginative work like yours that is quite natural; but with my mechanical stuff it's a sheer matter of industry. It's not the head that does it – it's the cobbler's wax on the seat and the sticking to my chair!' "[8]

But if this comment includes a measure of self-denigration as well as admiration for a superior novelist, it also contains a hard-headed realism. Like all professional writers, Trollope was acutely aware that art was only partly inspiration; the rest was hard work, and it is in order to debunk the romantic attitude to writing that he refers to himself crudely as a rustic driving pigs to market.[9] But an important insight into Trollope's underlying commitment to his art is given by his contemporary T. H. S. Escott, who remarks that '[f]ew writers, perhaps, have taken themselves more in earnest than Trollope'.[10] This is corroborated in Trollope's monograph on his friend Thackeray, which reveals his understanding that a writer possesses special gifts. A man should write a book, he says, 'because it is in him to write it, – the motive power being altogether in himself and coming from his desire to express himself'.[11] Thackeray also contains a homely description of the way Trollope himself worked by ceaseless observation and reflection: 'forethought', he affirms, 'is the elbow-grease which a novelist, – or a poet, or dramatist, – requires'.[12] This preparation for writing, the long gestation of characters and incidents, was rooted in the habit of day-dreaming which he had formed in childhood; indeed, in his later years much of his inner life, he tells us, was passed in the company of the Pallisers.[13] And although by his own admission Trollope was primarily a novelist of character, he understood the crucial importance of form. Referring to *Framley Parsonage*, he talks of the power of fitting the beginning to the end,[14] while his criticism of the novel of his young protégée, Kate Field, focuses on the fact that 'the end of [her] story should have been the beginning'.[15]

Of course these comments are not profound criticism. Trollope was not an intellectual critic; he wrote as a practising novelist. And in any case the bluffness of his critical remarks is often part of his defensive mask. However, most accounts of Trollope would have us believe that, although he was the son of a woman who in her day was a famous writer, and despite the fact that he was the close friend of novelists, dramatists and critics like Thackeray, George Eliot, Charles Reade, Bulwer-Lytton, George Henry Lewes, Sir Henry Taylor and Richard Holt Hutton, he was nevertheless a writer who possessed little theoretic conception of his art. In this book I am concerned to argue that this view, although abetted by Trollope himself, flies in the face of probability. Trollope knew better than most that art is artificial. Like most other writers he recognized that realism is only a convention, but unlike them he said so unequivocally:

'And yet in very truth the realistic must not be true – but just so far removed from truth as to suit the erroneous idea of truth which the reader may be supposed to entertain'.[16] Realism for Trollope is 'that which shall seem to be real'.[17] It should not surprise us then, that his art is altogether a more subtle and a more conscious business than his own cobbling metaphor suggests, or than critics have believed. However, in spite of the recent remarkable rise of critical interest in Trollope, the image of him as a rather pedestrian writer somehow persists. The sheer quantity, bulk and comprehensiveness of his writing throughout his career means that the form of his novels has not been given sufficiently serious critical attention. His work is too often equated with the study of the surface of social life, with the conventional or accidental ending, with lack of finesse in plotting and construction, with a garrulous interest in character and with padding and irrelevance. But the form of Trollope's novels is a striking aspect of his art, and it is his scrupulous concern with this area of his writing that forms the substance of this present study. And not art simply in the narrow formal sense, but also as an expression of the conventions within which the Victorian novelist wrote. Far from believing that Trollope needs to be rescued from the 'historicist trap', in my view the sheer complexity of the artistic achievement in his major novels can only be understood by a careful consideration of his art within the immediate historical context of contemporary critical theory.

The form of Trollope's novels encompasses both his moral vision of the world and his communication of it to the reader. It may thus be regarded as a relation between moral vision, structure and effect, which corresponds to the relation between author, novel and reader and which expresses that relation within the novel itself. Briefly then, Trollope's created 'world' and its expression inhere in the novel by means of form. It may be objected that my use of the term 'form' is too imprecise to be useful, but I hope that the following discussion and my reading of the individual novels will amplify and define it further. Of course there are many different aspects of form, just as there are many facets of vision and methods of communication, but those which Trollope employs with consumate skill seem to me, considering the weight of both internal and external evidence, to derive mainly from the major formal conventions within which the Victorian novelist worked: the drama, the omniscient author and the serial mode of publication. The influence of the drama on the art of such novelists as Dickens, Wilkie Collins and Charles Reade is, of course, well known. But its impact on the form of the Victorian novel was more pervasive than that. As S. W. Dawson has put it: 'it was not until the nineteenth century that the possibility arose of a dramatic form capable of surpassing the drama of the theatre in depth and vitality'.[18] It is significant, I think, that almost without exception the major as well as the minor novelists nursed an ambition to succeed in the theatre. Nearly all of them wrote plays, many of which achieved public performance. However, because the best of these writers felt the urgent need to give artistic expression to the dynamic thrust of social change in mid-Victorian England, they discovered that the only appropriate form for their work was the expansive form of the novel rather than the restricted form of the drama. This is immediately evident when we examine Trollope's own writing and compare the sweeping social panorama of *The Last Chronicle of Barset* with the cramped, stilted play *Did He Steal It?*, which he boiled down from the novel; or the maturity of moral insight and social observation apparent in *Can You Forgive Her?* which is so sadly absent from the earlier play *The Noble Jilt*, on which it is partly based. Trollope fully shared the Victorian writers' ambition for success in the theatre, and in spite of the fact that his two plays were still-born he nevertheless remained fascinated by the drama and was greatly stimulated by the contemporary critical debate about the possibility of creating a genuinely dramatic form in the novel. As a consequence, in the 1860s while at the peak of his fame, Trollope succumbed to the temptation to experiment that resulted in his astonishing production of a series of anonymous novels. Brief, single-plotted works, each is prefaced by a list of dramatis personae and falls into three well defined 'acts'. Moreover, each possesses dramatic compression and intensity together with a sense of closure and

7

completion, and Trollope clearly aims at the creation of a tragic, fatalistic world. However, his multi-plotted novels, which gained much greater maturity and artistic control during this decade, are also rooted formally in the drama, in this case the ampler conventions employed by the Jacobeans. In these novels the subsidiary plots form an ironic or even cynical counterpoint to the main plot, and the pattern is open-ended. Characters are given more freedom, life is less predictable and the action displays greater social complexity. This more flexible form supports the moral articulation of the novels in an unobtrusive way, not only because it takes hundreds of pages to work itself through, but also because it is embedded in the density of realistic detail. These novels too, in short, possess a far greater formal coherence than critics have recognized.

The narrative or rhetorical element in the mid-Victorian novel largely meant, at least for most contemporary critics and reviewers, the presence of the writer's authentic voice. And although some of the great Victorian novelists might be described as dramatists *manqués*, they saw themselves primarily as storytellers for whom the use of an authorial persona was particularly important. It is most evident in Dickens, George Eliot and Thackeray as well as in Trollope, but its widespread employment had, by the 1860s, become the focus of a fierce debate between those critics who favoured the dramatic form of the novel, which meant the virtual exclusion of the author (one might perhaps call them pre-Jamesian Jamesians) and those who, like George Eliot and Trollope especially, felt that the novel should tell a story. Those who championed the dramatic form, like George Henry Lewes, for instance, did so in the interests of greater artistic unity and formal realism. However, as moralists, George Eliot and Trollope agreed that the novel also had a clear ethical purpose which demanded a peculiar rhetoric of its own.[19] But Trollope made his rhetoric serve ends which were not merely moral but also mimetic and artistic. He made the garrulous, intrusive voice of the author the basis of his realism. In his manifold references to work, social and cultural institutions, leisure pursuits, moral attitudes and the like Trollope's narrative voice builds into the novel those laws by which its world operates, laws similar to those in the real world, in order to convince the reader of its truth without his having to refer outside the novel itself. This use of the author's voice is obviously very different from Dickens's great poetic, atmospheric set pieces, which draw the reader compellingly into the novel until he is no longer aware of its contiguity with the real world. However, although Trollope does achieve the fictional illusion of a self-contained world offered for our involvement, at the same time his numerous asides to the reader, sometimes witty, often cynically deflating, frequently inviting collaboration with the author, are concerned to remind us that art is only art, that fiction is merely fiction. Yet he rarely does so in such a way as to destroy the powerful illusion of reality that he has already achieved. And the effect is plainly moral. It prevents us from becoming too sympathetically immersed in the story, detaching us so that we can also judge its characters, their actions and their world. More importantly, by thus sustaining a profound tension between our imaginative sympathy and our moral scrutiny, Trollope asserts the need for moral relativism, for the necessity to attend scrupulously to the situation of the individual and the pressures exerted by his environment. It is essentially a fluid and open form which encourages us to seek a moral evaluation of the pattern of life presented to us, while reminding us that art is not life and that what we see as pattern may be neither whole nor wholly true. In short, we are enjoined to exercise our moral discrimination at the highest level.

Many mid-Victorian novelists such as Thackeray and the early Dickens for instance, were charged by contemporary reviewers with a formal slackness which was often laid at the door of the hectic convention of serial publication. The novelists' obligation to their public was made more onerous by the proliferation of magazines in the 1860s, each of which carried an instalment of at least one novel. It was a system which encouraged authors to write hand to mouth, and it tended moreover to foster a garrulous intimacy with the reading public. More seriously, the serial convention dictated a form which was rigid, mechanical and which aimed at moving the reader's emotions by a pattern of backward glance and rising intonation, by sensational action followed by curtain-line endings in order to secure suspense and excitement. Rhetorical in the worst sense, it militated against realism, especially the subtle moral realism which was Trollope's particular mode.

As Trollope makes clear in his *Autobiography*, he was well aware of these pitfalls even before he came to write his first serialized novel, *Framley Parsonage*, and he was determined to overcome them. Characteristically, because he is such a careful artist, Trollope achieves much more than that. By paying close attention to the unity and coherence of the serial part, by articulating formal patterns in the novel as a whole and by a judicious use of the author's voice, he creates a series of mnemonic devices which keep the world of the novel and the author's moral view in the reader's mind, achieving in each episode a sense of aesthetic completion together with the tension of foreshadowed development and a feeling of continuity. Thus in Trollope's hands even this obstinate convention is transformed into an art. Its pattern is given greater flexibility and possesses the rhetorical function of continually directing the reader's attention to the wider context of the writer's vision, while also serving our sense of realism, for it parallels our own intermittent apprehension of other people's lives as a continuing serial which we pick up and put down with fluctuating interest as they appear from time to time on our narrow horizons.

Trollope possesses the artistic ability to make a daring extension of the traditional novel conventions because his imagination is a powerful synthesizing force, holding in significant tension these separate aspects of the novel's form. The consequence for his fiction is an art which contains both the pattern and the inconsequentiality of life, the density of a fully realized social world together with the moral and psychological centrality of character. Of course this complex synthesis could only be fully revealed by an exhaustive and, to a certain extent, repetitive and even tedious analysis of a single novel. What I have opted to do instead is to examine these aspects of form separately in those splendid novels, *The Last Chronicle of Barset* and *Orley Farm*, in the fascinating experimental and anonymous works, *Nina Balatka* and *An Eye for An Eye*, and in the excellent and underrated novel, *The Claverings*. I conclude with a more general assessment of Trollope's major achievement in *The Way We Live Now* and *The Prime Minister*. My historical interest in the influences on Trollope's art is reflected in the way each chapter outlines the essential, immediate context of mid-Victorian critical debate on the novel. However, the greatest emphasis in this book falls on Trollope's uses of the drama and these chapters include, together with an examination of the nature of his debts to his vast reading in the Jacobean drama, a detailed account of his employment of the dramatic form in several major novels.

I ought also to explain why, unlike most recent critics, I have not chosen to deal with the bulk of Trollope's fiction, or with his development as a novelist. As my selection of novels indicates, this study is principally concerned with Trollope's writing in the 1860s and early 1870s. There are several reasons for this. Firstly, as the novelist most widely read by the Victorians, Trollope is a fruitful source for the study of generally accepted novel conventions. His contemporary, George Saintsbury, described his popularity thus : 'I do not know that I myself ever took Mr. Trollope for one of the immortals; but really between 1860 and 1870 it might have been excusable so to take him'.[20] And more recently Kenneth Graham has called him the 'High Priest of Victorian realism'.[21] Secondly, it was during this period that the formal conventions of the novel were first seriously discussed and, as David Skilton has demonstrated, Trollope's work naturally became the focus of this debate.[22] The third reason is that, in my view, the period spanning roughly 1860–75, coming after those years in which Trollope struggled to make his reputation with *Barchester Towers* and to consolidate it with the success of *Framley Parsonage*, represents the high-water mark of his writing career, the period during which he matured as a novelist and in which he paid the most serious attention to the practice of his art.

Although I am not really concerned in this book with literary biography, some knowledge of those aspects of Trollope's early life, critical interests and working habits which critics have tended to neglect is essential to a judicious understanding of his art as a novelist and should be given here in brief outline. As Trollope's library catalogue and his prolonged study of Jacobean plays demonstrate, he possessed a profound enthusiasm for the drama.[23] Perhaps it provided an important path back to the memories of amateur theatricals at Julians, the farmhouse near Harrow (later to be the model for Orley Farm) where he experienced probably some of the few bright spots in his solitary and miserable boyhood. Indeed, his family background was steeped in the theatre. His parents shared a particular devotion to Molière, whose works the family enacted, in addition to the usual Renaissance and Restoration drama, in the Julians drawing-room, and later in Brussels, Italy and Cincinnati.[24] Frances Trollope records how Mrs Trollope took her children to see her admired Mlle Mars as Elmire in *Tartuffe* in Paris,[25] and Thomas Trollope notes how the Trollope parents frequently underwent privations in order to appreciate the quality of Mrs Siddons's performance as Lady Macbeth from the pit.[26] Mrs Trollope particularly, threw herself into the world of the theatre, claiming the close friendship of William Charles Macready, Charles Keane, the Kembles, Henry Taylor ('Van Artevelde Taylor' as he was known after his famous historical play) and Mary Russell Mitford.[27] These and others less well known were frequent visitors to Julians, bringing the magical atmosphere of the theatre into the Trollope household.

Trollope's continued interest in the drama is evident during the period 1850–3 when, as his marginalia in his copies of the plays testify, he was engaged in an extensive study of the Jacobean drama and had just completed his first play. His studies recommenced, after a long tour of duty for the Post Office in Ireland, when he returned to London in 1859. The reason, I believe, was the fresh intellectual stimulus which stemmed from success and from new associations. The remarkable popularity of *Framley Parsonage* gained Trollope an invitation to George Smith's first *Cornhill* dinner in 1860. He was well liked and his new circle of friends soon included George Eliot and George Henry Lewes, Edward Bulwer-Lytton, Sir Henry Taylor and Richard Holt Hutton of the *Spectator*. His friendship with

Lewes in particular quickly blossomed. Temperamentally they
complemented each other, they shared an absorbing interest in
acting, the stage and French classical drama, and while Lewes
had been impressed by *Barchester Towers*, Trollope greatly admired Lewes as a critic and a theorist.[28] It is not surprising, therefore, that for a time in the 1860s Trollope was torn between
the neo-Aristotelian aesthetic, espoused by Lewes and Hutton,
which demanded unity and proportion of the dramatic novel,
and the Victorian novelist's instinctive desire, as W.C. Roscoe
noted, to give expression in a more ample and complex form
to his sense of a burgeoning society.[29] This problem was partly
solved for Trollope by his meeting with his mother's old friend
Sir Henry Taylor who, apart from being a famous playwright
himself, nurtured an abiding passion for the Jacobean drama
which rekindled Trollope's dormant enthusiasm for further
study.[30] This spilled over into his creative life and he gradually
perfected a more extensive dramatic form in order to embody
the social realism of his panoramic novels.

Another of Mrs Trollope's friends who also took Trollope
under his wing on his return to England was Edward Bulwer-
Lytton, whose interest, apart from his own novel-writing and
the drama, was the theory of the novel.[31] In the early 1860s
Bulwer-Lytton was working on a series of articles for *Blackwood's Edinburgh Magazine* within which one finds embedded
in embryonic form a theory about the rhetorical interplay of
sympathy with irony in the novel as a means of moving the
reader's emotions while at the same time stimulating his moral
judgement. It is a theory which Trollope repeats almost ver-
batim in his *Autobiography* and in his essay on prose fiction
and which, in my view, he first consciously employed in the
novel he was then working on, *Orley Farm*. And as far as the
serialization of fiction is concerned, Trollope tells us that by the
time he came to write his first serialized novel *Framley Parsonage* for the *Cornhill*, he had learned from the experience of
Dickens, Mrs Gaskell and Thackeray, the dangers of writing
hand to mouth. He was aware of how it impaired the unity of
the novel, how it tempted the author to sensationalize his
material; and because he had already thought long about the

problem he began to devise his own method of serial construction in the 1860s which came to maturity in his third serialized novel, *The Claverings*.

Although this study is primarily concerned with Trollope's art, I hope it also pays due attention to the intellectual substance of that art, for what a close examination of Trollope's practice as a novelist offers the critic who approaches it from a historicist point of view is a fresh perspective on the nature of his social criticism. For the most part critics have not given Trollope's penetrating critique of Victorian society the degree of serious attention that it deserves. For many, Trollope is still an avuncular, conservative figure and they frequently stress his affection for the rural squirearchy, his love of fox-hunting, his bland amusement at diocesan politics and his approving interest in the workings of the professions and the political world. This judgement is apparently strengthened by his own definition of his political creed as being that of an 'advanced conservative Liberal'.[32] But critics tend to emphasize 'conservative' rather than 'advanced', and regard him as being at his most radical a meliorist like Walter Bagehot with whom he has often been compared.[33] However, if we give due weight to Trollope's artistic statements and read his novels paying strict attention to the way their meaning is expressed by their form, we discover that not only is his criticism of English society and its institutions sharper than Bagehot's, but his support of the gradual movement towards democracy is also stronger. Trollope has a keener sense of the still basically feudal nature of English life and he is impatiently hostile, especially in his later novels, to its blind reverence for tradition, its exclusiveness, the rigidity of its class system and its lack of vision and energy. That his true sympathy is with the democrats is evident not only in his book *North America* in which he expresses his admiration for the new-found social mobility and independence of the labouring man, but in the novels as well, and particularly in his approval of men like Daniel Thwaite, Ontario Moggs, Mr Monk and Plantagenet Palliser. And because I believe that Trollope's attitude towards his world generally is rather more radical than critics have thought, it follows that I think the notion of his progress towards pessimism places the emphasis in the wrong quarter. If one thinks of the overwhelmingly tragic tone of an early novel like *The Macdermots of Ballycloran*, or the sardonic attack on the Civil Service in *The Three Clerks*, his satirical analysis of the legal system and its values in *Orley Farm*, his disenchanted view of bourgeois marriage in *The Claverings*, his condemnation of clerical politics in *The Last Chronicle of Barset*, quite apart from the heavy satire and profound pessimism of *The Way We Live Now* and *The Prime Minister*, it is clear that throughout his writing career Trollope possessed, in addition to the comic impulse, a mature, disenchanted vision of the Victorian world.

The appropriate place, it seems to me, to begin to seek the basis of Trollope's social criticism is at that point where the creative process is triggered into activity. And in this respect we are fortunate in knowing something of the extent to which he drew imaginatively on his vast reading in the Jacobean drama. Although, as C. J. Vincent has pointed out, Trollope is in a sense a Victorian Augustan, an heir to the tradition of Jane Austen and Fielding, he can equally be described with some justice as a Victorian Jacobean.[34] Although he was acutely aware of the limitations and absurdities of much of the drama, he discovered affinities with certain dramatists which reveal his cast of mind as having a good deal in common with Middleton and Fletcher – with Middleton's critique of city life and with Fletcher's concern for the individual. Moreover, like theirs, his realism always has a sharp cutting-edge, even in sunny novels like *Barchester Towers* or *The Small House at Allington*, which appear to sanction Victorian morals and manners. Like Middleton, his criticism is directed mainly at the middle classes, at their snobbery, conservatism, greed, hypocrisy and prejudice. Trollope makes the most comprehensive survey of middle-class life that we have in our literature because he wanted to explain to his fellow-Victorians why their society was not as healthy as they pretended. He examines those areas in which real power is vested – the Church, the law, the Civil Service, Parliament, the city and the squirearchy. Although controlled for the most part by ordinary, well-meaning men, as institutions they take on a life of their own. They seek to retain power in the hands of a privileged few and are dedicated with a ferocious though genteel intensity to preserving the *status quo*. That is why Trollope is always on the side of the outsider, even when, like Ferdinand Lopez, he is morally reprehensible. He is concerned to explore those situations in which isolated individuals like Mr Crawley, Miss Mackenzie, Lady Mason, or Lopez threaten the establishment, and in doing so he reveals the frighteningly uniform façade which society presents in its efforts to crush opposition and to preserve cherished illusions, such as the ideals of heroism, Christian faith, social mobility, justice, or the sanctity of hearth and home. These rest upon a fragile social consensus and their defence, Trollope demonstrates, is a process which results in the continual assumption of masks and the dangerous erosion of human individuality.

However, Trollope eschews absolutes. Even when he is at his most satirical, he recognizes much that is praiseworthy in the values of English life and traditions and has faith in the simple goodness of fallible people. His belief in the supreme value of the individual and his right to self-determination demands a moral relativism which makes allowances for the special case and for the intense pressures of a rapidly changing social environment. His fiction therefore encompasses contradiction as the finest realism should, and it is this refusal to reduce his vision of the world, this determination to preserve its multi-faceted quality, that gives to Trollope's novels their unique authenticity.

II
TROLLOPE AND
THE DRAMA

Trollope and the Jacobean Drama

TROLLOPE'S public reputation as one of the foremost exponents of realism in the Victorian novel and his private addiction to the Jacobean drama create an intriguing paradox; but even more fascinating is the influence of these plays on his writing of the novels. The parallels of moral and social pattern are partly due to Trollope's recognition of tensions in his own burgeoning society similar to those evident in the rapidly changing Jacobean world; and the Jacobean dramatists employ several socio-moral themes – the redemption of the prodigal, the impoverishment of the gentry by the rising merchant class, the scrutiny of aristocratic values, the newly subversive spirit of the independent wealthy woman and the testing of the response of feminine virtue to altered social conditions – which reappear in the novels that I wish to discuss in this section: *The Three Clerks, Miss Mackenzie, Ralph the Heir, Lady Anna, The Fixed Period* and *The Prime Minister*. However, the parallels between the plays and the novels are more than simply a general affinity of artistic interests. Since Trollope read and annotated 257 early plays, it is highly probable that some direct borrowing occurred. Indeed, he admits as much in his *Autobiography*: 'How far I may unconsciously have adopted incidents from what I have read, – either from history or from works of imagination, – I do not know. It is beyond question that a man employed as I have been must do so. But when doing it I have not been aware that I have done it'.[1] Moreover, his statement: 'I have found my greatest pleasure in our old English dramatists, – not from any excessive love of their work . . . but from curiosity in searching their plots and examining their characters'[2] suggests the strong likelihood of some specific indebtedness and in two instances at least, as Bradford Booth has demonstrated, Trollope's debts range from verbal echoes of Marlowe's *Doctor Faustus* in *Orley Farm* to his adoption of the plot of *The Old Law*, by Massinger, Middleton and Rowley in *The Fixed Period*.[3]

Surprisingly, in those novels under discussion Trollope does not conflate an amalgam of situations, plots and characters drawn from his immense reading in the Jacobean drama, but rather, with one exception, each novel displays his indebtedness to a particular play which gripped his imagination and which rose to the surface when he was groping for a piece of characterization, an embryonic plot, the development of a theme, or a unifying pattern. Since Trollope was studying the drama rather than poetry, apart from *Doctor Faustus* there are no verbal reminiscences, to clinch the matter of his borrowing. And moreover, although in the case of *The Prime Minister* his marginalia dating of Fletcher's *Women Pleased* offers corroborative evidence, for the most part Trollope's dating is of little assistance because it frequently records that he was reading the play for the fourth or fifth time. It is necessary, therefore, to look beyond verbal echoes, marginalia dating and the socio-moral themes which the plays and novels share, to similarities of characterization, parallels of situation, of plot development, emblematic pattern, the echo of characters' names, or to the presence in the novel of extraneous incidents which indicate a debt to a specific play. Indeed, the closeness of these parallels in the novels that I discuss puts Trollope's borrowing, I think, beyond doubt and reveals that his debts are more extensive than scholars have realized. The evidence also suggests, at least in the case of some novels, that they are more conscious than Trollope recalled them as having been when he wrote the *Autobiography*. It seems likely that with the passage of time his debts had faded from his memory of the novels, although they obviously lingered in the back of his mind.[4] Trollope found the whole ethos of the Jacobean drama a reflection of his own society and its problems. He was fascinated by the parallels that he observed between the social tensions of the Jacobean world and the Victorian class struggle: the similar intensification of economic and social competition, the waning of the aristocracy, the concomitant rise of the wealthy bourgeoisie and the emergence of a dominant middle-class ethic. But it was particular plays which provided the immediate catalysts for the operation of his imagination. Because Trollope did not simply transcribe the material that he adopted, an examination of the process of creative transformation affords us an insight not only into his artistic methods but into the shaping of his social criticism. Although John H. Hagan has described Trollope's mind as politically 'divided',[5] Trollope's treatment of the material that he borrowed from the Jacobean drama offers evidence that the true instinct of his mind was more radical than has been thought, and in those novels on which I wish to focus attention he anatomizes the moral anarchy that he felt lay just below the bland surface of middle and upper class Victorian society.

Trollope's *The Three Clerks* is more than merely a collection of comic autobiographical sketches of his early years as a post office clerk in the London of the eighteen thirties. Its prodigal son motif, developed in the parallel careers of the junior Civil Service clerks, derives from the contrasted careers of the apprentices in the satiric city comedy *Eastward Ho!* by Jonson, Chapman and Marston. Despite the fact that the structure of both the play and the novel is a very natural socio-moral pattern, there are a series of close parallels between them of characterization, structure, situation and incident. Alaric and Charley Tudor owe a great deal to the character of Quicksilver, an ambitious scapegrace; the puritanical clerk Henry Norman is modelled on the doggedly virtuous apprentice, Golding; and the goldsmith's daughters Gertrude and Mildred appear in the novel as Gertrude and Linda Woodward. A typical city comedy woman of the citizen class, Gertrude Touchstone's monomaniacal desire for social elevation, fostered by her weak-minded mother, finds a parallel in the intense social ambition of the Gertrude of the novel. There is a further parallel of situation between the marriage of Gertrude Touchstone and the impoverished gentleman Sir Petronel Flash, who seeks to gain her estate and Gertrude Woodward's match with the penniless Alaric Tudor, who wants her legacy. And in contrast, Mildred's dutiful acquiescence in her father's choice of his sober apprentice for her husband is paralleled in the novel by the virtuous Linda Woodward's passive acceptance of Henry Norman, a marriage which, like Gertrude's, is planned quietly by Mrs Woodward, whose sententious moralizing strikes a key note throughout the novel and who thus subsumes the functions of both Touchstone and his wife in the play.

The play's central, overt debate between prodigality and prudence, advanced on the one hand by the rascally apprentice Quicksilver and Touchstone's ambitious daughter Gertrude, and on the other by his virtuous apprentice Golding and his righteous daughter Mildred, is also fundamental to the clear moral design of *The Three Clerks*, in which the schematic moral contrast between the prudent clerk Henry Norman and his ambitious friend Alaric Tudor, who is 'no Puritan' immediately recalls the parallel of characterization in *Eastward Ho!*. Like Quicksilver, Tudor is frustrated by bourgeois values of thrift, industry and respectability and just as the Jacobean apprentice's social climbing is aided by money stolen from Touchstone, the Victorian clerk, who covets a seat in Parliament, advances his meteoric career by the theft of his ward's fortune. In both the play and the novel the criminals are tried and imprisoned, both repenting their folly, while the moralists, who preach to them while paying off their debts, are rewarded appropriately, Golding being elected a city alderman, while Norman inherits a country estate.

There are also further minor parallels of various kinds which give vitality and point to different areas of the novel. Quicksilver, for instance, also serves as a model for the third clerk Charley Tudor, the 'prodigal', who is reclaimed, like the apprentice, only after falling into the clutches of a money-lender and suffering temporary imprisonment. Indeed, he only narrowly escapes Quicksilver's fate. Quicksilver marries his whore, whose dowry is paid by the usurer Security, while Tudor nearly marries the barmaid of the 'Cat and Whistle', Trollope's Victorian equivalent to Sindefy, with a dowry provided by the landlady. The aristocratic confidence trickster Sir Petronel Flash, with his imaginary castle, reappears as the Honourable Undecimus Scott with his bogus fortune in shares; the pugnacious attorney Mr Chaffanbrass, is given life by the play's combative Lawyer Bramble; while the adventurers' projected voyage to Virginia is echoed by Alaric Tudor's final voyage to a new world. The most striking example among these minor characters and incidents, however – because it is an incident wholly superfluous to the plot – is the parallel between the Thames shipwreck at Cuckolds' Haven and the collision of Henry Norman's wherry with Chiswick Bridge, which indicates how Trollope could not prevent certain extraneous matter from creeping into the novel unawares.

Trollope's debts to *Eastward Ho!*, with its schematic moral characterization and its contrapuntal plotting, clearly influenced the form of *The Three Clerks*, with its three parallel and interwoven stories, and it is the nature of Trollope's debts to the play that holds the clue to his artistic intention. This goes beyond the superficial prodigal son theme for, as in the play, the truly central issue is how individual ambition may be reconciled with social order. With the growth of a highly complex society in the middle years of the nineteenth century power had begun to shift from the city to the Civil Service, and Trollope knew from his own experience that the ambitions of the intelligent public servant posed the problems of *Eastward Ho!* in a contemporary form. Alaric Tudor's dilemma, which mirrors Quicksilver's, is how to reconcile the paradox of society's simultaneous reverence for material success and for disinterested service. Like Quicksilver and Golding, each clerk nurses a private ambition, which for Charley Tudor is literary fame, for Henry Norman (like Golding) is public respectability, but which for Alaric Tudor represents the Victorian doctrine of individualism in its crudest terms. His growing cynicism is confirmed by his continual exposure in both his professional and domestic life to the double standards of middle-class morality and to its touchstone, Mrs Woodward. She accurately defines competition as the modern disease, but nevertheless strives to secure the three clerks for her daughters and acquiesces in her family's applause for Tudor's 'gumption', regarding him, like they do, as a 'winning horse'. Tudor's obsessive compulsion to compete, not only in the Civil Service but also for the prospective wife of his friend Norman, finally blights his life as, like Quicksilver, he rapidly loses touch with moral reality altogether.

As Trollope argues at length in Chapter XXIX, the modern world is governed by expediency. Convinced of this law by the Mephistophelean Undy Scott, Tudor commences a career of fraud which forms part of a whole series of parallels that includes not only the fiercely ambitious civil servant Sir Gregory Hardlines, but even the Prime Minister who, for the sake of a much needed safe vote, countenances the blurring of public and private interests implicit in Tudor's ambition to enter parliament. The Limehouse and Rotherhithe Bridge affair on which Tudor's fortunes hinge aptly symbolizes this ethos of political corruption, but the novel's central symbol for the fundamental clash between the old morality of social obligation and the new morality of self-help, is the new Civil Service competitive examination. The old patronage system recruited unambitious men like Henry Norman and Fidus Neverbend who help regulate burgeoning industrialization but allow the service to petrify into a system of self-perpetuating oligarchies. But the open examination, which foreshadows the emergence of a meritocracy, also threatens to bring social anarchy by admitting into the public service intelligent and unscrupulous men like Alaric Tudor, who employ their public role solely for private gain.

However, Trollope's satire, like that in *Eastward Ho!,* is two-edged. Like the authors of the play, he recognizes that ambition and energy are inherently admirable and that passivity too often masks moral torpor. Just as the self-righteous preaching of Touchstone and Golding is really little more than a defence of their narrow class concern, the puritanical homilies of Mrs Woodward and Henry Norman also conceal a fundamental self-interest. Their morality is tested at Alaric Tudor's trial where, as in the play, the man of virtue is in a position to restore the moral equilibrium. But in *The Three Clerks* Trollope employs the same situation to present a more tarnished world than that of *Eastward Ho!* in which comic reconciliation and social harmony are achieved. Unlike Golding, Henry Norman's forgiveness of his successful rival really masks a well-judged revenge, while on the public level a society wedded to his double standards requires more than the simple justice meted out in the play: it demands a scapegoat and Tudor is forced to emigrate. Nevertheless, in both the play and the novel it is society that is held responsible for the misdirection of the individual will and, as their parallel of emblematic pattern suggests, the moral worlds of *Eastward Ho!* and *The Three Clerks* include a clear-sighted account of the hollowness of social ambition. This is symbolized in the play by the illusory Eastward Castle which Gertrude Touchstone vainly seeks, and in the novel, more realistically, by the citadel of social acceptance which Gertrude Woodward tries to storm – the Chiswick Flower Show. Here in the close contiguity of the inner and outer worlds of London society she has a similar chastening experience of the emptiness of social victory for as Trollope points out: 'Where is the citadel? How is one to know when one has taken it?' (p. 185). She also witnesses the private hypocrisy of respected public figures and watches obsessive ambition progressively destroy her husband's peace of mind and, like the Gertrude of the play, as a result of her disillusioning initiation into marriage and society, Gertrude Woodward's private ambition is modified. But the fundamental problem of her innately competitive will remains. Unlike Quicksilver and Gertrude Touchstone, for whom there is a comic resolution and social reabsorption, for Alaric Tudor and his wife there is no simple answer. As Trollope demonstrates, in Victorian society there is no natural place for truly ambitious spirits and his sympathy at the conclusion of the novel is with its victims who emigrate, as the adventurers in the play desire to do, to a new world where competition with the natural environment offers their energy full scope and social value.

It is evident, I think, that Trollope's debts of character, plotting, situation and moral pattern bestow coherence and vitality on *The Three Clerks*, while the central issue of *Eastward Ho!* is

B

employed to deepen his own sombre criticism of contemporary society, a criticism which is consistent with his later trenchant satire in *The Way We Live Now*. And Trollope again transposes the Jacobean world into Victorian social terms in *Miss Mackenzie*, in which we can see a similar imaginative process at work. Faced with an admitted failure of invention, Trollope began to draw on D'Avenant's *News From Plymouth*, a farcical battle of the sexes dealing with a theme which fascinated him: the subversive power of the independent woman. He makes significant changes of character and milieu, however, for D'Avenant's boisterous port becomes Trollope's puritan spa town Littlebath, and worldly Lady Loveright, who judges her society's moral degeneracy with acerbic wit, is transformed into Trollope's mouthpiece for his own social criticism, the timid, middle-aged middle class spinster, Miss Mackenzie.

Once again Trollope's transposition involves parallels of characterization and details of situation and plotting. D'Avenant's play concerns three poverty-stricken sea captains who court rich Lady Loveright, her niece Miss Joynture and their affluent landlady the Widow Carrack. The plot of Trollope's novel hinges on the pursuit of the wealthy Miss Mackenzie, who lodges with her niece Susanna at Miss Todd's house in Littlebath, by three impoverished suitors. Trollope is also indebted to D'Avenant's technique of characterization. Like his sea captains, who are 'humour' figures, Trollope's lightly-sketched suitors represent hypocrisy, vulgarity and sheer dullness. While Seawit's intelligence is reflected in the cunning of the curate Maguire, and Cable's vulgarity is echoed by Mr Rubb the tradesman, it is evident that the prosaic integrity of John Ball owes a great deal to the stiff formality and innate honesty of Studious Warwell. Trollope also echoes D'Avenant in the smaller details of his plotting. In both the play and the novel the lady's niece urges the virtues of her dull but honest lover, who is ultimately accepted; and in the end the worldly suitors have to be content, in each case, with what they can get: in *News From Plymouth* Seawit marries Miss Joynture and Cable is trapped by the Widow Carrack, while in *Miss Mackenzie* Maguire is finally caught by Miss Mackenzie's friend, Miss Colza.

In both D'Avenant and Trollope the courtship ritual masks the crude reality of the wealthy single woman's social status as a mere commercial object. As such, Lady Loveright and Miss Mackenzie function as catalysts for the aggressively acquisitive forces in their respective societies, and although the stern morality of Trollope's spa town is far removed from D'Avenant's bustling seaport, in both worlds men thrive on women's social and sexual insecurity. In the cheerfully amoral world of the play this is part of an elaborate game, but in claustrophobic Littlebath it is insidiously concealed by a veneer of piety and here Trollope's severe criticism of the middle class evangelicals who prey remorselessly on the loneliness, frustration and neurotic guilt of middle-aged single women is sharpened by his debts to minor figures in *News From Plymouth*. The garrulous bore Sir Solemn Trifle is employed to flesh out the platitudinous hypocrite the Reverend Mr Stumfold, but a more striking model is the puritan 'humour' character Zeal, whose anti-Papist ranting is echoed by Trollope's curate Maguire.

Both Lady Loveright and Miss Mackenzie are singularly free spirits whose wealth, paradoxically, allows them the necessary freedom to assert the supremacy of moral rather than sexual or social values. They are feared as subversive forces because they courageously pierce the façade of public manners to reveal the shabby falsehoods and covert power that really make society work. In both D'Avenant and Trollope this transformation of vulnerability into moral armour goes hand in hand with the comic motif of the pursuer pursued, by which each potential lover is tested. But while Lady Loveright's social poise allows her to gauge Warwell's devotion by flirting nonchalantly with Seawit, Miss Mackenzie is tormented by her suitors' attentions and agonizes over her choice of John Ball. And in each case tension is added to the moral conflict by the strong undercurrent of sexual rivalry, for Ball bitterly resents the competition of Maguire and Rubb just as Warwell is frantically jealous of Seawit.

In the novel, as in the play, freedom is rooted in acute moral intelligence. For both women marriage must be founded on human equality, and Lady Loveright finally accepts Sir Studious

Warwell only when, for her sake, he has stripped himself of his wealth, books and pleasures; while Miss Mackenzie discards her romantic notions and marries her elderly, impoverished cousin principally because he does not threaten her hard-won independence. Furthermore, D'Avenant and Trollope both recognize that for women freedom must be exercised in the context of social healing. Paradoxically, Lady Loveright and Miss Mackenzie share, together with the need to assert their selfhood, a strong feminine instinct for self-sacrifice, and Lady Loveright's ambition 'to make a man, not take addition from him'[6] is echoed by Miss Mackenzie, who savours the combination of self-sacrifice and social power which her marriage offers. When her husband inherits wealth and a title Miss Mackenzie's match more closely parallels Lady Loveright's aristocratic marriage and her rejection of romantic self-delusion is fully rewarded. Clearly, within the moral framework of *News From Plymouth*, Lady Loveright's decision to love aright renders her match with Sir Studious Warwell a symbolic union of judgement and merit and it is echoed in Trollope's novel by Miss Mackenzie's marriage, which represents the fruitful combination of moral intelligence and human worth. Trollope's debt to D'Avenant thus goes deeper than simply their parallel interest in the power of the independent woman. His close echoing of the play's central plot emphasizes his moral preoccupation with the nature and value of personal freedom and his treatment of this problems gains considerable clarity of focus from his borrowing. However, his significant alterations of character and milieu contribute to the creation of a world which is darker and more threatening than that of the Jacobean dramatist, a recognizably Victorian world in which individual liberty is more difficult to achieve and to sustain.

In *The Three Clerks* Trollope successfully manages to fuse elements of autobiography with his debts to *Eastward Ho!*, but in *Ralph the Heir* the hiatus between the inheritance plot and the election plot marks, I believe, the gulf between his debts to Middleton's *Michaelmas Term* and his reminiscences of his own disillusioning experiences at Beverley in the election of 1868.[7] The plots are only tenuously connected through the relationship of the heir Ralph Newton with his guardian Sir Thomas Underwood who, like Trollope, vainly stands as a candidate in a borough which is subsequently disfranchised. Moreover, the subsidiary plot is in general more vividly compelling than the main plot. This is partly due to the depth of treatment accorded to the character of Sir Thomas Underwood, which was probably based on the complex personality of Trollope's own father, and also to the detail and atmosphere of the election scenes. The inheritance plot which is drawn from Middleton and is altogether different in style, contributes nothing to Trollope's account of contemporary politics because it is concerned with quite separate issues. Here Trollope preserves the basic situation of Middleton's play and in addition the hyperbolic behaviour of his tradesmen, together with the central pattern of character relations, but he also catches the distinctive tone and point of Middleton's satire. Like Middleton, a realist and a moralist, Trollope presents contemporary social tensions with unsentimental clarity. In both the play and the novel the city milieu embraces and symbolizes the central conflict between the impoverished gentry and the rising merchant class and the consequent corruption of rural values by the metropolis. In each case the targets of satiric attack are the avarice of the middle classes and the irresponsible use of capital inherent in a feudal system of inheritance, because as the old country estates pass into the hands of money-lenders and merchants the stability and values of the social order are threatened, while family life is poisoned by the frantic competition for property.

Middleton's city comedy types – the naïve young country heir, the wily city merchant and his rebellious wife and shadowy assistant – all recur in the novel; and there is, moreover, a clear parallel between the way Richard Easy is tricked out of his inheritance by a city woollen-draper and the way in which Ralph Newton and his estate fall into the blackmailing power of his London breeches-maker. Both Quomodo and Neefit, whose social aspirations are frustrated by their middle class background, are driven by an insane desire for social elevation and pin their hopes on their association with the landed gentry. The unspoken barter of sex for lands which motivates Middleton's world becomes explicit in Trollope as Neefit advances Ralph loans in return for a match with his daughter. But each merchant is governed so completely by his monomania that he finally overreaches himself and becomes merely a comic butt. Quomodo feigns death only to discover that his son threatens to ruin the estate and that his wife has made a match with Easy, while more realistically but no less comically, Neefit's impotent rage at his failure to blackmail Ralph is expressed in his smashing of the furniture of the Moonbeam Inn, and his humiliation is compounded by his daughter's subsequent marriage to a cobbler's son. Neefit, as the judge says of Quomodo in *Michaelmas Term*, is his own affliction.

Another important interest for both Middleton and Trollope is the way sexual and social rivalry feed each other and this forms the basis for several parallels of character and situation between the play and the novel. Just as Quomodo's daughter Susan is courted by the well-bred but dissolute gallant Rearage and by the social upstart son of a tooth-drawer Andrew Lethe, Neefit's daughter Polly is pursued by both the rakish heir Ralph Newton and Ontario Moggs, the cobbler's son. Similarly, while Quomodo and his daughter favour Lethe in opposition to his wife's preference for Rearage, Neefit's wife and Polly champion Moggs rather than Newton. Trollope has reversed some of the character relations and simplified this area of the plot, but, as in the play, the motive remains social victory by sexual intrigue and the social status of the suitors is still the key issue.

But essentially Middleton and Trollope are both concerned to examine not only bourgeois greed but the fundamental problem of what weak-minded and corruptible young men are to do with their lives while waiting for their inheritances. Both Richard Easy and Ralph Newton are plainly unfit to inherit their estates, which they tend to regard as useful collateral on which to raise loans, and their predicament points to the moral dangers of idle capital. Easy and Newton are both social parasites, content to batten on the wealthy merchants, and only bitter experience of their victims' wiles and a measure of luck encourage the young gentry to recognize, rather belatedly, their social responsibilities; for just as Easy's redemption commences with the fortuitous trial by which he regains his inheritance, Ralph Newton's reformation hinges on the timely death of his uncle. For the anguished Squire Newton, whose natural son cannot inherit it, the estate represents a tradition of order and social obligation. He is one in the long line of rural gentry portrayed in the past by novelists such as Fielding and Smollett. For these authors the estate could have a forceful symbolic significance as a seat and retreat for the finest values and the security of a passing world. But for the merchants, in both the play and the novel, the acquisition of a country estate offers the only kind of immortality materialism knows. For them it is a commercial possession, but also a symbol of social victory and a means of vengeance on the gentlemen they have served and despised all their lives. In social terms they pose a profound threat to the rural community, but both the play and the novel are also concerned to demonstrate how in private life the struggle for property destroys family relations. For Quomodo's son Sim the inherited estate becomes an irksome obligation, and Ralph's inheritance is the cause of bitter division in the Newton family and the source of the subtle discord between the squire and his son.

In *Ralph the Heir* Trollope's social criticism is given greater force by his adoption of the core of Middleton's plot and by his transposition of the pattern of conflicting forces at work in Jacobean society. But, thematically, while preserving Middleton's comic, satiric treatment of the aspiring merchant class, Trollope has shifted the balance of criticism from this area of society to focus on the underlying problems of capital and the archaic system of inheritance which underpins Middleton's plot. For Trollope, as for Middleton, it divides families, corrupts young heirs, intensifies the competition between city and countryside and increases the stranglehold of the commercial ethic on English social life.

As in the case of *Miss Mackenzie*, in the writing of *Lady Anna*, undertaken on board ship during a voyage to Australia, Trollope's imagination seems to have faltered and once again he turned for assistance to the Jacobean drama. But it is a particularly unusual novel because it is indebted to two different plays, one of which provided Trollope with the basis of his story, while the other helped him over a difficulty of plotting. In *Lady Anna*, unlike those novels previously discussed, Trollope's creative imagination was never really engaged with either the characters or the plots on which he drew. Rather, he deliberately embarked on what was frankly a thesis novel devoted to proving the superiority of education over birth and his borrowing provided him with the technical devices necessary to overcome obstacles to the prosecution of his argument.[8]

Trollope found a solution to the problem of arranging an encounter between a noblewoman and a commoner in the plot of the anonymous pseudo-historical romance *The Weakest Goeth to the Wall*, in which a noble family flee to a Flanders town where a tailor, Barnaby Bunch, protects the mother and daughter from their wicked landlord and squanders all his income in paying their debts. This is the basic situation of *Lady Anna*. Turned out of their home by the evil Earl Lovel, the Countess and her daughter are sheltered by a Keswick tailor, Thomas Thwaite and his son, Daniel. Trollope used Barnaby Bunch, whose humanity shines through his vituperation, as the model for his own rough-tongued tailor, whose staunch moral support of the two noblewomen also involves him in great financial sacrifice. But for a storyteller and a moralist this raised the challenge of arranging a credible situation in which an earl's daughter could marry a tailor 'without glaring fault on her side', as Trollope put it.[9] He found the answer in Ford's *The Fancies Chaste and Noble*,[10] a romance primarily concerned with a ritualistic trial devised in order to prove the virtue of noblewomen, in which Flavia's husband declares in open court that their marriage is null because of his pre-contract. These are exactly the grounds upon which Earl Lovel attempts to nullify his marriage to Josephine Murray and which, as in the play, prove false.[11] This legal plot is essential in gaining the reader's sympathy for the wronged Countess, but more importantly it enables Trollope to allow Anna to grow up in the same household as Daniel Thwaite and to fall in love with him without flouting either social or narrative propriety.

It is against a background of bitter class struggle that

Trollope's own testing of aristocratic virtues finds ironic definition, for the central legal battle over the noblewomen's rights
provides a vehicle for his covert examination of human values.
The rival claims of birth and education are formulated by
juxtaposition. Brought up in a tailor's family, Lady Anna is a
working class aristocrat, intensely aware of her ordinariness,
while Daniel Thwaite, well educated and possessing an innate
nobility, is obviously an aristocrat of the labouring class. But
Trollope's closer scrutiny of the claims of birth demonstrates an
appalling hiatus between social rank and human worth. Anna's
love and her moral education under Thwaite's powerful influence finally prove stronger than mere blood, and her insistence
on her pre-contract in the face of fierce psychological pressure
contrasts starkly with her father's cynical betrayal of human
obligations. And a similar parallel is drawn between the aristocratic Lovel family's readiness to consolidate their social position with the wealth derived from their son's abhorrent marriage
with a tailor's lodger (thus circumventing the necessity for a
lawsuit over the Lovel inheritance, which they might lose), and
the complex monomania of the base-born Countess, who has
so completely assimilated the corrupt values of the very family
that brought about her ruin that, in spite of her daughter's title
and probable independent wealth, she is prepared to kill Thwaite
in order to preserve the purity of the family blood.

Trollope felt that society was moving inevitably towards
democracy and in *Lady Anna* his sympathy is with the democrats who on the whole place personal values before class
allegiance, even when it involves them in self-evidently para-
doxical actions. By his quixotic sacrifice, giving succour to the
class he hates and which bankrupts and spurns him, Thwaite
transcends mere class antagonisms, yet his agreement with the
Countess that there can be no union between her class and his
affirms the notion of a hierarchy founded on birth. However,
his son Daniel, Trollope's spokesman in the novel, is both more
humane in his assumption of the simple equality of human
worth and more subversive in his conscious assertion of his
superior social value. Moreover, by demonstrating in the lives of
the radical tailors the traditional aristocratic virtues of concern

for moral and social obligations, Trollope satirizes the abstract notion of nobility based in some mystical way on blood, and the overtly symbolic marriage between an aristocrat and a member of the working class which closes the novel deliberately and ironically indicates that there is no innate difference between people. Unfortunately, in *Lady Anna* Trollope's attempt to graft elements of romance plotting onto a realistic study of Victorian social classes weakens both his grasp of character and the effectiveness of his realism. The argument, moreover, is allowed to rest on too hypothetical a case. It avoids the logical consequences of the issues of bitter class struggle it raises and in this instance one is forced to conclude that Trollope's social criticism is severely limited by the very plot material that he adopted from the drama.

The Fixed Period is another novel indebted to the Jacobean drama which fails because of its curious mingling of romance, fantasy and social realism. As Gamaliel Bradford noted, its plot is drawn from *The Old Law* by Massinger, Rowley and Middleton,[12] a play concerned with the testing of the nature and strength of man's fundamental humanity. When Duke Evander revives an ancient law calling for the death of men at the age of eighty and of women at the age of sixty, he makes in effect a searching examination of family loyalties and of the cohesive power of the whole social fabric. The response of the majority of the population to the old law is represented by Simonides, who can scarcely conceal his glee at the prospect of sudden wealth and position when he learns that his father, Creon, is to die. Leonides' son Cleanthes on the other hand, proves the exception. He is so grief-stricken that he even arranges a mock funeral in order to secure his father's escape. Families are everywhere divided by the cruel law, widows are courted in anticipation of their husbands' deaths and social life disintegrates. The play effectively demonstrates how social cohesiveness depends not on love or family loyalty, but on a materialist process of deferred expectations and on the sheer unpredictability of death.

Trollope's interest in the same disillusioning theme is embodied in his parallel plotting in *The Fixed Period*. In the island of Britannula the inhabitants have thrown off British rule and their new Government establishes a series of fresh laws designed to promote social efficiency and general happiness. The 'fixed period' is one of these. Citizens are to be sent to a 'college' at the age of sixty-seven to live in comfort and contemplation for a year while they await euthanasia. The family of Crasweller, the first man to fall victim to this law, crusade against it and they are aided by the President's son Jack Neverbend, who is courting Crasweller's daughter Eva. His rival Grundle however, eager to obtain her father's wealth, lends his support to the law in the Assembly. But unlike the authors of *The Old Law*, Trollope's concern with the human conflict between love and material self-interest is secondary to his satiric attack on utilitarianism, on its inhuman conception of social efficiency and on the tyrannical power of the state. The novel is a bitter satire on social planning, but it also constitutes a political nightmare so horrific that Trollope evades the issue by bringing in the British navy as a *deus ex machina*. The colony is in such consternation at the barbaric law that it gladly capitulates and returns to British rule on the day of Craswaller's incarceration. It has to be said that *The Fixed Period* is a poor novel, hovering uneasily between prophetic fantasy and social satire. With the exception of the President Neverbend, its characters are never convincing and in this case the result of Trollope's indebtedness to the Jacobean drama is one of the strangest novels in the English language.

It is remarkable that Trollope's finest political novel, *The Prime Minister*, is indebted to a Jacobean play, but this is corroborated by the dating of his marginalia. Trollope read Fletcher's *Women Pleased* on 23 March 1874 and began to write *The Prime Minister* on 2 April 1874, just ten days later, while the details of character and plot were still fresh in his mind.[13] He was deeply interested in the theme of Fletcher's play and this, together with elements of plotting, characterization and social comment, is carried over into the novel, informing both its main and subsidiary plots and binding them tightly together.

The villains of the play and the novel, both named Lopez, follow similar occupations: Fletcher's Lopez is a jeweller and usurer while Trollope's Lopez is a financial speculator whose father was a jeweller.[14] Like the Lopez of the play, who marries the wealthy Isabella in order to increase his scope for speculation, Ferdinand Lopez marries Emily to secure finance for his own ventures. To save money Isabella is denied proper food and clothing, while Emily is taken to live at her father's expense in Manchester Square. Isabella's desire for independence is paralleled by Emily's shame at her husband's fraudulent activities which makes a separation seem a moral as well as a personal necessity. Just as in the play Lopez's insane jealousy, fed by Rugio's wooing of his wife, widens the rift between them, when Emily shrinks from her unlovable husband his jealousy is intensified by the competition of her former lover Arthur Fletcher. Each young man fulfils the moral function of testing the woman's virtue and in each case the husband's suspicions are confirmed by his finding wife and lover together. Trollope also preserves the familial nature of the love triangle, for Isabella's lover turns out to be her disguised brother while between Emily's family and Fletcher's there is a long history of close ties.

The second love triangle in *Women Pleased*, which involves Isabella's brother Silvio, Claudio and the Princess Belvidere, is also echoed in *The Prime Minister* by the relation between Lopez, Fletcher and Emily. Like Silvio, Lopez is an interloper whose cardinal sin is social presumption, and Silvio's exclusion from the citadel where Belvidere is guarded by her mother is paralleled by Lopez's banishment from Manchester Square. And in the same way that Silvio uses his aunt Rhodope to gain access to Belvidere, Lopez employs Emily's aunt Roby to outwit Mr Wharton. On the completion of their furtive courtship, Lopez is ostracized by the Whartons. In the same manner the Duchess banishes Silvio, for Belvidere's marriage had been intended to cement a political alliance with the Duke of Siena – just as Emily's proposed match was expected to strengthen the connection with the Fletchers. Trollope is also indebted to Fletcher's plot for further minor details which he subsequently filled out. The violent rivalry between Claudio and Silvio is carried over into the novel when Lopez in a jealous rage pursues

Fletcher with a horsewhip; the supposed death of Claudio probably foreshadows Lopez's suicide, while the wilful Duchess's war with the Duke of Siena, which forms the political background to *Women Pleased*, anticipates the covert rivalry between the Duke and Duchess of Omnium in *The Prime Minister*.

But apart from these closely echoed details of plotting, Trollope is also indebted to the central theme of the play, which links its plots together : women's struggle to achieve 'maistrye' or 'their soveraigne Wills'. Like Fletcher, Trollope is passionately concerned with the woman's acute dilemma of how to reconcile her public roles and private identity and ambition. Women in Trollope's Victorian world are expected to assimilate the contradictions of a society which pays lip-service to ideals such as romantic love, the sacredness of the home and personal liberty, but where in reality they are supposed to function as pawns in the endless struggle for wealth and power. And the central symbol for the novel's thoroughly political and fragmented world, in which even marriage is an uneasy alliance made to preserve class privilege, is the Coalition. Like the Princess Belvidere and Isabella in *Women Pleased*, although they are women of different rank, the Duchess of Omnium and Emily Wharton are alike in rebelling against their coalition marriages. In *Can You Forgive Her?* Trollope is appalled at the way the sheer weight of social will forced the young Glencora to abandon her egalitarian passion for the scapegrace Burgo Fitzgerald for a purely political match with the pedestrian young Palliser; but in *The Prime Minister* he is even more critical of the way the middle classes, like the Whartons and the Fletchers, coyly idealize economic self-interest (I, 163), and he sympathizes with Emily's revolt against the crudely political nature of Victorian family life in marrying the outsider. For both Emily and Glencora however, marriage – the only area for individual fulfilment open to them – becomes a battleground for trenchantly opposed wills. Palliser hampers Glencora's efforts to organize the social aspects of his Government and Emily's dreams of furthering her husband's career are shattered by his secrecy and domestic tyranny. And because their husbands come to symbolize for

35

them society's dehumanizing betrayal of their selfhood, each unconsciously exacts vengeance.

The Victorian confusion of social and sexual roles is partly to blame in both cases. While Glencora has the ambition and the cynical utilitarianism necessary to keep the Coalition alive, Palliser is timid and thin-skinned. Angry that such a man must be 'jury, and judge, and executioner' (I, 364), Glencora endeavours to become the effective Prime Minister herself (I, 320–21), undermining her husband's political confidence until he feels that he is a mere figurehead (I, 195). In doing so she is gratifying a desire for a sexual as well as a social revenge on the husband she cannot truly love. Choosing a time when her husband's judgement is clouded, she secretly champions the mysterious interloper Lopez (who reminds her of Burgo Fitzgerald) in the Silverbridge election, and so contributes to the gradual collapse of the Government. Emily Wharton's militant feminism, her refusal to submit to her family's choice of either life-defeating virginity or a marriage 'within the pale' (I, 176) has a sexual motivation too. Her lover, Arthur Fletcher, treats her as his 'holy of holies' (I, 187) when she frankly wants to be 'mastered' by Lopez (I, 452). But, horrified by the crude realities of Victorian life which Lopez represents, she later retreats behind her family's tribal judgement of him as an abhorred foreigner. Trollope's treatment of Lopez becomes more sympathetic and his criticism of Emily more stringent as the schizoid quality of her nature emerges. Overtly a model Victorian wife patiently enduring her boorish husband, like Isabella and Belvidere in *Women Pleased* and like the Duchess of Omnium, she is working assiduously for her own triumph, coolly playing on his male vulnerability, his financial dependence, his social and sexual insecurity, until her passive assertion of blind will forces him into excesses, public humiliation and suicide. Characteristically, Emily responds to his death with a further piece of self-deception. Her abject penitence for the 'persistency of [her] perverse self-will' (II, 397) refers, she tells herself, to her social rebellion; but it more truthfully and accurately describes the final unrepentant triumph of her will in marrying Arthur Fletcher.

Like Fletcher in *Women Pleased*, Trollope is fiercely critical of a society that classes its women as outsiders and ignores their legitimate claims to selfhood expressed in terms of social value. One of the dominant ironies of the novel is that while it is the women who possess will and energy, they are made subject to the crushing weight of social convention invoked by weak men like Palliser, Wharton and Fletcher. Trollope portrays Victorian society as totally enervated, desperately in need of people of vision and drive, and inevitably, he suggests, women of powerful will may become a frustrated and subversively destructive force. As in the play, this theme is closely woven into the structure of the novel, binding together its subsidiary plots and giving it both vigour and formal precision. *The Prime Minister* offers the fullest example of Trollope's debts to a play thoroughly permeating a novel from the larger elements of character and structure down to the smaller details of plotting, and I believe this is mainly due to the fact that *Women Pleased* was still fresh in his memory, informing his imagination as he wrote.

Trollope's debt to the Jacobean drama is more extensive than scholars have supposed; and his borrowing, which spans his entire career as a novelist, contributes to both his successes and his comparative failures. Plainly, *Ralph the Heir*, *Lady Anna* and *The Fixed Period* suffer from Trollope's inability to assimilate fully his various debts, but *Miss Mackenzie* on the other hand, is redeemed from conventionality by his adoption of D'Avenant's spirited comedy. Because of its debt to *Eastward Ho! The Three Clerks* is developed with a surer sense of form and artistic purpose than critics have recognized, and similarly *The Prime Minister* gains greater moral penetration and clarity of design from Trollope's borrowing from Fletcher. These debts are equally important in shedding further light on the nature and workings of Trollope's imagination. Essentially, it is a synthesizing imagination, which utilizes traditional forms and ideas by transposing them into Victorian social terms. However, Trollope clearly felt that his world was altogether more complex, darker and more bewildering than that offered by the comedies and romances on which he drew. He transforms them into sombre novels, possessing a bleaker and a more trenchantly satirical social criticism. And this treatment of his adoption of characters, plots, themes, situations and incidents from the Jacobean drama suggests, in my view, that the innate bias of Trollope's mind is more radical than critics have believed.

Scene and Form

The power of Trollope's form is a striking but still relatively disregarded aspect of his art. This is partly due to his undeserved reputation as a mechanical craftsman, but it is also because the expansive nature of his novels resists post-Jamesian critical notions. Against James's view of mid-Victorian novels as 'baggy monsters' needs to be set the judgement of W.P. Ker, who noted Trollope's affinity with the *Comédie Humaine* but considers him the greater artist because '[h]e is a dramatist, and Balzac is not'.[15] In the dramatic novel, as in the drama, the individual scene is a subject in its own right and as the smallest unit of the action it is an important source of the reader's insight into the meaning of the novel. Trollope has an instinctive sense of its form and function, but his achievements in the use of scene are also rooted in his careful study of the early drama. His marginalia frequently insist that scenes must possess dramatic fullness and aesthetic completeness,[16] and in an article on Henry Taylor he argues that it is by means of its scenes that drama 'forces the reader to identify himself . . . with the images and creations of the author'.[17]

Trollope's close interest in the relation between the individual scene and the ampler form of the novel emerges in his remarks on the function of the scene together with a scenario in an article for *Good Words*:

. . . rules as to construction have probably been long known to [the novelist]. . . . They have come to him from much observation, from the writings of others, from that which we call study, – in which imagination has but little immediate concern. It is the fitting of the rules to the characters which he has created, the filling in with living touches and true colours those daubs and blotches on his canvas which have been easily scribbled with a rough hand, that the true work consists.[18]

These 'rules as to construction' constitute the basis of the scenarios to be found among Trollope's work sheets. But the vitality of character so vividly presented in his novels resides in the dramatic scene, and its creation is the 'true work' which demands imaginative power :

The first coarse outlines of his story [the novelist] has found to be a matter almost indifferent to him. It is with these little plotlings that he has to contend . . . Every little scene must be arranged so that, – if it may be possible, – the proper words may be spoken and the fitting effect produced.[19]

This shaping process is not determined by any vague pictorial aesthetic, although Millais found Trollope's novels a pleasure to illustrate. It is much more than an intense visualization of the action for it involves a careful structuring of these 'little plots' in which 'incident or the character was moulded and brought into shape'.[20] An important aspect of Trollope's solution to the problem of form in the novel is his employment of scene in conjunction with a scenario composed of points of development in plotting and characterization, which allows flexibility in planning and yet achieves precision and point in execution. His artistic gains lie in his use of closely related techniques which are translated from the dramatic to the fictional form.

G. G. Sedgewick's perception that the drama is an ironic convention is also true of the dramatic novel.[21] In its scenes the reader looks from the real world into a world of illusion, obtaining an elevated view of it and observing it with a mixture of detachment and sympathy. Irony is the essential tool of both the dramatist and the dramatic novelist for in the scene what strikes the reader most is not the portrayal of inward character but the dynamic relation between characters in conflict. The scene is an oblique means of communication with the reader because the author's voice comes through a seemingly objective presentation. Its central irony resides in the reader seeing his own wisdom confirmed by events. In the well-known confrontation between Mr Crawley and the Bishop of Barchester in *The Last Chronicle of Barset* this kind of irony is potent on several levels. In the Bishop's presence the perpetual curate of Hogglestock assumes a studied meekness which the reader knows to be the political strategy of a proud, forceful man and despite his initial blandness, the reader is aware that the Bishop is not only timid but impotent in the matter of Mr Crawley's preaching from his own pulpit. Nor is Mrs Proudie's submissiveness natural, but is the result of a prior quarrel with her husband over the legality of the Bishop's 'inhibition'. There is thus an opening irony of manners which requires a moderation of pace, for their self-control depends on the rigorous suppression of emotion.

The ironic movement of the scene, the recognition of the curate's power, is given impetus by his prior insight into the Bishop's misery. His wry smile of understanding goads Mrs Proudie to the rudeness which invokes Mr Crawley's magisterial rebuke: ' "Peace, woman . . . The distaff were more fitting for you" ' (I, 192) that has the Bishop on his feet. There is a high irony in the down-at-heel curate lecturing the Bishop and his wife, but it is an irony compounded of recognition and reversal of fortune as Mr Crawley ignores the palatial trappings they had relied on to subdue him and forces instead a reluctant acknowledgement of his intellectual and political strength. Instead of the Proudies sacrificing the obscure man in their political battle with the Framley set, he uses them to gain a temporary but immensely satisfying victory over the forces that are crushing him. As one of the older order of clergy in Barsetshire, Mr Crawley presents in its most potent form the challenge of the ascetic life of priestly authority, but blinded by their limited political aims the Bishop and his wife fail to recognize the curate's spiritual integrity and feel only the humiliation of their defeat. For the reader there is not only the primitive identification with the underdog in his fight against institutional oppression, but the perception of the ironic emergence of the true nature of revolution within the Church.

In Trollope the ironic nature of the dramatic scene works in conjunction with dialogue as the revealing medium of the details and motives of a situation. In *Orley Farm* the scene of debate at the Bull Inn, Leeds, between the Hamworth attorney Dock-wrath and the commercial traveller Moulder, demonstrates Trollope's fine dramatic control. Here dialogue, characters and theme are synthesized as conflicting parties embody contrasted ideas. The generation of the action focuses the reader's attention on the dialogue itself, which produces a strong dialectical force propelling the scene's emotion and action. The debate centres on Dockwrath's refusal to abide by the unwritten rules concerning the use of the commercial room of the hotel where he has taken up residence, which Moulder attempts to enforce. The irony lies in the obese, bullying traveller's assumption of the role of prosecuting counsel, while the gaunt young lawyer staunchly defends his commercial interests, and the commercial men staying at the hotel form the jury. The setting of the 'trial', the commercial room, completes the visual irony, and the legal form of the argument with its dialectical pattern, lends an ironic richness to the dialogue. Moulder's case, that because Dockwrath is not a commercial man he is not entitled to the privileges of the room, is defended by the attorney on the grounds that he is a commercial lawyer, and the ironies of this statement illumine the whole scene. In one sense Dockwrath is truly a commercial man for he runs a lodging house in Hamworth, but Moulder, aware only of the lawyer's intention to deceive, takes the assertion as a lie. As the reader knows, however, Dockwrath has just completed an errand to Groby Park to sell legal information and thus in an invidious way he has indeed become commercial. Moreover, he consciously associates himself with the business ethic by using their room and he matches the arrogance of the commercial men in the legalistic battle in which they are engaged by invoking the law to defeat the obvious justice of Moulder's claim. The dialogue of the scene thus cooperates with its ironic structure to bring about a balanced development of the action, elaborating and intensifying its impressions and giving direction to the reader's moral interest. Its synthesis is the uneasy compromise as the travellers leave the room to Dockwrath, both sides claiming victory. But the failure in communication only masks the corrupting association of self-interest as Trollope obliquely suggests the degrading collaboration of the law with commerce and its capacity to pervert justice.

The dramatic scene in the novel is a fairly limited area of time and its significant impact depends upon the reader's sense of closure and completion. This effect demands a formal rhythm and tempo which is traced in the smaller climaxes that help to shape its meaning. For instance, in the scene in which Mr Crawley visits the Bishop's palace this development depends initially on the opening irony of manners which the reader has to recognize and which is revealed by the characters' manoeuvring for dominance. The rhythmic pattern of the whole interview is carefully composed as the Bishop's blandness is shaken first by the curate's ready acquiescence and then by his wife's interruption. The minor crisis is marked by silence, the bewildered shaking of the Bishop's head and Mr Crawley's smile of sympathy. After the silence, which allows the reader a fraction of time to assimilate what he has 'seen', the tempo rises again as Mrs Proudie stridently responds to this challenge; and the changed pattern of speech conventions, as Mr Crawley's careful argument begins to overwhelm the Bishop and as Mrs Proudie's interjections gather venom, is a measure of the altered balance of power which leads naturally to the climax. As the implacable confrontation which underlay the opening politeness is revealed in the curate's open rebuke, they jump to their feet in response to the attack and the curate marches out.

The rhythm of this scene is Trollope's basic means of organizing the reader's understanding of the emerging irony and it is instructive to measure its success against the same scene in his subsequent play, *Did He Steal It?*. Much of its point is lost by making Mr Crawley a schoolmaster and Dr Proudie a local magistrate. But Trollope also destroys the whole structure of the encounter. The ironic effect of the preliminary tactics is missing, for they both sit. The dramatic rhythm is further nullified because in the play Mr Crawley is defensive from the outset and his 'I am ... guiltless before the law' is much less dramatic than in the novel where he makes his subtle early challenge to the Bishop over its interpretation. Similarly, Mrs Goshawk's antagonism emerges too early. Her 'I am glad you

obeyed our summons' and 'Yes, sir; and Mr Goshawk is express-
ing his opinion . . .' are lines which are given in the novel to
the Bishop. Her vigorous attack and Mr Crawley's early capitulation thus prevent any possibility of dramatic growth. Except
for minor alterations, the dialogue is identical with the novel,
but the interview is flat and undramatic. Mrs Goshawk bears
all the burden of the conversation and her husband is little
more than a mild echo, so that the reader misses her usurping
interruptions and the comic dislocation that allows the curate
to take the initiative. His fine closing lines are retained but they
miss their biblical irony and in fact lose their impact altogether
because Mr Crawley has already addressed them to his wife.
In the play they merely mark the close of a vulgar squabble,
and their function as exit lines is denied by the need for dramatic compression which forces Trollope to continue a discussion
at the end of the scene between Mr Crawley and Grace about
Mrs Goshawk's son Captain Oakley. This conflation prevents
Trollope from rescuing any vestige of dramatic significance from
the scene. It is a strange paradox that scenes in Trollope's novels
are more truly dramatic than in his two plays, but he needed
the imaginative scope of the scenario to keep true scale in his
scenic structure and detail.

Within the limited area of time that the scene constitutes the
dramatic writer's sense of space is also important in creating its
rhythm and Trollope excels in presenting sharply detailed and
composed groups set in a potentially dramatic relation to each
other. The dramatic scene is often a microcosm of the conflicting
human forces in the novel and in *Barchester Towers* this is true
of Mrs Proudie's reception. Scale is kept by Trollope's careful
use of a clear social perspective. It is the first confrontation of
the political forces of the diocese after Mr Slope's divisive
sermon and is a gesture made to cement its factions. Its function
of papering over the cracks is imaged in Mrs Proudie's efforts to
hide the dowdy appearance of her cheap furnishings. Gesture
and grouping chart the currents of the emotional action as some
kind of attack is expected from the Grantly set. But it comes
from an entirely unexpected source because, of all people, the
Bohemian Stanhopes share an instinctive complicity to subvert

43

Mrs Proudie's political efforts. The irony is carefully prepared as the guests arrive; as their father hides in a corner of the crowded reception room; as Madeline makes arrangements for the positioning of her sofa; and scale is kept as the Bishop becomes entangled first with the fascinating 'Madame Neroni' and then with her brother Bertie.

The central movement of the scene, the comic attack on Mrs Proudie's hypocrisy, is more than finely-judged farce. The sudden exposure of the underproppings of her finery is the perfect dramatic image for her inherent vulgarity, given point by her furious 'Unhand it, sir!' (I, 97) in response to Bertie's proffered assistance. It is as though the runaway sofa has obeyed the collective will of the assembly in order to prick her arrogance as she achieves her aim of capturing attention, but only as a figure of fun. The irony of Mrs Proudie's comic reversal prompts the reader's recognition of her dehumanizing moral stupidity. However, there is also a muted effect of sympathy as the uneasy equilibrium of the reception is disrupted to reassert the schism in the diocese between those who rejoice at her exposure and those who do not. While the reader partly identifies with the helpless victim at the centre of the room, he also sympathizes with the figures clustered in the background as their excitement at the mishap grows out of their awareness of its social scope and meaning.

Trollope's gift for conferring space and movement on his characters is due to the extra dimension which drama allows. This depends to a large extent on his economical use of settings which gain emblematic significance for character through the accumulation of detail. Trollope makes the reader aware of the emotional background of a scene while focusing on the foreground action. In *The Claverings*, for instance, the moral atmosphere of Clavering Park is given in the scene of Sir Hugh's homecoming after the death of his infant son. A fearful repressive moral area is suggested as the night air strikes his wife shivering at the top of the staircase, and she feels his chill egoism in the way he meticulously removes his street clothes in the hallway before coming up to greet her. The breath of cold air, the delay, the hand nervously grasping the banister rail are all given from Hermione's point of view and they summarize the atmosphere of indifference and blind will in which she is trapped.

Trollope's dramatic realism also depends to an important extent on the characteristically fine balance he achieves between character and setting. Places affect actions. As Lily Dale knows, the gardener in the greenhouse is a different person from the gardener in the house. People are aware of the value and meaning of place and this is turned to comic effect in Mrs Proudie's reception and the curate's visit to the palace, as character adroitly steps outside its conventional limitations. But in Trollope's works characters usually reflect their surroundings although they are not determined by them, and setting thus possesses a quiet relevance to human action. The cold secretiveness of Sir Hugh Clavering is imaged in his square stone house, half-shuttered against intruding eyes, while Ullathorne Court is described in more and warmer detail because it is full of the life and passion of the Thornes for the old ways. The sham of the rich Broughtons is reflected in their Bayswater residence, 'not made of stone yet looking very stony' (*The Last Chronicle of Barset*, I, 244); but the ultimate withdrawal from life is presented in the insane Mr Kennedy whose house, a mere set of 'Ionic columns' through which the visitor passes to the 'broad stone terrace before the door' (*Phineas Finn*, I, 124) symbolizes his emptiness.

Trollope occasionally employs setting to focus objectively the inward mind of a character in a state of crisis and this is deftly achieved in *The Last Chronicle of Barset* when Mrs Dobbs Broughton hears of her husband's suicide: 'Everything was changed with her, – and was changed in such a way that she could make no guess as to her future mode of life. She was suddenly a widow, a pauper, and utterly desolate, – while the only person in the whole world that she really liked was standing close to her. But in the midst of it all she counted the windows of the house opposite' (II, 260). While it realistically evokes her state of shock, setting here also suggests her emotional void and her lack of moral perception. Even the sophisticated Dalrymple is aghast at the vacuum which is revealed and in this scene the

London world is shown to be very different from that of Barsetshire, where the parallel death of Mr Harding is a source of moral insight and self-evaluation.

In Trollope's comedy, too, setting has complete dramatic relevance. It is not the rhetorical scene-setting of Dickens, but there is nevertheless a covert and joyful collaboration between setting and character in *Barchester Towers* after the Archdeacon's first introduction to the new bishop, his wife and his chaplain, when Mr Harding mildly exclaims that he will not find it possible to like Mr Slope:

'Like him!' roared the archdeacon, standing still for a moment to give more force to his voice; 'like him!' All the ravens of the close cawed their assent. The old bells of the tower, in chiming the hour, echoed the words; and the swallows flying out from their nests mutely expressed a similar opinion. Like Mr Slope! Why no, it was not very probable that any Barchester-bred living thing should like Mr Slope! 'Nor Mrs Proudie either,' said Mr Harding.

The archdeacon hereupon forgot himself. I will not follow his example, nor shock my readers by transcribing the term in which he expressed his feeling as to the lady who had been named. The ravens and the last lingering notes of the clock bells were less scrupulous, and repeated in corresponding echoes the very improper exclamation. (1, 42).

In Chapter XIX 'Barchester by Moonlight' Trollope achieves a counterpoint of mood by a dramatic and functional use of the time of day. Eleanor Bold, Mr Slope and the Stanhopes, taking a walk on a summer night, discover that the old city, so mundane and so busy with the petty cares of its inhabitants by day, has undergone a breathtaking transformation, and its beauty stills their quarrelsome natures. The scene creates a temporary emblem of harmony which suggests the possibility of beauty and order in a world of disequilibrium and ferment. It heightens by contrast the ensuing scenes of battle in the diocese, for although Barchester people have the moral capacity to appreciate such rare moments of equipoise, they are ironically incapable of achieving them in the social world.

Thus in a fundamental way Trollope's use of the dramatic scene to articulate the meaning of the novel depends on his careful planning of the scenario.[22] There is, for example, an apparently minor scene which occurs at the physical and moral centre of *The Way We Live Now* in which Father Barham, the Roman Catholic priest from Suffolk, pays his audacious visit to the great commercial man, Melmotte. The priest's background has been meticulously drawn. He is an obscure figure on the very fringe of English society, while Melmotte is its centre and catalyst; and while Barham is an English gentleman, Melmotte is a foreign Jew. This quiet but deliberate contrast serves to draw attention to their moral likeness. Melmotte's devotion to credit, unsupported by any underlying fiscal reality, is essentially similar to Barham's faith in the dogma of his Church, for credit is divorced from capital in the same way that dogma has become estranged from faith. The priest's employment of any means to secure converts is not unlike Melmotte's weird capitalism. The priest will use Melmotte's money to buttress his Church just as the entrepreneur is manipulating religious groups to gain support for his bid to enter parliament and extend his capacity for credit. Further, each loves the exercise of power for its own sake and each comes to believe in his own infallibility. However, Barham is a religious fanatic in an age in which wealth has become the new faith. As Trollope points out: '[i]t seemed that there was but one virtue in the world, commercial enterprise, – and that Melmotte was its prophet' (I, 411). Everyone is involved in the new world and the implication of the Church in this scene indicates the scope of the corrupting association.

The emblematic and satirical value of the scene, however, lies in its ironic structure which produces a careful reversal of the reader's expectations. Instead of a lecture by the Victorian clergyman to the arrogant rich man, the priest himself comes on a speculative enterprise and Melmotte's 'Who the d[evil] are you?' (II, 55) has a mordant irony. It is also potentially a scene of moral recognition, but although Barham is given the rare opportunity of catching Melmotte off his guard he is too bigoted to perceive the depths of his deceit. In an earlier scene the Bishop of Elmham has been discussing with Barham, in a smug, pseudo-religious way, Christ's coming to the Romans. Here the priest is face to face with the Antichrist of the modern world but, ironically, in spite of all the evidence, Barham falls prey to the process of fantasy creation which sustains Melmotte's power and by an exercise of specious casuistry goes away believing the brutish man to be a good Catholic. Surprisingly, it is a process that traps Melmotte as well. As Trollope comments at the close of the scene, these gaudy and grandiose preparations for the Emperor of China's dinner demonstrate that 'the most remarkable circumstance in the career of this remarkable man was the fact that he came almost to believe in himself' (II, 57).

This scene is also a place where the reader's vision rests while there is a subterranean movement of the action. There is a concealed structural irony, for the scene in fact represents the apex of the two men's careers. It is Barham's most audacious venture before he retires to the obscurity of Suffolk, and Melmotte is soon to discover that the tide of rumour has turned against him and his wheel of fortune has started its downward turn. But the main impact of the scene is as a symbol of the world of the novel as a whole. The mediation of the needy aristocracy between the entrepreneur and the priest, the angry incoherence of the conversation, the murky quality of human intercourse encompassed by the tinsel trappings of unfettered materialism make it a potent symbol for Trollope's modern hell.

In the dramatic novel then, scenes have a relevance to the form of the novel as a whole. They present clues to its meaning; for the reader's search for significance in a Trollope novel must always be in the abstract, and yet at the same time dramatic, conflict of ideas and modes of action. This essentially spatial pattern, however, is rooted in the temporal development of the novel. At the beginning the reader wishes to know why the conflict of wills is necessary and the function of the opening scene is to create the dramatic environment which contains it. In *Barchester Towers* the comic disequilibrium in society is focused in the incongruity between the ideal of the Church and its reality as a merely temporal institution. Like the battle between the old and the new, this fundamental split is already present as Archdeacon Grantly watches at the bedside of his dying father, torn between his desire for a bishopric and his love for the gentle old man. This inner conflict is evoked emblematically by the entry of Mr Harding, who stands at the kneeling man's shoulder, the embodiment of his conscience, as Grantly repents of his naked ambition. Although the scene is muted, the rare inside view of Grantly that we are given deftly serves to set apart the elegaic mood of the old world from the comic world of the new bishop, a world of power struggles rather than inner moral strivings. What is more, the conflict overlaps with Trollope's political world from the start; there is an emblematic aptness in Grantly's use of the new-fangled telegraph to wire his urgent message to London and in the demise of the old ministry which makes an ironic parallel with his father's death. But the full relevance of this finely-judged opening scene is only apparent at the conclusion of the novel when the unworldly Mr Harding defeats the divisive tactics of the Archdeacon by renouncing the deanery in favour of Arabin in order to maintain the necessary delicate balance of diocesan power. Just as the anarchic Madeline Stanhope's uncharacteristic efforts at reconciliation succeed on the social level, so in the political sphere Mr Harding demonstrates surprising insight and force as he re-establishes equilibrium in the clerical world. Grantly's self-regarding desire for power, which his old friend thought unseemly, is thus nullified as the emblematic significance of the opening scene is translated into fact.

One important aspect of Trollope's realism is his ability to employ dramatic structural techniques in the novel so that scenes transcend the individual novel and span the years, making a larger temporal pattern. Trollope's recognition of the function of Mr Harding in Dr Grantly's inner life at the beginning of *Barchester Towers* allows his death, the serenity of which reminds Grantly of his father's saintliness, to make the parallel quietly emphatic. This scene provides the Archdeacon with an astonishing moment of understanding of the deeper nature of his relation with his father-in-law. It prompts him to make the alien judgement that the old man he had often scorned had 'all the spirit of a hero' (*The Last Chronicle of Barset*, II, 421), and this revelation that the meek old man has been a father-figure to the bullying, worldly cleric and the source of the conscience that moderated his actions is a profound psychological and moral insight which provides the reader with the shock of recognition that realism demands. Yet Trollope had prepared for it in the quiet opening scene of *Barchester Towers*.

This kind of temporal placing and ironic balance is apparent in Mr Crawley's interview with the Bishop. The irony of his infuriating smile gathers increased significance in the life of Mrs Proudie as it drives her to unparalleled interference in Church matters when she humiliates her husband in front of the powerful Dr Tempest, so undermining his authority in the diocese that he wishes her dead. The collapse of her marriage and the removal of the comic mask has an ironic point for it reveals that in truth it was she who was dependent on her husband. When he sinks into apathy and gloom, she dies. This recognition, which accompanies her reversal of fortune, is a source of moral discovery and it enforces the sense of contradiction between appearance and reality, which is shown to be an integral and surprising part of the reality of human life. And it sends the reader searching back over the cumulative growth of her monomania which was there unheeded in her meeting with the Archdeacon at the beginning of *Barchester Towers*. In retrospect the battle with the rebellious curate emerges as something different from what the reader was led to believe. It presented an opportunity for moral recognition and growth that was not grasped. Not only that, but the scene of their encounter was in fact an ironic turning-point in their lives; for as Mr Crawley's smile fed her anger and set her on a destructive path it also marked a change in the psychological health of the curate and foreshadowed his ultimate vindication.

Such scenes are part of the evolution of cause and effect in the lives of the characters and the most important of them are necessary in a fundamental sense, for they are part of the dramatic rhythm of the novel. They mark a major point in the narrative where the characters experience a break between motives and effects and have to adjust to altered circumstances. They are important moments of moral recognition and the first and most prominently placed is that in which the first cycle of the action culminates and which checks its momentum. Most obviously this is true of the scene of Lady Mason's abrupt and unexpected confession to Sir Peregrine Orme that she forged her husband's will and is in truth guilty of the crime for which she is being tried. It is one of the central dramatic scenes in *Orley Farm*, tense with the emotions of love and shock, of recognition and reversal, and it results in each of the lovers having to re-evaluate their future relation. The rest of the action develops out of the changed balance of forces. And these pivotal scenes are carefully prepared for. In *The Last Chronicle of Barset*, for instance, the clash between the palace and Mr Crawley is anticipated in the opening discussion by the Walker family which outlines for us the scope of the conflict; by Mrs Proudie's mindless opposition to the Framley set; by Mr Crawley's trenchant rejection of Mr Thumble's message and by the joyful and faintly silly martyrdom of his long walk to Barchester. The sequence of cause and effect is broken by the Proudies' recognition of the difference between the probabilities as they estimated them – that Mr Crawley would be cowed and submissive at the palace – and the altered necessities that lie ahead of them as this assumption proves totally false.

The conclusions of Trollope's novels frequently embody the conventional recognition scenes of the drama. They are often a complex set of scenes which complete character and structure and which possess unusual moral significance. They show how the forces that shaped the conflict also give meaning to its conclusion, for in the dramatic novel the end is implied in the beginning. In *The Claverings*, for instance, the quietly emblematic final scene is one which completes the major ironic reversal in the novel as the super-jilt, Lady Ongar, who has failed to regain Harry Clavering's love, talks to his future wife, the prudent Florence Burton, in the same grounds of Clavering Park where she had refused him in the opening scene in favour of wealth and position. She recalls her prophecy that she would return to Clavering only when Harry is married, and observes that it is now being fulfilled. But the concealed irony, which even in the bitterness of self-mockery she is too generous to reveal to the naïve Florence, is that the prudence which took Harry away from her was not the result of his deepest instinctive choice, but the product of social forces he was not strong enough to withstand. Seen in these terms, the marriage which ends the novel is not a conventional gesture of hope for the future but is, instead, inconclusive and bitterly ironic.

Trollope's scenic method of presenting character and developing action is varied. Not all scenes are crises. In most of Trollope's vast, panoramic novels there are a number of quiet domestic scenes with a less immediate commitment to plot. These serve to familiarize the reader with character before it is set in action, like the Walkers' conversation about Mr Crawley at the beginning of *The Last Chronicle of Barset;* or to give added depth to the novel's perspective by suggesting the unremittingly normal background of daily life, like the Noningsby scenes in *Orley Farm* or, as in *The Bertrams*, those quiet domestic scenes which obscure private tragedy. And sometimes they capture the moral atmosphere of a social group like the Burtons in *The Claverings*, whose class attitudes have a crucial function in the narrative. But another kind of scene which possesses a convincing reality for the reader is that in which the action is hidden beneath an exterior surface on which nothing very much appears to be happening. For instance, in *The Eustace Diamonds* Lucinda Roanoke's love of hunting at first seems no more than an expression of a healthy athleticism and sociability. However, the scene in which she meets Sir Griffin Tewett in the hunting field is fraught with the concealed tensions of covert manoeuvring as her aunt, Mrs Carbuncle, seeks to marry her to the highest bidder. The odious Sir Griffin is attracted by Lucinda's physical power and her curious hatred of sexuality, and the hunter swiftly becomes the pursued. The scene of the hunt thus gains a complex emblematic significance for the perverted sexuality of the society of *The Eustace Diamonds* and it turns Lucinda Roanoke's life in the direction of personal tragedy.

Trollope's realism is most effective in those scenes devoted to the portrayals of ordinary family life like the conversation between the Duke of Omnium and his sons at the breakfast table in *The Duke's Children.* But the character of the Duke himself is best revealed in *The Prime Minister* in one of those odd little scenes which are so often related to plot and theme in an unobtrusive way when, in the middle of the great political entertainment at Gatherum, the Prime Minister disappears for a walk in the grounds with old Lady Rosina De Courcy. Their discussion of the merits of cork soles emphasizes his absorption in mundane matters like decimal coinage. But this scene has wider implications, for the Duke is sensitively aware of the vulgarity of the party from which he has temporarily escaped and recognizes his conspicuous lack of the tact and *bonhomie* necessary to the leader of a Coalition Government. More disturbing for him is the fact that his wife, in organizing these gatherings, is beginning to dominate not only the uneasy coalition of their marriage but (he fears) the Government as well, for, witty and gregarious, she is the truly political creature of the two. His walk with Lady Rosina is thus not simply an expression of the greater ease that he feels in the company of the old Whig aristocracy, nor merely an escape from the tedious duty of seeing to his guests; but his absence from the huge party on such a frivolous pretext offers a covert challenge to his wife's efforts and to the principle of coalition itself in both private and public life. As the novel reveals, it is the Prime Minister who helps to sabotage the Government, and at the very time when, ironically, he was becoming subtly enamoured of power.

In his complex employment of the dramatic scene then, Trollope's aesthetic sense consistently serves his realism. This aspect of his art is so well concealed that it has been overlooked, but in the major novels his scenes are all thematically placed and related and they make an unremitting contribution to his moral vision. Trollope's art depends to a large extent on his judicious use of scene and scenario, but in a real sense it derives from the conviction that what he dramatized really was dramatic.

III
THE FORM OF
THE STORY

The Open Form: *The Last Chronicle of Barset*

THE sheer scope and complexity of a panoramic novel like *The Last Chronicle of Barset*, which Trollope believed was his best work, are basically an expression of his need to give some kind of articulation to the growth and crowdedness of his world. For this reason Jerome Thale, for instance, argues that plot is not important as an element in the structure of this novel and he stresses instead the spatial quality of its design. He reminds us that Trollope himself regarded plot as 'the most insignificant part of a tale' and as merely the 'vehicle' for the narrative.[1] Jerome Thale therefore views the form of *The Last Chronicle of Barset*, with its gradual accumulation of situations and events in spatial patterns, as analogous to painting or music.[2] However, in my view traditional plotting does have an essential function in Trollope's design of the novel and a closer analogy to the multiple plotting in *The Last Chronicle of Barset*, with its parallels and contrasts of character and situation, juxtapositions and criss-crossing of lives and worlds, is not painting or music, but the Jacobean drama.

Ruth apRoberts has argued cogently that as a moralist, Trollope's preferred form, the 'shaping principle' of his fiction as she terms it, is the neatly circumscribed moral situation of novels like *The Warden*.[3] As I shall argue later in this chapter, there is some truth in this view, but we should remember that like his close friend George Eliot Trollope was a diligent observer of the larger world of English society and in his best fiction acute personal moral dilemmas are worked out in an organic relation to the wider circles of social life that encompass them. In *The Last Chronicle of Barset* he succeeds brilliantly in amplifying this principle into an appropriate form for a panoramic study of English social life for as its title implies, the novel is not simply the story of Mr Crawley and the missing cheque, but is a sustained moral exploration of a whole contemporary world: the story of society at a point of change. And in order to achieve this Trollope employed traditional techniques of dramatic plotting.

Of course the term 'plot' has long been a stumbling block in Trollope criticism, partly because Trollope himself employs it in two different senses in his *Autobiography*. When he speaks of plot as the 'vehicle' for the story it is clear from the context of his discussion of Wilkie Collins's sensational novels that he means the external mechanics of the narrative design. However, elsewhere in the *Autobiography* Trollope minimizes the care he expends on the narrative; he stresses instead his serious artistic attention to the function of subsidiary plots and makes it clear that his solution to the form of the story lay in his examination of the technique of multiple plotting:

Though [the novelist's] story should be all one, yet it may have many parts. Though the plot itself may require but few characters, it may be so enlarged as to find its full development in many. There may be subsidiary plots, which shall all tend to the elucidation of the main story, and which will take their places as part of one and the same work . . .'[4]

Thus plot, in its traditional sense, is fundamental to the form of the story in *The Last Chronicle of Barset*. The techniques associated with multiple plotting provide a dynamic means of combining the thematic concentration of the moral fable with a comprehensive study of a whole world. The subsidiary plots form compositional centres in the novel, each embodying a different aspect of its dominant theme. The story is thus an integrating power, bringing all the plots and characters into significant relation, and it is finally revealed as a static moral design as well as an organic creation. In *The Last Chronicle of*

Barset there are a number of plots competing for the reader's moral attention. There is the poverty-stricken curate accused of theft; his daughter's love for the Archdeacon's son; the continued saga of John Eames's courtship of Lily Dale; and the problems of the artist Conway Dalrymple, making his way among the parvenus in London. These constitute the moral centres which compete for the reader's sympathy and judgement. The fundamental design is made by parallel and antithesis of character as well as by the similarity and contrast of the human situation. And it is essential for the reader to grasp these relations in order to follow Trollope's narrative in its fullest moral sense.

The Last Chronicle of Barset is a study of the possibilities for moral heroism in a world of fluctuating ideals and as such it is the exception to Trollope's consistent refusal, on the grounds of realism, to admit heroes into his fiction.[5] He feared the spread of bureaucracy and the commercial ethic and felt that the modern world, with its restrictive codes, its shifting ethical standards and corrupting pursuit of money had shrunk spiritually and offered little scope for acts of individual heroism.[6] However, Trollope still had faith in the sustaining and civilizing power of traditional cultural values fostered by the Church, by the rural community and by a strong literary heritage. He felt also that heroes were more than ever needed; not in the Carlylean mould, nor the Biedermeier heroes of cheap Victorian fiction, but as individuals who possessed the rare and peculiar kind of moral heroism which such traditional values help to shape. This is the unifying theme which informs Trollope's sophisticated narrative design. The form of *The Last Chronicle of Barset* is, I think, both more complex and more precisely articulated than Trollope has been given credit for and it is also the product of a more profoundly moral intelligence than Trollope has usually been allowed.

The major unifying characters of *The Last Chronicle of Barset*, Mr Crawley and John Eames, consistently advance its central moral concern as each in his way attempts to be a modern hero. The complete social and personal contrast between the ascetic country curate and the complacent young London civil servant, who never meet in the novel, draws attention to their parallel stories. At the conclusion Trollope makes it clear that it was not his intention to write 'an epic about clergymen'. Had this been his aim, he would have taken 'St Paul for [his] model' (II, 452). But in Mr Crawley's despairing battles with poverty, the law and the Church this is exactly the pattern of heroic martyrdom that he proposes to himself. It is part of his belief and part of his nature. His reading of the Greek drama and his identification with the great deliverer 'Eyeless in Gaza, at the mill with slaves' (II, 232) give him the inspiration he needs to prosecute a satisfying victory over the timid Bishop and his termagant wife. The battle for his pulpit makes the curate something of a hero in Barsetshire, but what spoils his claim to epic heroism is the rooted egoism that makes the image of a martyr attractive to him.[7] While Mr Crawley is making a stand against the foundering ideals of the Church, Eames's more limited idealism is expressed in his romantic constancy to Lily Dale, which bestows on him the conscious role of a 'hero of romance' (II, 322). This is given spurious substance in London by the myths, current at the Income-tax Board where he works, that have grown out of his thrashing of his rival Crosbie, so that 'Mr. John Eames had about him much of the heroic' (I, 147). In Barsetshire Mr Crawley is a poor and faintly silly figure, humbling his finely-honed intellect in the service of the Hoggle End labourers, while Eames, floating emotionally between the values of London and those of Barsetshire, accommodates himself uneasily to the insistently commercial ethos of the metropolis.

There is a pointed difference between the great epic heroes from whom Mr Crawley derives his strength and the potential heroes of *The Last Chronicle of Barset*. Since Victorian social life no longer offers the opportunity for heroism on a meaningful scale Trollope shows how, instead of the hero mirroring and amplifying the aspirations of his society, in contemporary life the potential hero has to battle against its collective will. The presence in this novel of idealistic rebels in conflict with major Victorian institutions and codes makes a large moral generalization. The political nature of ecclesiastical life is ironically exposed by the integrity of the curate's revolt. Belief in the sanctity of the priesthood dictates his cumulative battles and as sides are taken the schism in the diocese widens. This forms part of a larger pattern in the novel, for while the Church in Barsetshire is ruled by a weak, hen-pecked bishop, the Income-tax Board in London is run by the arrogant bully Sir Raffle Buffle. John Eames, his private secretary, resents his sycophantic position. He cannot be bothered to preserve the insidious illusion of industry that Buffle's ego demands. The superbly farcical scene in which Eames counterbluffs his superior in order to gain leave of absence to aid Mr Crawley makes a fine parallel with the curate's climactic interview at the palace, where Mr Crawley's equally shrewd political instinct quickly discerns and challenges the real source of diocesan power.

Rebellion is one of the counterpointed themes which bind the story. The major ironic effect of these scenes is that the true rebel in each case is the figurehead of the institution being threatened. Buffle's blatant abuse of power is an open secret in the Civil Service, which nevertheless allows him to retain his position, while the 'inhibition' that Mrs Proudie makes her husband send Mr Crawley is strictly illegal. As everyone in the diocese knows, the subversive force in Barsetshire is not the rebellious curate, but the Bishop's wife. There is a similarity of situation, but there is a difference of moral emphasis. Eames attacks the bureaucratic heavy-weight of the Civil Service from the strength conferred by his financial independence, while the curate has to construct his rebellion from political weakness and poverty; but Mr Crawley's revolt is in truth sincerely con-servative, while Eames's insouciant rebellion differs only in degree from his superior's self-regarding pride. Egoism is the root of moral failure in *The Last Chronicle of Barset*. This is illumined by the cluster of minor figures. Neither Mr Crawley's quest for sympathy among the labourers at Hoggle End nor Eames's soliciting of support from his wealthy patroness is in keeping with the demands of heroic dignity. What is more, the curate's relinquishing of his pulpit is the deliberate choice of an unnecessary martyrdom. Pride makes Mr Crawley's best actions perverse and this is something of which he is partly aware. Ironi-cally, Eames also succumbs to his own kind of myth-making, falling into the clutches of an aggressive London girl and almost wilfully losing Lily Dale, who has come to love him as a man, if not as a god. The parallel though separate and discrete development of their stories makes a dominant structural irony, which serves the function of moral emphasis as the wheel of fortune turns for both men, as in a morality play. At the conclusion of the novel the romantic hero, rejected for the last time by Lily Dale after his 'epic' pursuit of the Dean, is left weeping over a rail in a deserted street. For Mr Crawley, however, life reveals a different solution. His battles arise partly from thwarted ambition, so his elevation from the stylized posture of a radical defender of the poor to the status of a vicar is appropriate and embarrassingly human.

This is only one of a number of interlocking relations which advance the novel's central concern against a complex, densely realized social background. Like Eames, Major Grantly fails to achieve heroic stature in spite of all his moral striving. Trapped between the claims of rank and romantic heroism, he gives in to social pressure; not to the disguised materialism of his father the Archdeacon, nor even to the approbation of his class, but to the more subtle power of the novel's women. They view Lily Dale's refusal of John Eames and the Archdeacon's battle with his son as a threat to the romantic feminine love code, which in turn masks a hard-headed devotion to marriage. Just as Eames allows the women to plead his cause with Lily, so too Major Grantly is persuaded by the collective feminine will of Barsetshire society. His equivocation is resolved by a conversation with the austere but warm-hearted schoolmistress Miss Prettyman, and by a parallel encounter in Silverbridge High Street with the subversive millionairess Mrs Thorne, whose contempt for timid conformity to social rules, brusque dismissal of the affair of the 'trumpery cheque' and frank delight in romantic sacrifice, bring the staid Major to the point of reluctant decision.

One function of the interwoven plots is to create a pattern of moral correspondence in the reader's mind through juxtaposition. The meeting of Eames and Grantly on the railway train down to Guestwick, as each journeys to propose to his respective young lady, effects a natural transition from London to Barsetshire. But more importantly, it is also the meeting of different lives. Trollope's plots are really different versions of the same human predicament and here they meet, as they are designed to do. The deft juxtaposition of the points of view of the two men in the railway carriage, each pretending to read but pondering instead the difficult endeavour ahead, probes their claims to romantic heroism. Trollope's tone and the reading direction in the chapter title, 'A Hero at Home', alert the reader to the fact that Eames is a little too self-conscious and rather weary of his fruitless role. Trollope's ironic deflation also extends to the Major who, unlike Eames, anticipates an easy victory, but is conscious at the same time of his sacrifice and is not relishing the 'task' before him. While Eames's journey is the result of his friend Dalrymple's taunting, Major Grantly's trip is prompted by the social skill of the Barsetshire ladies. Moreover, just as Eames's lapses from constancy follow the examples of London life, so the Major's devotion at Allington is inspired, not by his easy victory but by Grace Crawley's selfless refusal of him. As Trollope comments sardonically, 'Half at least of the noble deeds done in this world are due to emulation, rather than to the native nobility of the actors' (I, 314). The moral distinction between the two men comes out in their contrasted capacity to learn. Grantly accepts the reprimand to his narrow egoism, but Eames fails to understand that he simply lacks the kind of heroic qualities that Lily Dale demands and he remains trapped by his illusions. What the weight of the novel's social panorama obscures it is the function of such a deft juxtaposition of plots to reveal.

For much of the novel the lives of these two men, which crisscross and run parallel before diverging, chart similar successes and failures; but the spirited girls whom they pursue both achieve a quiet moral victory. Grace Crawley and Lily Dale have contrasted origins and destinies, but they share an acuteness of moral sensibility which makes marriage problematical for them. And it prompts them to seek perversely heroic solutions to their dilemmas. Grace's sheltered life at the Hogglestock parsonage sharpens her suffering under the stigma of theft which her father has incurred. Nevertheless when Major Grantly finally proposes, she rejects the social approbation that such a marriage would confer on her disgraced family, feeling that her motives must be clearly above suspicion. For Lily Dale, who is older, the moral issue is more complex. In the past is her heartless jilting by Adolphus Crosbie; in the present is the choice between a tempting but dangerous marriage with him, or the social acclaim of a joyless match with John Eames. Her struggle to escape the illusions of her past is morally fine, but its conclusion is deliberately ambivalent.[8] Away from the security of her mother's house at Allington, Lily Dale is less pert, less wise too. The atmosphere of the metropolis, with its suggestion of new standards and wider possibilities, is morally unsettling. It makes correct decisions difficult. The London scenes are therefore all scenes of crisis for Lily Dale just as those in Barsetshire are for Grace Crawley. London is the place of her disenchantment as her encounters with Crosbie at the picture-gallery and in the park force her to accept how shabby her 'Pall Mall hero' really is. She cannot accept either man as hero or husband. In reaching this decision her adolescent egoism is gradually transmuted into the sustaining pride of self-denial and self-conquest. There is, Trollope suggests, something heroic in her final endorsement of the letters 'O.M.' in her book, but there is also something perverse and human.

The continuing story of John Eames and Lily Dale bulks large in *The Last Chronicle of Barset* because part of its function is to link the contrasted worlds of Barsetshire and London. In Barsetshire the illusory claims of epic and romantic heroism are soon discredited. They cannot flourish in a healthy moral climate. But in London people inhabit a world of fantasy. Here the unknown artist Conway Dalrymple, who deifies on canvas the leaders of the commercial world, becomes a celebrity overnight. The hero of the 'city' and the 'artist hero' are both the focus of society's escapist and perverted quest for romantic ideals. Here in the metropolis a further minor parallel is made between Dalrymple and John Eames. Eames's languid self-approval incurs heavy authorial irony as he is introduced as 'our hero' whose heroism lies merely in the fact that he moves among 'very respectable people' (I, 243). Dalrymple and Eames both employ their heroic roles to make a misplaced assault on the inner sanctum of this society; but through inexperience the young innocents are ensnared by its destructively neurotic women. Dalrymple quickly tires of the shallow, theatrical Mrs Dobbs Broughton while Eames, initially the more critical of the Broughton set, is completely beguiled by the wily, sophisticated Madalina Demolines.

The first fourteen chapters of *The Last Chronicle of Barset* read as if it were a novel with a central figure, concerned solely with Mr Crawley and the moral dilemma created by his supposed theft of Lord Lufton's cheque. By Chapter XIV rumour has spread and Barsetshire is alive with clerical scandal. Then the story moves rather abruptly from the curate to John Eames and the narrative never returns to Mr Crawley with quite the same concentration. His private agony takes its place in the rotating pattern of the other plots. The reader who desires tragedy may be disappointed by this movement, but it is strictly functional and its aim is the achievement of a realistic treatment of human issues. The obscure country curate cannot become a tragic St Paul figure in the modern world. His life has to be placed in perspective by the wider milieux of London so that it is swallowed up and forgotten in the bustle of the larger commercial and social world.

Trollope employs the techniques associated with multiple plotting to create structural effects that bind the story while permitting it to expand. This involves him in problems of transition, which are overcome by cross-cutting from one world to another. This makes for formal emphasis while stressing human variety. The first major transition from Barsetshire to the metropolis, the cross-cutting from the private scene at Allington between Lily Dale and her mother, with its fullness of human sympathy, to the public vulgarity of the Broughtons' dinner-party in Chapter XXIV is deliberately abrupt, morally complete and achieved with just the right modulation of narrative tone. Trollope's sympathy for Lily Dale's brave confrontation of her fear of moral cowardice contrasts with his sharp condemnation of Eames's smug acceptance of shoddy London ways. The transition, which is carefully related to plot and character, is made through the silent presence in the scene of Lily's agony of the two rivals, the would-be hero of romance, John Eames, and her former 'Apollo', Adolphus Crosbie. This relation is neatly reversed in the following scene at the Bayswater party where she makes a powerful impact on their hostile encounter, and both are ironically unaware of her decision to renounce them.

This patterning of interwoven plots and milieux produces a series of moving contrasts which gives *The Last Chronicle of Barset* its social richness and moral density. It also acts as a formal correlative for Trollope's apprehension of the shared surface of human life and creates an appropriate form for his investigation of a whole society. Since the hero is essentially an isolated figure, it is the crowdedness of the social world which often conceals from him the ironic correspondence of his predicament with those of other people. Mr Crawley, for instance, knows nothing of the poverty of Mr Quiverful. Moreover, the proximity of parallel lives can offer alternative examples to follow or reject. For Grace Crawley, the Miss Prettymans' lives as schoolmistresses, lonely and tainted with sexual and social failure, present the alternative to marriage. This is why they press her courtship with such vigour and agonize over her selfless refusal of Major Grantly. While for Lily Dale there is constantly before her the pre-nuptial joy of Emily Dunstable, which tempts her to salvage some happiness for herself in a marriage with John Eames. And what enhances the integrity of the moral choices of Grace and Lily is their quiet but stubborn refusal of easy alternatives.

Trollope also insists that heroic action must be viewed realistically in the context of life's limiting conditions of time and chance. Life offers various options which become irrevocable as past choices alter the present and also serve to make present comparisons. While, for Eames, Crosbie's presence in London gives continued support to his feeling of heroic dominance over the man he once thrashed, it is also a nagging reminder of his failure to achieve heroic stature in Lily Dale's terms. And in the same way, Dean Arabin forms part of the conscious burden of worldly failure that Mr Crawley has to bear. The reversal that has taken place in the lives of the Dean and the curate is, of course, one aspect of Trollope's criticism of the Church. While both were fine scholars at the university, in the political world of the Church one rose and the other fell. But this is also partly why one is a potential hero and the other is not. The intervening years of disappointment and frustration have nurtured Mr Crawley's revolutionary zeal, while the Dean has slipped into well-bred sloth. Indeed, Dean Arabin's success represents only one of a series of paths that were open to Mr Crawley, as his triumphant interview with the Bishop and his temperamental similarity to the Rural Dean Dr Tempest suggest. The curate is himself aware of this and it provides more fuel for his rebellion, for the kinds of lives which he covets and which might have been his, are precisely those lives that he feels morally compelled to shun. Not all Trollope's connections are as emphatic as this or we would lose the sense of naturalness which *The Last Chronicle of Barset* so richly provides, but they are strong enough to give a sense of unity in diversity, which is one of its dominant moral effects. The presentation of similar lives with different endings is a fundamental aspect of Trollope's realistic and moral sense. It places moral heroism firmly in the context of the variability of human growth and the continual narrowing of present choices.

Several critics dislike the shift in focus away from the story of Mr Crawley, the disreputable nature of the new characters who are introduced and the change in tone from the tragic to the satirical. However, this movement is thematically important. Barsetshire and London are clearly segregated areas of moral experience. The supposed theft of the cheque is a big scandal in Barsetshire, while in London thieving clergymen are almost commonplace. And similarly, Barsetshire's definitions of heroism and those of London are very different and must be allowed to comment on each other, especially since, as Trollope observes, metropolitan life is beginning to alter the country ways. He therefore insinuates into the narrative, quietly and without strain, many connections between Barsetshire and London. And in the modern world the strongest link is financial. Archdeacon Grantly draws a substantial income from London property; his son Charles preaches at a famous London church; Mrs Thorne's ointment millions allow her to keep an ostentatious house there and Eames's legacy assists him to prosper in London in the Civil Service. In Barchester the palace is invaded by evangelical Londoners and the ancient cathedral close is threatened by the desecrating hands of the Ecclesiastical Commission. The influence of metropolitan values is extended as London increasingly becomes the source of Barsetshire wealth and power and as it meddles more and more in provincial affairs.

Part of the contrast between the two worlds is made in scenes which overlap in time, thus drawing them to the surface of the reader's moral attention. As Eames's trip to Barsetshire coincides with Mr Crawley's visit to London, the potential hero of Barsetshire is being tried by the hard-headed reality of the city, while the romantic hero of the metropolis is being tested by the moral context of the country. The bewildered Mr Crawley is engaged on a painful quest for the truth of his moral condition and in baring his heart to the vulgar, shrewd, but generous lawyer, Mr Toogood, the shy and fastidious curate undergoes a penitential exercise in humility. The setting of Eames's crisis at Allington is more quietly emblematic. The frosted garden of the Small House makes an image of the dead relation with Lily Dale which he refuses to recognize. The strength and tact with which Lily rejects her opportunity to avoid the blight of spinsterhood means that Allington comes to stand in the novel as the emblem of the country's power of almost too self-conscious moral scrutiny. Eames returns to London with the knowledge that he is 'vain, and foolish, and unsteady' (I, 372), but its unreal atmosphere quickly absorbs him once again and he manages to turn failure into romantic martyrdom on an 'heroic' scale.

In the pattern of interwoven plots an important effect, as one plot is replaced with another, is structural irony. This is especially powerful in the cross-cutting between Chapters XL and XLI, from Mr Toogood's aggressively homely hospitality in London to Mr Crawley's ill health at Hogglestock. Here Trollope relies on the power of gossip and rumour, the connecting and relating agents *in The Last Chronicle of Barset*, to assist the transition. Mr Toogood defends Mr Crawley before the urbane Silverbridge attorney Mr Walker, but he is forced to admit the justice of the popular opinion that the curate is a 'queer fish' (I, 414). The subsequent shift in scene to the curate's house is a movement from the city to the country, from city affluence to an interior marked by poverty and from the measured tone of professional debate to the human agony. Neither man has seen him like this. Prostrated by the journey to London and by overwork, his delirious revelation of the truth about the missing cheque spills out unremarked. This demonstrates how Mr Crawley's queerness, his inability to recall money given in charity, is part of his heroic strength as well as one aspect of his human failure. Because the crowd scene is segregated from that in which the curate is presented in isolation the reader turns with greater sympathy from the misunderstanding group to the scarcely-known man. Since, as the novel demonstrates, heroes nowadays are 'queer', public discussion obscures their private suffering, just as rumour makes what is private public and unbearable.

The most important effect of the pattern of rotating plots in *The Last Chronicle of Barset* is the deliberate ironic undercutting of one story by the next. Eames's shallow heroics are set beside the greater generosity of Major Grantly and their limited rebellions are in turn undercut by the tenacity of Mr Crawley's courageous revolt against the Bishop. It is a complex moral design which reveals only finally their complete moral stature. We discover with a shock that Mr Crawley's revolutionary fervour and intellectual arrogance overlie an innate conservatism and humility of almost heroic magnitude. When Mr Toogood and Major Grantly bring news that he will not now have to stand trial, the curate astounds them by remarking that in his clearer moments he had known all along where the cheque came from. What his pride and jealousy have concealed is that he really does believe in the superiority of Dean Arabin and was too humble to contradict his friend for a second time. When Major Grantly exclaims 'I call that man a hero' (II, 354) it is difficult not to agree. Even worldly Mr Toogood does. But it is a heroism qualified by the development of the novel as a whole and by Mr Crawley's assimilation at its conclusion into the easier conventions of polite ecclesiastical society as he is transformed into an establishment figure.

This process of deferred judgement is partly due to the progress and treatment of character. Our interest in Mr Crawley involves a changed response to him as he alters under the impact of political strife from a self-pitying, maudlin figure to a formidable rebel. However, all the claimants to a degree of moral heroism present different versions of failure when they are set beside the gracious humility of old Mr Harding, who emerges as the novel's most consistent rebel and its only true moral hero. This dominant irony, which Trollope allows to surface late in the novel, is deliberately concealed by the bustle of the various stories competing for our attention, all of which are finally set beside that of Mr Harding to be judged. Trollope's hero is an odd, saintly old man, simple, selfless and apparently ignored in all diocesan affairs. But he possesses to a profound degree the quality of sympathy which is such a healing force in Trollope's divided world. Just as in *The Warden*, when he battled successfully with his powerful, bullying son-in-law the Archdeacon over relinquishing Hiram's Hospital, and in *Barchester Towers*, when with rare political shrewdness and love for the Church he renounced the deanery in favour of Arabin, he is still a tenacious though sweet-tempered rebel. In *The Last Chronicle of Barset* he triumphs not only over his worldly daughter, for he thinks highly of Grace Crawley, but over the whole diocese because he is almost alone in refusing to believe that a Barsetshire clergyman could be a thief. And he strenuously asserts Mr Crawley's innocence in the teeth of all the evidence, risking ridicule as a senile and foolish old man.

Mr Harding represents Trollope's ideal of heroic goodness. He has unlimited faith in the Church and in humanity. It is his sympathy for Mr Crawley which prompts the letter to his daughter Eleanor, the Dean's wife, that finally discloses the origin of the cheque. It is Mr Harding's profound sympathy and clarity of moral vision that allows him to discern and remedy the cause of Mr Crawley's martyrdom and he is the source of the profound reversal of fortune in Mr Crawley's life. His last and most selfless act is that of ensuring that his own living, St Ewold's Parsonage, will go after his death to the curate whom he has scarcely known, but in whom he has recognized those marks of spiritual distinction needed in the higher service of the Church. In the scene at Mr Harding's death-bed, with its marvellously controlled pathos, his moral influence over the bluff Archdeacon is so strong that St Ewold's is promised for Mr Crawley with a squeeze of the hand. The origin of the old man's moral power lies in his complete unworldliness and in the unfeigned love that people bear him. With a few quiet words he contrives to close the breach between Henry Grantly and his father. And even after his death he is still a pervasive presence whose healing power is at work in human lives. The Bishop remembers him as the only person in the diocese who genuinely mourned the death of Mrs Proudie and his presence at Mr Harding's funeral prompts the Archdeacon's surprising inward pledge of future peace in the diocese. This healing web of profoundly emotional responses to the moral presence of the old man repairs the fabric of human life in Barchester. In a strange way Mr Harding's moral heroism also invariably produces the shrewdest and healthiest political solutions. Grantly is profoundly moved by the death of his old friend. Pacing before the deanery fire, in a rare moment of moral insight there bursts from him the alien judgement that the odd old man he had often scorned had 'all the spirit of a hero' (II, 421). This revelation has all the weight of the novel's structure behind it; for Trollope places it at the centre of a number of interlocking stories and allows it to emerge late in the narrative with the maximum of ironic effect. He is concerned to show that in an increasingly materialistic, political and self-absorbed society the truly effective revolutionary is a conservative and a man with no pride. The moral hero of *The Last Chronicle of Barset* is the 'unheroic' hero.

The movement away to London a third of the way through the novel means that such heroism is placed in a much wider social context. Trollope wishes to demonstrate how the decline of moral heroism is connected with the spread of materialism and the corresponding loss of human scale in modern life. For much of the novel's length the technique of balance and counter-point is employed to advance this vision. The shifts from the country to London and back are made in terms of the moral atmosphere of places like the open fields of Allington which is the setting of Lily Dale's self-sacrifice and an emblem of the country's power of moral discrimination; or the secretiveness of dingy Hook Court, the origin of Dobbs Broughton's tinsel splendour and the scene of his suicide. These places can bear the weight of emblematic significance for the lives of the people who live there because they are first realized on a physical and human level. One powerful effect of the contrapuntal structure of the London and Barsetshire plots lies in Trollope's emblematic use of scenes which take their place in the balancing masses of the novel. In particular he employs two such scenes to show how the focus of idealizing tendencies in modern times has changed; it is no longer the local parson as it was in the days of Jane Austen, but the city financier. The occasion of the drinking of the last of the 1820 port at Plumstead is, for old Mr Harding, an occasion for quiet nostalgia for the days when clergymen were gentlemen; when they danced and played cards. But when the Archdeacon makes this a source of bitter contrast with the present, Mr Harding's scrupulous conscience forces him to take a radical stance and denounce the idleness of former days. Nevertheless, the drinking of the wine confers an almost sacra-mental quality upon the past, which is intensified by their acute sense of mutability. The corresponding scene at the Broughtons' dinner-party is in striking contrast as we move from the clergy-men's quiet conversation to the forced gaiety and concealed tensions of the secular world of Bayswater. There is a complete change of tone as Broughton vulgarly boasts of the price of his '42 Bordeaux. For him it merely represents success, and is part of his posture as a hero of materialism. Here in the contrast between Barsetshire and London the emblematic patterning of the ecclesiastical and the secular, the past and the present, is full and complete.

These emblems are local and temporary, but there are two emblems which Trollope employs recurrently : the painting of Jael and Sisera on which the artist Dalrymple is engaged, and

Mr Crawley's books. The painting functions as a metaphor for the London scenes as the books do for those in Barsetshire. They indicate how the achievement of some kind of moral heroism depends on people retaining links with a strong cultural tradition. The painting represents the perversion of art and history, for Dalrymple is simply pandering to the commercial man's desire to attain a kind of heroic immortality. More significantly, like Sisera the London men are betrayed into the treacherous hands of rapacious women and the dominance of the female will marks this society as neurotic and nihilistic. The grotesque scenes at the Broughtons' house serve cumulatively to extend the meaning of the picture, which becomes suddenly explicit when Dalrymple rips it apart in the presence of Mrs Van Siever. He does so because he recognizes that its absurd illusion gets in the way of human reality and by this action he asserts his preference for the sober honesty of Clara Van Siever, even with her poverty, to the sham heroism conferred on him by art and wealth. It is a small heroic gesture, but one which Trollope shows is increasingly difficult to make in the modern world.

As I have already suggested here, Trollope retained a strongly held faith in the sustaining moral force of a cultural heritage. And while culture is prostituted in London, what fortifies Mr Crawley, by contrast, in his battles against an oppressive world are his tattered books of heroic mythology. After the challenging visit of Mr Thumble with the Bishop's 'inhibition' the curate returns to a zestful examination of *The Seven Against Thebes*. Mr Crawley conceives of his martyrdom in heroic as well as in Christian terms and he identifies strongly with heroic figures. Yet he talks disparagingly of *Samson Agonistes* – 'Agonistes indeed!' (II, 232). Even with the support of an intellectual tradition, in Trollope's balanced and realistic view moral heroism is still a human and fallible affair.

The novel's emblematic pattern also extends to the sphere of money. Trollope's potential heroes all strive to combat the crushing pressures of bureaucracy and rigid social attitudes, but they struggle hardest against the corrupting power of cash. Again there is no hiatus between the realistic surface of the novel and its metaphorical significance. In Barsetshire Lord

Lufton's missing cheque gives an initial impetus to the story, but thereafter its main function is emblematic. It stands for the worldliness of Barsetshire and its poorest curate's ignorance of financial affairs, but it also charts the moral movement in the country, which is to care less about the cheque and more about the welfare of Mr Crawley and his family. The worldliness of London, in Trollope's view, has reached irredeemable proportions. Here people are linked only by commercial bills. Emblems of trust in the business world, ironically they become the focus of intrigue and revenge. The origin of Broughton's wealth, they pay for his wife's romantic fantasies; they are the cause of his suicide and they finally ruin Crosbie and Musselboro. These elusive commercial bills, with their power to blight and destroy, form the shifting base of a rootless society. And in *The Last Chronicle of Barset* Trollope uses them to mark the end of the intimate, morally vital world of *The Warden* and to foreshadow his horrifying vision of the nihilistic world of *The Way We Live Now.*

The Last Chronicle of Barset possesses a remarkable depth of temporal and moral perspective, and this is bestowed on it by Trollope's unique use of time. His introduction of all the major figures of the Barsetshire novels is not simply his means of taking an elaborate farewell of them, as some critics have suggested. Rather, he examines their moral development in order to see whether his generalizations about humanity hold true. And he makes this daring perspective entirely relevant to his central moral concern, as life offers them a second chance to affirm or deny their moral directions. For instance, Lady Lufton's fear of her son's entanglement with the socially insignificant Lucy Robarts in *Framley Parsonage* is repeated in the lives of Archdeacon Grantly and Grace Crawley, a situation on which Lady Lufton's advice is sought. She has plainly learned from her earlier experience and the Archdeacon and Grace profit from her generous and rebellious modernity. Similarly, John Eames's heroism in *The Small House at Allington* where he thrashed Crosbie and saved Earl De Guest from a bull, is fully tried in *The Last Chronicle of Barset* and is found to be badly flawed by egoism. Lily Dale on the other hand, learns from her juvenile infatuation and in this novel achieves a perversely heroic triumph, but it is a triumph heavily qualified by Trollope's measured irony: 'My old friend John was certainly no hero, – was very unheroic in many phases of his life; but then, if all the girls are to wait for heroes, I fear that the difficulties in the way of matrimonial arrangements, great as they are at present, will be very seriously enhanced' (II, 371). The most obvious instance of this kind of repeated situation is the testing of Mrs Proudie's egoism, since her encounters with Mr Crawley and Dr Tempest exceed her comic interference in *Barchester Towers*. She possesses Mr Crawley's heroic power of will, but in her it has become a purely destructive force and she has to die. But most important is the manner in which, for old Mr Harding, his past is repeated in the Bishop's hounding of Mr Crawley, which recalls his own past moral battles over Hiram's Hospital. Like Mr Crawley, Mr Harding in *The Warden* also made a painful journey to London to consult a disinterested lawyer about a delicate moral dilemma and he likewise decided, after examining his conscience, on a course of humble submission. Mr Crawley is exhorted by Dr Tempest not to relinquish his living for the sake of a mere ideal, just as Mr Harding was harangued by the Archdeacon for his absurd scrupulosity. And Mr Harding's determined and generous response to Mr Crawley's predicament in this novel affirms the moral parallel.

In his portrayal of Mr Crawley and Mr Harding in *The Last Chronicle of Barset*, Trollope reveals simultaneously his admiration for the revolutionary heroic ideal and his awareness of the need for a conservative, sustaining cultural context. Carlyle's response to the new, unheroic, materialistic age, was to turn in *Past and Present* to the social values of the Middle Ages. But Trollope's past extends only as far as the world of Jane Austen and the youth of Mr Harding, which is evoked in the drinking of the port. The end of the era of *The Warden* is realized emblematically in Mr Harding's violoncello. Like Mr Crawley's books, it is an appropriate emblem for a supporting culture, but its function is also quieter and more personal and denotes, for Trollope, the quintessentially heroic. What it comes to signify is given in the scene in which his tiny granddaughter

Posy succeeds in getting weird melodies from its ancient strings, while Mr Harding recalls the earlier days when he played to the fractious bedesmen in the idyllic garden of Hiram's Hospital. Mr Harding has been a creative moral force in people's lives, a healing, unifying power in society, and the emblem of the child playing on his violoncello represents Trollope's hope for the continued functioning of innocence and harmony in human relations. For Trollope this is the task of the moral hero and in *The Last Chronicle of Barset* he employs the story in one of its most complex forms to examine the paradox that in the modern world, true revolutionary moral heroism is rooted in a Christian spirit of humility and self-sacrifice.

The Closed Form: Trollope's Experimental Novels

Trollope's short novels, as Ruth apRoberts has pointed out, are important to the critic interested in the form of his fiction.[9] However, those novels which he wrote anonymously at the peak of his fame in the 1860s have been virtually ignored.[10] But they are of particular interest because, standing cheek by jowl in the long list of Trollope's fiction with broad studies of the Victorian social milieu like *The Last Chronicle of Barset* and wide-ranging socio-political novels like *Phineas Finn*, which are in general balanced, relatively sanguine books, these short, intense, bleakly deterministic novels represent, in my view, Trollope's endeavour to significantly modify the mode of realism that he had established by the early 1860s and to articulate once more the tragic philosophy of life which dominates his earliest novel, *The Macdermots of Ballycloran*. These novels thus express the darker side of Trollope's mind, which for the most part he had hitherto kept strictly under control.

As his deliberate decision to bring the Barsetshire series to a close indicates, Trollope felt that he had reached a watershed in his fiction. He realized increasingly, as he makes clear in his *Autobiography*, that his growing interest in the psychology of character rather than in social commentary demanded a different form. In the novels of the 1860s we find, for instance, several potentially tragic figures like Lady Mason, Hugh Clavering, Mr Crawley or Mr Kennedy, whose inner lives often occupy an important place in the novels, but whose individual tragedies are engulfed by Trollope's overwhelming social preoccupations. By contrast, in his experimental novels as I have called them, *Nina Balatka, Linda Tressel, The Golden Lion of Granpère* and *An Eye for An Eye*, Trollope wanted to penetrate beneath the façade of social manners, the nexus of roles, rules, laws and attitudes which govern our social responses, in order to explore their complex psychological causes and frequently tragic effects. And he also introduces something which had virtually disappeared from his fiction since *The Macdermots of Ballycloran*, the vision of human lives as being subject to fate. This is clear if we compare his treatment of Mr Crawley with that of Nina Balatka, Linda Tressel or Fred Neville. In a fundamental sense Mr Crawley's character can be regarded as his destiny: the proud curate's fate is to a great extent in his own hands and we watch him choosing freely both his initial rebellion and his later submission to authority. The world of *Nina Balatka* is ruled by the dead weight of history, which is only narrowly thwarted by unpredictable impulses of human generosity; while in *An Eye for An Eye* blind fate governs the lives of all the characters and finally overwhelms the novel's central figure, Fred Neville.

In particular, *Linda Tressel*, Trollope's second anonymous novel and a powerful and gloomy book, reveals his interest in abnormal psychology and his new fatalism. Linda's destiny is shaped both by her character and by social circumstance. Her crime is that she falls in love with a young revolutionary Ludovic Valcarm, and she is therefore relentlessly persecuted by her Calvinist aunt, in whom Trollope explores the corrosive effects of religious fanaticism: 'To Madame Staubach's mind a broken heart and a contrite spirit were pretty much the same thing. It was good that hearts should be broken, that all the inner humanities of the living being should be, as it were, crushed on a wheel and ground into fragments, so that nothing should be left capable of receiving pleasure from the delights of the world' (p. 294). As her instrument of oppression Madame Staubach chooses her dull, middle-aged lodger Peter Steinmarc, but when Linda runs away from him, horrified at the prospect of such a marriage, he too reveals a strong sadistic streak: 'He wanted to be her master, to get the better of her, to punish her for her disdain of him, and to bring her to his feet' (p. 350). Indeed, Linda's whole society becomes her adversary; for even when she flees to her dead father's old friend Herr Molk, as soon as he learns the identity of her anarchic lover, he too joins in the condemnation. However, Linda cannot escape with Valcarm because she is torn between her profound need for love and sympathy and her conviction of guilt, the result of the prolonged religious indoctrination which has rendered her weak and submissive. This deep psychological torment emerges symbolically in her dreams about Valcarm, who would come to her 'beautifully, like an angel, and, running to her in her difficulties, dispersed all her troubles by the beauty of his presence. But then the scene would change, and he would become a fiend instead of a god, or a fallen angel; and at those moments it would become her fate to be carried off with him into uttermost darkness' (pp. 250–1). Linda cannot free herself from the tyranny of her aunt's peculiar religion: 'The doctrine had been taught her from her youth upwards, and she had not realized the fact that she possessed any power of rejecting it' (pp. 362–3). And once she accepts the degree to which her character and her life have been thus determined, the only logical resolution of her dilemma is death.

The corollary of Trollope's decision to dramatize more intensively the psychology of his characters and the operation of an unremitting fate was the necessity of experimenting with a different form. He had to make a break with the multi-plotted novel with its gallery of figures and several centres of interest and return to the 'closed' form of the single-plot novel, a form even more tightly and logically articulated than a carefully developed situation such as we find, for instance, in *The Warden*. And the taut structure of *Nina Balatka* and *Linda Tressel*, together with the lists of dramatis personae which Trollope, unusually, gives us at the beginning of these novels, suggests to me that he was conscious of their affinity with the drama.

The question that has teased Trollope readers for so long is why he should have chosen to publish these novels anonymously. Trollope's own explanation of such a daring venture at the height of his popularity and just two months after his attack on the pernicious practice of anonymity in the *Fortnightly Review* has never seemed to me to be very convincing. According to Trollope, writing in his *Autobiography*, by the mid-1860s he was a rich and successful novelist and wondered whether 'a name once earned carried with it too much favour'. He set out, therefore, to test the hypothesis that it was an author's name rather than the value of his work that attracted the reading public to a new novel and he decided 'to begin a course of novels anonymously'.[11] I think that there is some truth in R. C. Terry's view that this unusual experiment is yet another instance of Trollope's continual need to prove himself;[12] but the main reason, it seems to me, has to do with the nature of the novels, and Trollope himself, in his *Autobiography*, draws our attention to their unusual features: their foreign settings, local colouring, elements of romance and their pathos. He speaks of these as hallmarks of his new identity as a writer, but just as the roles of disinterested liberal and unintellectual storyteller are two of the many masks that Trollope employs in the *Autobiography* to shield himself from possible criticism, or even ridicule, so too, in my view, is the whole question of identity. On the practical level, he knew that his reputation rested on the splendid social comedy of the Barsetshire novels and naturally enough he was unwilling to risk alienating his faithful readers by making a sudden and dramatic change of style under his own name, although his identity was quickly discovered by Richard Holt Hutton who reviewed *Nina Balatka* in the *Spectator*. But the fundamental reason for his decision to publish anonymously lay, I believe, in his dissatisfaction with the mode and form of his realistic fiction in the 1860s, and the cloak of anonymity, which freed him both from critical hostility and from obligations to his regular readers, allowed him the scope to give full play to his tragic vision, to experiment with psychological realism and to develop a different form in which to articulate it.

Although *An Eye For An Eye* was finally published in 1879 with Trollope's name on the title page, like *The Golden Lion of Granpère*, I include it with *Nina Balatka* and *Linda Tressel* because in addition to being written roughly contemporaneously with them, it bears their unmistakable stamp. It explores intense social conflict rooted in religious divisions, incorporates a deterministic view of life and develops a single, tragic crisis which takes place in a foreign setting. Moreover, from a formal point of view it represents a development in Trollope's experiment with the 'closed' form of the novel. Bearing this in mind, its long-deferred publication, always something of a mystery to Trollope scholars, can be seen as probably due to the comparative failure of his earlier anonymous novels, for by the time he eventually decided to publish *An Eye for An Eye* the dramatic form of the novel had begun to find broader critical favour.

In my view then, taken together these novels represent a highly self-conscious attempt to transpose the form of the drama into fictional terms and as such they must be viewed in the context of Trollope's interest in contemporary critical theory. As Richard Stang has demonstrated, the mid-Victorian debate about dramatic construction and unity in the novel created a significant body of critical opinion in favour of more artistic rigour. Neo-classicists in particular, such as Trollope's friends G. H. Lewes and R. H. Hutton, preferred the 'closed' form of the intensively dramatic novel, although others such as Fitzjames Stephen and Charles Kingsley complained that theorists looked too much to the French well-made play for their model, rather than to the ampler form offered by Shakespeare.[13] In his experimental novels Trollope employed the criteria of economy, proportion, selection and unity advocated by Lewes and Hutton, but what is most striking about them is the way in which their single plots articulate so clearly both the nature of the dramatic conflict and the growth of its intense crisis. As on the stage, the conflict of opposed wills creates a correspondence of character and situation which is mirrored emblematically in the sharply contrapuntal arrangement of scene and setting, and the development of the crisis possesses a complementary temporal rhythm that gives to sequential interest a moral intensity. This places on Trollope the obligation to provide the kind of climactic scene which is rare in his novels, the function of which is to resolve the crisis and reveal its full significance and the justification for which lies in the concentration and economy demanded of the 'closed' form.

The change in Trollope's stance as a realist in *Nina Balatka* is due in no small measure to the influence of G. H. Lewes. The novel was written in 1865 immediately after Trollope's return from Prague, which Lewes had visited earlier and which inspired the central illustration in his well-known article on art as a means of discovering the Ideal in the Real:

We remember walking through the Jews' quarter in Prague, when it had for us only a squalid curiosity, until the sight of a cheap flower or two in the windows, and a dirty Jew fondling his baby, suddenly shed a beam as of sunlight over the squalor, and let us into the secret of the human life there. The artist who depicted only what we saw at first, would not have been so real as he who also depicted the flowers and affections; and not being so real, he would not have been so poetical.[14]

In *Nina Balatka* Trollope takes up Lewes's challenge to the realist to penetrate to the deeper relation between character and its social environment and he avoids novelistic cliché in his treatment of the Jews by evoking powerfully the deterministic ethos of the Prague ghetto but by revealing at the same time the deep-rooted humanity of its secret life, although in the end this works against his tragic vision.[15]

The novel's basic pattern derives from the stark nature of the tragic social schism in Prague between Jews and Christians. Whereas the Christians are marked by a crippling egoism fed by their traditional role as racial oppressors, the Jews, shackled by their ghetto spirit, are nevertheless torn between self-interest and social impulse. Trollope's general moral classification of character is evident in the broad contrast he makes between the kindly patriarch Stephen Trendellsohn and the gentile virago Madame Zamenoy; and between the Jews' treatment of the orphaned Ruth Jacobi, which stresses the communal caring engrained in Judaism, and the Christians' ostracism of their

relatives, old Balatka and his daughter, whom they have bank-
rupted. Trollope reveals a world of poisoned human relations,
and the racial conflict in the divided city shapes the novel's central moral concern: the intense struggle that takes place between
the contrary human impulses of fidelity and treachery, between
a tentative movement towards social integration and sheer brutal
nihilism. These forces are intensified in the lives of Anton, the
young Jewish visionary and his Christian fiancée Nina, whose
struggle to break out of the vicious circle of history and to
unite Prague by their marriage gives them important status at
the centre of the conflict.

Trollope's moral sense and his dramatic impulse reinforce
each other in a pattern of correspondence of character and
situation which reveals the ironic confusion of racial labels and
moral tags. Anton's mature, sacrificial love for Nina, which
threatens to alienate him from the other members of his race,
is opposed by the adolescent sexuality of his petulant Christian
rival, Ziska Zamenoy; while the Jewess Rebecca Loth's superbly
disinterested humanity contrasts with her rival Nina's more
limited and selfish love. However, Trollope's clear moral pattern
can shift. It does so, for instance, in the scene where Anton
stands looking up at the lamp in Nina's window while inside
she sits pondering the implications of her love for the Jew. As
in the theatre, it makes a split scene which provokes a spatial
reading and creates a collective image of inside and outside,
light and darkness, warmth and cold, that underlines Anton's
increasing isolation in the gloom of his engrained Jewish suspicion of the Christians. But Anton and Nina are only partly
representative of their respective factions. The moral contrast
between them – between his reluctant impulse towards
treachery and her tenacious affirmation of loyalty – is also a
fundamental aspect of their personal relation, and by thus revealing their full humanity Trollope emphasizes the deep irony
of their personal commitment. Trollope also seeks to overcome our conventional response to the moral conflict in another
way for, ironically, one of the most destructive elements at work
in the divided city is not stereotyped Jewish avarice, but the
bitterly competitive will of the Christians. The Zamenoys'

rampant materialism is reflected in their smart New Town suburban house, which is reached by straight, functional, ugly streets, while the Balatkas' home, hidden in a tangle of back-streets in the picturesque Kleinseite district, images the consequent imprisoning effect of their poverty.

Trollope's tragic sense of the clutch of history is also expressed in this novel by the unity of place which he achieves. Its characters are set in close proximity to one another in order to shape the action all the time, but in addition the social and geographical milieux of reactionary Prague create a significant counterpoint which defines emblematically and with great economy the broader context of racial strife. Just as the empty Hradschin Palace, peopled by Nina with happy lovers, rises in the moonlight out of Balatka's house, Nina's need of a sustaining illusion grows out of her social ostracism; but as a potent emblem of a repressive regime, the palace of the old kings of Bohemia places Nina's dreams of social integration in a deeply ironic perspective. And its parallel Jewish emblem, the ancient synagogue which similarly overshadows the Trendellsohns' house in the ghetto, and in the centre of which is 'a cage . . . within which five or six old Jews were placed, who seemed to wail louder than the others' (p. 84) focuses Trollope's view of Judaism as an inextricable tangle of religious faith and social history. The ghetto, like the Kleinseite, is a claustrophobic spiritual area and the synagogue with its cage, like the empty palace, functions as an emblem of the imprisoning forces of history from which Nina and Anton, on behalf of a whole generation, strive to free themselves.

Trollope's pessimistic view of the limited possibilities for meaningful social action is mirrored in the inevitability of the plot of *Nina Balatka*, each section of which is also a well-marked succession of crises, stimulating and satisfying an interest of their own while advancing the narrative. The first section defines the nature of the conflict in Prague and reveals how in the twelve short days following her engagement to Anton both factions spurn Nina; the second section, which covers the next twelve days in which they contrive to bring about her isolation and submission, culminates in Rebecca Loth's surprising visit to tempt Nina to take part with her in a joint sacrifice for Anton;[16] while the final section, spanning only four days, moves swiftly through Anton's treachery, old Balatka's death, Nina's complete social alienation, her attempted suicide and her rescue by the Jewess. But while time articulates the rhythm of the novel, it also bestows on it a measure of unity, emphasizing Trollope's profound sense of the tragic ironies possible in a world darkened by hatred. Nina's reflection at the beginning of the novel that her twenty-first birthday in a month's time will bring her freedom is balanced at its conclusion by her bitter reverie before her attempted suicide. The wedding day that she has been joyfully anticipating almost becomes the day of her death.

Time also repeats itself in a way that the reader recognizes, although the characters do not, as they are continually forced to re-emphasize their moral directions. As racial fears take on different guises Anton is tempted to forsake Nina, first by the Zamenoys' lies, then by Ziska Zamenoy's attempted bribery and finally by the misplaced zeal of Souchey, Nina's servant. Each time, in spite of himself, his suspicions harden and he moves further towards his act of betrayal. And similarly, Nina undergoes three separate periods of temptation to abandon her Jewish lover. There is Ziska Zamenoy's offer of marriage and social acceptance, her father's dire poverty and sickness and, finally, Rebecca Loth's subtly attractive temptation to make an idealistic gesture of renunciation of Anton as proof of her love for him. In the moral confusion that reigns in Prague, wrong courses can be pursued from the highest motives, but Nina recognizes Rebecca's proposal as fundamentally divisive and negative. However, in contrast to Anton's abject surrender to traditional racial fears, Nina's thrice-affirmed fidelity makes a striking parallel with the redemptive power of the Jewess's remarkable faithfulness in sending her forlorn Christian rival food and clothing and in appearing once more just in time to save her from suicide. In a similar way, the pattern made by Nina's three spiritual crises, which take place on the Moldau bridge that symbolically as well as physically links Jewish and Christian Prague, makes the larger generalization.

Her temptation to betray, as she believes, Christianity for Judaism, is defined in ironic terms for her by the statue of the Catholic saint, drowned for refusing to betray the secrets of a queen's confession. Each period of trial is resolved by Nina's clinging to her choice of a husband from among the Jews, but is also accompanied by the gradual unbalancing of her mind which leads with frightening logic to the inevitable final scene.

This scene, which is central to Trollope's careful exploration of Nina's tortured consciousness, reflects back on a whole series of events, for Nina's reverie on the bridge encapsulates the development of her obsession with suicide. As her progressive isolation from a caring world engenders unbearable feelings of spiritual alienation and guilt Lotta Luxa's malicious prediction that the Jew would jilt her, which is symptomatic of the mindless hostility that infests Prague, becomes reinforced in Nina's mind as she reflects that Lotta's second prediction of suicide by drowning must also be fulfilled (p. 177). For Nina the river is no longer simply a divisive feature of the Prague landscape, but has become a personal, malignant force and an agent of the fate that Lotta Luxa has forseen. In her agony and confusion, suicide appears to Nina at different moments to bestow personal, social and metaphysical significance on her wretched life. It is a revenge on Anton, a perverted test of her capacity for fidelity, a spiritual quest, God's retribution and a personal atonement for the whole history of social evil in Prague. But her instinctive identification in her final moments of despair with St John of Nepomucene illumines both the fragility and the sanctity of simple human faith as the only worthwhile value in a torn world. However, it is not the saint's legendary power which saves Nina from becoming the tragic victim of historical forces, but the strenuous love of her Jewish rival, who ironically embodies the power and the function of the dead Christian saint, and whose final appearance as Nina's redeemer we have been led to anticipate. By his pairing of these two women at the conclusion of the novel, Trollope stresses their totally sacrificial fidelity as representing the only possible hope for social harmony. But Anton, corrupted by the ghetto mentality, recognizes this too late and, coming as it does after he has almost caused Nina's death, their reunion clearly provides an inadequate foundation upon which to build a new society.

The emphatic parallel which Trollope makes between the Jewess and the Christian, together with the hurried reconciliation between Anton and Nina and their exodus from Prague to seek a new life in a more tolerant society, are all huddled up in a brief epilogue, which produces a weakened and faulty ending to the novel. But this is not Trollope shirking tragedy, for the avoidance of a tragic conclusion has been foreshadowed. Rather, it proceeds from Trollope's artistic commitment to divided aims. He is attempting to reconcile Lewes's idealistic notion of the triumph of humane impulses over historical adversity, embodied particularly in Rebecca Loth, with his own deeply tragic instinct, expressed in his dramatization of the tortured psychology of Nina Balatka.[17] I believe it is of equal significance that it also stems in part from Trollope's acknowledgement of the law of dramatic economy, which as yet he had only imperfectly adapted to the novel.

However, in *An Eye for An Eye*, written in accordance with the strict neo-classical rules favoured by Hutton, who praised its simplicity and proportion,[18] Trollope allowed his gloomier vision full rein and produced a bleakly deterministic tragedy. From the beginning there is an almost Aeschylean sense of fate brooding over the protagonists as the absurd conflict between freedom and duty is developed by the rigidly schematic pattern of characters arranged in blindly hostile groups. The tragedy is dependent on the gulf that exists between England and Ireland, Protestants and Catholics, aristocrats and commoners, rich and poor. The Scroope family in Dorset and Mrs O'Hara and Father Marty in Ireland battle dourly for control of the will of Fred Neville, the novel's central character, in accordance with their differing notions of obligation, which the former see as his duty to an abstract, idealized conception of social rank, and the latter as his more particular human obligation to Kate O'Hara, who is expecting his child. The focus of the novel is the psychology of Neville, whose choice constitutes its crisis. And what gives him importance at the centre of its conflicting claims is his very ordinariness, for Trollope's tragic vision has none of the grandeur of heroic tragedy. He is introduced as a particular kind of chooser, who sees situations only in terms of black and white alternatives and who equivocates when events prove to be intractable. His romantic notions of freedom are shown to be pathetically inadequate in the context of the clashing fatal imperatives of the conflict, and he is murdered. Few plays, which by their nature aim at compression and concentration, attempt more than this and Trollope resolves his plot with dramatic lucidity and, I think, with genuine tragic power.

As in *Nina Balatka*, the reader's moral attention is economized by the selection of a few foreground characters. However, in *An Eye for An Eye* the conflict of wills is not open and visible, and so instead of employing shifting moral groupings of character Trollope uses a strict surface pattern in order to provoke our reading of the underlying myopia. The sharp contrast that he makes between the high-minded Scroopes and the equivocal Mrs O'Hara and her devious priest, with their limited political horizons, masks the covert parallel which only slowly emerges; for in this novel self-interest takes on many guises and is a morally levelling factor. The stark contrast between the driving forces of the action, the wild, amoral Mrs O'Hara and the decorous, religious Lady Scroope, who engage in a tenacious struggle to effectively limit Neville's will, is rendered deeply ironic by their clear moral identification. Like Mrs O'Hara's absurd pride in her daughter's blood, which makes Neville an attractive victim, Lady Scroope's fanatical commitment to the claims of birth renders her prevention of a match between the heir and the Irish peasant girl imperative, and the scene in which Mrs O'Hara confronts Neville with the result of her scheming finds its parallel in Lady Scroope's sober exhortation to him to place his obligation to Scroope before his immediate duty to the wronged girl. Similarly, the overt distinction between the rivals Sophia Mellerby and Kate O'Hara masks their basic commitment to the same moral category, for both employ sexual politics to feed their wills. And the other pair of would-be rivals, Fred Neville and his brother Jack, are also explicitly contrasted and covertly compared. The man of reason makes a striking contrast with the man of feeling, who naïvely believes that 'to be free to choose for himself in all things, was the highest privilege of man' (I, 62–3). Jack, who is the spokesman for Scroope, makes the intellectual statement which summarizes the expediency of the Scroope ethos and the deterministic philosophy which informs the world of the novel, when he remarks that '[c]ircumstances are stronger than predilections' (I, 90). However, in chasing Sophia Mellerby's fortune in order to redeem his position as a younger brother, Jack Neville is in secret competition with the Scroope world. And his cynical manipulation of circumstance, like his brother's thoughtless pursuit of his predilections, is rooted in egoism and hedged around with equivocation, as are all human actions in this novel.

The pattern of An Eye for An Eye is further developed by Trollope's use of the paired scene. Each section of the novel contains reciprocal scenes of temptation and debate. The subtle presence of Lady Scroope in the apparently private and random encounter between Sophia Mellerby and Fred Neville at Scroope, surrounded by ancestral portraits reminding him emblematically of his duty, is balanced by the sexually charged scene with Kate O'Hara on the Irish coast, in which her mother's hand is crudely in evidence. At Ardkill Cottage Neville is devoted to Kate, but at Scroope Manor he realizes her lack of fitness to be a countess and he takes refuge in fantastic equivocal schemes which would allow the couple to spend their married life on board a yacht. And while his movement between England and Ireland makes a physical correlative for his vacillating nature, the careful pattern which these scenes make also serves to give a roundness to his character which the other figures lack. We can watch the fluid movement of his consciousness crystallizing to points of decision and then dissolving again under the pressure of circumstance.

In An Eye for An Eye Trollope also articulates time in a special way by evoking vistas of the past, because time governs the tragedy. A brief flashback judiciously intercalated into the narrative reveals that the reclusive Earl's involvement with his heir's prospective marriage is, after all, deeply egotistical; for his son, the previous heir, broke the old man's heart by rejecting his choice of a bride and marrying instead a French prostitute.

And similarly, we learn of Mrs O'Hara's wretched marriage to a well-born rake and his subsequent abandonment of both her and her child. Trollope carefully places these revelations early in the novel so that by the end of its opening section they make a strong ironic parallel. Just as for Earl and Lady Scroope Neville's possible marriage to a low-born, penniless, foreign Catholic girl threatens a tragic repetition of the past, so too for Mrs O'Hara the fledgling lord's imminent desertion of her pregnant daughter foreshadows a renewal of her own past grief and guilt. Neville's butterfly romance is thus placed in a profoundly ironic perspective by these juxtaposed histories of other people's past choices which are now working on him with dedicated intensity. In truth his freedom is more limited than any one of the characters knows and Jack Neville's earlier statement is invested with redoubled ironic force as others' lives impinge on Fred Neville's actions with cumulative and tragic effect.

Trollope intensifies the psychological pressure placed on Neville and gives an added sense of inevitability to the development of the plot by allowing him no scenes into which to escape. And an important measure of temporal unity also contributes to this effect, for the action spans Neville's one year of freedom with his regiment before he settles down to his domestic duties. This constitutes the limited period within which Mrs O'Hara must contrive to secure him for her daughter and which Lady Scroope has to thwart her. The rhythm of this crisis is mirrored in the novel's structure. The ensnaring of Neville, which occupies the long opening section, takes from October until March; the rapid piling up of events in the central section occurs during the next three months; while the resolution of the conflict, during which time suddenly becomes crowded and urgent, takes a mere three days in midsummer. But it is Fred Neville's character, his continual denial of the very existence of a crisis, that governs the ironic form of *An Eye for An Eye* and Trollope therefore also employs time for its shock value. The decisive suddenness of the Earl's death and Neville's easy assumption of his new role leads inevitably to his murder. Clearly chance rules with a fine impartiality over the world of the novel and is

part of its meaning. While the particularity of Neville's character is destiny, the casual juxtaposition of the lives of the
Scroopes and the O'Haras is chance. And the accident of
Neville's interposition at the heart of this conflict of similar
but separate destinies, which he is utterly unfitted to resolve,
generates a powerful sense of the operation of fate in human
lives. The mimetic adequacy and tragic power of *An Eye for
An Eye* depends, not on Trollope's presentation of the 'Ideal'
behind the 'Real' as in *Nina Balatka*, but on his ability to convey a sense of strictly conditional freedom.

Coincidence, then, forms an important part of the novel's
structure and takes its place in the pattern of foreshadowing
which focuses our attention on the final scene of Fred Neville's
murder. This is first anticipated in the early flashback by which
we learn of Mrs O'Hara's own desertion, her social isolation,
her physical power, her incipient madness and her strange
obsession with the claims of blood (I, 38–9). Our expectations
are heightened by the horror with which she foresees her own
fate befalling her daughter and her determination to avenge it
(I, 44, 47); by the violence she offers her gloating husband when
he returns, and by Neville's own premonitions when he leaves
Scroope and as he nears the Irish cliffs. Trollope thus renders
Neville's death necessary both in dramatic and in psychological
terms. By ruining her daughter's life as well as her own, Mrs
O'Hara has incurred a double guilt, and in thrusting Fred
Neville from the Heights of Moher she exacts a double vengeance. The phrase 'an eye for an eye', which she repeats exult-
antly in the asylum, thus possesses an obscure but profoundly
personal significance and encapsulates at the same time Trollope's tragic vision of human destiny. But his sense of the
appropriate dramatic form, of closure and completion, is perhaps most in evidence in the final scene. The place of Neville's
misdeed becomes the arena for his great retribution and the focal
point of his illusion of freedom is abruptly transformed into
the place of his death. The ironic effect of this almost casual
revolution of fortune's wheel is completed in the temporal
scheme of the novel, for his year of freedom in Ireland is ended
and it is once again midsummer. Although the character of

87

Neville, a man unable to choose until the possibility of making a true choice has long passed, is central to the novel, the psychology of the two women who dramatize the terms of his choice so urgently is also important. And Trollope finally draws the parallel between the insane Mrs O'Hara and the penitent Lady Scroope, locked away in the asylum and the chapel of the manor house, to emphasize their collective guilt and to amplify the tyranny of the imprisoning claims of the past. It is a pattern which stresses Trollope's profound awareness of the strange, ironic contingency of human life and in common with his other experimental novels it also summarizes his bleakly tragic, 'un-Trollopian' vision.

IV
THE RHETORICAL
DESIGN

The Rhetoric of *Orley Farm*

MID-VICTORIAN critics distinguished between the dramatic
novel, which they praised for its unity, autonomy and realism,
and the novel that was dominated by the author's voice, which
they felt to be lax and inartistic. Reviewers displayed a marked
preference for 'showing' rather than 'telling' and those novels
which were constructed on the basis of 'scene' instead of 'summary' received loud and often undiscriminating praise.[1] As
Trollope was the rising star among the novelists at this period,
it was natural that his methods should become the focus of
this particular debate and several reviewers readily identified
in his novels what they considered to be his abuse of the author's
voice. The *Saturday Review*, for instance, was critical of his
procedure in *The Small House at Allington* because: 'Mr Trollope . . . sets a very bad example to other novelists in the fre-
quency with which he has recourse to the petty trick of passing
a judgment on his own fictitious personages as he goes along,
in order that the story may thus seem to have an existence
independent of its teller, and to form a subject on which he can
speculate as on something outside himself'.[2] Henry James on
the other hand, who believed that the novel should have the
same kind of validity as history, complained that Trollope
destroyed this autonomy by taking delight 'in reminding the
reader that the story he was telling was only, after all, a make-
believe'.[3] This critical confusion about the function of Trollope's narrative voice mirrors the Victorian critics' general

89

uncertainty as to whether the novel should be viewed primarily as art or as history. And this debate has continued for so long in Trollope criticism precisely because Trollope's rhetoric mediates continually between life as something to be lived and fiction as something that is made.[4]

Essentially, both Henry James and the *Saturday Review* critic are complaining that Trollope's method puts the reader in a false position. I believe, however, that the creation of a stable relation between the author, his reader and the world of his fiction is a fundamental aspect of Trollope's rhetoric. Indeed, he had enunciated his conception of this relation as early as *Barchester Towers*, in Chapter XV :

> Our doctrine is, that the author and the reader should move along together in full confidence with each other. Let the personages of the drama undergo ever so complete a comedy of errors among themselves, but let the spectator never mistake the Syracusan for the Ephesian; otherwise he is one of the dupes, and the part of a dupe is never dignified. (p. 130).

Trollope never allows his reader to become his dupe, but in spite of this assertion (which is itself of course part of his rhetorical procedure in *Barchester Towers*) and Henry James's confidence that Trollope 'never juggled with the sympathies or the credulity of his reader',[5] his narrative voice does continually manipulate the reader's response. At the beginning of *Orley Farm*, for instance, it achieves several effects which depend on establishing a firm relation with the reader. 'It is not true', Trollope tells us in his opening sentence, 'that a rose by any other name will smell as sweet. Were it true, I should call this story "The Great Orley Farm Case". But who would ask for the ninth number of a serial work burthened with so very uncouth an appellation?' (I, 1). Trollope's whimsical revelation of the nature of his story and his bluff admission of a certain professional sharpness function to bind the reader to him, but this 'little slap at credulity', as Henry James called this use of Trollope's authorial tone,[6] also enforces from the beginning the reader's clear sense of the novel as fiction rather than history. And yet within a few sentences the narrative voice begins to establish the autonomy of the novel's world. Trollope ceases to talk of 'this book of mine' and discusses as if they were historical truth those 'legal questions which made a considerable stir in our courts of law' (I, 1). The reader quickly learns, therefore, that Trollope's fiction inhabits the interface between art and life and that his narrator frequently mediates between both.

But Trollope's almost imperceptible shift from fiction to fact is most important in creating the novel's illusion of a self-contained world, and throughout the novel the narrative voice is continually active in building up the reader's sense of his entering a unified world with its own set of rules which works just like real Victorian life, in order that he may participate fully in the fiction offered for his sympathy and judgement without the necessity to keep referring outside the novel to his own experience. Trollope's narrator builds into this world a system of detailed correspondences which occur, for example, in the sphere of work, which makes up such a large area of *Orley Farm*. Its legal world is given solidity as we learn that barristers come into their prime in their fifties instead of in their forties like other professional men, that it is not quite the thing for a barrister to wait upon an attorney, or that there is as complex an etiquette among commercial travellers as among lawyers; we discover that there is a strict hierarchical order among housemaids, chambermaids and cooks; and we learn too about the financial prospects of chemists' assistants in London.[7] And Trollope's capacity to mediate between his reader's world and his fictionalized world also depends upon his creation of shared conventional values. His narrator praises public schools, inveighs against public examinations and extols domestic contentment; and he does this so successfully that the critic for the *National Review* called his review of *Orley Farm*, 'Trollope as the voice of the English middle class'. But Trollope also invests his world with a psychological density by means of generalized observations that the reader can recognize. There are the shy, awkward men like John Kenneby who nurse an intense inner life; there is the truth that 'there is nothing perhaps so generally consoling to a man as a well-established grievance' (I, 81), and there are glimpses into the psychology of officialdom: 'To the policeman's mind every man not a policeman is a guilty being, and the attorneys perhaps share something of this feeling' (II, 207).

Trollope's ability to secure the reader's commitment to a realistic world seemingly contiguous with his own is essential to the creation of a stable relation between the author, the reader and the fiction. And this effect of stability is fundamental to Trollope's moral rhetoric which seeks to dislocate his reader's secure, conventional ethical response without making a complete rupture with the author or his fictional world. Trollope never quite dupes his reader, nor does he ever quite remove the overwhelming impression in the reader's mind that he has entered an autonomous, realistic world. But he does create the important effect of a profound and continuous tension between art and life, because in spite of his elaborate pretence that the novel is history, he also constantly draws attention to its patent artifice and nowhere more obviously than when he introduces Lady Mason to the reader at the commencement of *Orley Farm*:

I trust that it is already perceived by all persistent novel readers that very much of the interest of this tale will be centred in the person of Lady Mason. Such educated persons, however, will probably be aware that she is not intended to be the heroine. The heroine, so called, must by a certain fixed law be young and marriageable. Some such heroine in some future number shall be forthcoming, with as much of the heroic about her as may be found convenient; but for the present let it be understood that the person and character of Lady Mason is as important to us as can be those of any young lady, let her be ever so gracious or ever so beautiful. (I, 12–13).

Here Trollope reminds us forcefully of the conventionality of art and of those laws of fiction which we have erected to minister to our egotistical desires: our need of youthful heroines like Madeline Staveley, whom he has promised to introduce, or marriages like that between Madeline Staveley and Felix Graham at the conclusion of the novel, or a simple system of reward and punishment. In drawing attention to this pattern of wish-fulfilment in fiction, Trollope is undermining his reader's moral security, challenging his sense of the completeness and meaning which fiction offers and reminding him at the same time of the fluidity and insecurity of life. But this narrative address also functions as a clear reading direction for Trollope does in fact find much that is admirable and even heroic in the lovely woman who boldly forged her husband's will, courageously survives two trials and finally stands exonerated. And by thus disrupting the novel's conventional morality, Trollope complicates our response both to fiction and to life. The form of the novel is thus extended and made more flexible and realistic as its moral categories and conventional patterns are probed and questioned.

Clearly Trollope's subtle rhetoric serves his moral vision. Like the majority of mid-Victorian critics, who were in no doubt that the highest art should convey moral lessons,[8] he felt that novels had taken the place of sermons,[9] and in his *Autobiography* he declares himself unequivocally a moralist.[10] The corollary, of course, as Trollope well understood, is that 'the novelist, if he have a conscience . . . must have his own system of ethics'.[11] Ruth apRoberts has described Trollope's moral position as so advanced as to be defined as 'Situation Ethics',[12] and certainly in *Orley Farm* his sustained defence of Lady Mason, who successfully defies all moral, legal and fictional codes, seems to fit her analysis of Trollope's strenuous exercise of moral pragmatism. For instance, in that intense scene of Lady Mason's confession of guilt to Sir Peregrine Orme, where Trollope charts the conflict between her necessary moral empiricism and his moral absolutism, the situation clearly calls for the conventional reader's condemnation. However, we have been already made aware that she possesses the instincts of a lady and that her confession is wrung from her by a generous love. And moments of moral sensitivity and inner torment like these suddenly evade the straightjacket of fictional convention and register in the reader a profound moral shock. For Trollope has forced us to identify with a remarkable character in an extraordinary moral situation; has required us in effect to test our own system of values, and has made us uncomfortably aware of the simplified demands we habitually make both upon art and upon life.

And yet I do not wholeheartedly agree with Ruth apRoberts

that Trollope is a moral relativist simply. In spite of all his attacks on the kinds of novel conventions that demand among other things a nemesis,[13] I believe that Trollope, like George Eliot, has a strong sense of a natural justice at work in the world. But its mode of operation takes no account either of traditional fictional or Victorian ethical conventions; it rather works within and through character and produces the self-torture of isolated individuals like Louis Trevelyan, Julia Brabazon or Lady Mason. There is a working out of reward and punishment in *Orley Farm*, but the reader finds it at the same time both reassuring and disconcerting, because it affirms the strength of moral impulses in human lives, yet it bypasses the simple conventional patterns of the novel and overturns social mechanisms.

Trollope's rhetoric clearly revolts from didacticism – from the garrulous intimacy that he objects to in the Thackerayan narrator, for instance.[14] As he remarks in a letter to Kate Field about the manuscript of her novel: 'Your reader should not be made to think that *you* are trying to teach or to preach, or to convince. Teach, and preach, and convince if you can; – but first learn the art of doing so without seeming to do it.'[15] For Trollope, as I have been suggesting, this art eschews equally both narrative sermonizing and the cruder patterns of wish-fulfilment. The key to our understanding of Trollope's moral rhetoric resides in the great importance he attached to his relation with his reader and in the absolutely central place that character holds in his art. His major figures are neither wholly good nor wholly bad, but 'mixed' and as such they demand both our sympathy and our judgement. We are led to feel compassion for villains like George Vavasor, Ferdinand Lopez and even Augustus Melmotte, and we are also made alive to the weaknesses of worthy people like Mr Crawley, Mark Roberts, Harry Clavering or Lady Mason. In my view, what moulds Trollope's flexible relation between the author, his characters and his reader, and is at the same time fluid enough to mediate between fictional pattern and moral truth, is a complex rhetoric of sympathy and judgement.

One of the more interesting and surprising aspects of Trollope's rhetorical art is the way it developed out of the mid-Victorian debate about the form and function of the novel.

A prominent participant in this discussion was Trollope's friend, the novelist and student of fiction, Edward Bulwer-Lytton, who was an advocate of the dramatic in fiction but who also argued for a freer form for the novel. One of his particular interests was the relation between the author and the reader and in 1860 and 1861, when Trollope was engaged in writing *Orley Farm*, Bulwer-Lytton was working on a series of articles, some of which dealt with this subject, later to be published in *Blackwood's Edinburgh Magazine* under the title 'Caxtoniana'.[16] It is probable that Bulwer-Lytton discussed his ideas with Trollope, but in any case there is a striking similarity between their views. Like Trollope, Bulwer-Lytton is suspicious of novels which appeal only to the intellectual reader and he maintains that their characters must embody compelling emotions with which a miscellaneous audience can establish sympathy.[17] In his lecture, 'On English Prose Fiction', Trollope puts it this way :

It all lies in that. No novel is anything, for purposes either of tragedy or of comedy, unless the reader can sympathise with the characters whose names he finds upon the page . . . Truth let there be; — truth of description, truth of character, human truth as to men and women.[18]

Bulwer-Lytton and Trollope also agree that the reader can only share the author's knowledge of his characters if their creator has first been sympathetically involved in their lives. In his *Autobiography* Trollope gives us his well-known description of this process of identification :

[the novelist] desires to make his readers so intimately acquainted with his characters that the creations of his brain should be to them speaking, moving, living, human creatures. This he can never do unless he know those fictitious personages himself, and he can never know them well unless he can live with them in the full reality of established intimacy.[19]

But the rhetorical process is more complex than this, for the author's moral intellect is also at work judging his characters. This is where the emphasis falls in Bulwer-Lytton's early essay, 'On Art in Fiction',[20] and Trollope elaborates his position in his *Autobiography* :

[the author] must argue with [his characters], quarrel with them, forgive them, and even submit to them. He must know of them whether they be cold-blooded or passionate, whether true or false, and how far true, and how far false. The depth and the breadth, and the narrowness and the shallowness of each should be clear to him.[21]

What Bulwer-Lytton and Trollope are outlining is a creative paradox, an imaginative co-operation between sympathy and judgement, since the author's uncompromising critical intellect should be as strong as his moral identification. And the reader, in making this kind of moral scrutiny, needs to be distanced from the characters, an effect which is best achieved by the use of irony; for while sympathy serves to suspend the reader's judgement, irony serves to sharpen it. It is this continual interplay between sympathy and irony that forms the basis of Trollope's moral rhetoric in *Orley Farm* and it clearly is a method flexible enough to include both 'scene' and 'summary', to mediate between the conventions of the novel and the evolution of natural justice which depends on much subtler relations between character and form, and to articulate connections between the autonomous social world of the novel and the moral situation of the tormented woman isolated at its centre.

Although it was admired by George Eliot and Trollope himself thought it one of his best novels, in recent times *Orley Farm* has been frequently misread. Bradford Booth believes that it is artistry *manqué*,[22] Robert M. Adams calls it a 'patchwork affair' which 'does not prove its moral as novels must',[23] while Robert M. Polhemus's view of Lady Mason as a 'deeply flawed woman' throws his interpretation of the novel off balance.[24] These misreadings have occurred, I think, because critics have tended to ignore the novel's subtle rhetoric. In my view *Orley Farm* owes a great deal to Bulwer-Lytton's theory. It would be difficult to exaggerate how thoroughly Trollope's creation of a rhetorical design, shaped by the complex interplay of sympathy with irony, informs the novel at all levels. And this design is perfectly adjusted to the novel's central unifying concern, the complex nature of moral judgement. For its main issue of how to judge the enigmatic Lady Mason, whose trial forms the catalyst for Trollope's sardonic vision, engages all the major

characters and the reader is immediately involved in the process. As his mock apology later in the novel suggests, Trollope
regards Lady Mason not merely as a criminal, but also as a
social victim and as a good and even heroic woman. At the
same time he also alerts the reader to the process that lies at
the heart of the novel's rhetorical pattern:

I may, perhaps be thought to owe an apology to my readers in that I
have asked their sympathy for a woman who had so sinned as to have
placed her beyond the general sympathy of the world at large. . . . But
as I have told her story that sympathy has grown upon myself till I
have learned to forgive her, and to feel that I too could have regarded
her as a friend. (II, 404).

Beneath this disarmingly simple defence of Lady Mason lurks
the ironic assertion that *Orley Farm* possesses a rhetoric designed
to challenge the Victorian reader's blind allegiance to the conventional morality of the nineteenth-century novel. But more
importantly, *Orley Farm* is one of Trollope's most sustained
assaults on the moral code of the Victorian middle classes, for
which he felt such a high price was being paid in human misery.
And in this novel two distinct but fundamental aspects of the
code are inseparably entangled: the Victorians' profound belief
in the infallibility of the law as the custodian of public morality
and in the sanctity of womanhood as the regulator of moral
conduct in the home. Trollope employs Lady Mason's guilt,
which threatens both of these myths and automatically incurs
punitive responses, to demonstrate how the impossibly high
ideals which they enshrine serve to display society's unhealthy
contempt for human frailty. What is more, the inflexibility of
this absolutist morality, which masks its extreme fragility,
resting as it does on a consensus of will, undermines the strength
of the private conscience and makes responsible judgements
difficult, if not impossible.

The intensely dramatic scene of Lady Mason's confession,
which occurs midway through the novel, is designed to carry a
heavy rhetorical burden and its multiple perspectives of sympathy and irony suggest the true complexity of moral scrutiny.[25] A sympathetic effect is created by the profound realism

of its psychological undercurrents. Just as, having been sold as bankrupt stock on the marriage market by her ruined parents and cheated by her avaricious husband Sir Joseph Mason, Lady Mason employs his commercial ethic to defeat him, so in relation to another father-figure, her potential husband Sir Peregrine Orme, she sacrificially adopts his straight-jacket morality to save him from public disgrace. But she is not a moral chameleon. Her powerful response to both base meanness and high-minded generosity is in each case a splendid assertion of the fundamental empiricism of the personal conscience in human relations. However, in the shocked reactions of the aging baronet Trollope strikingly reveals two powerful yet disparate elements of neo-Calvinism at work in the Victorian world. A fixed code cannot be reconciled with the equally strong claim of the sanctity of the private conscience and our sympathy for Lady Mason is accompanied by an ironic distancing in judgement on Sir Peregrine Orme, who invokes blinkered absolutist notions of repentance and restitution. The subtle, ironic movement of the scene makes his social reflex the surrogate for the average reader's moral response to her sensational crime and flagrant breach of feminine mythology, while at the same time he is encouraged to identify with the warm response of Sir Peregrine's daughter-in-law, Mrs Orme. Although she is the main representative of saintly Victorian womanhood in the novel, Mrs Orme makes a mature, compassionate assessment of Lady Mason's unique human situation which involves a moral relativism that ironically runs counter to the canons of public respectability, and which is vindicated as the scene illumines Lady Mason's motives and foreshadows her agonizing retribution.

Lady Mason's role as a social victim is the long-delayed but inescapable effect of her passion for equity and her cheating of the law to obtain it. Because she never thought of her action in forging her husband's monstrously unfair will as anything but just and has never considered it from the point of view of social ethics, the revelation of Sir Peregrine's moral horror is a traumatic experience. Paradoxically, Trollope's concern to secure our balanced moral judgement means that he is never entirely neutral or objective and Lady Mason's prostration in the fireless room, huddled in a shawl, suffering the chill of moral exclusion, makes a covert though powerful appeal as an emblem of her state of mind. It works in conjunction with the complex flow of the reader's sympathy and emotion: admiration for her self-sacrifice, fear as she contemplates the future and an element of physical suffering that sharpens our response to her mental anguish, which is effectively evoked through Mrs Orme's instinctive gesture of human warmth and approval in lighting the fire and ministering to her immediate needs.

Mrs Orme's indefinitely deferred judgement of Lady Mason marks her as the chief spokesman for Trollope's rhetoric of sympathy and this is balanced by Felix Graham's fitful role as ironist. By this means Trollope effectively avoids intrusive moralizing, but he is careful that neither spokesman fully represents his own moral vision. The fledgling attorney is obsessed with arriving at an abstract legal judgement of Lady Mason's case, while Mrs Orme is absorbed by the human need. One is concerned with justice, the other with equity. However, their main function is to present, from opposite points of view, cogent reasons why the reader must eschew simple, definitive moral judgements. Felix Graham's ultra-idealistic posture serves to emphasize that it is no good looking to the law for equity in human affairs. Its double standards are most clearly in evidence at the emblematically futile legal congress in Birmingham, the ironic centre of society's purely commercial values. Graham's sympathy for the visionary speaker Von Bauhr exposes the gulf which exists between the heady pretensions which the congress enshrines and the rooted cynicism of its participating lawyers; for Mr Chaffanbrass's sneers form an appropriate commentary on the frantic attempts of Lady Mason's lawyer, Mr Furnival, to get the case against his client quietly dropped. And in private life the moral chaos of the legal system is aptly summarized in a parallel domestic scene by Judge Staveley's participation in the emblematic fumbling chase of blind man's buff during the Christmas celebrations at Noningsby, where the human face of the law and also its fallibility are exposed: ' "Justice is blind," said Graham. "Why should a judge be ashamed to follow the example of his own goddess?" ' (I, 223). Graham, of course, confuses justice with equity because his faith in the law is divorced from his contempt for the system, but like all the main characters in attacking one double standard he is trapped by another, for his sweeping condemnation of Lady Mason and her lawyers, which makes a submerged parallel with the harsh judgement of her made earlier by Sir Peregrine Orme, is only partly directed at the legal situation. As his theoretical attempt to train a wife implies, what he really loathes is Lady Mason's breaking of a deeply-cherished myth. His idealism is ultimately rooted in egoism and it is in this context that the irony of Judge Staveley's fatherly reprimand: ' "Graham, my dear fellow, judge not that you be not judged" ' (II, 122), which lies quietly at the heart of the novel's rhetoric, cuts through these moral ambiguities and includes the reader within its frame of reference.

Trollope's placing of his central moral statement midway through the novel marks a shift in its rhetorical weight. As Graham's role as spokesman is undercut by the dichotomy between his public posture and his private life, so Trollope stresses the wholeness and integrity of Mrs Orme's point of view. Just as he employs the interpolation from Molière's *L'École des Femmes* to discredit Graham as the spokesman for idealism in the novel, so in the moral relation between Lady Mason and her Good Angel, Mrs Orme, he draws on elements of Marlowe's *Doctor Faustus*.[26] As Mrs Orme is suddenly thrust from her sheltered life into the public arena of Lady Mason's trial she is most strongly contrasted with Felix Graham, whose high-mindedness crumbles into petulant frustration at the inequity of the legal process, while Mrs Orme, in spite of her knowledge of the woman's guilt, courageously supports the wretched Lady Mason. Trollope's rhetoric of sympathy is at work in the intense moral relation between the two women which serves to deepen our understanding of Lady Mason as the second trial duplicates the first. The present agony is felt the more keenly as the past is more fully revealed. A widow, with a son Lucius Mason's age, Mrs Orme alone is competent to judge the nature of Lady Mason's temptation, the desperation of her desire to preserve her innocent son's good name and the quest for equity which makes victory at the second trial a moral as well as a psychological imperative. And her refusal to do so gains a special significance. She recognizes the fundamental incompatibility of rigid public ethics and the fluid inner life of personal conscience, and unlike the idealists, Sir Peregrine Orme and Felix Graham, she rejects the static view of human character that an inflexible moral system implies; for she has observed how twenty years of lonely anguish suffered on behalf of her penniless son and her scrupulous act of conscience to protect Sir Peregrine Orme have ennobled Lady Mason. She not only sympathizes, but she is morally in her debt.

The relation between the novel's social realism, its treatment of character and its rhetorical design is partly articulated by Trollope's use of masks. As Lady Mason's story demonstrates, character may not simply be related to the rhetorical structure, but may in a meaningful sense *be* that structure, for the inevitable unfolding of her story is also the progressive revelation of her character. The emergence of Lady Mason's inner nature develops the novel's central contrast between public and private judgement as Trollope exploits the ironic gap which exists between her public mask and her private face. Her mask is unwillingly assumed and worn with sorrow, and its unpeeling in the course of the novel is a sympathetic as well as an ironic process. Pity for her is most strongly felt immediately before she goes to the court, in a scene charged with high irony when she breaks down before her son's priggish resentment at her reticence, but dare not let him learn the cause of her distress. Her subsequent movement from the private to the public ordeal elicits admiration for her sheer power of will as she carefully restores for the trial the impenetrably composed façade that she had first assumed for the same occasion twenty years before. And inside the courtroom this mask allows Trollope to explore the relation between the inward and the social worlds in greater depth. The main irony which the public mask reveals is that, despite the effective myth, public judgement, unlike the law, bears no relation to the rigid yet fragile bourgeois morality it is supposed to represent, but is a crude and frighteningly casual process. Public faces are intended to deceive and the packed

courtroom at first believes Lady Mason innocent. For the specta-
tors, however, the operation of the law is simply diverting
theatre and when the evidence points plainly to her guilt they
merely alter their mode of illusion and applaud her coolness for
the accomplished mask of a heroine forger. For the larger world
there is no double standard because there exists no standard
at all.

This is the world of Moulder, the commercial traveller, whose
ethics dominate the novel. And Trollope's ironic method includes the use of Moulder as his temporary spokesman, who
assumes a position which is being attacked by the author (II,
215–17). The victim and his point of view are allowed to take
over completely and his words condemn him utterly as Trollope employs the device of the mask and the accompanying
shock in a deadly form. His method is a kind of *reductio ad
absurdum*. The commercial code underpinning the law (which
we have already witnessed in the confrontation between
Moulder and the attorney Dockwrath at the Bull Inn, Leeds)
which Sir Peregrine cannot bring himself to believe and which
Felix Graham deplores, is frankly applauded by Moulder. He
enjoys the sale of truth and stories of the guilty escaping justice
by feeing sharp lawyers, and will wager ten pounds on Lady
Mason's acquittal. And the intimidation of honest witnesses
also appeals to his bullying nature, but it is the sovereign impartiality of wealth that calls forth his hyperbole: ' "Unfair!"
said Moulder. "It's the fairest thing that is. It's the bulwark
of the British Constitution" ' (II, 216).

It is from this threateningly amoral world of the masses, of
frank hedonists like Moulder and his fellow commercial traveller, Kantwise, 'pigs out of the sty of Epicurus' (I, 246) as Trollope calls them, that the middle classes retreat into defensively
rigid codes. But as Trollope shows so clearly, these unattain-
ably high standards result in people erecting complex façades
to evade the constant moral scrutiny of daily life. Worn as a
matter of habit they are also a means of avoiding claims on one's
humanity. This is what links men as different as the nostalgically
conservative Sir Peregrine Orme and the abrasively radical
Felix Graham. Their human responses freeze into clumsy and

inappropriate moral postures. And in *Orley Farm* these masks are also emblematic of double standards of behaviour and judgement. Sir Peregrine Orme and Felix Graham also share a blind faith in the law which means that at first they are easily deceived about Lady Mason. To the crafty lawyers, however, who know that the verdict of the courts represents justice rather than equity and for whom humanity's façades are their stock in trade, her guilt is transparently obvious. Yet they too are absolved from making a responsible judgement, not by their beliefs, but by their professional roles. Legal etiquette forbids that they mention her guilt and the system of advocacy requires that they conceal it. Ironically however, while as lawyers they uphold public morality, when their masks slip a little they are revealed as men who are bored by the dull proprieties of Victorian society and it is as men, rather than as lawyers, that their interest and sympathy are aroused by the beautiful woman's secret guilt.

The assumption of masks baffles the achievement of justice and equity and it also stultifies human intercourse. More importantly, however, as the precise regulation of conduct puts an intolerable strain on the individual personality and the mask is increasingly used to evade self-scrutiny, it threatens the inward life. The ironic shock of recognition that in Joseph Mason, Lady Mason's persecutor, mask and face have become identical, distances us in judgement on his horrifying egoism. Ostensibly his mindless rigidity of outlook simply reflects the impersonal law of equity which rules his life and to which he clings long after it has become absurd and destructive. But at a deeper level this constitutes a complex façade employed to cover his flight from self-judgement. His paranoiac concern with equity, which he confuses with justice, is really an obscure source of self-justification: 'Justice, outraged justice, was his theme. Whom had he ever robbed? To whom had he not paid all that was owing? "All that have I done from my youth upwards." Such were his thoughts of himself' (II, 239). Clearly this mask has a different function and value from Lady Mason's and the moral contrast between the two antagonists is brought out by Mason's own 'trial'. It occurs in a fascinating moment, made powerful by the complex interplay of sympathy with irony, when Lady Mason enters the courtroom and confronts her accuser: 'As she thus looked her gaze fell on one face that she had not seen for years, and their eyes met. It was the face of Joseph Mason of Groby, who sat opposite to her; and as she looked at him her own countenance did not quail for a moment. Her own countenance did not quail; but his eyes fell gradually down, and when he raised them again she had averted her face' (II, 248). This moment encapsulates their shared experience of the past, confirms Lady Mason's moral superiority and secures our moral commitment to her at her moment of most intense crisis. At the same time it also ironically foreshadows the function of the law in achieving equity, for Mason is soon to be trapped by his obsession. The passion for justice which he has projected onto the law renders him the victim of its brutal and inefficient commercial system. He thus falls by the code he has lived by and this fleeting moment becomes emblematic of the way outraged natural justice brings about nemesis in the fulness of time.

This is an important aspect of the rhetorical design of *Orley Farm*, a novel which challenges our allegiance to the kind of simple morality enshrined in the traditional conventions of the novel, which encourages our acceptance of the need for moral relativism and yet which also includes a realistic vision of a natural moral order, firmly rooted in antecedent human experience, asserting itself through character and the fluctuating ironies of life. The conclusion of Lady Mason's trial reaches a point of moral equilibrium which embodies a synthesis of our contrary impulses to sympathize and to judge. And it is to this point that Trollope's elaborate, complex but subtle rhetoric has imperceptibly led us. Although her acquittal, which avoids the obvious injustice of a verdict in favour of the vicious Joseph Mason, corresponds to our sympathetic knowledge of her innate nobility, the trial also engineers her public shame and her retribution. The private principles of equity and moral empiricism are vindicated while the public myths of legal infallibility and feminine purity are preserved. In the larger development of the novel the growth of our sympathy for Lady Mason is balanced by Trollope's achievement of an aesthetic distance so that we can judge life's victims with critical detachment.

This depends on our awareness in *Orley Farm* of the quiet presence of the traditional tragic pattern of hubris (pride), hamartia (an error of judgement) and nemesis (divine retribution), governed by a natural moral law, which gives shape to Lady Mason's life and binds it firmly to the social world of the novel. It includes all the egoists within its scope and the precise form of their retribution has an ironic appropriateness. Trollope makes it clear that Lady Mason's excessive love for her unworthy son is a subtle form of egoism and that her passion for equity is tainted by pride in her vengeance on an unjust social order. And in reclaiming the land from Dockwrath when her son comes of age she re-enacts her original crime and sets in motion the train of events which leads inexorably to her second trial. It is not the crime, but her refusal to accept the second chance that life offers her to alter her moral direction, that brings upon her the very fate she has striven to avoid, the ruin and humiliation of her son. And similarly, Joseph Mason's scheming for vengeance under the cloak of justice achieves no more than simple equity in the return of the farm to him, which occurs independently of the legal process. His faith in the law, which appeared to enshrine his harsh ethical code, merely ensures his moral defeat. Its true function as the catalyst and preserver of popular illusion is demonstrated in Lady Mason's victory, and Joseph Mason is left nursing an insatiable obsession. For his step-brother Lucius the ready espousal of public values also brings about his private anguish. He too becomes the ironic victim of his own fantasies, because it is his conceit in his new role as a landowner that resurrects the old legal battle and his nemesis comes at the moment of his mother's shocking confession immediately after the trial, which humbles him in the very instant of his triumphant vindication. Even Sir Peregrine Orme is brought within the scope of retributive justice for, although Trollope overtly protects the reputation of the weak, he also insists on their share in the common guilt. Sympathy for the saddened old man is subtly balanced by one of the novel's most poignant ironies. When, after a great inner struggle, Sir Peregrine has courageously succeeded in revaluing the moral outlook of a whole lifetime and has broken free of the imprisoning attitudes of Victorian mythology, it is Mrs Orme, his paragon of womanhood, who strenuously invokes them afresh in resolutely opposing his marriage with Lady Mason. Her earlier presence in the courtroom at Lady Mason's side, a pairing emblematic of their shared moral convictions, really concealed a potent irony which Trollope permits to surface late in the novel with devastating rhetorical effect. In spite of her undoubtedly generous humanity, even Mrs Orme cannot reconcile the contrary demands of the neo-Calvinist ethic, the claims of the private conscience and those of public standards, when an issue touches her closely. But this in turn conceals a further irony. It is essentially a false dilemma employed to mask her true commitment because, while in preventing the match she is overtly defending the family's good name, in truth, like Lady Mason, she is really protecting the financial security and prospects of her son. Mrs Orme's ironic capitulation to the commercial ethic demonstrates, perhaps more than anything else in the novel, the destructive power of a rigid moral code and its corrupting function of cloaking squalid self-interest.

In many ways *Orley Farm* is Trollope's *Measure for Measure*, but especially so in the way it raises ethical problems rather than resolves them; and although it does not have a moral to 'prove' it is clearly the product of a profoundly moral intelligence. By means of its multiple perspectives of sympathy and irony Trollope reveals how contemporary social mythologies grow out of a contempt for humanity and he stresses the almost schizoid lives they compel people to live. Trollope emphasizes that moral scrutiny is a delicate and complex process and he urges a compassionate yet responsible judgement of human frailty. And he does so by probing our assumptions about the conventions of fiction, by unsettling our familiar search for pattern in both fiction and life and by showing us how the springs of natural justice are located in character. In *Orley Farm* rhetorical design, social realism and moral vision are artistically unified because, as Bulwer-Lytton and Trollope agree, they are intimately related in the act of imaginative creation.

Serial Design in *The Claverings*

Trollope is central to any study of the serial method of publication in the middle years of the Victorian period in the first place because of his great popularity with the mass of the reading public, since it was largely through the medium of the magazines that his contemporary reputation was made.[27] Thackeray, for instance, keenly felt his rival's success while *Framley Parsonage* was appearing in the *Cornhill* concurrently with the early chapters of his own novel *Philip*. As he wrote to Mrs Baxter: 'I think Trollope is much more popular with the Cornhill Magazine readers than I am: and I doubt whether I am not going down hill considerably in public favour.'[28] From the instant success of *Framley Parsonage* in 1860 until the end of Trollope's career almost all his novels first greeted the public in instalments, and a further reason for his significance as a serial writer was his willingness to experiment with the convention in response to the fluctuating pressures of the literary market. Many of his novels were serialized in magazines like the *Cornhill*, the *St Paul's Magazine*, *Blackwood's Magazine*, *Macmillan's Magazine*, or *Good Words*, and others, like *Orley Farm* or *Can You Forgive Her?*, appeared in monthly part issue, a system which was popular until the publication of *The Vicar of Bullhampton* in 1869 and 1870 marked its decline.[29] The shilling part issue had been popular with the novel-reading public by virtue of its cheapness and for its particular quality of suspense, but it was gradually killed by the shilling magazine which sprang up in the 1860s and which, as Trollope recognized, dealt the market a severe blow: 'The public finding that so much might be had for a shilling, in which a portion of one or more novels was always included, were unwilling to spend their money on the novel alone.'[30] Trollope and his publisher, George Smith, fought the incursion of the magazine by experimenting with thirty-two weekly issues at sixpence per issue. *The Last Chronicle of Barset* first appeared in this form and despite its conspicuous lack of success the experiment with sixpenny parts was repeated with *He Knew He Was Right*, this time with a different publisher, Virtue. The other form of publication which Trollope tried as a desperate response to the stiff competition from the magazines was the singular production of *The Prime Minister* in eight massive monthly issues, but it was by then an outmoded method of publication and this no doubt contributed to the novel's comparatively poor sales.[31]

Trollope's readiness to accommodate the literary market and his editors in his methods of publication is matched by his almost incredible precision in planning his serials. His work sheets reveal that he provided exactly forty-eight pages of manuscript for each instalment of *Framley Parsonage, The Small House at Allington* and *The Claverings*,[32] and although these first two novels were only partly written when publication was already in progress, his work sheets for *Framley Parsonage*, for instance, show careful preliminary planning with chapter titles decided beforehand and the serial divisions clearly marked. The result of this forethought is a manuscript remarkably free from revision and *The Claverings* displays a similar diligent preparation.[33] Trollope's obligation to achieve this kind of accuracy was determined not only by the length of the magazine page and the space allocated to the novel in its layout, but also by the specific nature of his contract with the editor. *The Claverings*, for example, which was written for the *Cornhill*, was to consist of 'sixteen numbers of 24 pages each'.[34] As a rule, Trollope did his utmost to oblige his publishers in the matter of serial instalments, and the serial once planned admitted of little alteration. But he was also very much concerned with the question of balance and continuity in the narrative, and with the equalizing of tensions and ironies. Thus his response in 1863 to a request from Edward Chapman for last-minute revisions was terse and insistent: 'I can not make it shorter than it should be, in order that it might suit the periodical',[35] and he concludes a letter to Arthur Locker in 1881 about the difficulties encountered in serializing *Marion Fay* on a note of testy pride: 'No writer ever made work come easier to the editor of a Periodical than do I'.[36]

However, the fundamental importance of Trollope's art as a serial novelist lies, I think, in his extraordinary attention to the way his novels were presented to the reader, and he had very firm views about the pernicious effect of the convention of serial publication when he came to write *Framley Parsonage*: 'I had felt that the rushing mode of publication to which the system of serial stories had given rise, and by which small parts as they were written were sent hot to the press, was injurious to the work done.'[37] He knew that his friend Thackeray scrambled frantically from one instalment to the next, alternating between lethargy and panic, and this method was forced on Trollope himself when Thackeray wanted *Framley Parsonage* in a hurry for the *Cornhill*. However, as Trollope makes abundantly clear in his *Autobiography*, he did not commence writing the novel until the development of its plot was firmly fixed in his imagination, and his comments on the dangers inherent in the serial mode of publication underline his artistic sense of the novel as a complex unity which he refused to allow the regular and mechanical demands of the instalment to impair:

It had already been a principle with me in my art, that no part of a novel should be published till the entire story was completed. I knew, from what I read from month to month, that this hurried publication of incompleted work was frequently, I might perhaps say always, adopted by the leading novelists of the day . . . I had not yet entered upon the system of publishing novels in parts, and therefore had never been tempted. But I was aware that an artist should keep in his hand the power of fitting the beginning of his work to the end.[38]

The convention was also suspect, in Trollope's view, because of its seductive ease of production which led to idleness,[39] and he considered that this is what mars the form of Thackeray's fiction, for he finds *Vanity Fair* 'vague and wandering, clearly commenced without any idea of an ending',[40] while in *Pendennis* 'You feel that each morsel as you read it is a detached bit, and that it has all been written in detachments'.[41]

In spite of Trollope's clear artistic intentions *Framley Parsonage*, which constituted his serial baptism, is also episodic, as the critic for the *Westminster Review* noted: 'The habit of writing a story in periodical instalments is almost always fatal to that coherence and proportion without which no work can lay claim to any really artistic merit. The consequence of this mode of publication is that "Framley Parsonage" is rather a series of anecdotes than a well-knit tale.'[42] However, after the resounding success of *Framley Parsonage* George Smith naturally wanted another novel from Trollope and his next contribution for the *Cornhill*, other than the stopgap *Brown, Jones and Robinson*, was *The Small House at Allington* which, in spite of its almost equal rapidity of production, displays more care both in the design of the novel and in the construction of the serial part. Trollope deliberately rounds off each instalment so that the reader is seldom left in a state of suspense. There is never any doubt, for instance, at the end of Part IV about the engagement of Lily Dale and Adolphus Crosbie and when Earl De Guest is attacked by a bull, the crisis has passed by the close of the instalment when he has been saved by John Eames. Indeed, in only four parts of the twenty in which the novel was published is there a slight note of tension at the end. But it is in Trollope's next *Cornhill* novel *The Claverings*, a persistently underrated study of Victorian class and sex warfare, that his mastery of the convention of serial writing is most evident. By this stage in his career Trollope had consciously rejected Mrs Gaskell's method of simply ignoring the limitations that the convention placed on a writer and breaking off the story when an instalment had to end, so that serialization had a minimal effect on the novel's form;[43] and similarly, he instinctively avoided Dickens's method of writing in 'blocks' from number to number for sensational effect. He endeavoured instead to utilize the serial divisions in such a way that they contribute to the novel's coherence and unity, while significantly developing its rhetorical design.

Trollope recognized that the serialized novel had to fall into parts coherent enough to stand on their own, for the reader expects the aesthetic satisfaction of contemplating a completed whole. Each number thus presents its own problems of achieving unity and diversity of interest together with a sense of coherent development. In the first instalment of *The Claverings*, chapters I–III, where the reader needs an immediate grasp of what the novel is in the fullest sense 'about', Trollope secures several formal effects to direct our attention to his essential moral concern. He also gains our interest through the arousal of a strong sense of expectation and continuity. The number opens on a crisis in the lives of the novel's central figures as Julia Brabazon coolly jilts Harry Clavering in the autumnal garden of Clavering Park in favour of a simply materialistic marriage. Julia's whimsical, affectionate taunting of Harry with his poverty, his lowly status as a school usher and his immaturity colours her worldly cynicism and reveals at the same time the tension of her suppressed love for him; but for her the claims of the inner life have to yield to those of financial necessity. The burnt grass of late autumn forms an appropriate background to the end of their courtship and the more distant emblematic vista of the square, sombre stone mansion of Sir Hugh Clavering, whose cynical diplomacy the reader quickly learns is responsible for the destruction of Harry's youthful hopes, has a significance which expands as the number progresses. Trollope recognized the importance of presenting the novel's main concerns as early and concretely as possible; for while *The Claverings* is a rich and varied study of Victorian marriage, social class, materialism and the conflict between youth and age, its organizing theme, which is placed squarely before the reader in this opening scene, is the powerful tension between the promptings of the inner emotions and the diplomatic prudence that rules Victorian social life. Other interests are interwoven with it, giving it definition and expanding its significance, but this important theme is given progressive definition in the remainder of the number in Julia's careful refusal of Harry Clavering's rashly proffered life savings to help her out of her financial plight and in her discussion with her sister, in which she makes a cold appraisal of the strategic wisdom of her forthcoming marriage to the infamous Lord Ongar. For as Hermione admits, her own worldly match with the almost pathological Sir Hugh Clavering has become a living nightmare.

Trollope's careful balancing of middle class milieux, which

is such an excellent feature of the novel's moral pattern, is also employed to produce an essential measure of unity in the opening instalment. His deft contrast between the rectory, with its well-bred, languid air of untroubled prosperity, the oppressively soulless atmosphere of Clavering Park and the Burtons' lower middle class home at Onslow Crescent, with its busy air of contented domestic routine, serves to articulate his moral vision; for underlying the surface differences of these varied households and marriages there is a powerful similarity of myopic response to the novel's central issue, the tyranny of social will. The constricting ethos of class rigidity which expresses this will is indicated by the dominant subject of the opening instalment, the choice of a career. In the central chapter, 'Harry Clavering chooses his Profession', the rector sneers at his son's choice of a socially demeaning career in civil engineering and, since this occurs after he has been jilted by Julia Brabazon and before her mercenary marriage to the prematurely senile aristocrat, a connection is made by its placing between the flanking chapters which gives a sense of aesthetic completion to the close of the instalment. It does not end on a high note of anticipation, but on a profoundly ironic parallel of character made from Lady Ongar's point of view as she leaves the church after her wedding:

And as she stepped into the chariot which carried her away to the railway station on her way to Dover, she told herself that she had done right. She had chosen her profession, as Harry Clavering had chosen his; and having so far succeeded, she would do her best to make her success perfect. Mercenary! Of course she had been mercenary. Were not all men and women mercenary upon whom devolved the necessity of earning their bread? (p. 32).

Despite the apparent finality of this conclusion, enough narrative hints have been intercalated into the first instalment to ensure the continued interest of the serial reader. There is the measured tone of irony in which Julia Brabazon and Harry Clavering are introduced, there is the early promise of Julia herself, a character too interesting to be lost to the story, and the reader is also informed of her husband's premature senility; then there is the advancement of Harry's career and a hint of development in our knowledge of the unattached status of the Burtons' daughter, Florence. Once the reader has grasped the nature of the potential love triangle he looks forward to further developments in accordance with his well-schooled sense of probability. At the close of the first instalment then, Trollope has achieved the essential serial emotion – a sense of completion together with the tension of foreshadowed development.

However, Trollope was not so much concerned with keeping his reader guessing as with balance and continuity, and he aims at retaining as much of the novel as possible in the reader's consciousness. As he reads on he becomes aware of those various points of interconnection and formal relations of character and situation through which Trollope expresses his moral sense of the underlying sameness of human lives. The major function of this everchanging pattern is to direct the reader to the novel's central concern and to keep it in his view throughout the progress of the serial. All the contrasted marriages of the novel, for instance, are prudent matches based on economic self-interest and at best they are uneasy, diplomatic marriages. The rector's wife has given him up and he feels acutely her lack of respect for him; Cecilia Burton, restive at her husband's humdrum, cautious prudence, engages in a prolonged though unconscious love affair with Harry Clavering (for her efforts to secure him for her sister-in-law go well beyond the bounds of reason and propriety); while Hermione's marriage, which she later bitterly contrasts with that of Mrs Clavering, is a hell of boredom and despair. This pattern of cautious social decorum, personal diplomacy and emotional sterility extends to all the family relations of the novel and Trollope draws attention to these in his chapter titles, which serve as reading directions: 'Sir Hugh and his Brother, Archie', 'Count Pateroff and his Sister'. And indeed, this latter pair, with their comic pseudo-allegorical names, Sophie Gordeloup (gardyloo!) and Count Pateroff (with its hint of cynical sexual conquest) serve, by their almost professional diplomatic expertise, to draw attention to the covert cynicism and inhuman calculation which tarnish English family and social life.

Thus in the early numbers of *The Claverings* Trollope employs a design which creates a formal mnemonic for both author and reader. Once the relation of character or situation has been grasped the appearance of its parallel at a later stage in the serial completes the pattern and bestows on its movement a mnemonic as well as a moral value. The initial impact of this design is made by juxtaposition within the three chapter serial unit. The reader's curiosity is naturally focused on the flanking chapters, each of which is constructed around a coherently developed scene, and the connection between them is made by a reflexive movement of the mind prompted by a sense of closure and completion. In Part II, Chapters IV and VI, 'Florence Burton' and 'The Reverend Samuel Saul', are brought into careful ironic balance because the courtship of Fanny by the curate, who like Harry Clavering wishes to marry his master's daughter, later provides a mirror of the struggle between Harry and Florence Burton. The correspondence is one of character and class reaction. Mr Saul's social concern makes a pointed contrast with Harry Clavering's egoism, while the rector's horror at his curate's effrontery in threatening traditional class boundaries is the response of a narrow class sympathy similar to that shown by Mr Burton. This pattern, lodged early in the reader's mind, is the source of several later ironies when the curate quietly exposes Harry Clavering's bourgeois confusion of social role and moral value as he makes uncomfortably explicit the parallel between them, and when Fanny Clavering's revolt against the outmoded class structure, like her brother's vacillation between Florence and Julia, testifies to a profound emotional hunger which society seeks to deny. Similarly, the instinctive generosity of Florence Burton in her dealings with Harry Clavering and the selfless tact of Mr Saul in his treatment of Fanny, are emphasized when the pattern made in Part II shifts again and Trollope brings them together in mutual recognition of each other's true worth.

However, this is not Trollope's sole technique for securing a formal mnemonic in the serial. He employs the larger elements of form, but often he uses local detail. The habitual action which expresses character can also take on a mnemonic function. Theodore Burton's habit of dusting his boots with his handkerchief is at once an expression of the man and of his class. Harry Clavering in his youthful pride and ignorance substitutes the class image for the man, and refuses to dine with him, and when he does eventually visit the Burtons at Onslow Crescent he cannot imagine how the lovely Cecilia can love a man who dusts his boots in that manner. His response to the Burton household, which moves from condescension to agreeable surprise, is ironically matched by Burton's cool, measured assessment of the interloper, which Trollope sardonically underscores: 'What would Harry have said if he had heard all this from the man who dusted his boots with his handkerchief?' (p. 85). Burton's characteristic habit is referred to repeatedly in Part III so that when the next confrontation between him and Harry Clavering, due to the growing alarm at Onslow Crescent at Harry's estrangement from them, occurs much later in Part IX of the serial (Chapters XXV–XXVII), Trollope can be confident of the mnemonic value of this trait as registering Burton's moral superiority and he calls the chapter simply 'The Man who Dusted his Boots with his Handkerchief'. Here Burton is his wife's diplomatic envoy sent to secure Harry for Florence, and his handling of the meeting with such tact and delicacy creates in Harry Clavering an ironic reversal of his earlier narrow judgement – of which he is embarrassingly conscious: 'And this was the man who had dusted his boots with his pocket-handkerchief, and whom Harry had regarded as being on that account hardly fit to be his friend!' (p. 276).

Trollope secures the variety necessary within the serial instalment to avoid excessive formalism through the mobility of Harry Clavering at the centre of the novel, which is consequent on his crossing class boundaries both in his chosen sphere of work and in his courtship of Florence. In Part III, Chapters VII–IX, Trollope juxtaposes the two moral areas of the novel which make increasingly conflicting claims upon him: the world of Bolton Street where Lady Ongar lives and that of Onslow Crescent, and the third chapter, 'Too Prudent by Half' which closes the number, gains in irony from the preceding closely-linked scenes. Harry's first encounters with the beautiful widowed Lady Ongar and the homely Burtons are thematically important. Harry is dumbfounded by Julia's cynical maturity, her coy appeals to nostalgia and her seductive assault on bourgeois prudery: ' "It is only the world, – Mrs. Grundy, you know, – that would deny me such friendship as yours; not my own taste or choice. Mrs Grundy always denies us exactly those things which we ourselves like best. You are clever enough to understand that" ' (p. 74). From this challenge to the prudent life, diplomatically made, but with an undercurrent of powerful feeling, Harry Clavering has to readjust to meet the world of Onslow Crescent. And Trollope's abrupt change of moral and social atmosphere is masterly. His criticism of puritan materialism is directed precisely at the way it unconsciously informs the lives of warmly realized folk like the Burtons, but to his surprise Harry Clavering finds it attractive. His astonishment at Lady Ongar's altered bearing is matched by the evaporation of his class prejudice as he watches the builder of drains and bridges expertly preparing gravy and decanting wine. But, ironically, although Cecilia ostensibly preaches her husband's conformist work ethic, like Julia Ongar she covertly challenges constricting class claims and also sexual ethics, selecting Harry Clavering as the object of an unconsciously rebellious flirtation. These contending influences, so obviously distinct yet linked by the fundamental need to challenge the crushing power of social will, cancel each other in Harry Clavering's consciousness and the third and closing chapter, 'Too Prudent by Half' is charged with irony as Florence Burton's complacency, nurtured by the materialism and feminine dominance of the bourgeois ethos, prompts her to delay their marriage at the very time when the Burtons' cosy domestic world is being threatened afresh by Lady Ongar, who employs Harry's innate knight-errantry in a romantically diplomatic mission to Count Pateroff.

Harry Clavering's physical movement in the novel is a correlative of his vacillation throughout the serial between the contrary and exclusive choices of a passionless but prudent marriage and a spontaneous but tarnished romance, summarized by these two worlds, geographically placed and related but morally discrete and separate. Such places are part of the formal mnemonic of the serial because they are the source of the attitudes which the characters carry around with them and which make such powerful claims on them. But more significantly, by employing a central and typical figure to link the novel's different worlds, Trollope solves the serialist's problem of achieving unity and coherence. Harry Clavering dominates the first ten of the sixteen instalments and his dilemma focuses sharply two contemporary human concerns. He is trapped in a network of rigidly defensive class attitudes which run counter to economic individualism and the absorption of the middle classes by the metropolitan mercantile world. And he is also caught in the clash between society's inflexible idealization of romantic love and the reality of unpredictable human passions. He finds it increasingly impossible to distinguish between the promptings of conscience and of self-interest, between moral and class values, between love and passion. It is profoundly ironic that Harry Clavering's dilemma should be the only force linking the fragmented society of the novel and his faltering endeavour to vindicate love and social mobility as healing forces only reveals the more compellingly the slender threads that connect a community based only on a consensus of will.

Of course Trollope recognized that this method alone is not enough to guarantee sustained serial interest and the movement away from Harry Clavering's enveloping point of view is to a series of alternating actions which are the source of the dominant serial emotion, irony. The management of the transition is aided by publication in parts, but it is important that such shifts are smooth if the narrative continuity is not to be lost. In Part IV, Chapters X–XII, there is the familiar moral pattern of correspondence between the chapters 'Florence Burton at the Rectory' and 'Lady Ongar takes possession' and in part this derives from the basic serial device of the author's and the reader's omniscience and the characters' ignorance. Florence is warmly embraced by the fastidious rectory family where she begins to reap the social benefits of her love, while at Ongar Park her solitary rival, ostracized by her family and by society at large, begins to taste the bitter fruit of her more forthright, calculating materialism. Florence Burton looks to the future with confidence while Julia Ongar reaches the nadir of despair and self-loathing. The transition in Part IV from Clavering to Ongar Park and away from the centrality of Harry Clavering in the narrative, is made by the central chapter, 'Sir Hugh and his Brother, Archie'. The movement is achieved by means of a split scene which creates a highly formal effect. The fierce quarrel between Sir Hugh Clavering and his uncle, the rector, in the Clavering drawing-room allows Hermione Clavering the opportunity to try to negotiate Harry's agreement to Sir Hugh's mercenary scheme of marrying Julia Ongar to his brother. While the uneasy diplomacy of family life has overtly collapsed and has turned into open wrangling, it is at the same time covertly strengthened by Trollope's emblematic use of the inner room where the dehumanizing bartering with human lives points to the lack of any real moral connection. As Harry Clavering moves from the alcove into the drawing-room there is an ironic correlation of mood between his inner disquiet and their open discord and the irony is underlined by Florence's welcoming smile. But the reader's interest has been firmly located on Julia Ongar and the context of shoddy diplomacy is appropriate to the accompanying movement from the bitter group scene, of which she is the still and invisible centre, to its alienated member; for it is pharisaical social prudence that incarcerates her at Ongar Park and it is to the powerful Sir Hugh Clavering that she owes her position as social victim. Trollope's switching of the reader's vision in the last chapter of the number to Julia Ongar's spiritual desolation means that his gaze can be allowed naturally to rest there as her solitude is next broken by the shadowy figure from her imprisoning past, Count Pateroff.

After Part X the central movement of the serial is furthered by Trollope's method of cross-cutting, which is more than the mechanical alternation of sombre and comic – although this is important for retaining the reader's interest – because it creates a significant ironic pattern. His cross-cutting, for instance, from the conclusion of Part XII when Archie Clavering makes his final comic proposal to Julia Ongar to the tense battle between her and Cecilia Burton at the beginning of Part XIII, is made through the emblematic relations of character and milieu. Archie's club, the Rag, stands for the world of the gaming table and the race-course and he and Cecilia obviously represent different moral areas of Victorian society. Although Archie is shallow and malleable, Trollope does not treat him harshly for he has weighed himself and recognizes his limited moral worth. But Cecilia Burton by contrast possesses the rooted egoism of the novel's varied women, together with the smugness of a moral as-surance bestowed on her by her social background. But although the moral movement from the world of the Rag to that of Onslow Crescent is full and complete, they are deftly linked and com-pared in the ironic juxtaposition of the visits of Archie and Cecilia to Lady Ongar. Archie Clavering's bid for Julia's wealth is at least made open-eyed and with an easy-going cynicism, but Cecilia Burton's wild imprudence is marked by the passion of bitter rivalry. What is more, as Julia Ongar emphasizes to her, the love code she purports to defend in striving to gain Harry Claver-ing for her sister-in-law falsifies human relations. Although both gambles fail, each gambler is given the opportunity to make a fresh moral evaluation. For Archie Clavering it merely brings confirmation of what he already knows, but for Cecilia Burton, blinded by an unacknowledged love for Harry Clavering and by narrow class attitudes, her confrontation with the funda-mental claims of the inner life of the emotions affords her neither moral awakening nor a truthful reassessment of the dangerous realities of feminine power. Trollope stresses the central importance of this power in the world of the novel by his employment of a similar technique in the final instalment. Here, Mrs Clavering's manipulation of her despised husband in order to smooth the way for her children's marriages is ironic-ally juxtaposed with the preceding Chapter XLVI, 'Madame Gordeloup retires from Diplomacy', as Trollope neatly places the subject next to the means of satiric comment. Both women have done untold damage to human relations in the novel, Mrs Clavering from a sense of duty to the binding obligations of the feminine love code and Sophie Gordeloup from a forthright materialism and a frank delight in malice.

The prolonged and frequently interrupted reading of a serial-ized novel means that there is a constant danger that the reader might overlook some important element of the novel's moral pattern, like the quiet contrast which Trollope makes in the opening number between the sisters, Hermione Clavering and Julia Ongar. By the middle of the serial this parallel might have begun to escape the reader's attention and the function of the internal structure of Part VII is to enforce the moral design of their contrasted fortunes, as the death of Hermione's infant son heralds the collapse of her loveless marriage, while Julia Ongar is escaping the claims of her own past and regaining Harry Clavering's love, with its accompanying promise of social acceptance. Then the wheel of fortune, turned as so often in Trollope by social forces, revolves once more under the impetus of feminine diplomatic pressure and at the conclusion of the novel the contrast is made again. This time the context is one of parallel as both sisters, similarly betrayed by society's perverted values, resign themselves to widowhood: the one acutely aware that she has thrown away life's rich possibilities, but morally though not socially redeemed, the other socially irreproachable but still the prisoner of her peevish egoism.

Harry Clavering's sudden capitulation to this powerful collective feminine will, expressed by Florence and Cecilia Burton and by his mother, and subscribed to by the Burton and Clavering families and by the whole ethos of Grundyism which euphemistically cloaks their political will, creates the difficulty of too complete a climax, for his decision to marry Florence comes just over midway through the novel. Trollope handles it with shrewd realism; the unbalancing effect of little Hughy's death, Harry's illness and his mother's bedside intervention on behalf of Florence have psychological weight and truth, but it raises the problem of how to redirect the serial reader's interest and expectations. But because Trollope did not, like Dickens and Thackeray, write from instalment to instalment, he always has such problems under control and he avoids the difficulty by shifting the focus of interest away from Harry Clavering's moral collapse to the society responsible for it. Trollope places his capitulation at the beginning of Part XII and the remainder of the number directs the reader's attention outwards to the wider social movement of the novel; to the parting of Sir Hugh

Clavering and his wife, to Archie Clavering's final visit to Lady Ongar and the growing storm over Fanny's courtship by the curate, so that several issues are kept in suspension for the next instalment.

In *The Claverings* Trollope's serial unit also has several minor but important functions. It is frequently employed to introduce a figure who is later thrown into a dynamic relation with another character, like Florence Burton, whom the practised serial reader could see on Harry Clavering's horizon in Part I; or in Part V, Chapters XIII–XV, when Count Pateroff's mock-sinister diplomacy at the Blue Posts throws in Harry's way the insuperable barriers of the vacuous Doodles and the ponderous military gourmet Colonel Schmoff. The conclusion of a number often assists the reader by establishing the stage reached in Harry Clavering's moral struggle, but it also frequently presents the morally emphatic recognition by a character of some fact or relation previously hidden from him by social manoeuvring or by the engrossing nature of his own egoism. Part II, for instance, ends with Fanny Clavering's startled realization that she is being pursued by her father's curate, a relation which requires the growth of moral sensitivity and self-knowledge. This kind of unwilling recognition is also Julia Ongar's experience at the conclusion of Part IV as loneliness compels her to concede the futility of her materialist ethic. The serial unit also makes a submerged movement in the narrative which creates a subdued but noticeable impact. In the early parts of the serial the central chapter has its own function of introducing new characters, but towards the conclusion it deals with partings and supports the thematic undercurrent of social dislocation. This is elaborated in a series of chapters entitled 'How Damon parted from Pythias', 'Desolation', in which the death of little Hughy creates a vacuum at the heart of the novel, 'Parting', 'How to dispose of a Wife', and 'Showing what happened off Heligoland', in which the death of Sir Hugh Clavering and his brother is reported. And the only central chapter to deal with a reunion, that of Harry and Florence, is given the ironical title, 'The Sheep returns to the Fold'.

One of Trollope's methods for achieving that clear sense of

progression essential for retaining the serial reader's interest is foreshadowing, which creates an ironic perspective within which present actions are given added significance. A major source of anticipation is the repeated situation, which also embodies Trollope's realistic and moral sense of life giving people second chances. As Mr Saul's fortunes are charted against Harry Clavering's throughout the novel, each meeting with Fanny offers the curate a further opportunity to renounce his daring assertion of human values, just as Julia Ongar's return forces Harry Clavering to choose anew between personal and social claims; and while Fanny is repeatedly tempted to betray her class values, Florence Burton is ready to abandon hers. But Trollope's more subtle technique for securing a sense of continuity is his unobtrusive employment of ordinary images which take on the expressive identity of character so that their recurrence later in the serial has a mnemonic effect. They summarize neatly the moral direction of the protagonists at various stages of the story and are carefully intercalated into its varied moral and social contexts. The 'bargain-price-reward' motif, which Julia Ongar eventually learns to transcend, finds its satirical value in the gambling men's talk of the mastery of mares and fillies. But whereas Julia Ongar regarded her marriage as an unpleasant contract, albeit one made on the basis of scarcely concealed cynicism, Captain Boodle and Archie Clavering see marriage in brutal terms as an exciting risk. However, the way in which the novel's women collectively defend the social security afforded by marriage is similarly dehumanizing and is effectively defined by their repeated use of the images of 'sheep' and 'sheep-fold' by which they designate the roles of men and home. This is more insidious because the cosiness of the image falsifies the central importance of the moral and social issues raised by Harry Clavering's dilemma and it masks the energy with which the women govern through the trivialization of urgent human problems. Balancing the 'sheep' imagery is the image of the 'butterfly-in-the-sunshine' used so often by Harry Clavering to describe the superficial attractiveness of his apparent freedom, which is later converted into the truer and more compelling image of the 'moth-and-the-candle'. And there is also the important image foreshadowing an ironical reversal, which Harry Clavering employs when he finally commits himself to Julia Ongar: ' "I must bear what men say. I do not suppose that I shall be all happy, – not even with your love. When things have once gone wrong they cannot be mended without showing the patches. But yet men stay the hand of ruin for a while, tinkering here and putting in a nail there, stitching and cobbling; and so things are kept together. It must be so for you and me" ' (p. 266). This extended image is immediately relevant to all the relationships in the novel, but its potency lies in its reversal in the larger development of the narrative; for while Harry is speaking feminine society is mustering its forces, and it is the women rather than he who patch his relationship, not with Julia Ongar but with Florence Burton, into a superficial whole.

Trollope recognized that towards the conclusion of the serial recollection, aided by the habit of re-reading, is an important source of the reader's moral understanding and in the final instalment of *The Claverings* it creates a profoundly ironic perspective. The encounter of the rivals, Julia Ongar and Florence Burton, is the point to which the reader's anticipation has been directed throughout fifteen instalments and Trollope invests its formal prominence with moral weight. Both Julia and Florence have achieved a measure of moral growth in the course of the novel, Julia through her remorse and her self-sacrifice and Florence through her selfless insight into Harry Clavering's true nature. It is fitting that the only two people who are capable of transcending the limitations of wealth and class and who have been kept apart for so long should finally meet at the conclusion of the novel to revalue their experiences. As in the opening number, Clavering Park forms the consciously ironic background to Julia Ongar's confession of her love:

'It was here, on this spot, that I gave him back his troth to me, and told him that I would have none of his love, because he was poor . . . Now he is poor no longer. Now, had I been true to him, a marriage with him would have been, in a prudential point of view, all that any woman could desire. I gave up the dearest heart, the sweetest temper, aye and the truest man that, that – Well, you have won him instead, and he has been the gainer.' (p. 503).

This explicit acknowledgement of her reversal of fortune binds the serial and invests its conclusion with a moral and aesthetic completeness. But not quite. Behind the bitter, self-mocking irony, containing as it does in her references to Harry Clavering's fidelity and oblique comment on Florence's prudence in marrying him a realistic element of feminine revenge, is concealed nevertheless a sordid world of diplomacy, and Julia Ongar tactfully keeps from the ingenuous girl the shocking truth about the powerful social pressures that, with appalling caprice, have bestowed on her the man she loves. The marriage with which the novel ends is thus not merely a conventional happy ending, nor the pledge to the future or to social harmony that we find in romantic comedy; rather, as the logical conclusion to this subtle study of Victorian class and sex warfare, it is plainly, ironically, and even tragically, inconclusive.

V

THE ACHIEVEMENT

In this concluding chapter I would like to focus attention on the two novels which, in my view, together with such excellent works as *The Last Chronicle of Barset* and *Orley Farm*, will in the long run sustain Trollope's growing reputation among readers and critics alike: *The Way We Live Now* and *The Prime Minister*. Although they develop further several of Trollope's familiar themes which I have already traced in the course of this book – the relation between personal identity and the shaping forces of the environment; the individual's response to the changing values of his society; the tyranny of social convention; problems of will and ambition; the dilemma of the outsider and the highly political nature of English social life – these two novels stand apart not only because they are more artistically conceived, but also because they are rather more profound. After his great success in the 1860s, Trollope had reached a stage in his career when he felt the need to attempt a larger assessment of his age and to make a mature statement about the direction in which he considered English life was moving.

Although *The Way We Live Now* is a masterly satire and *The Prime Minister* is a magnificently documented study of political realism, it would be a mistake to regard their worlds as being totally dissimilar. In the first place *The Way We Live Now* is a good deal less gloomy and *The Prime Minister* is rather more sombre in tone than critics have recognized. And secondly, as I will discuss later, there are grounds for thinking that Trollope regarded them as contiguous and complementary studies of the major sources of power in the modern age, presenting from different perspectives a coherent judgement of Victorian society. Although the majority of Victorians felt that free enterprise and parliamentary government were the twin bulwarks of the English way of life, in these consecutive novels Trollope's detailed examination of their pervasive effects on the whole range of public and private behaviour amounts to a quietly subversive revelation of the moral vacuity and inertia which for him these social systems had come to symbolize.

The Way We Live Now

When it was first published, *The Way We Live Now* was very unpopular. The *Saturday Review*, whose response was fairly typical, objected to 'the incivility of Mr Trollope's title. "The way *we* live!" '[1] But a further reason for its unpopularity may well have been its topicality and uncomfortable relevance. The novel was written at the height of the financial boom of the 1870s and Melmotte's fraudulent venture, the South Central Pacific and Mexican railway, which dominates much of the novel, may have been drawn from the real-life scandal about the misleading prospects of the Honduras Ship Railway, which had failed the previous year. A third reason was undoubtedly the novel's trenchantly satirical tone. Irony governs its texture and is manifested in almost every conceivable form. Most obviously it is present in the title, for far from presenting a celebration of high Victorian progress, the book is overwhelmingly negative. Proposed elopements and marriages fail, the projected railway is, of course, never built, fortunes are not made, since even fraud is ultimately unsuccessful; and after the death of its chief perpetrator, Melmotte, no moral lessons are drawn and social life is allowed to continue as before, ruled by the same sordid conventions. Essentially the novel is characterized by the way people conspicuously fail to achieve anything even in their own strictly limited terms.

However, perhaps a more fundamental reason for the lack of success of *The Way We Live Now* with contemporary readers is the way that Trollope's irony continually disrupts the relation between the author and the reader. There is a disturbing ambivalence between the expectations which a practised Trollope reader brings to the novel and the authorial stance implied in the title. On the one hand there is an element of reassurance for the reader in Trollope's satiric exaggeration, as for instance in his handling of Melmotte's preposterous dinner for the Emperor of China, but on the other hand his sense of moral security is upset by the author's balancing technique of understatement, for example in his treatment of the spiritual poverty of the Church. And there resides an equally disturbing use of irony in Trollope's treatment of character. His reader's anticipation of the familiar many-sided study of individual moral dilemmas as people strive to achieve an equable relation with their society is frustrated because in *The Way We Live Now* people's problems are simply 'operational' – purely political dilemmas of how to gain some personal advantage or neutralize attacks on their social positions. The reader is thus left striving to read moral situations of which Trollope's characters stubbornly refuse to admit the existence. And this absence of firm authorial guidance creates a disorienting experience akin to that of the figures within the world of the novel itself. In several respects, therefore, and not least in the way Trollope has cut his reader adrift, *The Way We Live Now* is a self-consciously modern novel.

Trollope himself, overreacting as he sometimes did to criticism, remarked that the novel contained good satire but was too exaggerated.[2] However, it is by no means wholly satiric. Indeed, as we have already observed, as a realist and a moralist Trollope strenuously eschewed simple moral absolutes and while his satiric assault on modern capitalism and its ethos is powerfully substantiated in its own terms, the world which he thus exposes for our judgement is inhabited by ordinary, frail men and women trying to do their best for themselves and their families in a time of great social flux and moral uncertainty. There are, moreover, gleams of sanity and goodness as the world that Trollope presents is endlessly qualified and humanized. Melmotte is clearly a modern monster, but he is equally a naïve and pathetic victim;

Mr Longestaffe's harsh, confused morality is shown to proceed from his sense of being stranded between the old world and the new; while the unscrupulous Lady Carbury achieves a muted kind of redemption through her love for her unworthy son. The satiric force of *The Way We Live Now* is thus balanced by Trollope's simultaneous provision of a wonderfully realistic and delicate treatment of human problems which evokes a large measure of sympathy for little people trapped by historical circumstances beyond their understanding or control. Trollope does not, however, shirk the implications of his satire and allow the novel to veer towards comedy and comic solutions as James R. Kincaid suggests; rather, in my view, he manages to combine, without any sense of strain, both an absolutist moral stance and a high degree of moral relativism.[3] He recognizes that people both make and are made by their society and that the individual's crucially important struggle to assert and maintain his identity through marriage, business, or politics now takes place within a dangerously uncertain environment and is subject to altered pressures. Of course, to the extent that people and institutions are responsible for creating a malevolent social ethos they are vulnerable to the scourge of the satirist, but equally, when they are forced by society to consistently deny their individuality so that life becomes devoid of meaning for them, our response must be one of sympathy.

The main focus of Trollope's satire is the capitalist system, which in his view had fostered an increasingly intense struggle for wealth and power; however, his venom includes not only the entrepreneurial class, represented by Melmotte,[4] but the parasitic establishment figures like the Grendalls and also the multiple moral failure of social institutions such as the Church, the political parties, the city and the press, all of which either openly or covertly support the debased values which Melmotte stands for. Even more painful for contemporary readers must have been the way that Trollope's remorselessly logical analysis of the way in which the money ethic has permeated human affairs destroys a whole collection of cherished myths – the puritan work ethic; the doctrine of self-help and social mobility; the belief in the heroic qualities of the captains of industry and commerce; the aristocratic creed of *noblesse oblige*; the comforting faith in the sanctity of true love and domestic bliss; or the lingering notion that England was still a Christian country – all of which have been swept away.

Because, in the modern world life is no longer fruitful or joyous, but fraught with anxiety and despair, the novel is full of unnatural relations. Women like Madame Melmotte, Lady Pomona, Lady Carbury and Mrs Hurtle are or have been terrified or humiliated by their bullying husbands; children like Lord Nidderdale and Marie Melmotte are pawns in their parents' struggle to accumulate wealth and position; alternatively, like Felix Carbury, they cold-bloodedly batten on their parents, or, if like Dolly Longestaffe they have financial independence, they are rebellious and unloving; while lovers such as Marie Melmotte, Hetta Carbury, Mrs Hurtle and John Crumb are deceived and jilted. Two examples in particular demonstrate the perversion of human relations that occurs when social pressures override the need for self-determination. For the Victorians it would not have been uncommon to find a member of the impoverished squirearchy like Mr Longestaffe trying to make a financially sound match for his daughter, but the reader is astonished and disturbed to discover that she feels constrained to engage actively in selling herself. Still more interesting is the relation between Lord Nidderdale and Melmotte towards the close of the novel. The lonely city magnate is so far gone in lies and illusions that he can gain satisfaction even from a 'simulated confidence' with the young man (II, 225). But this perverted psychology, which suddenly and surprisingly humanizes Melmotte, testifies to the underlying need of people even as thoroughly cynical as the great financier himself, to make an intimate human contact for, as Trollope is concerned to demonstrate throughout the novel, people cannot for ever escape the claims of their own humanity.

Yet for the most part people have become so conditioned to the impersonal ethic of free enterprise that they are only dimly aware of the extent to which, within little more than a generation, it has transformed English life. The modern world is urban, secular and capitalist and the old moral values of the Christian order of Barsetshire, although still alive vestigially in people's language and frame of reference, have been overlaid by a new and frightening nihilism. As Hetta Carbury recognizes, there has come into being 'a newer and worse sort of world' to which they all now belong (I, 71). Throughout the novel Trollope juxtaposes the old values and the new in a surprisingly extensive satirical counterpoint of patterns of animal and biblical imagery in order to chart this shift in the whole spiritual frame of the contemporary world. The competitive commercial ethic has produced a post-Darwinian social jungle. Indeed, the young men of the Beargarden Club frankly admit that they inhabit a world in which people 'prey on each other'. The arch-capitalist Melmotte is described variously as a 'commercial cormorant', or a 'wolf and a vulture', who would skin people if he could get money for their carcases. And his aristocratic 'curs', Lord Alfred Grendall and his son, denounce him as a 'brute'. The wild American, Winifred Hurtle who, like Melmotte, is in love with power, is defined by a similar cluster of images as a 'wild-cat', a 'tigress' and a 'beast of prey'. It follows that in this world those who are not predators are victims. Lady Carbury offers herself to her son like a 'pelican' and in return is tortured by him like a 'butterfly upon a wheel'. A corollary of this general process of dehumanization is that people now display the whole range of animal instincts. Felix Carbury, for instance, who is judged by his uncle to possess the 'instincts of a horse', turns a social event into an act of bestiality, asking his mother when the 'animals' are coming to 'feed'. And Madame Melmotte observes, after deriding Marie as a 'pig, ass, toad, dog' when she refuses to be sold into marriage, that even love is simply a 'beastly business'.

Indeed, there is a profound absence of any significant inner life in most of these new people and Trollope's contrapuntal pattern of biblical imagery indicates the moral and spiritual frame that they have abandoned. Lady Carbury, who like the Longestaffes occasionally attends church when in the country where it is still a mark of class and fashion, is merely doing her social duty by discussing her soul with the surprised Bishop of Elmham. We also learn that Felix Carbury and Georgiana

Longestaffe never read the Bible and that the American entrepreneur Mr Fisker has never prayed in his life. Moreover, when
the Bible is referred to, it is invoked in the strict service of self-
interest. Lady Carbury employs it in defence of her son's idleness
(I, 364), while Lady Pomona uses it to buttress her opposition to
her daughter's marriage with a Jew (II, 263). In reply Georgiana
turns the Scriptures against her parents, accusing them of feeding her stones and serpents (II, 424). Surprisingly, one of the few
people who does read the Bible and who even quotes it to the
astonished Felix Carbury, is the amiable young Lord Nidderdale,
but his belief in refraining from throwing the first stone is really
little more than a variation of Beargarden hedonism (I, 209).

In Trollope's view the modern world has abandoned the
Christian faith for a new religion. It now 'worships' Melmotte
(I, 331) whose faith is utilitarian and materialistic: 'It seemed
that there was but one virtue in the world, commercial enterprise, – and that Melmotte was its prophet' (I, 411). Because
people vaguely sense that they are stranded between two worlds
they look to men like Melmotte to give a spiritual dimension
to the new commercial order so as to allay their profounder
apprehension of the appalling emptiness of their lives, and their
thwarted religious instinct thus finds a new and perverted mode
of expression. But the main symbolic role that Trollope assigns
to Melmotte, ironically, is that of the Tempter, whose success
represents nothing less than man's second Fall. This satirical
function grows unobtrusively out of local, realistic detail. Melmotte's inversion of the whole moral order is quietly suggested
by his habit of conducting business on Sundays and by the way
in which, both as a social entertainer and as a forger, he turns
night into day. As Melmotte's reputation grows, Mr Longestaffe
comes to feel that he is a great 'necromancer' and a Medea
figure, and the theme of conjuring is sustained by the grand
illusion of 'fairyland' that Melmotte creates for the great ball
(I, 115). Hints of the diabolical also accumulate throughout the
novel until they constitute one of its central satirical statements,
as the black magician is gradually transformed into the devil
himself. Melmotte's wife, for instance, believes that he is as
'powerful as Satan', while the lawyer Mr Squercum regards

himself as the 'destroying angel of this offensive dragon' (II, 258, 230). Indeed, in several important respects Melmotte's career makes a parallel with that of Milton's Satan. Driven by the law from a life of luxury on the Continent where he had finally overreached himself, Melmotte seeks to build his own kingdom in London, Trollope's modern hell. He re-establishes authority over the social world through his cohorts Lord Alfred Grendall and his son by the sheer force of his egoism, and the illusion of unlimited power that he creates is given a defiantly symbolic presence when he has his own Pandemonium built for the great dinner. Yet although Melmotte regards himself as the absolute ruler of his kingdom, the city, and as a god-like being who can dine with the brother of the Sun, once more like Satan he falls through overweening pride as he comes 'almost to believe in himself' (II, 20, 57). And this symbolic pattern is extended to include the Beargarden Club, several of whose members have been drawn into Melmotte's financial orbit; for at the closing of the club, which coincides with Melmotte's death, Mr Lupton ironically describes it as a Paradise that they have forfeited, while the religiously inclined Lord Nidderdale meditates with unconsciously dark humour on the consequences of the fall of Adam (II, 431, 437).

Although Trollope's satiric use of biblical parallels emphasizes the perversion of values in contemporary life most people cannot give proper expression to the change that they feel has taken place. Mrs Hurtle, an American and an outsider, is the exception. She frankly celebrates the alteration. Indeed, she is Melmotte's chief apologist, defending him and the system he represents in almost Nietzschean terms and affording it a quasi-spiritual dimension. What she worships in him is the will to power, comparing his stature with that of George Washington and Napoleon. Such a man, she says, rises above mere honesty because power transcends morality. And it is Mrs Hurtle who makes explicit Trollope's interest in the connection between the exercise of power in the modern world and the mythology of heroic capitalism, because she believes that 'wealth is power, and that power is good' (I, 246). Moreover, in her view, commercial power greatly outweighs that of mere politicians or political systems.

One of the fundamental ironies of the novel is the way that not only English society but Melmotte himself become the willing victims of this superficially attractive philosophy. The American entrepreneur Hamilton K. Fisker puffs him up into a commercial 'hero' and when he entertains the Emperor of China he is finally accepted as such by the nation (II, 45). And because he aims at unlimited power, he inevitably also endeavours to become a 'political hero' (II, 171). But Melmotte eventually finds himself trapped by the myth-making process. When his fraud is discovered and his career is finished, he still feels hopeful that he may yet be able to transform himself into a criminal hero so that his reputation 'would not all die' (II, 298). And he eventually chooses suicide partly so that something of the mythology he has striven to create may remain intact.

However, before he dies Trollope allows us a rare interior view of this enigma, partly in order to satirize the popular Victorian myth of social mobility based on economic individualism by revealing that instead of being a Dick Whittington figure, Melmotte is an obscure, illegitimate, foreign Jew, who has scaled the pinnacle of the English commercial world by manipulating its rapacity and credulity. But the central thrust of Trollope's satire is directed at the fact that, like the traditional hero figure, Melmotte symbolizes his society's values. In truth people have created him out of their own deepest needs, both material and spiritual, and just as his reputation for wealth and power depends upon his exploitation of society he is in turn a creature of its collective will, its servant and victim as well as its leader and hero.

If Melmotte provides the measure by which Trollope intends us to judge English life, we must take into account the important American element in the novel, which critics have tended to overlook, in order to assess the significance of what Melmotte represents, for to witness free enterprise in its most modern form we must look not to Melmotte but to Fisker. And in this connection Trollope's formal mastery coincides with his satiric intentions, because while Melmotte stands at the heart of the novel linking all its characters in his web of commerce, Fisker remains in the shadows on the novel's periphery. Melmotte represents the older order of European capitalism, bound up with quasi-spiritual needs, with the social mythologies and complex traditions that finally baffle him. Fisker on the other hand, exemplifies how insidious and unheroic the new form of free enterprise really is. Unlike the lugubrious, monosyllabic Melmotte in whom we witness the machinery of commerce ponderously at work, Fisker is mercurial, good-humoured and intelligently audacious. An instinctive manipulator, he first selects the respectable Paul Montague as a dummy director in order to gain credence for the proposed railway venture and then employs the wealthy Melmotte to attract needy men of rank to its board in order to complete the cosmetic operation. After the financial débâcle in London he is still around to pick up the pieces, turning the failure of the company in Europe into the making of its San Francisco branch and walking off with Marie Melmotte's fortune into the bargain. He is the new international man, acutely aware that San Francisco is now a suburb of London and that he can play off England against America in order to facilitate a rise in his railway shares. The American element in the novel is important primarily because it demonstrates how England is being sucked into the much larger world of western capitalism with its brutal realism and frontier ethics. For all his cosmopolitanism and arrogance, Melmotte, like the English, is essentially provincial and naïve. And this is his undoing. He becomes obsessed, not only with the creation of his own mythology, but with the class system of his adopted country, making fatal errors of judgement about the power of rank before the law and misjudging too the inbuilt strength of its snobbery, which effectively excludes him from society's inner circles. Fisker, by contrast, never makes the mistake of believing in the myths that he assiduously cultivates and it is his anonymity and his clinical manipulation of the system and its figureheads on an international scale that make him and his kind so dangerously invulnerable and modern. If Melmotte is Trollope's yardstick for the decline in the English way of life, Fisker represents his grim warning about the direction in which he felt contemporary society was inevitably moving.

The urgency of Trollope's prophetic note is intensified by his examination of the tyranny that the free enterprise system exerts over English life. One of his chief satiric triumphs in *The Way We Live Now* is his revelation of the way in which the ethic of the market-place has so permeated people's consciousnesses that ordinary intercourse has come to obey the impersonal laws of supply and demand. The strongholds of traditional values, the Church, the political parties, the press, marriage and social gatherings have degenerated into areas where human value is measured in cash. Just as in the commercial world the rising price of Melmotte's railway shares is based on his conjectured wealth and their fall is contingent on the collapse of this illusion, so in private society tickets for his grand dinner stand 'very high in the market' until the last moment when rumours of an impending social fiasco cause their value to plummet (II, 88). Even friendship is shown to be subject to the same impersonal laws as Lady Monogram trades her social assistance to Georgiana Longestaffe in return for her allocation of tickets, feeling that she has been cheated in her bargain when they turn out to be worthless. More poignantly, Georgiana, who has always overvalued herself in the marriage market, desperately lowers her price as she grows older. Parallels such as these, which are multiplied in the novel, record how people have traded away their precious individuality, reducing themselves in the process to the status of vulnerable objects.

Money permeates the atmosphere of *The Way We Live Now*. It is the focus of people's aspirations and fears. We learn how much they earn writing novels and newspaper articles, how much they sell their homes for and what they win or lose at gaming or in the share market. Trollope's detailed realism allows the neutrality of cash to stand as an important ironic symbol for personal relations in the modern world and as such it makes most of the formal connections between them, throwing into weird juxtaposition widely diverse areas of society. But at least money is in a sense real. Credit, which in fact effectively governs people's behaviour, is not. Melmotte's wealth is a carefully fostered illusion, sustained by the community and subject to rumour. Trollope exploits for satiric effect the parallel between the spurious activities of Melmotte's railway board and the ceaseless gambling at the Beargarden Club. The one deals in worthless share scrips, the other in valueless IOUs. Just as people fear that Paul Montague will reveal that Melmotte is a swindler, nobody at the Beargarden wishes to know that Miles Grendall cheats at cards, for these acts would involve the acknowledgement of a real world of solid objects and moral absolutes that must be suppressed. Trollope maintains the contrapuntal relation between these two groups throughout the novel, for the existence of the one is dependent on the social currency of the other, and the collapse of Melmotte's empire coincides with the closing of the club. By this neat but entirely natural formal parallel, Trollope emphasizes the fundamental irony that in reality the doctrine of economic individualism rests on a mindless conformism. Indeed, the most chillingly ironic statement in the entire novel comes from Melmotte as he instructs his railway board in the morality of free enterprise: 'Unanimity', he intones, 'is the very soul of these things' (I, 381).

This flight from reality is evident not only in the larger social world but in its microcosmic symbol, the Beargarden Club, where it is focused more intensely. Bereft of moral conviction and lacking faith in themselves and in society alike, the young men evade the truth about the awful hollowness of their existence by regarding life as a tedious game. The game, indeed, emerges as a potent metaphor for the nihilism of the new world. In the competition for the 'Marie Melmotte Plate', Felix Carbury feels himself to have been 'checkmated' by her father, but nevertheless he decides to 'carry on the game' (I, 223; II, 154); Lord Nidderdale wants to enter business simply because commerce might prove more exciting than whist or loo (II, 225); while for Dolly Longestaffe even Melmotte's suicide is less awful than having nothing to amuse him (II, 433). This shocking reduction of death to the level of a game of cards demonstrates how formidable are the barriers erected against the intrusion of moral reality. The notion of the game not only serves to orchestrate the competitive elements of social life, creating a buffer against uncomfortable truths, but it affords at the same time a set of rules that effectively absolves the players from individual responsibility.

Much of the burden of Trollope's satire lies heavily on the governing classes represented by the Longestaffes, the Monograms, the Nidderdales and the Grendalls, whose misplaced pride in their rank and their need to maintain it with acquired cash turn them into Melmotte's bitterly resentful lackeys. And there is a high irony in the fact that Melmotte covets English titles and distinctions which Trollope shows to be debased. But his satire casts a wide net and there is a characteristic double-edged irony in the way he offers Mrs Hurtle as a symbol of emancipated American womanhood for our judgement, while employing her at the same time as a vehicle for his criticism of English life. Her commitment to energy and freedom from conventional constraints comes as a breath of fresh air blowing through the novel. She argues with conviction precisely what Trollope demonstrates, that in England the possibility for the kinds of achievement she advocates is limited by the laws of inheritance which prevent young noblemen from becoming their own masters; by a class system which fosters marriages based on rank and wealth; by the way women are repressed and subdued and by the manner in which English social life is governed by the trivial canons of good taste. As an independent outsider she is an accurate analyst but her conclusion that England is a 'soft civilization' is underwritten by the fact that she is in love with several aspects of English life and by those qualities that she exemplifies in her personal relations (I, 445).

However, as I suggested earlier, Trollope's world is not totally dark, nor is it treated in a uniformly satirical way, for *The Way We Live Now* also contains a realistic examination of human dilemmas intensified by a period of great flux. Because people often find themselves in situations not of their own choosing and from which there is little possibility of escape there is a moral relativism and sympathy at the heart of Trollope's judgement of character which makes allowances for the oppressive influence of the new environment. Mr Longestaffe's offensive treatment of his daughter's suitor, the honourable Jew Mr Brehgert, contrasts strongly with his dealings with the evil Jew Melmotte, to whom he is prepared to sell his birthright, Pickering. Longestaffe's situation is a subtle study of racial hatred and moral confusion, but it is qualified by the fact that he feels himself to be trapped by circumstances beyond his control. Indeed, by a curious twist of psychology he even takes pride in his depressed condition because it both confirms his status as being above that of the rich parvenus and justifies his inertia and his appalling prejudices. And in his misconceived loyalty to the past, Longestaffe makes a surprising parallel with Roger Carbury, Trollope's moral norm in the novel, who is nevertheless perverse in his insistence in handing on Carbury Manor to his nephew, who is certain to ruin the property, simply from a blind reverence for tradition. But although both men exhibit a moral smugness that Trollope finds distasteful, he understands their instinctive grasping at the old ways. And not only the gentry, but self-consciously modern people are also muddled by the changing times. Although as an American Mrs Hurtle cherishes her love of heroism and power, at the same time her woman's instinct for self-sacrifice leads her into a love affair with an effete young Englishman who in her heart she despises. But because, like Roger Carbury, she is morally alert she recognizes the powerful irony at work in the contrary impulses that chart her moral confusion. However, for the most part people are intensely aware of the desperate nature of their predicaments without being able to apply to them any moral remedies. The reader watches the way individuals become trapped in situations by a remorseless logic that proceeds out of the way they live. Often such dilemmas arise from their inability to recognize moral claims. Georgiana Longestaffe, for instance, loses Mr Brehgert because of her prolonged, mercenary negotiations over his London house, a course which is consistent with her market philosophy and is a source of dark humour. But like most of the novel's characters, she is not treated as a tragic figure because she regards herself as a marketable commodity and thus denies her selfhood.

All Trollope's varied patterns of character and situation serve to stress how moral alternatives are restricted by the new environment, how individual growth is warped or stunted and how idealism founders. There is the parallel between Ruby Ruggles, the servant girl, and Georgiana Longestaffe who both come up to London from the country husband-hunting among men of rank and fortune and have to be schooled into the realistic limitations of age, class and the treachery of the metropolitan world. But the fundamental irony for people living in an atomistic society is that they have to face their problems alone, unaware that other people confront similar dilemmas. Trollope employs his familiar pattern of rotating stories to record the bleak uniformity of this world and of the pressures that can overwhelm the isolated individual, and this is a profound source of the reader's sympathy. This is particularly true of the main victims in the novel, its various women. Like Lady Carbury, Mrs Hurtle fights to overcome the plight of the single woman in a predatory society and both of these women are finally redeemed. But perhaps a closer and more surprising parallel is that between Winifred Hurtle and Marie Melmotte. The only women in possession of independent fortunes and the freedom to assert their right to self-determination, they chart the lonely struggle of romantic idealism. At the opening of the novel no two people are more dissimilar, the one a fierce, widowed American and the subject of scandal, the other a timid, young European Jewess. But both share the feminine instincts which girls like Georgiana Longestaffe and her English sisters have long ago learnt to suppress. And although their golden idols, as Marie Melmotte calls Felix Carbury, turn to clay, they love the clay nevertheless, only to be bitterly disillusioned. These women of spirit (for Marie Melmotte matures rapidly during the course of the novel) also offer independently judgements of English life which coincide with telling effect. Ironically the European Jewess comes to feel degraded by her contact with the aristocracy, while the American regards society as being in the grip of a terrible paralysis. But they cannot escape, as Hetta Carbury can, to the rural world of Suffolk. For them America, with all its vulgarity and violence, offers the only, tainted alternative and soured and despairing, their final escape there at the close of the novel in the company of Fisker constitutes their muted tragedy.

Such people require our sympathy, and in the course of the novel Mrs Hurtle is transformed from a satirical symbolic force into a woman distinguished by her capacity to care. Similarly, false and foolish though she is, Lady Carbury also has claims on our compassion because of the rare naturalness of her love for her worthless son. And Trollope has considerable residual sympathy too for the young men of the Beargarden who are not entirely wicked or vicious, but whose lives are cramped and empty of purpose. However, the main sympathetic figure, who recognizes moral problems for what they are and acts accordingly, is the traditional Trollopian character, Roger Carbury. His rural world is Trollope's only viable alternative to the modern age and the centrifugal form of the novel, radiating out from Melmotte at its centre, demonstrates how the rural characters on its periphery are sucked into the tainted London world. Father Barham, the priest, is duped by Melmotte's display of wealth, while the servant, Ruby Ruggles, is dazzled by Felix Carbury's rank. But Roger Carbury remains undeceived. He cares deeply about people and although he is portrayed as crusty, romantic and sententious, putting himself in the wrong with Paul Montague and making a fool of himself over Hetta Carbury, he is ruled by good nature and good sense. He represents the old-fashioned Christian virtues exemplified by his traditional Anglicanism, his acts of practical charity and by his position as the figurehead of a close-knit community rooted in the permanence of the Church and the land. Of course Trollope does not offer us rural Suffolk as the perfect pre-lapsarian world. It is a backwater, out of touch with changing times and all it can hold out as an alternative to an atomistic, nihilistic society is an outdated feudalism. Just as Trollope's treatment of American values constitutes his warning about the future, Suffolk is his nostalgic picture of what society has irretrievably forsaken.

Although Trollope has produced a novel in which moral laws appear to be in abeyance, it does not follow that they no longer exist, or have no force. As I have been arguing, *The Way We Live Now* combines a satirical, absolutist stance with the creation of a realistic moral world in which unnaturalness cannot for long be sustained without some form of retribution. This arises logically out of human behaviour and Lady Carbury's book, 'The Wheel of Fortune' provides an appropriate symbol not only for her own life but for the working out of the process of natural justice in the world. This creates a pattern which is best realized in the meteoric rise and fall of the novel's central figure, Melmotte. It grows naturally out of his whole way of life. He is brought down by a paradox of the system by which he lives. When he most desperately needs money to pay off the purchase of Pickering, rumour of his debts and the consequent fall of his railway shares prevent him from raising the necessary capital. And although he has used his daughter as his private bank, she chooses the moment of his greatest need to assert her personal independence. What is more, he becomes the victim of his own strategy of total deceit, because by the time she realizes that for the first time her father is telling the truth her decision to help him comes too late. Moreover, his contemptuous forging of Dolly Longestaffe's signature to the title deeds proceeds from the fact that he is cocooned in a world of illusion which is ironically shattered by Dolly's unshakeable adherence to reality. But the most telling irony of all is the fact that since in Melmotte's world everything, including human life, has a market value, when he becomes aware that his own has fallen to zero he accepts the brutal logic of the market-place and commits suicide. And it is at this point that we realize with a shock that he scarcely existed at all in his own right, but primarily as the expression of an impersonal social will.

All the other major characters suffer similar profound reversals of fortune. There is a dark irony in the fact that the Jewish banker Mr Brehgert judges Georgiana Longestaffe to be too mercenary for him. Unable to believe that he could wish to be free of a high-born Christian lady her failure is terrible to her and faced with the reality of age and loneliness she despairingly runs off with a penniless curate. She pays the penalty for her willing acquiescence in the destruction of human values, not, however, in the sufferings of conscience, for repentance is bound up with the kind of moral awareness that is largely absent from this novel, but from a clear recognition of life's missed opportunities. And this pattern is multiplied. For all her idealism, Mrs Hurtle believes at heart in the supremacy of the will and she is constrained by this to try to intimidate Paul Montague. But because he prefers softer women this very procedure guarantees her failure. However, for Lady Carbury the wheel of fortune is turned by the power of love and this is sufficiently rare in the novel to draw attention to itself. In spite of her mercenary nature, her hypocrisy and her pathetic attempts to manipulate editors, her sacrificial love for her son, which Trollope describes as 'pure and beautiful', is the one redeeming feature of her character which attracts Mr Broune and results in his proposal of marriage (II, 211). This change in fortune is accompanied by a moral growth as she repents her past life, echoing Thackeray's narrator in *Vanity Fair*, as having been 'all vanity, – and vanity, – and vanity!' (II, 462). She recognizes the falsity and emptiness of her life, the poverty of her literary talent and her cruel neglect of her daughter. Her worthless son is taken off her hands and unlike almost all the other characters she is enabled to make an optimistic start to a new life based on sober moral realism.

It was not for nothing that Trollope had originally designated Lady Carbury as his 'chief character'.[5] She dominates the opening of the novel and strikes its satirical keynote. But as it progresses Melmotte becomes the organizing centre of Trollope's satire, while Lady Carbury forms the focal point of the group of character relations which belongs to the novel's realistic mode, which humanizes it and softens the absolutism of its satire. More importantly, in a world in which people's continual mortgaging of the present for an uncertain future, fostered by the competitive system that they have brought into being, merely guarantees frustration, Lady Carbury's experience offers the promise of a kind of redemption and the continuation of basic human goodness. Trollope's hope for the future lies not in the old ways of life that Roger Carbury represents, but in man's recognition that the prolonged abrogation of moral and spiritual values against his own deepest instincts is futile and self-defeating.

The Prime Minister

It is remarkable that a contemporary critic should have regarded Trollope's masterpiece as marking his 'decadence', but in fact the *Saturday Review* again condemned it as severely as it had his previous novel and the other reviews were almost universally unfavourable.[6] This may have been due partly to the fact that, although it maintains a consistently realistic tone and there is a marked absence of satire. Trollope's account of Victorian political life in *The Prime Minister* is more deeply pessimistic than his treatment of the free enterprise society in *The Way We Live Now*. However, his examination of the ways in which capitalism and parliamentary government fail to fulfil human aspirations are not documentary studies but rather parables of the modern age. But although Palliser's Coalition Government has no greater historical authenticity than Melmotte's railway board, both function as large metaphors for the real world and of course, as several critics have observed, in *The Prime Minister* Trollope draws on Victorian politics in the interests of realism, mediating imperceptibly throughout the novel between fiction and history.

Because, in these novels, Trollope is concerned with different aspects of what is essentially the same world, he creates several links between them. Most obvious is his introduction into *The Prime Minister* of a younger Melmotte in the person of Ferdinand Lopez, the Portuguese Jewish speculator. Although more humanized, anglicized and sophisticated than Melmotte, like the great financier, he is, Trollope tells us, 'a self-seeking, intriguing adventurer, who did not know honesty from dishonesty when he saw them together' (I, 275). Both men are absorbed in the struggle to gain admission into English society and both in their different ways try to use marriage as a route to social status and wealth. Moreover, both strive to enter Parliament and when their careers finally crash in ruins both commit suicide. Fundamentally, both men are given the function of testing the values of English life and in *The Prime Minister*, as in *The Way We Live Now*, the outsider is the main linking agent in the novel. Not only is Lopez the centre of the important subsidiary plot, but his attempt to carve a place for himself in society brings him into contact with virtually the whole spectrum of the Victorian world: the middle class strongholds of the Whartons and the Fletchers, the seedy city world of Sexty Parker, the subterranean world of the working classes represented by Tenway Junction, and the politico-social arena of the Prime Minister himself, Gatherum. However, unlike Melmotte, the younger man employs traditional English methods to obtain his goal by marrying into the moneyed middle classes. But because Lopez tries to behave like an English gentleman he is much more vulnerable than Melmotte, and Trollope's scrutiny of the various ways Lopez is snubbed and thwarted, for all the wrong reasons, makes this novel more disillusioning than *The Way We Live Now*.

The contiguity of these two novels is also suggested by Trollope's repeated use of the 'special case', which he employs for satiric effect in the former novel, but with even more devastating realism in *The Prime Minister*. He does so in order to reveal disturbing truths about the fundamental nature of power. In the earlier novel his placing of a brutal figure at the pinnacle of English commercial life constitutes a satiric indictment of the tyrannical system under which people are content to live. By contrast, in *The Prime Minister*, Trollope selects as his representative political figurehead his ideal statesman, Plantagenet Palliser and puts him in charge of the best Government, theoretically, that can be devised, a non-partisan Coalition serving the national interest, which nevertheless fails from a lack of political will. But like Melmotte, Palliser quickly discovers the limits and the ultimate futility of power. Indeed, in both novels real power is shown to be elusive, for both Melmotte and Palliser are really the instruments of others, of Hamilton K. Fisker and the Duke of St Bungay. But in the broader sense, too, they are agents of their society and when they are no longer useful as credible figureheads, its communal assent is withdrawn and they fall.

Although, like Walter Bagehot with whom he has been frequently compared, Trollope regarded politics on one level as an exciting game and Parliament as the best club in London, more importantly he shared with his fictional Prime Minister two unshakeable convictions; first, that 'to serve one's country without pay is the grandest work that a man can do, – that of all studies the study of politics is the one in which a man may make himself most useful to his fellow-creatures'; and second, that his position as an 'advanced conservative Liberal' was the most rational that could be held.[7] Although they are meliorists, both Palliser and Trollope are more in sympathy with the whole movement towards democracy than was Bagehot, for instance.[8] Trollope's statement of his belief in political evolution in his *Autobiography* – that while Conservatives wish to maintain social distances, the Liberal 'is alive to the fact that these distances are day by day becoming less, and he regards this continual diminution as a series of steps towards that human millennium of which he dreams' – is amplified by his Prime Minister in a rare moment of confidence to the astonished Phineas Finn :

Equality would be a heaven, if we could attain it. How can we to whom so much has been given dare to think otherwise? How can you look at the bowed back and bent legs and abject face of that poor ploughman, who winter and summer has to drag his rheumatic limbs to his work, while you go a-hunting or sit in pride of place among the foremost few of your country, and say that it all is as it ought to be? You are a Liberal because you know that it is not all as it ought to be, and because you would still march on to some nearer approach to equality . . . (II, 321–2).[9]

However, one of the novel's central ironies is the fact that Palliser's innate diffidence will not permit him to fire men with speeches like this in the House. His political dream is too private for the hurly-burly of parliamentary debate and it therefore resists translation into dynamic political action.

Several critics, including Bradford Booth, Robert Polhemus, Ruth apRoberts and John Halperin, have debated the success or failure of Palliser's political career.[10] However, for me, and I think for Trollope too, that is not the strictly relevant issue. For all its political realism, *The Prime Minister* is a parable and in it Trollope employs the 'special case' – the unique conjunction of his ideal statesman with a Coalition Government – in order to reveal the processes of Victorian political life as a way of assessing the political health of the nation. He creates a situation in which there exists the possibility of a truly representative, patriotic Government guided by reason and led by an unambitious, conscientious statesman. However, in spite of the old Duke's claims that the Government has achieved the limited success he anticipated, Trollope shows how in meaningful political terms it has failed conclusively and how Palliser's hopes of doing something grand for his country are dashed. The failure is the result of the clash between Palliser's character and the nature of political reality. As Trollope tells us in his *Autobiography*, his ideal statesman lacks moral elasticity: 'I had . . . conceived the character of a statesman [as being] superior . . . But he should be scrupulous, and, as being scrupulous, weak.'[11] And this judgement is endorsed by Trollope's political realist, the Duke of St Bungay, who remarks that Palliser 'has but one fault, – he is a little too conscientious, a little too scrupulous' (II, 441). But equally, in Trollope's view, the Coalition fails because that is in the nature of coalitions; as he points out in his biography *Lord Palmerston*: 'Political coalitions are never firm because they are formed of individual men, and each man has a heart in his bosom in which he carries memories of the past as well as his hopes for the future.'[12] In the real political world partisan politics and personal ambition can never be suppressed for long.

During the many discussions of politics in the novel, a great deal of cant is talked about coalitions; how single party government is natural to English society and how coalitions are always feeble because they are based on compromised principles. It is certainly true that the Duke's administration is offensive to Mr Boffin's staunch, patriotic Conservatism and that the Radicals are disgusted at being led by such a mild man as Palliser, but as Trollope was well aware, the great majority of politicians simply resent sharing power. And the fundamental malaise of Victorian partisan politics is summarized in the way the old Duke regards the Coalition as a means of delaying reform, which results, as Mr Boffin complains, in a 'death-like torpor' (II, 3). However, politicians of both parties concur in approving of the way the Government has effectively stifled reformers like the Home Rulers, the economists and the philosophical Radicals and also approve of the way they share between themselves the spoils of office. Indeed, St Bungay himself admits that policies are only useful for creating a majority in the House. And like the old Duke, who also regards the Coalition as an essential device to buy time until another Liberal administration can be formed, all Trollope's politicians believe the regaining of party power to be of far greater importance than mere policies. This much is evident even to an observer like Mrs Finn, who recognizes that politics has nothing to do with reform and that there is never anything special to be done either by Conservatives or Liberals. There is genuine horror, therefore, when a Reform Bill, which has the support of the Prime Minister, is presented by the Coalition, and it is ironic that Mr Monk's county suffrage measure is finally lost by the development of a Liberal majority and the demise of the Coalition. But there is a much darker irony in Lady Glencora's shrewd assessment of political realities from the point of view of her own coterie: ' "I don't think it makes any difference as to what sort of laws are passed. But among ourselves, in our set, it makes a deal of difference who gets the garters, and the counties, who are made barons and then earls, and whose name stands at the head of everything" ' (I, 64).

Throughout *The Prime Minister* Trollope is concerned to demonstrate the opposing claims of politics as the focus of national aspirations and those of Realpolitik. And Palliser finds himself at the centre of this conflict. Almost alone among Trollope's politicians he is a statesman of genuine vision, who is also in touch with the realities of the workaday world outside the hothouse of politics. He can devote himself with equal delight to the extension of the franchise, decimal coinage, or to discussing the merits of cork soles. But ironically he is plainly unsuited to the Realpolitik of managing a *laisser-faire* Coalition.

He obstinately sets his face against short-term expedients and Trollope's revelation of his political creed fairly late in the novel does much to explain his sense of frustration at realizing the futility of power. His private vision feeds his misery at failing to define for himself 'the past policy of the last month or two' (I, 194). And against his colleagues' advice he supports Monk's bill as a small step along the road to democracy. Moreover, not only does Palliser lack the requisite charm, tact and thick skin to be an effective Prime Minister, but he continually allows moral values to get in the way of political decisions. By ignoring parliamentary traditions, like the appointment of the law officers of the Crown, by which he offends Sir Timothy Beeswax, and by his decision not to appease the powerful brewers' lobby, he inadvertently threatens the Coalition itself. And his political blunders accumulate. He snubs Sir Orlando Drought, refuses to interfere in the Silverbridge election, pays Lopez's election expenses and, most eccentric of all, he bestows a Garter on Lord Earlybird. Ignoring the advice of St Bungay – ' "You will offend all your own friends, and only incur the ridicule of your opponents" ' (II, 279) – Palliser believes that by acknowledging a meaningful relation between the Government, the aristocracy and the world of the ploughman he is giving public recognition to the concept of the nation as a community of interests. In the event, as his old mentor had predicted, he astonishes Lord Earlybird, disgusts his powerful supporter Lord Drummond and educates no one. Indeed, Palliser himself is unable to sustain the gesture, coming to feel like his colleagues that it is quixotic.

Apart from his scrupulosity and his love of virtue, Palliser's main political flaw is his innocence of the many-layered depths of cynicism around him. He is the unwitting tool of the old Duke, who regards him as a convenient patriotic symbol to hold the Coalition together in a way that a more nakedly political figure could not, and whose resignation, when the Government has run its course, will not damage a Liberal regrouping. A hard-headed realist, St Bungay treats politics with a curious mixture of patriotic devotion and frank cynicism, regarding it as a dignified but worthwhile game. And Trollope supplies the metaphor : 'As a man cuts in and out at a whist table, and enjoys both the game and the rest from the game, so had the Duke of St. Bungay been well pleased in either position' (II, 367). Long in political years and honours, the old Duke leaves the highest place to Palliser, not from natural diffidence, nor from aristocratic disdain, but quite simply because he does not want to surrender his real power as a king-maker. Similarly, the rest of Trollope's lesser politicians, like Phineas Finn, Sir Timothy Beeswax, Lord Drummond, or Barrington Erle, all respected figures, are so obsessed with power that they collectively sacrifice principles for place and pay in the Coalition, or alternatively use it as a springboard from which to launch a new ministry. This deep-rooted cynicism, shared by political wives like Mrs Finn and Glencora and so often masked by convincing political arguments and courteous eloquence – especially by the old Duke – constitutes one of Trollope's main criticisms of the political world. Contemporary politics, he felt, were partisan, static and ultimately sterile.

Trollope's view of Victorian politics, as revealed by the 'special case' which he examines, gains its effectiveness partly by being set against a densely realized background. He is very perceptive, for instance, about the many component parts that make up a coalition and how these agree with differing degrees of cohesion and cordiality. He details too the grasping of the good things of office, the in-fighting, the back-stairs intrigues, how opposition to the Coalition arises from the personal ambition of those who serve in it and the way politics is interwoven with social life. True power resides with a small coterie of Whig and Conservative aristocrats, and because Glencora instinctively realizes that for the Coalition to be a success political antagonists have to be bound by social rather than political ties she accordingly opens up Gatherum to the Government on a grand scale. Trollope also achieves a greater sense of realism by introducing a wider perspective. He makes us aware of the gulf that exists between what the newspaper-reading public is told and what the politicians themselves know about the daily health of the Government. And he reveals how the fragility of the Coalition can be laid embarrassingly bare by Glencora's

tactless joke at one of her parties about the necessity for minis-
terial obedience.

Tolstoy was surely right in believing that in *The Prime Minister* Trollope had written a 'beautiful book'.[13] And his mastery
lies not only in the breadth and maturity of his treatment of
politics, his psychological insight and his social observation, but
in his comprehensive grasp of the form of the novel. This is
particularly in evidence as he develops the theme of coalition
which articulates its different social, geographical and moral
areas.[14] Trollope's characteristic formal techniques emphasize
the way political life is shaped by personalities and individual
experience is dominated by political instinct. At the beginning
of Chapter IX, for instance, the focus moves from a discussion
of the projected gatherings by means of which Glencora intends
to cement the Coalition and gain a measure of real power for herself to the dinner-party given by the vulgar Mrs Roby, who has
assembled an ill-assorted group of guests in order to enhance her
own social prestige. Like Glencora she is using her unwilling
husband, whose brother is in the Government, in order to extend
her sphere of influence and enter the fashionable world. Moreover, she also employs the occasion to plot the coalition marriage of her niece Emily Wharton and Ferdinand Lopez. Like
Glencora's parties, Mrs Roby's dinner is aimed at getting people
to embrace publicly in a spirit of false harmony what they de-
plore in private, as Mr Roby, who detests his brother and Mr
Wharton, who dislikes Lopez, have to do on this occasion. Indeed
a further link with the world of the Pallisers is made by the
subject of dinner-table conversation. Here in private Mr Roby,
a party whip and a thoroughly professional politician, reveals
the true nature of the Duke's patriotic Government and corrobo-
rates the insights offered by Mrs Finn and Glencora : ' "The truth
is" he says, "there's nothing special to be done at the present
moment, and there's no reason why we shouldn't agree and
divide the good things between us" ' (I, 104).

This small-scale local articulation of one of the novel's main
themes forms part of a much larger emblematic pattern. Glencora's great parties at Gatherum, which represent the Coalition
in the popular mind, also find their private counterpart in

Lopez's dinner-party at his father-in-law's house in Manchester Square. Just as at Glencora's gatherings, which Palliser describes with some force as vulgar, there is a loose association of politicians, parasites, bores and hangers-on, so Lopez has recruited to his dinner-table a bunch of disreputable people who might be useful to him. Both Glencora and Lopez are encouraged by the sheer scope of their ambition to replace true hospitality with utilitarian, professional catering in houses that have never been home to them. While Glencora pursues reputation and power, Lopez strives for money and influence. In each case the voice of conscience is present but unheeded, for just as Palliser turns up unexpectedly at Gatherum and expresses his censure, Mr Wharton appears, like Banquo's ghost, halfway through the Lopez banquet to the consternation of his guests. What these gatherings reveal, like the structure and machinery of the Government itself, is that all attempts at coalition are concerned basically with reducing people to objects of political will. Consequently they are tasteless, joyless and divisive, and serve only to lay bare the atomistic social relations which it is their overt purpose to conceal beneath a spurious, temporary unity.

Trollope's development of his moral vision by means of counterpoint extends to his treatment of the middle classes in the large balancing mass of the novel. His criticism of the political world as being in-bred and based on aristocratic patronage is equally applicable to the powerful landed classes. Just as Glencora thinks of the old Duke as a king-maker and her husband as a surrogate king, John Fletcher is known to his family as 'king John'. They too are autocratic and insular, living in rural kingdoms on the Welsh border run on almost feudal lines. What Trollope draws attention to by these parallels is the division of power between the political world of London and the gentry of the shires. It is an arrangement which suits both groups. They respect each other's claims to power and each is content to leave the other alone. But the parallels between them are closer even than this, for like the Coalition Government, the Wharton–Fletcher alliance has been formed primarily to protect class interests. Although, like Sir Alured Wharton, the Fletchers feel that their traditional obligation to the local

F

community requires that they should lose a little money on their farming, it is a moral luxury that they can afford only because their real wealth is made elsewhere. In fact it is founded on those very politics of coalition which they overtly abhor. It comes from marriages, like the projected match between Arthur Fletcher and Emily Wharton, where Mr Wharton's £60,000, made from a lifetime's work as a commercial lawyer is to be added to the Fletchers' acres in a union of money and land. Indeed, the whole existence of the landed classes, Trollope suggests, is underwritten by the continued coalition with city cash, an uncomfortable truth that provokes their uneasy, defensive sneers at city wealth and city life. But this coalition also shares another significant feature with the public world of Westminster politics. It is only a temporary hiatus between single-party governments. The Fletchers are content to absorb Wharton money so that the Whartons also become in time an extension of the Fletcher party, which is the eventual outcome of the courtship of Arthur and Emily. This political instinct, developed over centuries of acquisition, and which binds families into one 'party' is, as Glencora recognizes, what makes them impregnable.

As the world goes the Whartons and Fletchers are the bedrock of society – sober, sensible, useful and even kindly people. But their political solidarity of an almost tribal kind represents a fundamental narrowness of heart, a resistance to change and a denial of any sense of national community. And when their partisanship is manifested through prejudice it can be morally vicious and destructive. They admit with some pride that they are prejudiced people, meaning by this their possession of an instinctive moral rectitude, an old-fashioned standard of gentlemanly conduct which is the fountainhead of honour and a guarantee of the rightness of their social position. But in truth it is a sure political instinct which enables them to embrace, without any sense of guilt, a cynical and utilitarian view of humanity. Their morality is fully tested by their treatment of Emily Wharton and Lopez. Their overt judgement of Lopez is made in terms of his foreignness and his relative poverty. And he is doubly marked as an outsider because he is neither sufficiently wealthy nor secure enough socially to cultivate prejudices of his own. But what really outrages them is his opposition to the Wharton-Fletcher alliance and he is quickly identified as a political enemy. Political to their fingertips, the Fletchers drop Emily immediately upon her marriage, ostensibly because she has disgraced herself, but in truth because they resent Lopez's success in winning her over to the opposition. And in formal terms Trollope tactfully reinforces this point by the electoral contest between Lopez and Arthur Fletcher at Silverbridge, which makes a parallel with their equally political battle for Emily's allegiance. However, since after Lopez's death Emily's money is still intact, it becomes expedient to welcome her back into the party. After a long debate the Fletchers decide on a policy of forgiveness; they manipulate her emotions unashamedly at her brother's wedding until she acquiesces finally in marrying Arthur Fletcher, something, ironically, that she had long set her heart on, having repented her excursion into the wilderness.

In his treatment of the personal lives of the middle classes Trollope mirrors unerringly the ruling principles of the larger political world. Striving for power, they survive on covert coalitions which they are ashamed to acknowledge publicly and which for the most part they conceal successfully even from themselves. As in the larger world the overwhelming reason why Lopez is resented, snubbed and excluded is that his ambitions come to symbolize for his social enemies the possibility of a genuine coalition between the different classes, between the establishment and outsiders and between the spheres of finance and politics. This is an anathema to people like the Whartons and the Fletchers for it represents a possible movement towards a more open and dynamic society and a permanent shift in the whole balance of social power. They bulk large in the novel precisely because their rigidity, inertia and partisan politics are symptomatic of the paralysis that Trollope felt was gripping English life.

The middle classes fear not only what Lopez symbolizes but also his obvious political gifts, for he is all political instinct. Significantly, we first encounter him at the Liberal Reform Club where he curries favour with Everett Wharton. Then he uses

Emily's aunt to gain access to her, plays on his heroism in rescuing Everett from the thieves, trades on Mr Wharton's loneliness and exploits his business partner Sexty Parker's greed. Thick-skinned, sharp-witted, charming and plausible, Lopez fastens on people's weaknesses and exploits them remorselessly. For him every meeting is a political event, each encounter with his father-in-law is a series of careful manoeuvres for advantage, and it is a measure of his political acumen that he manages to ingratiate himself with Glencora and gain entry to the great world of Gatherum. But Trollope is concerned to present a balanced view of Lopez. He is so utterly devoid of principles, Trollope tells us, as to be almost an innocent, who 'had no inner appreciation whatsoever of what was really good or what was really bad in a man's conduct' (II, 203). More importantly, Trollope makes it clear that his complete lack of moral values is simply irrelevant to the kind of judgements made of him by the Wharton–Fletcher clan, whose own mode of behaviour, like his, is rooted in political expediency; and Trollope makes a careful parallel between Lopez's cynical manipulation of people and that of the irreproachable figures like the old Duke, Glencora and the Fletchers. Lopez is hated because he lives as the world lives, not as it pretends to live. Trollope's measured sympathy for him becomes increasingly evident in those interior views that we are given of him shortly before his suicide, in which we are made aware of his genuine love for his wife and his sorrow at the ruin of Sexty Parker and his family. But although Lopez is a predator, Trollope affirms that in a real sense he is also society's victim. That other thorough politician, Glencora, who is deeply implicated in his unfortunate career, knows only too well how society musters its forces against the outsider and she is honest enough to share the blame, as she remarks to Mrs Finn: ' "I have a sort of feeling, you know, that among us we made the train run over him" ' (II, 425).

In this chillingly pessimistic study of the tyranny, the gradations and the limitations of power, Trollope's placing of Lopez's attempt to enter Parliament at the formal and moral centre of the novel is of greater significance, in my view, than critics have recognized. By this means Trollope suggests the possibility of the kind of coalition which he feels to be necessary, acknowledges how ambiguous it must necessarily be, and how it is inevitably denied. Although Lopez wants a seat in the House in order to advance his career, in the real, tainted world modern men like him who have drive and energy even though their personal morality is dubious, are needed as desperately as people like Palliser, who have a larger vision, who recognize the existence of the real world and are prepared to govern it. It is this utterly unlikely coalition of political idealism and self-help which the political world requires in order to rediscover its energy and sense of direction. But, such is Trollope's deliberately ironic use of the 'special case' that both Palliser and Lopez are badly flawed symbols. His ideal statesman is too honourable and scrupulous to dirty his hands and become an effective politician, while the dynamic new man is too innately corrupt to be able to envisage the national interest.

Nevertheless, the Silverbridge election, I think, offers the novel's central statement, although it does so equivocally. And several personal and political relations hinge on its outcome, giving it a dramatic as well as an emblematic significance – Emily's marriage, Glencora's reputation and influence, Palliser's integrity, as well as Lopez's career. But the possibility of the emergence of a new political style based on this kind of symbolic coalition between the Liberal Prime Minister and the foreign interloper founders precisely because it is at this point in the novel that its two plots converge with complex and telling effect. It is part of both Trollope's moral design and his social criticism that Lopez is offered and fails to gain the one seat in England that seems certain, and that he is refused the dowry he has every right to expect. In both cases, trying to emulate the English, he relies mistakenly on their tradition of fair play, but is defeated by politics masquerading as morality. Mr Wharton, whose social and racial prejudice is extreme, reneges on his moral obligation, ostensibly to protect his daughter, but really in order to retain power over Lopez's actions. And by doing so he confirms Lopez's role as an outcast and contributes to his estrangement from Emily and to his eventual suicide. Palliser's reaction to Lopez's candidacy is similarly governed by a confusion of motives. His resistance to Glencora's interference in the election has as much to do with their political rivalry as it has to do with the issue of electoral purity. Although he feels that he must endorse reform, his action, as the Duchess well knows, runs counter to tradition and is rank bad politics. Moreover, his decision is also morally dubious because it stems partly from a growing intoxication with public displays of virtue. The profound irony of this central episode in the novel is that the possibility for advancing Trollope's liberal ideal of bringing closer together the different classes, the worlds of work and of politics, the qualities of vision and dynamism, idealism and political skill, founder on the rocks of prejudice, pride and political naïvety. It reveals not only Trollope's mature breadth of political vision, but also the depths of his pessimism, as English political and social life fail so comprehensively.

Like Anna in *Anna Karenina*, whose suicide his resembles, Lopez feels keenly the defeat of his attempt to enter society on its own terms. And since, as an outsider, he equates success with social acceptance and advancement, he finally bows to its assessment of his worthlessness and kills himself with the same appalling logic as does Melmotte. And Lopez's choice of Tenway Junction for his suicide is also a significant aspect of Trollope's social criticism. It makes a daring counterpoint late in the novel with the great world of Gatherum as Lopez returns from the drawing-rooms of polite society to die in the workaday world. These milieux are symbolic of the social extremes of the Victorian age. They present more than simply a contrast between Government and governed, rich and poor; they symbolize the gulf between past and present. Gatherum, the elegant home of the Whig coterie, is the symbol of an era that has outlived its usefulness. Tenway Junction, by contrast, is a potent symbol of an industrial age, propelled by the impersonal forces of change, which the aristocracy and the middle classes strive to resist. Its emergence as an important symbol late in the novel serves to place in perspective all the preceding political discussion. Essentially, Trollope is employing a reductive process, for from this point of view all the politics in *The Prime Minister* are seen as little more than manoeuvrings in a vacuum, quite unrelated to the larger modern society that has to be governed.

Politics dominates the world of *The Prime Minister* not only in terms of its larger themes, but also in the area of intimate personal relations, for here too people inevitably become objects of another's will. This is one aspect of the surprising parallels which Trollope draws between Glencora and Lopez, who tries to rule Mr Wharton through his wife Emily. Similarly, Glencora, who is admired by that professional politician, Barrington Erle, because she is totally lacking in scruples, manipulates her husband in order to strengthen her political influence. And this is brought out in her conversation with Lopez about the Silverbridge candidacy: 'She certainly had a little syllogism in her head as to the Duke ruling the borough, the Duke's wife ruling the Duke, and therefore the Duke's wife ruling the borough' (I, 237). And what goes for the borough goes for the country as well. Indeed, in every area of life we find people being constrained to act in a political way. Like Lopez, they are always 'in the inner workings of their minds, defending themselves and attacking others' (I, 5), a process which produces façades and evasions of truth and turns meetings into encounters which alter the balance of political forces in personal relations. And nowhere is this more evident than in Trollope's superbly subtle study of the uneasy coalition marriage of Glencora and Plantagenet Palliser, a marriage threatened by political rivalry, because their private relationship is thoroughly interwoven with politics. Discovering that neither tenderness nor respect can replace the innate sympathy necessary for a harmonious life, they are always fighting against each other, Palliser because he shrewdly suspects that the old Duke selected him for his wife's gregariousness and utilitarianism, and because her popularity reduces his political stature; Glencora because she is desperately competing with her husband and subconsciously working for his fall. She in particular is acutely conscious of the irony of their roles for, as she tells Mrs Finn: ' "They should have made me Prime Minister, and have let him be Chancellor of the Exchequer. I begin to see the ways of Government now. I could have done all the dirty work" ' (II, 186). And she sets up her own rival 'cabinet' with Mrs Finn, which becomes a symbol of her covert battle with her husband for political supremacy that lasts throughout the novel. This situation breeds a feeling of insecurity in Palliser and he is driven to assert his authority through 'unpolitical', subversive actions which will shake the Coalition while leaving him morally impregnable. His quixotic gift of the Garter, for instance, is a consciously statesmanlike act, but it also serves to assure him of his possession of authority and, more importantly, draws attention away from his wife. Yet, paradoxically, he is increasingly unhappy as Prime Minister and wishes the Coalition could be brought to an honourable conclusion. Trollope succeeds with splendid psychological realism in showing Palliser desperately striving to reconcile these tensions, which arise out of the politics of marriage, in a way that will be seen neither by the public world nor by his own conscience as in any way dishonourable.

However, what people fear most in political life, Trollope reveals, is not conflict or compromise but the corollary of ambition – failure. This is what Palliser, especially, dreads and Trollope points out that this is why people like him cling to power long after it has ceased to be rewarding (I, 304). Because, as Palliser admits to Phineas Finn in an unguarded moment, he is only truly alive when he is immersed in political activity, he equates political defeat with personal inadequacy. It is the complex tensions that this engenders, rather than the corrupting effect of power, that lead him to grow imperious, comparing himself, when he has finally lost office, to Caesar who cannot consent to serve under Pompey. It is a triumph of Trollope's astute characterization that his Prime Minister is so morally alert that he is profoundly aware and ashamed of this process in himself, but like his jealousy of his wife it is something he finds himself powerless to alter. Of course Glencora, too, fears failure, but in her case it stems from her sense of her inadequacy as a woman. Since her marriage is unfulfilling, she puts all her emotional capital into her political schemes and she cannot bear the feeling of personal defeat that accompanies the collapse of her grand parties. She realizes with shame her lack of the dignity required of a truly great lady and that her endeavours have been slightly ridiculous. And Lopez, whose career makes a strong parallel with Palliser and Glencora, also fears public failure more than anything, even death. However, inexorably, and in Trollope's view inevitably, all the coalitions in the novel, matrimonial, social and political, end in shame and a bitter sense of defeat, creating in the process a formal pattern which helps to chart its underlying political rhythms.

In addition to the dread of failure, what all the characters share in this thoroughly political book, is the profound sense of living in a much ampler world than that of ordinary people. Palliser indeed finds the floodlit stage unnerving, feeling that both he and his administration are being judged against the backcloth of history, while Glencora urgently seeks her place in history too (I, 321). This awareness of the drama of political life is further developed by Trollope's intercalation into the novel at several important points pertinent references to Shakespeare. Lopez, for instance, describes himself to Mr Wharton as a romantic Shakespearean merchant, believing that he inhabits a sphere of heroic entrepreneurship in which petty morality does not apply. To Sexty Parker on another occasion he calls himself a Shylock in business, which serves to emphasize his role as the focus of racial prejudice. Like Shylock he is a rather ambiguous social victim, tricked by a middle class lawyer of irreproachable background. However, Mr Wharton's racial disgust and covert hatred emerge as he violently compares himself to Brabantio whose daughter has been stolen from him by a black, and when he echoes Hamlet's morbid distinction between his father (Hyperion–Fletcher) and Claudius (a satyr–Lopez). And in a novel which, as I discussed in an earlier chapter, draws on Fletcher's *Women Pleased* and in which John Fletcher uses the early drama to furnish a moral guide for his brother (I, 179), it should not surprise us to discover not only references to *The Merchant of Venice*, *Othello* and *Hamlet*, but also to *Macbeth*, *King Lear* and *Coriolanus*, a play which anticipates some of the political themes of *The Prime Minister*. Trollope employs these references both as a way of indicating his characters' acute self-knowledge and of registering their sense of living in a world that is much larger than life. Palliser compares himself with

Coriolanus, the high-minded hero who will not bend to the vulgar for approval, and Glencora sees her situation mirrored in that of Lady Macbeth. She acknowledges the workings of fate, testifies to her husband's high integrity, but at the same time recognizes her innate ambition and her powerful influence over his actions. Similarly, when Palliser refuses to nominate a candidate for Silverbridge she likens him to Lear foolishly surrendering power, and near the conclusion of the novel she compares him sadly to Othello whose occupation has now gone. These various postures which the characters strike echo the Shakespearean tragic themes of family feuding, political conflicts, racial hatred and revenge, and in a cumulative way they serve to emphasize the lust for power and the reduction of people to instruments of political will which, for all its superficial decorum and urbanity, *The Prime Minister* is really concerned with.

Finally, however, an important function of these Shakespearean echoes is that of ironic reduction. They form a contrast from the point of high art, of genuine political action, of real tragic significance, by which we are enabled to judge the smallness of the world of *The Prime Minister*. We recognize the ultimately inconsequential nature of its politics and the inability of its people to reach the heights of energy, will and passionate commitment of the Shakespearean figures, or to be imbued as they are with a sense of destiny. Trollope's superbly artistic employment of these subtle parallels not only draws attention to the fine low-key realism of his mimetic art, but it also offers his telling judgement on the moral stature of the Victorian world.

NOTES

I INTRODUCTION

1 C. P. Snow, 'Trollope: The Psychological Stream', in *On the Novel* ed. B. S. Benedikz (London, 1971), p. 3.

2 James R. Kincaid, 'Bring Back *The Trollopian*', *Nineteenth Century Fiction*, 31 (1976), p. 5.

3 R. C. Terry, *Anthony Trollope: The Artist in Hiding* (London, 1977), p. 54.

4 Frederick Locker-Lampson, *My Confidences, An Autobiographical Sketch* (London, 1896), p. 331.

5 *An Autobiography*, p. 314.

6 *An Autobiography*, p. 310.

7 *An Autobiography*, p. 136.

8 Frederic Harrison, 'Anthony Trollope', *Macmillan's Magazine*, XLIX (Nov. 1883), p. 54; *Studies in Early Victorian Literature* (London, 1895), p. 203.

9 *An Autobiography*, p. 120.

10 T. H. S. Escott, 'Anthony Trollope, An Appreciation and Reminiscence',

Fortnightly Review, LXXX (Dec. 1906), p. 1102.

11 *Thackeray*, p. 169.

12 *Thackeray*, p. 122.

13 *An Autobiography*, p. 274.

14 *An Autobiography*, p. 120.

15 *Letters*. p. 217.

16 *Thackeray*, p. 185.

17 *Thackeray*, p. 186.

18 S. W. Dawson, *Drama and the Dramatic* (London, 1970), p. 79.

19 See George Eliot, 'Leaves from a Note-Book', in *Essays*, ed. C. L. Lewes (London, 1884), p. 358; Trollope, *An Autobiography*, pp. 126, 190.

20 George Saintsbury, *Corrected Impressions* (London, 1895), p. 175.

21 Kenneth Graham, *English Criticism of the Novel 1865–1900* (Oxford, 1965), p. 21.

22 David Skilton, *Anthony Trollope and his con-*

temporaries (London, 1972).
23 See Victoria and Albert
Museum Library, Forster
Collection, F.S. 8vo 8968,
Trollope; Catalogue of His
Books (London, 1874); see
also *Marginalia*.
24 F. E. Trollope, *Frances
Trollope: Her Life and
Literary Work* (London,
1895), vol. I, 89–90, and T. A.
Trollope, *What I Remember*
(London, 1887), vol. I, 180–1.
25 F. E. Trollope, *Frances
Trollope*, vol. I, 246–7.
26 T. A. Trollope, *What I
Remember*, vol. I, 25.
27 A. G. L'Estrange, ed., *The
Friendships of Mary Russell
Mitford* (London, 1882), vol.
I, 160, 228, 239.
28 Anthony Trollope, 'George
Henry Lewes', *Fortnightly
Review*, n.s. XXV (1879),
pp. 15–24, and *Letters*, p.
252. Many of Lewes's
critical notices were collected
and published in *On Actors*

and the Art of Acting
(London, 1875) at Trollope's
suggestion, and the volume
is prefaced (pp. v–xii) by an
'Epistle to Anthony Trollope'.
29 W. C. Roscoe, 'De Foe as a
Novelist', *National Review*,
III (1856), pp. 380–2.
30 T. H. S. Escott, *Anthony
Trollope: His Work,
Associates and Literary
Originals* (London, 1913), p.
142, and Henry Taylor,
Correspondence, ed.
E. Dowden (London, 1888), p.
75.
31 Escott, *Anthony Trollope:
His Work, Associates and
Literary Originals*, p. 182.
32 *An Autobiography*, p. 253.
33 See especially Asa Briggs,
'Trollope, Bagehot and the
English Constitution',
Cambridge Journal, V (1952),
pp. 327–38.
34 C. J. Vincent, 'Trollope : A
Victorian Augustan', *Queen's
Quarterly*, LII (1945), pp.
415–27.

II TROLLOPE AND THE DRAMA

1 *An Autobiography*, p. 100.
2 *An Autobiography*, p. 315.
3 Bradford A. Booth,
'Trollope's *Orley Farm*:
Artistry *Manqué*', in *From
Jane Austen to Joseph
Conrad*, ed. R. C. Rathburn
and M. Steinmann.
(Minneapolis, 1958), pp. 153–
5.

4 Ruth apRoberts refers to
Bradford A. Booth's
discoveries in her study,
Trollope: Artist and Moralist
(London, 1971), and A. O. J.
Cockshut notes Trollope's
more general affinity with the
early dramatists in *Anthony
Trollope: A Critical Study*
(London, 1955).

5 John H. Hagan, 'The Divided Mind of Anthony Trollope', *Nineteenth Century Fiction*, 14 (1959), pp. 1–26.

6 *The Dramatic Works of Sir William D'Avenant*, ed. J. Maidment and W. H. Logan, 5 vols (London, 1873), vol. IV, 131.

7 Trollope writes that had he given himself a fair chance, 'by continued labour [Middleton] might have excelled all the Elizabethan dramatists except Shakespeare', *Marginalia*, PR2711 D8 As. Col., *The Works of Thomas Middleton*, ed. A. Dyce, 5 vols (London, 1840), vol. IV, 635. Charles Reade recognized the innately dramatic quality of *Ralph the Heir* and drew heavily on it in his play *Shilly-Shally*.

8 What convinced Trollope of the novel's merit was his readers' horror at the social heresy it proclaimed, see *An Autobiography*, p. 298.

9 *Letters*, p. 308.

10 Trollope thought the play 'obscure', although he admired the moral tone of Ford's work, see *Marginalia*, PR2521 G5 1869 As. Col., *The Works of John Ford*, ed. W. Gifford, revised A. Dyce, 3 vols (London, 1869), vol. II, 321.

11 Trollope's work sheets indicate his concern with the precise formulation of the Earl's claim, which he had checked by a lawyer friend, and they demonstrate Trollope's assessment of its importance in the novel, see *Papers*, MS. Don. C.10., p. 7.

12 Quoted in Bradford A. Booth, *Anthony Trollope: Aspects of His Life and Art* (London, 1958), p. 129. Trollope read *The Old Law* in 1876, see *Marginalia*, PR2711 D8 As. Col., *The Works of Thomas Middleton*, ed. A. Dyce, 5 vols (London, 1840), vol. I, 120.

13 *Marginalia*, PR2421 D8 1843 As. Col., *The Works of Beaumont and Fletcher*, ed. A. Dyce, 11 vols (London, 1843–6), vol. VII, 94. As Inga-Stina Ewbank has pointed out in 'Anthony Trollope's Copy of the 1647 Beaumont and Fletcher Folio', *Notes and Queries*, 204 (1959), 153–5, this copy is in the library of the Shakespeare Institute. From his marginalia dating in this edition it is evident that for some reason *Women Pleased* was one of only a few Fletcher plays which Trollope omitted to read during his first period of study in the Renaissance and Jacobean drama in the years 1850 to 1853.

14 There are other echoes in *The Prime Minister* of the names of characters in *Women Pleased:* Silvio's aunt is named Rhodope, while Emily's aunt is called Roby, and the name of Emily's lover, Arthur Fletcher, may be an unconscious echo of that of the play's author.

15 W. P. Ker, 'Anthony Trollope', in *On Modern Literature*, ed. T. Spencer and J. Sutherland (Oxford, 1955), p. 146.

16 *Marginalia*, PR1263 D6 As. Col., *A Select Collection of Old English Plays*, ed. R. Dodsley, 12 vols (London, 1825–7), vol. VI, 202; *The Works of Beaumont and Fletcher*, ed. A. Dyce vol. VI, 538–9, vol. VIII, 324.

17 Anthony Trollope, 'Henry Taylor's Poems', *Fortnightly Review*, I (1865), p. 130.

18 Anthony Trollope, 'A Walk in a Wood', *Good Words*, XX (1879), p. 600.

19 Trollope,'A Walk in a Wood', p. 600.

20 Trollope, 'A Walk in a Wood', p. 597.

21 G. G. Sedgewick, *Of Irony, Especially in Drama*, (Toronto, 1948), p. 32.

22 *Papers*, MS. Don. C.10., pp. 15–21. Trollope's planning of a scenario for *The Way We Live Now* is particularly interesting because it clearly indicates his original intention to put Melmotte on trial for forgery instead of having him commit suicide. See P. D. Edwards, 'Trollope Changes His Mind: The Death of Melmotte in *The Way We Live Now*', *Nineteenth Century Fiction* 18 (1963), pp. 89–91.

III THE FORM OF THE STORY

1 Jerome Thale, 'The Problem of Structure in Trollope', *Nineteenth Century Fiction*, 15 (1960), p. 147.

2 Thale, in *Nineteenth Century Fiction*, 15, p. 149.

3 Ruth apRoberts, *Trollope: Artist and Moralist*, (London, 1971), p. 39. She regards the multi-plotted novels as 'elaborations of this unit' (p. 48), but in my view this underestimates their dynamic quality.

4 *An Autobiography*, p. 205.

5 Trollope continually defends this practice, in the concluding chapter of an early novel like *The Three Clerks* and at greater length in Chapter 35 of *The Eustace Diamonds*.

6 See Mario Praz, *The Hero in Eclipse in Victorian Fiction*,

trans. Angus Davidson (London, 1956).

7 Ruth apRoberts has an interesting discussion of this aspect of Mr Crawley's character in *Trollope: Artist and Moralist*, p. 104.

8 Juliet McMaster in her article, ' "The Unfortunate Moth": Unifying Theme in *The Small House at Allington*', *Nineteenth Century Fiction*, 26 (1971), pp. 127–44, argues persuasively that there is a strong element of masochism in the relation between Lily Dale and John Eames in *The Small House at Allington* and *The Last Chronicle of Barset*.

9 She argues that they 'display and define the Trollopian unit of structure', *Trollope: Artist and Moralist*, p. 46.

10 An exception is William A. West, 'The Anonymous Trollope', ARIEL, 5 (1974), pp. 46–64, which makes an interesting general assessment of these novels.

11 *An Autobiography*, p. 175.

12 R. C. Terry, *Anthony Trollope: The Artist in Hiding* (London, 1977), p. 37

13 Richard Stang, *The Theory of the Novel in England 1850–1870* (London, 1959), p. 122. Stang noted that Trollope's friend Henry Taylor also favoured the intensively dramatic novel.

14 G. H. Lewes, 'Realism in Art: Recent German Fiction', *Westminster Review*, LXX (1858), p. 496.

15 This is probably the reason for Trollope's high regard for this novel, which he considered to be better even than his much more popular work, *The Eustace Diamonds*, see *An Autobiography*, p. 296.

16 R. H. Hutton, who admired *Nina Balatka* and who immediately identified its author, points to this scene as the moral centre of the novel, see Smalley, *Critical Heritage*, p. 269. He also shared Lewes's and Trollope's concern with the 'Ideal' in fiction. For a fuller discussion of Hutton as a critic of Trollope see David Skilton, *Anthony Trollope and his contemporaries* (London, 1972).

17 It is significant that Trollope's later recollection of this novel was that it ended 'unhappily', *Letters*, pp. 282–3.

18 Donald Smalley ed., *Anthony Trollope: The Critical Heritage* (London, 1969) pp. 445–8.

IV THE RHETORICAL DESIGN

1 See, for instance, 'British Novelists – Richardson, Miss Austen, Scott', *Fraser's Magazine*, LXI (1860), p. 21.

2 Smalley, *Critical Heritage*, p. 209.

3 Henry James, *Partial Portraits* (London, 1919), p. 116.

4 This debate was sharply focused by Robert Scholes and Robert Kellogg in *The Nature of Narrative* (London, 1966), where they argue the case for the novelist as creator rather than as *histor*.

5 James, *Partial Portraits*, p. 103.

6 James, *Partial Portraits*, p. 116.

7 Trollope's wide knowledge is revealed in his *London Tradesmen*, ed. Michael Sadleir (London, 1927), pp. 12–22.

8 See Richard Stang, *The Theory of the Novel in England 1850–1870* (London, 1959), pp. 48–51.

9 *An Autobiography*, p. 126.

10 *An Autobiography*, p. 186.

11 *An Autobiography*, p. 190.

12 Ruth apRoberts, *Trollope: Artist and Moralist* (London, 1971), p. 52.

13 See Trollope's *The Three Clerks*, in which Charley Tudor's editor "specially insists on a Nemesis", p. 214.

14 *Thackeray*, p. 201.

15 *Letters*, p. 218.

16 They were later collected and published under the title *Caxtoniana* (London, 1875).

17 Compare Edward Bulwer-Lytton, 'On Certain Principles of Art in Works of Imagination', *Blackwood's Edinburgh Magazine*, XCIII (1863), p. 552 with Trollope, 'On English Prose Fiction as a Rational Amusement', in *Four Lectures*, ed. M. L. Parrish (London, 1938), p. 124.

18 Trollope, *Four Lectures*, p. 124.

19 Compare *An Autobiography*, pp. 199–200 with Edward Bulwer-Lytton, 'The Sympathetic Temperament', *Blackwood's Edinburgh Magazine*, XCII (1862), pp. 540–1.

20 Edward Bulwer-Lytton, 'On Art in Fiction', *Pamphlets and Sketches* (London, 1875), p. 352. This article first appeared anonymously in the first volume of the *Monthly Chronicle* in 1838 under the title 'The Critic'.

21 *An Autobiography*, p. 200.

22 Bradford A. Booth, 'Trollope's *Orley Farm*: Artistry Manqué', in *From Jane Austen to Joseph Conrad*, ed. R. C. Rathburn and M. Steinmann (Minneapolis,

1958), pp. 146–59.
23 Robert M. Adams, 'Orley
Farm and Real Fiction',
Nineteenth Century Fiction,
8 (1953), p. 37.
24 Robert M. Polhemus, The
Changing World of Anthony
Trollope (Berkeley and Los
Angeles, 1968), p. 79.
25 As Trollope makes clear,
although a 'trial' novel, Orley
Farm is not concerned with
arousing suspense, and his
insistence on this point may
have been an attempt to
dissociate it from the
sensationalism of such
contemporary successes as
Miss Braddon's Lady Audley's
Secret.
26 The parallel from Molière is
between Felix Graham and
Arnolphe who, fearing he
will be cuckolded, has a
peasant's daughter Agnès
brought up in complete
ignorance of the world.
While he is absent Agnès
meets and falls in love with
Horace, just as Mary Snow
does with Albert Fitzallen.
Both the play and the novel
show how human nature
cannot be circumvented by
strategy. See also Bradford A.
Booth, in From Jane Austen
to Joseph Conrad, pp. 153–5.
27 George Saintsbury also
makes this point in
Corrected Impressions
(London, 1895), p. 172.

28 The Letters and Private
Papers of W. M. Thackeray,
ed. G. N. Ray (London, 1946),
vol. IV, 236.
29 See Kathleen Tillotson,
Novels of the Eighteen-
Forties (Oxford, 1954), p.
29.
30 An Autobiography, p. 236.
See also Michael Sadleir,
Trollope: A Bibliography
(London, 1928, repr. 1964),
p. 78.
31 Papers, MS. Don. C.10., pp.
24–5.
32 Papers, MS. Don. C.9., pp.
72–3, pp. 125–6, pp. 146–7.
33 Papers, MS. Don. C.9., p. 146.
34 Papers, MS. Don. C.9., p. 142.
35 Letters, p. 137.
36 Letters, p. 458.
37 An Autobiography, pp.
120–1.
38 An Autobiography, p. 120.
39 Thackeray, p. 38.
40 Thackeray, p. 95.
41 Thackeray, p. 201.
42 Smalley, Critical Heritage, p.
133.
43 Dickens experienced
difficulty with Mrs Gaskell
over the publication of
North and South in 1855, and
the manuscript of Wives
and Daughters shows why
Dickens had the editorial
labour that he did, for,
written on large sides of
paper, the story goes on
without a break even for

chapter divisions; see John
Rylands Library, English

MS. 877, Wives and
Daughters (c. 1864–6), 920 ff.

V THE ACHIEVEMENT

1 Smalley, *Critical Heritage*, p. 401.

2 *An Autobiography*, p. 305.

3 James R. Kincaid, *The Novels of Anthony Trollope* (Oxford, 1977), pp. 164–5.

4 There are several similarities between Melmotte and Dickens's Merdle, although the precise nature of Trollope's debt is by no means clear: 'According to Escott, Trollope denied the possibility of his having been influenced by Dickens, saying, *"The Way We Live Now* appeared in 1875; I only read *Little Dorrit* on my way to Germany in 1878".* Now, somebody is mistaken here; for Trollope not only read *Little Dorrit* in the monthly numbers as it appeared (1856–7), but he wrote an article on it!' Bradford A. Booth, 'Trollope and *Little Dorrit*', *Nineteenth Century Fiction*, 2 (1947), p. 237.

5 Quoted in Michael Sadleir, *Trollope: A Commentary* (London, 1961 edn.) p. 426.

6 Smalley, *Critical Heritage*, p. 426.

7 *An Autobiography*, pp. 250–1, 253.

8 See Asa Briggs, 'Trollope, Bagehot and the English Constitution', *Cambridge Journal*, V (1952), pp. 327–38.

9 *An Autobiography*, p. 253.

10 See Bradford A. Booth, *Anthony Trollope: Aspects of His Life and Art* (London, 1958), pp. 99 and 101; Robert Polhemus, *The Changing World of Anthony Trollope* (Berkeley and Los Angeles, 1968), p. 208; Ruth apRoberts, *Trollope: Artist and Moralist* (London, 1971), pp. 145–6; and John Halperin, *Trollope and Politics* (London, 1977), p. 222.

11 *An Autobiography*, pp. 308–9.

12 Anthony Trollope, *Lord Palmerston* (London 1882), p. 163.

13 N. N. Glisev, *Chronicle of the Life and Work of L. N. Tolstoy 1818–1890* (Moscow, 1958), p. 315.

14 Robert Polhemus makes this point (in *The Changing World of Anthony Trollope*, p. 198).

SELECT BIBLIOGRAPHY

This is primarily a selected list of works which I have found useful in writing this study. I have kept it reasonably concise because both James R. Kincaid, in *The Novels of Anthony Trollope* (Oxford, 1977) and R. C. Terry, in *Anthony Trollope: The Artist in Hiding* (London, 1977) have included fairly comprehensive bibliographies of general works on Trollope, while David Skilton, in *Anthony Trollope and His Contemporaries*, (London, 1972) and Donald Smalley, in *Trollope: The Critical Heritage* (London, 1969) have published extensive selections of Victorian reviews and criticism. Specific editions of texts and other documents by Trollope are given in the Note on References, p. x.

BIBLIOGRAPHIES

Helling, Rafael, *A Century of Trollope Criticism* (Helsinki, 1956).

Irwin, Mary L., *Anthony Trollope: A Bibliography* (New York, 1926).

Ray, Gordon N., *Bibliographical Resources for the Study of Nineteenth Century English Fiction* (Los Angeles, 1964).

Sadleir, Michael, *Trollope: A Bibliography*, (London, 1928, supplemented 1934, reprinted London, 1964).

Sadleir, Michael, *Nineteenth Century Fiction, A Bibliographical Record*, 2 vols (London, 1951).

Smalley, Donald, 'Anthony Trollope', *Victorian Fiction: A Guide to Research*, ed. Lionel Stevenson (Cambridge, Mass., 1964).

Smalley, Donald, ed., *Trollope: The Critical Heritage* (London, 1969).

GENERAL WORKS ON TROLLOPE

Banks, J. A., 'The Way They Lived Then: Anthony Trollope and the 1870's', *Victorian Studies*, 12 (1968), 177–200.
Booth, Bradford A., *Anthony Trollope: Aspects of His Life and Art* (London, 1958).
Booth, Bradford A., 'Trollope on the Novel', *Essays Critical and Historical Dedicated to Lily B. Campbell* (Berkeley and Los Angeles, 1950), pp. 219–31.
Booth, Bradford, A., ed., *The Letters of Anthony Trollope* (London, 1951).
Briggs, Asa, 'Trollope, Bagehot and the English Constitution', *Cambridge Journal*, 5 (1952), 327–38.
Brown, Beatrice C., *Anthony Trollope* (London, 1950).
Clark, John W., *The Language and Style of Anthony Trollope* (London, 1975).
Cockshut, A.O.J., *Anthony Trollope: A Critical Study* (London, 1955).
Edwards, P.D., *Anthony Trollope: His Art and Scope* (London, 1978).
Escott, T.H.S., *Anthony Trollope: His Work, Associates and Literary Originals* (London, 1913).
Fredman, Alice G., 'Anthony Trollope', *Columbia Essays on Modern Writers*, (New York, 1971).
Hagan, John H., 'The Divided Mind of Anthony Trollope', *Nineteenth Century Fiction*, 14 (1959), 1–26.
Halperin, John, *Trollope and Politics: A Study of the Pallisers and Others* (London, 1977).
Harrison, Frederic, *Studies in Early Victorian Literature* (London, 1895).
Hennedy, Hugh L., *Unity in Barsetshire* (The Hague and Paris, 1971).
James, Henry, 'Anthony Trollope', *Partial Portraits* (London, 1888), pp. 97–133.
Ker, W. P., 'Anthony Trollope', *On Modern Literature*, ed. T. Spencer and J. Sutherland (Oxford, 1955), pp. 136–46.
Kincaid, James R., 'Bring Back *The Trollopian*', *Nineteenth Century Fiction*, 31 (1976), 1–14.
Kincaid, James R., *The Novels of Anthony Trollope* (Oxford, 1977).
McMaster, Juliet, *Trollope's Palliser Novels: Theme and Pattern* (London, 1978).
Mizener, Arthur, 'Anthony Trollope: The Palliser Novels', *From*

Jane Austen to Joseph Conrad, ed. R. C. Rathburn and M. Steinmann (Minneapolis, 1958), pp. 160–76.

Polhemus, Robert M., *The Changing World of Anthony Trollope* (Berkeley and Los Angeles, 1968).

Pollard, Arthur, *Anthony Trollope* (London, 1978).

Pollard, Arthur, *Trollope's Political Novels* (Hull, 1968).

Pope Hennessy, James, *Anthony Trollope* (London, 1971).

Ray, Gordon N., 'Trollope at Full Length', *Huntingdon Library Quarterly*, 31 (1968), 313–40.

apRoberts, Ruth, *Trollope: Artist and Moralist* (London, 1971).

Sadleir, Michael, *Trollope: A Commentary* (London, 1927).

Skilton, David, *Anthony Trollope and His Contemporaries* (London, 1972).

Smalley, Donald, ed., *Anthony Trollope: The Critical Heritage* (London, 1969).

Snow, C. P., *Trollope* (London, 1975).

Stebbins, L. P. and R. P., *The Trollopes: The Chronicle of a Writing Family* (London, 1946).

Terry, R. C., *Anthony Trollope: The Artist in Hiding* (London, 1977).

Thale, Jerome, 'The Problem of Structure in Trollope', *Nineteenth Century Fiction*, 15 (1960), 147–57.

Trollope, F. E., *Frances Trollope: Her Life and Literary Work* 2 vols (London, 1895).

Trollope, Thomas A., *What I Remember* 2 vols (London, 1887).

Walpole, Hugh, *Anthony Trollope* (London, 1928).

GENERAL STUDIES ON THE NOVEL

Booth, Wayne C., *The Rhetoric of Fiction* (Chicago, 1961).

Friedman, Alan, *The Turn of the Novel* (New York, 1966).

Graham, Kenneth, *English Criticism of the Novel 1865–1900* (Oxford, 1965).

Harvey, W. J., *Character and the Novel* (London, 1965).

Mendilow, A. A., *Time and the Novel* (London, 1952).

Miller, J. Hillis, *The Disappearance of God: Five Nineteenth-Century Writers* (Cambridge, Mass., 1963).

Miller, J. Hillis, *The Form of Victorian Fiction* (Notre Dame Indiana, 1968).

Praz, Mario, *The Hero in Eclipse in Victorian Fiction* tr. Angus Davidson, (London, 1956).

Scholes, Robert, and Kellogg, Robert, *The Nature of Narrative* (London, 1966).

Stang, Richard, *The Theory of the Novel in England 1850–1870* (London, 1959).

INDEX

Fictional characters are referred to in *italic*.